Sommerstall Academy

Dear reader, make sure to read the trigger warnings for this book on
www.jarahwrites.com

Also by Jarah Aurel:

Arcane
Untangle Me
Serendipity
Only you
Piece by Piece
In Shadows We Rise
Little Nymph
Effervescent

Jarah Aurel

Sommerstall Academy

© 2023 Jarah Aurel
ISBN: 9798317111656

This book is a work of fiction. Names, characters, places, and incidents are either a product of the author's imagination or are used fictitiously. Any resemblance to actual people living or dead, events or locales is entirely coincidental.

To the girls that like to be treated right and seen without trying

Chapter 1

Florence

Honestly, I've been wanting to get hit by a car for a while now. Therefore, I really shouldn't complain now that I'm lying flat on my back on the hard concrete like a bug and just as unable to get up.

Stupid, heavy backpack!

For the record, I really did not wish for this to happen right in front of school just as all the students file out of their buses and onto the sidewalk a few feet away from me. I also didn't anticipate the Vehicle hitting me being a bus.

"Are you okay?" the old driver asks, crouching down next to me. All around us, more students gather, some reaching for their phones to point their cameras at me. *No, I'm not okay,* I think. *I am mortified.*

I try to slip out of my backpack with some remaining dignity only to wince as I realize that my shoulder hurts like a female dog. Dammit! I don't have time to get it checked out with my law exam this afternoon.

If I miss it, Miss Yeng will be angry, which is the last thing I want. The old lady is seriously scary, and she doesn't like staying after school so a student can write a make-up test. I speak of experience, and the memory of her cold, dead eyes boring into me as I try to focus on the made up case on the paper is enough to make me shudder.

The only silver lining is that it's Friday. Maybe my classmates will forget all about my little incident here over the weekend and by the time Monday rolls around, I can blend in once again. One can only hope.

"Can you hear me?" the bus driver repeats slowly, dragging me from my thoughts. His face has taken on a pallid sheen, his eyes wide with panic at the thought of having broken my head. *Note to self, zoning out after being hit by a bus is not the right time.*

"Yes. Sorry, yes. I'm all right," I assure him, brushing him off with a wobbly smile. To really sell it, I try to get back to my feet once more, ignoring the agony in my shoulder and the stars that dot my vision when the thick straps of my backpack drag me down.

Clearly noting my struggle, the bus driver jumps in to help, his careful hands grabbing me by the elbows. "Hang on, let me help you. Oh gosh, I'm really sorry. I didn't see you. Do you need a ride to the hospital?" he gushes as he pulls me to my feet. I feel so bad for making this old man worry this much when it was my fault for crossing the street with my attention elsewhere, I can hardly look into his eyes.

I shake my head instead, looking at my blouse as if I had to straighten it. "That's okay, really. Have a good day." With a parting smile in his vague direction, I rush to the sidewalk and try to disappear in the crowd of students. That, at least, turns out to be a simple task seeing as all the scholars of Sommerstall Academy are heading to their first period now that I'm no longer stuck on my back like a dead bug.

Attraction over. My cheeks can stop burning now.

But I'm not that lucky, and as I think back to how I managed to get hit by a bus that drove about 5 mph on a street I cross every day, I feel my blush intensify with embarrassment. All I can say is that it was not my fault. If *he* hadn't caught my eye from where he was sitting inside that bloody vehicle, looking brooding and mysterious, I would have noticed that the bus ahead of his was starting to drive.

I didn't possess the self-control to keep my eyes from straying his way. I never do.

And so, with his dark messy hair, disheveled by the big headphones he always had on, and the intense look in his eyes as he looked outside the window with absolutely no regard or attention for me, I was wholeheartedly distracted. Who wouldn't swoon over an attractive man oblivious to one's existence.

I hope the courtesy extends to this incident so that he didn't notice me be hit by a bus either. If he saw me like that, I would have to switch schools, and that would be a shame since I live basically one street over from this one.

I'm just thankful I didn't drive to school today. That would have been a whole different sort of commotion, and if anything would have happened to my Vespa, I would have cried. On a nice spring day like today though, the helmet-hair just wasn't worth it, so I chose to take the fifteen-minute walk upon myself instead.

With my head still ducked low and my arm cradled to my chest to appease my throbbing shoulder, I enter the classroom and sit down at my desk. School starts in ten minutes, so I can still read. I should have time for at least five pages if no one interrupts me.

Thank God for small mercies. A distraction in the form of three mouthwatering males taking care of their mate is exactly what I need to forget I made a fool out of myself in front of all my peers.

I take my book out of my backpack, trying not to wince as I move my left arm. Luckily, I always carry my current read inside a protective bag, so today's fall hasn't damaged it. With my record, "rather safe than sorry" is the key to survival. The tight ball of anxiety in my gut relents a fraction knowing there's one less thing to worry about.

"Hey, Lorence! I heard you came face to face with a bus this morning. How's that for a first kiss?" my classmate Orion jaunts on his way to his chair on the opposite side of the classroom.

Lorence. I hate that nickname, which, naturally, is exactly why he keeps using it.

"Probably better than yours," I fire back, and for a second, he actually looks impressed. Or shocked. Who can tell with this guy? Before he can remark on my uncharacteristically bold reply, I mumble "Sorry, that was mean," not wanting to cause a scene and drag this interaction out when the reprieve of fiction is waiting for me. I turn back to my book and sink deeper into my chair. *What is wrong with me?*

Today really is a cursed day, and I'm not able to lose myself in the written words when Orion starts talking to his friends, Liam and Marcus, at a volume so loud I wonder if they want to entertain the entire room. It takes my everything not to let it agitate me. Honestly, some people have no respect for others. It's eight am. I don't care about the results of a stupid soccer match.

I sink deeper into my chair, scrunching my face up as if that could help me focus on the story in my hands. Instead, I'm interrupted once more, this time by a much kinder voice.

"Morning Flo. I heard what happened. Are you okay?" Benji asks as he enters the room. He stops near my chair, leaning down to pull me in a sideway hug. It's slightly awkward since I'm sitting and he's a giant, but I appreciate any hug I can get.

Even at eight am, the smell of weed clings to him, and when he pulls back to grin lopsidedly, I note the redness in his eyes. His ginger curls are messy atop his head, like he couldn't be bothered to style them, and the sight of his disheveled state brings a genuine smile to my lips. At least I'm not the only one who surely looks out of sorts after my stunt on the street.

"Yeah, I'm fine, thanks." I look past my friend as a glimpse of black hair catches my eye. Elija walks past Benji, sending me a nearly imperceptible smile before sitting down next to Orion.

I can feel my cheeks heat like they always do when he does that. It's the height of our interactions, and it shouldn't mean anything to me like I'm sure it means nothing to him, but like the crazy deluded girl that I am, I feel my heart skip a beat. I try to hide my gooey eyes since everyone else would think I'm crazy to melt over an impassive smile he grants all our classmates he never speaks to. Just like me.

I don't know what it is with this guy. I can usually handle people smiling at me. Hell, I smile at everyone I cross paths with. He's the only exception. Maybe it's his unruly black hair, his chains and rings, his cute brown eyes, or those soft-looking lips- Oh, never mind. I already got hit by a bus once thinking about Elija. That should be my last and final sign to drop this obsession.

I drag my gaze back to Benji's only for him to lift a thick, orange eyebrow knowingly. I laugh, embarrassed at having been caught staring, and shove my friend away.

He chuckles knowingly to himself as he heads toward his friends, and I track his movement to subtly get another look at Elija despite myself. Who am I kidding? I will never manage to stop fantasizing about him, and honestly, school would be a lot more boring if I did. To his right, I notice Jamie's already in his seat, which means their group is now complete.

More students file into the room, smiling at me in greeting, and I'm too busy returning each one to read a single page before class begins. I deflate when the bell rings and I know I'll have to wait for the sweet relief of the romantasy story for another while.

The next forty-five minutes consist of me trying to focus on the teacher's lecture as I fight the urge to look at a certain guy on the other side of the room. The only thing possibly better than reading because my deranged mind makes up stories of its own when I look at him. Improbable scenarios where his smile lingers and his gaze contains longing for me.

Even after a year of being in the same class, the scenarios haven't gotten old. It's embarrassing that I still get excited every time I see him. It's not even like we've exchanged more than two sentences in all the time we've known each other. Still, he just somehow piques my interest and it hasn't waned since the first day of the school year.

That's why Friday is a highlight. It's the day when most people go out for lunch while I stay in the classroom to do my homework or study. Elija and some of his friends, for their part, often return to the room in a matter of minutes.

Even though the two of us don't speak, without the distraction of a teacher up front, I keep catching him staring at me just as much as I get caught myself. I'd be scared he thought I was a creep if it weren't for that small smile he keeps flashing me. *That smile, dammit.*

As soon as our first period is over, I make a move to pick up my book. I need this. Need the break from reality to wash away the lingering discomfort at the thought of my scene before school. I wish my mind didn't make such a big deal out of this, but I can't shake the oppressive feeling in my stomach knowing I made such a fool out of myself.

The only thing that can help me now is mentally vanishing into a whole different world, but before I can start reading, Benji calls my name. "Flo! Come over here!" I raise my head to find him waving as if we were miles apart rather than a few feet.

It's hard to be mad at him for the insistent interruption when I know he means well. He probably sees me by myself in the breaks with my nose buried in books and thinks I'm a sad loner. I sigh to myself and come to terms with the fact that I won't get to read this time either. I close the book, line it up perfectly with the side of my desk, and get to my feet to walk over to the guys.

"Hey, flower girl," Jamie greets me with a bright smile. Out of the six guys, he's probably the one I'm the least nervous around. With his happy-go-lucky attitude, his constant jokes and the ever-present smile on his lips, he leaves no room for my shyness.

Of course, Benji's chill to hang out with. And then, there's Elija. Although that is different. I've interacted with him the

Chapter 2

Florence

Hours later, I'm done with all my studying and homework. That means there's nothing left to distract me from my throbbing shoulder and racing thoughts. Despite the lingering pain, the test in the afternoon went fairly well, so unless my grade still somehow turns out to be a fluke, I won't have to ask for extra credit. It'd be a damn good thing too considering that's another thing Miss Yeng hates.

I reach for my phone rather absent mindedly, but once it's unlocked, I don't know what to do with it. Scrolling through social media, as tempting as it sounds, only ever makes me anxious and twitchy, but the distracting pain in my shoulder keeps me from diving into a strange world.

I wonder if something is seriously wrong with it, but then again, I'm sure I'd be in pure agony if that was the case. It's only been like twelve hours since I obtained the injury, so what's to say this isn't normal? I did crash onto it with my entire body weight, so I can't blame it for hurting. Right?

Maybe I'll ice it if it isn't better by tomorrow. That's what the athletes in the books I read always do when they're hurt, so it can't be all that wrong.

I tap away on my screen without much thought, opening a new text thread and typing in a message I'll never send like I often do. I'm not a confrontational or even brave person, but sometimes when I can't get something out of my head, I'll type

Already, this talk puts the overall wordcount between us up to its double. Perhaps this day isn't cursed.

Our interaction of the day ends at that, and I return to my own desk since the other guys come back into the room. I try to focus on reading but, as usual, they talk too loudly for me to lose myself in a different world.

"Elija, you're coming to the gym after school, right?" Marcus asks, and I give up on trying to read. Instead, I stare at my book, trying not to look like I'm eavesdropping.

"Can't today," he tells his friends.

"Why? You always tag along on Tuesdays and Fridays," Liam pushes.

Meanwhile, I had no idea he worked out. He's always wearing hoodies that conceal his body. All I know is that he's a few inches taller than Benji and his shoulders fill out the thick sweaters like no one's business.

"I have a doctor's appointment to get that birthmark on my side checked," he mumbles, his voice so low I nearly don't catch the words. He's usually more quiet and subdued compared to his noisy friends, and the fact that I have to strain my ears to hear him makes me feel ten times worse for snooping.

Without missing a beat, Jamie reaches for his friend's hand, grasps it tightly, and speaks dramatically, "Listen to me, Sunshine. We'll get through this. You won't die on my watch."

I try to stifle a laugh but know I failed miserably when Elija looks at me. Our eyes clash for a second before I tear mine back to my book, my skin burning from my neck to the tips of my ears.

Smooth, Florence. Real smooth.

Without a word, he places them on my head, and I pause the music playing on the one AirPod I'm still wearing to listen to whatever he wants to show me.

He does that sometimes; letting me listen to a certain song he likes while he gauges my reaction. He doesn't talk much, but I think this is his way of showing affection. I, for one, adore it.

Today's song is R&B soul like always, and I enjoy the vibes with my eyes closed, not caring what I look like with those big speakers on my ears. When it's over, I hand the headphones back to my friend, trying not to wince because of my shoulder, and take his phone to show him a song I've been listening to recently.

When he shuts his eyes to take it in, I become painfully aware of someone else's attention. I meet Elija's gaze with a smile, and with a grin of his own, he reaches for me.

I'm stupefied for a second, thinking he'll touch me or something, but he merely plucks Benji's phone out of my hand instead. My heartbeat slows as he types something into his own and sits back down.

"It's a song I like," I explain quietly since I'm pretty sure he starts playing it himself. I know the two guys listen to similar songs, so he should probably be warned that this is one of mine.

"I know," he says to my surprise. He goes back to scrolling through his phone, and I tear my eyes from him.

Not once have I been nervous about showing Benji something I liked, but with Elija listening to it, I suddenly feel self-conscious. *It doesn't matter if he won't like it*, I repeat to myself. Still, I really hope he will.

"I like it," Benji tells me suddenly. I smile at him before glancing at Elija again. He meets my eyes at the exact same moment, smiling. That's all it takes to make me blush like a preschooler.

"It's great. I love the beat," he tells me, making the pressure bleed from my shoulders. *He loves the beat.* It takes everything I've got not to squeal at the minuscule sign of his approval.

out of him as if he couldn't help it. His late reaction makes me think he tried to keep the comment to himself but ended up changing his mind.

It's such an untimely mock that Jamie bursts out laughing in apparent disbelief. "What is wrong with you?" he snorts.

I've been wondering the same thing about the white-haired guy, but it doesn't seem to be personal. He tends to mock people for no reason whenever he gets bored, so I just ignore him.

He is merely another rude person blessed with a beautiful shell. Their whole friend group consists of handsome members. So much so that I'm wondering whether that's some sort of condition.

Orion's hair is the lightest shade of blond, and his eyes are as blue as the sky on a clear day. He's attractive in a slightly dangerous way with those hard features and sharp angles.

Turning to me, Jamie adds, "Sorry, as you can tell, we haven't yet succeeded at teaching our parrot proper manners." Orion turns to glare at him. "Oh, don't worry, Cupcake, you'll get there," Jamie adds sweetly, petting his head. At the touch, Orion gets up from his seat and starts chasing him through the room.

There's some laughter amongst our classmates until the teacher for our next class arrives and puts a stop to the show.

The rest of the morning passes blissfully uneventfully.

When the bell finally announces the start of our lunch break, I feel the usual anticipation growing. Everyone gets out of the room while I start on my homework. Less than ten minutes later, Elija sits back down at his desk along with Benji. They eat their food in silence, both of them wearing headphones same as me.

Since I feel no eyes on me for once, I'm able to focus on the worksheet ahead of me. When I'm done, I consider getting my book out to read, but another urge takes over, and I find myself taking a seat opposite my friend. Benji smiles at me before taking off his headphones.

I let my eyes trail over him quickly; brown, slicked-back hair, grey eyes, and always dressed to the nines. A bit extravagant for school, but I couldn't imagine him pairing anything as casual as jeans with the shirt embroidered with the Academy's sigil we're all forced to wear.

He'd be handsome if it weren't for his need to act like he's better than the rest of us simply because he has unlimited access to daddy's money.

Benji rolls his eyes before burying his head in his arms, no doubt done with the day. I smile at the way his orange curls splay against the sleeves of his green sweater, like a band of fiery flowers on a field, before turning my attention to Liam.

"I guess I am," I reply with my smile intact. He doesn't bother me enough to make a dent in my mood.

If anything, I feel bad for him. He's not exactly pleasant most of the time, and I think not even his friends truly like him. They've been rolling their eyes at him for as long as I've known them. Despite all the watching I've done, I haven't figured out why they still hang out with him, though.

Not that Liam seems to care about them much more. I'm pretty sure he only uses them for invites to parties or because it looks good to the rest of the school to be friends with Marcus.

Speaking of the devil. "You'd sue anyone for no real reason," Marcus reminds Liam, dragging the attention away from me. I smile at him for that.

Opposite to Liam, he seems like a nice guy even though he wouldn't have to be. As captain of the academy's soccer team, he could probably act like a jerk and still be drooled over by most of the students. Not that I blame them. His brown, wavy hair that almost reaches his neck, paired with those hazel eyes do make a good combination. The workouts and practices he attends almost every day don't hurt the image either.

He's not as easy-going as Benji or as sweet as Jamie, but he seems down to earth. Very intimidating at times but not mean.

The silence stretches on for a few seconds, only for Orion to break it. "I guess I am," he finally mocks me, the words bursting least, and I wouldn't exactly say I'm not jittery around him. He makes me a whole different sort of nervous.

Not in a bad way, though. It's not like he intimidates me like some of his friends.

"Hi, Jamie. Benji, what'd you call me over for?" I inquire, fighting the urge to fidget as I stand awkwardly before their row of desks.

"You looked so lonely over there." Benji winks and I get the feeling this is him trying to be a wingman because he noticed my straying eyes earlier. I stifle a laugh.

"I was just about to read," I say, clearly disappointing him by not playing along.

Before we can fall into an awkward silence, Jamie asks, "So, no scratch from the accident earlier? All limbs still attached to the right place?"

That's what I like so much about him. He always knows how to keep a conversation going and tends to make the people around him smile in the process.

He throws his head back to get his blond hair out of his eyes and kicks his feet on the table in an easy matter.

"Yes, sir," I say with a fake salute. Then, catching myself, I quickly put my hand back down and try to cover my embarrassment with a laugh. That's another something that'll keep me up at night. Knowing Elija is looking at me only makes it worse. He just saw every second of me making a fool out of myself.

Besides, what I said isn't strictly true. My shoulder is still throbbing and hot while my arm from the elbow down feels weirdly cool and tingly. Oh well. No use in dwelling on it or announcing to the world what a clumsy idiot I am. Nope, that is a secret better kept to myself.

"I would sue that bus driver if I were you. Of course, if I were you, I wouldn't have gotten hit in the first place, but you're always tripping over things, aren't you?" Liam asks from where he's sitting, looking as smug as ever.

out messages and then delete them again, pretending I shoot them off and actually speak my mind.

But today, the pain in my shoulder must numb my brain because I click *send* before my mind can run interference and stop my fingers from doing something so reckless. It's only when the message goes out with the signature *swoosh* that my eyes widen and my heart stumbles a step.

"No. No, no, no. Oh my god," I mumble to myself, staring at the screen wide-eyed. "This can't be real. Oh, no." I drop my phone in my lap, bringing my hands into my hair agitatedly even as my shoulder screams at the movement. I just keep shaking my head in disbelief as I stare at the cursed gadget on my lap.

This can't be real.

I grab my phone once more, willing the message away as if I could undo my actions through sheer will of thought. "Come back. Please," I wail desperately, my heart beating out of my chest as I stare at the text I decided to initiate my first ever online interaction with Elija with.

Me: So, are you dying?

Of course, I couldn't text him something normal either. Nope, I had to come across as a psychopath. I groan in despair. *Cursed. Flipping. Day.* What do I do now? If I delete it, he'll wonder what I deleted, and I'll make it awkward. If I leave it at that, he'll think I'm murderous or something.

I have to fix this.

Frantically, my fingers go back to moving over the screen, but with every message I send off, I bury myself deeper and deeper in my own grave until a cold sweat beads my forehead and my heart is racing with disdain at myself.

Me: Oh shoot, that sounded so weird. I didn't mean it like that.

Me: I just overheard Jamie at lunch so I figured I'd ask.

Me: I was joking.

Me: But I shouldn't have. Dying is no laughing matter, of course. Especially you dying.

Me: I mean, not that *you* dying would be any more tragic than anyone else dying. I just mean because I texted it to you. Not that you specifically are special or anything.

Me: Oh my god, not that you're not special! I'm sure you're very special to your family. And friends.

Me: Please, never read this or forget this ever happened.

Me: I know this sounds like I'm a total wacko, but I'm not, I promise.

Seriously, what is wrong with me? As far as texting your crush goes, this is as nightmarish as it gets. I should have left it at the first text. Or stopped after the second. Now, he'll think I'm a weirdo with stalking tendencies. Who sends nine messages in a row? Oh my-

My phone pings and my head snaps to the device with the sort of desperation I'm unused to.

Elija: Hey Florence

Elija: Yeah, turns out it's nothing, and dw I'd be concerned if u hadn't overheard with the way Jamie was yelling.

Elija: How's your shoulder btw?

Oh

My

God

A new, warm sensation joins my curdling mortification, warring with it for dominance in my gut. He noticed I hurt my shoulder? That means he must have paid some serious attention to me, doesn't it? He noticed when not even my parents did. And that *Hey Florence*? Suddenly, I love my name. I don't think I've ever heard him say it, which should totally be illegal. I'll have to hear it from his lips sometime.

I can't believe he actually replied to my spew of nonsense. I'm getting excited like a kid on Christmas, and it's so embarrassing but I can't stop grinning. I force myself to wait a few minutes before answering so as not to seem too desperate. Although that train has probably left the station when I texted him nine times in a row within one minute.

Me: It's fine, thanks :)

I cringe and throw my phone away once more. I officially renounce texting. I am way too bad at this.

But Elija doesn't seem to cringe as badly as I do because he answers after a minute.

Elija: U should ice it.

Elija: Maybe go see someone if it's still bad on Monday…

Something fuzzy settles in my chest. His messages are almost enough to make me think he's concerned for me. So, despite not wanting to stupidly get my hopes up, I soak it up.

Me: Will do, thanks

Me: It barely hurts anymore, though :)

And again, I cringe slightly.

Elija: That's great to hear

Elija: I gotta go now, have a good night. And remember to keep me in mind when the urge to sound like a wacko arises again;)

Me: So much for forgetting it ever happened... Have a good night too.

And so, I surrender to the horrible day and start going down the rabbit hole on social media, watching endless videos about books from fellow book worms in the hopes that it'll take my mind off the fact that I'll have to change schools.

It's the last period on Tuesday afternoon, and I am more than ready to go home. I stayed up late last night since my parents had left for their trip and I forgot about the time. They're enjoying the beach while I enjoy my freedom. That was the plan, at least.

Turns out gym class isn't very enjoyable after skipping breakfast and lunch in my hurry and having slept for four hours. In my defense, I was finishing up a drawing on my iPad and couldn't put it aside.

I read a marvelous fantasy book last Sunday and it really inspired me. I started off with a simple portrait of a few of the characters and started bringing them together yesterday. The background took me a really long time since I just couldn't seem to get it right. The final result was worth the effort, though.

That doesn't make me feel any less stupid now. Normally, I know how to be home alone. Practice makes perfect, right? Wrong, apparently, since I made an amateur's mistake yesterday.

My parents have always worked a lot, but after I turned thirteen four years ago, they started taking more vacations and work trips. At first, they checked up on me every day, telling me when to study, eat, and go to sleep but that has long since stopped. They trust me more now, and usually, that's well deserved.

My thoughts break off when a softball hits me right in the face.

"Sorry!" Lynn screams from where she's standing on the other side of the field. I try to smile and brush her off.

"Good throw," I tell her as I leave the gym on shaky legs. She's a sweet girl. I don't want her to feel bad. Seeing as my surroundings are tilting, I really think I need some water, though, so I make my way toward the bathroom.

Halfway there, I stop short, trying to blink my surroundings back into focus as they blur. *Not again,* I think.

It's no use. The familiar cold and exhaustion start spreading through me, making my body feel a hundred pounds heavier and my brain go numb. Before I black out and break my face, I lower myself onto the ground as best as I can. I'm out before the back of my head even hits the floor.

Chapter 3

Elija

I hate volleyball. Honestly, why? It's not like I love sports that involve a ball in general, but I can tolerate most of them. Volleyball? Not so much.

First off, it hurts, and not in a good way. Every time I deflect the ball – or whatever you're supposed to call what I'm doing here – my wrists feel like they're set on fire. My skin is red and the way my bones beneath hurt can't be healthy. My body is very clearly telling me to quit, but my teacher has other plans. *Sadistic jerk.*

As if the ensuing pain of touching the ball isn't bad enough, it's literally all you can do. I mean, there's a net dividing you from your opponents. The only fun thing about sports is ramming and pushing the people you play against. Here? There's no such luck.

"Come on, dude! You should have gotten that one!" Marcus yells after we lose another point thanks to me. His competitive nature is really showing, and I bite my tongue to refrain from telling him there's nothing to gain whether we lose or win.

"One more attack coming from Orion and my wrists will break," I mumble, hoping no one hears me whining. I'm not proud of my behavior but this really isn't fun and Orion is exerting himself with every slam of the ball in my direction. I think he's getting a kick out of showing off how good he is at this.

"Oh, we're so sorry, Princess. Do you want us to kiss it better?" Jamie asks in between breaths. Of course, his sarcasm is still intact while his asthmatic ass is fighting for air.

I flip him off as I walk toward the ball, but my eyes move to the gym's glass doors on their own accord, gravitating toward a familiar silhouette like she's a magnet of the opposite pole. It always does.

As I look at Florence, I realize I've never seen her with a high ponytail before. She often has her brown hair pulled back by a hair clip, but this is different. It looks good, of course, but less like her. It's too rigid, not soft and light enough without any strands out to frame her pretty face.

I scan her outfit, hoping I don't come off as a creep. When my eyes settle on the small pattern of daisies on the sleeve of her shirt, I can't help but smile. There's always, and I can't stress this enough, *always* some kind of flower or plant to be found somewhere on her clothes.

Whenever that's not the case, she's probably wearing her customized Converse. They're white with little sunflowers all over them, which I'm sure she painted herself.

Even her necklace, the one she never takes off, has a flower pendant.

"Dude, we're waiting!" Marcus suddenly pulls me out of my daydream, making me realize I've been staring for too long. I raise my eyes to hers to check if I've been caught, only to realize something is wrong. Her eyes are heavily lidded, and I watch as she starts swaying on her feet. *What the hell?*

Before I can react, the she sits down on the floor and her body goes limp. I wince when the back of her head hits the stone and rush out of the gym without another thought.

"Florence?" I ask uselessly, kneeling down beside her. I hear the guys coming after me.

"What the hell is wrong with her?" Benji asks, sounding more alert than I remember ever hearing him. He kneels down at the other side of her, gently cupping her face while telling the others to get a teacher. My irritation spikes unexpectedly as I look at his hands on her cheeks, no matter how irrational. She didn't give him permission to touch her. I suppress the urge to push him away.

Instead, my attention is drawn back to Florence as her body starts jerking and convulsing wildly.

"Hey what is going on here? Get away from her!" our gym teacher, Mr. Bonks demands as he rushes over. My blood runs a little hotter at the accusatory note in his voice. Like I or my friends would ever hurt Florence.

"I saw her fall, sir. I don't know what happened," I explain while Benji keeps calling her name. Her body twitches twice more before she goes limp again.

My heart is racing as I reach for her wrist to check for a pulse, calling her name again. The jackhammer in my chest calms when I feel her heart beat strongly against my fingers, and her chest falls and rises with steady breaths. Still, her skin is an unnatural shade of white, dark circles underneath her eyes that look nearly black and even her lips have lost all their color.

"Back up. Give her some space to breathe," Mr. Bonks says before pushing me to the side to take my place. He does exactly nothing to help her and I'm fighting down the urge to reclaim my position.

Finally, a soft groan sounds from Florence, and I step closer to her once more, my anger forgotten.

"Florence?" I ask softly. Her eyes flutter open weakly, and I'm so relieved to see those emerald irises I could hug her. I don't, of course. Instead, I smile down at her in jarring relief.

She looks dazed, but it slowly gets better.

Finally, her eyes leave mine and move to my chest and arms. I try really hard not to smile because she looks so confused as she takes her time checking me out. This might very well be the first time she sees me without the barrier of a thick hoodie, and I wonder if she knows that too even in her state.

She clears her throat, swallowing a few times before bringing her eyes back to my face. "You have tattoos," is all she states. My cheeks heat, liking her eyes on me a little too much when she's clearly still a little out of it. Her eyes are still a little glazed, her lips softly parted.

I hear Benji laugh quietly and Mr. Bonks clears his throat. "Are you all right?" the man asks her.

Her pale cheeks grow slightly pink as she nods and tries to sit up. I notice her mistake at the same time as she does since she curses quietly before going limp yet again, her eyes rolling back in her head. Thankfully, Benji is able to catch her head so she doesn't hit it again.

This time, her body doesn't convulse but she does groan quietly before reopening her eyes with visible effort.

"What the hell, Flo? Tell us what you need," Benji says as he wipes the sweat off her forehead.

Florence swallows a few times and I realize her throat must be dry. I turn toward Marcus and tell him to get some water.

"Legs," she whispers quietly, still looking dazed. I gaze at her legs, trying to stay on topic despite the sight of the long, smooth expanse of her bare skin beneath her shorts.

"Oh, of course. Lift her legs a bit. And someone get a piece of chewing gum or something. She needs sugar," our gym teacher says, finally starting to be useful. I do as he ordered, lifting her legs on my lap while Benji holds her head and Marcus helps her drink. As soon as she's chewed the gum Jamie brought her, some color returns to her complexion.

"Sorry," she says shyly, looking anywhere but at me.

"Do you need anything else? Should I call someone?" Benji asks her.

"No, I'm good, thanks. I'll just eat something at home." She smiles at her friend, and I feel the absence of her attention like it's something physical and uncomfortable. Why won't she look at me like that? Whenever I meet her eyes in class, she looks away after a second but at Benji, she smiles for several beats.

I softly lay her legs back down on the floor before getting up and returning to the gym. She should be fine now, and I imagine she'll be more comfortable with a smaller audience. No matter that the last thing I want to do is leave her. Like, ever. It's more important that she's not uncomfortable in her vulnerable state.

Chapter 4

Florence

It's been three days since I passed out at school and the memory of it still has me cringing. I'll never go to bed late on a school night again. Especially since my dazed self decided to make an even bigger fool out of myself by checking Elija out in front of everyone.

I don't even want to know what I must have looked like; white as a sheet of paper and layered in sweat. Meanwhile, he looked so frustratingly beautiful. I really don't know why he won't wear tank tops more often, especially in summer. No idea how he survives in those hoodies all year.

Now knowing the round, molded shoulders and defined tattooed arms he's hiding, I understand it even less. I might have been dazed, but I wasn't blind. His arms are mouthwatering, and I might have recalled the image of them when I was failing to fall asleep that night. Imagining what they would have looked like next to my face as he caged me against a wall.

I'm becoming unhinged.

The way he left me as quickly as possible was a slap in the face. It's silly since I didn't need his help anymore and he had no reason to stick around, but I didn't even get the chance to thank him.

I've been going mad ever since. There's just no way to get a good read on that guy. He has been acting as always but now my mind is working overtime trying to decipher what every little gaze or smile could mean. What if I'm making a complete fool out of myself, reading into something that isn't there?

He probably smiles at everyone. What if he's in a relationship? Oh geez, I wouldn't know since I never talk to him. Would him having a partner make me a homewrecker? Maybe I've been looking at him suggestively and am making him uncomfortable.

"Florence?" My head snaps up and I'm greeted by an expectant-looking Mr. Hank. The teacher raises a greying eyebrow, and my heart drops a bit. Since when do I zone off so badly in class? I've never had to ask a teacher to repeat a question.

"I'm sorry, I didn't catch that," I tell him while tapping a familiar rhythm with my finger on my thigh. The smile on my face feels forced but I keep it up in an attempt to smooth the line between my teacher's brows.

"We were talking about the trip in two weeks. You said you had a tent for twelve people, right?" he asks.

"Right. Yes, I do." My smile starts feeling a bit more natural every time I repeat my rhythm. It's a trick I learned when I first started getting anxious. I don't even remember how I came up with that melody, but it helps to feel it on me.

Mr. Hank clears a few more things up about the annual camping trip before the class is dismissed and my classmates leave for lunch.

Since I managed to forget my book at home today, I end up listening to music and thinking about the camping trip. I already asked my parents if I could use our old tent for the trip this year and they agreed. After last year's disaster, as they called it, they didn't need much convincing.

Last year, the school didn't organize enough tents for all the students, leaving us to sleep in our sleeping bags beneath the stars. I loved it. Feeling the soft breeze skim my skin and listening to the rustling leaves in the wind lulled me to sleep as nothing else could.

My parents disagreed. They didn't think it was magical, they thought it was barbaric, sleeping amongst the bugs and worms like animals. Their words, not mine. Other than that, they were sure all the creeps were watching me sleep.

Honestly, what creeps?

Sure, there are idiots at this school like at any other, but I can't think of a creep. Besides, I'm sure there are more interesting subjects to watch if it came down to it.

I look up from my hands, my thoughts forgotten when the door opens. Today, Elija is alone as he enters the classroom, and my heart skips a beat with excitement. He smiles at me before sitting down and eating his food.

Meanwhile, I force myself to keep my eyes on my phone so they won't stray over to where he is. Maybe I should renounce my prior statement. Maybe I'm the creep parents should be worried about. I hate that idea.

I'd do my homework or study but there aren't any exams coming up and I've finished all my assignments early. I'm left to twiddle my thumbs.

Once Elija has finished his food, I gather all my courage and look at him.

"A song for a song?" I ask, trying to keep my voice even. The guy across from me looks up, clearly puzzled.

"Sorry?" he asks. I can feel my cheeks heat up but I refuse to look away.

"I'm not in the mood for any of the songs on my playlist and Benji's not here to show me anything new. If you want, you could tell me a song to listen to and I'd tell you one in return." Elija nods slowly, a smile forming on his lips as he gets up and walks over to me.

He stops on the opposite side of my desk, forcing me to look up at him from where I'm sitting as if to accentuate how tall he is. I don't think he does it on purpose, but the fact still becomes glaringly obvious to me. He hands me his phone, oblivious to how I'm lusting after him, and I give him mine.

I've been thinking about this for the last twenty minutes, so I know what song to play for him. It's similar to the one he liked last week, one with a real band and drums instead of all that electronical stuff, so I hope he'll enjoy it too.

He, having had a lot less time to prepare, thinks about his choice for a few seconds. I watch him as he types something on my phone, and I could have sworn I saw a blush rise up his neck.

Maybe I make him nervous too? Maybe he feels this weird pull toward me like I do to him? Maybe-

My thoughts break off as the first note of his song meets my ears. My chest deflates a little, my silly hopes shriveling as *FRIENDS* by Marshmello starts playing. Speaking of hints.

I laugh a little to cover my embarrassment.

Then, I do what I do best in uncomfortable situations. I open my silly mouth. "Okay, hint taken," I tell him, still smiling over the uncomfortable knot in my throat.

Clearly, I wasn't slick about my glances and now I'm just bothering him while he's trying to enjoy his lunch break. It was stupid of me to even propose doing this. Or maybe not, because at least now I know what he wants, or rather doesn't want from me. It was just dumb to imagine or tell myself there was anything between us in the first place. I mean, we don't even talk to each other, for Pete's sake.

"What? What hint?" he asks, frowning. I point to my phone.

"It's fine. I wasn't trying to make you uncomfortable or anything. I just always like finding new songs." I laugh again, all the while I can't get *liar, liar, pants on fire* out of my mind.

Elija takes a closer look at my screen and his face breaks out in a grin. "I'm sorry, I didn't mean to put on that song." It's his turn to chuckle. "Please un-take whatever hint you took." My cheeks burn up impossibly hotter as I hand him my unlocked phone again. The song that starts playing next is *friends* by Chase Atlantic.

"There you go," Elija says, setting my phone back down.

My confusion returns with full force. Great. Did he really make a mistake or did he feel bad for the flustered mess I turned into? If it was a mistake, am I supposed to read into the lyrics of the song that's playing now? I guess it does mirror my confusion about us a bit but what if it's really just a song he likes? This is too stressful.

"You have great taste in music," he tells me after a few minutes.

"Thanks. I love Chase Atlantic." I check the time and feel my eyebrows draw together. "Shouldn't the rest of the class be back by now?" I ask Elija.

"Why would they? Our last period has been canceled." *Back up, what?* "You didn't know that?" his tone suggests he already knows my answer.

"No. Why are you still here, then?" I ask.

"I was going to wait for my bus, but," he trails off, checking the time on his phone. "It left about two minutes ago." I curse inwardly. Two minutes, that means I'm the reason he's stuck here until the next bus arrives. I'm about to apologize when he raises a hand to stop me. "Don't worry about it," he tells me with a knowing smile.

"How long will you be stranded here?" I ask him.

"A bit less than an hour. Don't apologize," he adds hastily, so I laugh instead.

"You're an idiot for not telling me. I wouldn't have gone berserk on you if you had left," I assure him. Then, almost automatically, I apologize for calling him an idiot. He laughs at me.

"It's fine. You can call me whatever you want," he brushes me off with a subtle wink that's just the right amount of teasing. I want to ask him if "*Mine*" is included since I saw that on Instagram once, but I think better of it. This is the first time we're having an actual conversation so I'm trying not to come off too strong.

Instead, I stretch my back before muttering, "These chairs are murder."

"I don't mean to keep you here. I'm sure you'd rather go home or do whatever your usual Friday afternoon activity is." I quickly shake my head but stop myself before I tell him that I'll gladly endure uncomfortable chairs just so I could hear his voice some more.

"I certainly won't leave you here alone after making you miss your bus. But." I chew on my lip and avert my eyes, looking at his rings as I work up some courage. "I live five minutes away. You could wait with me until the next bus arrives. Only if you want to, of course. I'll tell you, though, the chairs at my place are a lot more comfortable."

I say all that as nonchalantly as possible. As if this wasn't the first time I've ever invited anyone home, especially with no parents around. If they knew I just asked a guy over, they'd probably go ballistic. As it is, they won't be home for another six days.

"Are you sure? You don't need to feel guilty, I could find something to occupy myself with here if it's a problem," he assures me.

This, ladies, gentlemen, and gentlepeople, is what I'm talking about. He would wait an hour longer to go home and wouldn't be mad. Wouldn't blame me for his wasted time or demand I owe him something. There isn't an ounce of scorn on his face, solidifying the sense of safety I've always felt around him.

It's what propels me to say, "I'm sure, come on."

I grab his wrist, catching myself too late to pull back again. With the intention of not making more of a fool out of myself, I keep my hand where it is and gently start tugging him away. I'm just glad he could grab his backpack on our way to the door.

I pretty much speed walk out of the building and toward the parking lot, scared my hand will grow clammy and nasty. When we finally reach my Vespa, I hand him my helmet. It's cute how he tries to fight me on the topic, insisting I need it more if we fall. In the end, he doesn't stand a chance of winning the argument. I'm my parents' daughter after all, and I refuse to let a backpack take the risk of not wearing any protective gear even for a short drive.

Looking at my bike, he says, "Why am I not surprised it's mint-colored?"

"What's wrong with that?" I ask him, trying to see what he does when he looks at my baby.

"Nothing's wrong with it. It suits you." Judging by the gentle smile teasing his lips, I'll trust that the comment is genuine.

I get on first before telling him, "Get on. You can place your feet there. Just hold on tight, okay?" I don't hear his response over my heart pounding in my ears, but his strong arms wrap around my waist from behind the next second, spanning around me entirely.

That's enough to distract me, and when I don't move for too long, Elija speaks up. "Any moment now," he teases me. What he didn't anticipate was that feeling his warm breath fanning against my neck wouldn't do anything for my focus.

I pull myself together and start driving home. As soon as I gain speed and the warm air turns to a cool wind around me, I'm able to relax. It's always been like this. No matter how stressed I am, one minute on my bike and I feel better.

I tilt my head back slightly, still watching the road but relishing in the feeling to drive without a helmet for once. I'm always responsible when it comes to that, but I have to admit driving like this with a cute guy at my back awakes so much adrenalin within me that it feels like I'm floating.

"Easy, there. If you go any faster, it'll get expensive." Elija laughs behind me. Checking the speed I'm going at and realizing he's right, I force myself to slow down a tad.

"Sorry," I yell back, only partly meaning it.

We arrive at my place way too soon and I lead him into my room, never one to linger in the living room that's way too big to be in alone.

"Are your parents not home?" he asks while scanning my room with meticulous intensity. I'm suddenly glad I always keep it tidy. There would have been no recovering if I had dirty laundry lying around.

"Nope, they're in the Bahamas. They take small vacations about once a month." I sit down on my bed and watch him look at the ripped-out book pages on my wall.

Of course, I bought second-hand books in bad conditions to do it. I'm not a monster.

"They just left you behind to fend for yourself, huh?" he says it so lightly I feel silly for taking it personally. Truth is, I do feel like they abandon me sometimes. Like they jump at any chance to get as far away from me as possible.

Not wanting to let Elija know he hit a soft spot, I take extra care to keep my smile in place. I'd say he's quite perceptive since he was the only one that could tell I hurt my shoulder a week ago, but practice has made my act rather convincing.

"Yes, my life is truly challenging," I swoon dramatically and get to enjoy his soft laughter in return.

"So no siblings?" he asks me as he moves on to check out the pictures and plants on my desk.

"Nope. What about you?"

"Three. One older brother, Kai, and two younger siblings, Daniel and May." There's an easy smile resting on his face, a dreamy expression crossing his eyes, and I'm embarrassed to admit it evokes envy inside of me. I wonder what it would have been like to grow up with siblings. Maybe my parents would have stuck around more.

"I'm sure you keep your parents on their toes," I say lightly. Elija seems to be done examining the room and sits down on my chair. He looks comfortable in my space, almost natural even though he sticks out like a sore thumb with his black clothes and chains amongst all the light green and white.

"My brother and I help a lot with the twins. They're from my mom's current marriage and just turned five," he explains. I find myself taking in every word he's saying, making sure I remember all the new information for later. I can't believe I know so little about him, and yet it still somehow isn't awkward hanging out alone.

"That's really nice of you." We share a smile.

"Do you want to watch a movie?" he suddenly asks. I consider telling him he'd miss his next bus if we did that but decide against it. I'm fairly sure he's aware of that, so who am I to put a bumper on his attempt to spend more time with me.

Or maybe he doesn't want to talk to me for an entire hour and that's why he suggested it... I shove the nagging thought aside and choose to be positive about it.

"Sure, your pick," I offer.

"Mhh. What about Harry Potter? Judging by those pictures over there, I'd say you like it." He points at the small display of Harry Potter-related things on top of my desk extension, and I beam at him.

"Lucky guess," I tease before patting the bed next to me. I'm already sitting at the far edge, so I hope it's not inappropriate or giving him any ideas. He doesn't seem like the type of douche that would jump at the opportunity to make out during a movie on a first meeting, and I'm not even sure he likes me like that, so my nerves stay on the jittery side instead of the worried one.

"You can sit down if you want." My TV is placed opposite my bed so it's the most comfortable way to watch a movie from here.

Elija sits down where I pointed to, looking a lot less flustered than I feel. Maybe this is a regular thing for him? Hanging out on girls' beds. I only ever see him with his friends around school, but that doesn't mean anything. We don't exactly hang around each other either...

"Which one's it going to be?" he asks once he's settled, turning my way and banishing my wayward thoughts. Coming face to face with him with so little space in between us has my heart rate picking up impossibly more. I'm sure my cheeks are flaring crimson by now.

"You've made the best-possible choice once, you can't go wrong from here on." He seems to think about it.

"How about we start with the first one?" he asks, and my heart skips a beat. This just can't be good for my health. Is this him implying we do this again sometime? My cheeks are starting to hurt because of the constant grin I'm entertaining.

Without another word, I pick up my remote control and put on the movie. *Thanks, Netflix, for taking it on.* As soon as Dumbledore appears on the screen, sweet, familiar homesickness of the best kind settles in my chest. I should probably not still be this obsessed with it considering I'd be of age and in my last year at Hogwarts by now. It doesn't matter, apparently, since I'm this close to squealing.

Yeah, I'm mentally holding two fingers really closely together.

When the characters on screen start talking, I bite down on my cheek so I don't speak along. I usually watch these movies alone and have long since learned most of the dialogues by heart. That means I always act the scenes out as they play.

I won't allow myself to do that in front of Elija, though. He'd probably get sick of this whole idea before I could say "bloody hell", and I don't want to annoy him.

"You okay?" the guy beside me asks, capturing my attention.

"Yeah, why?" He points at my leg, which is bouncing even more than usual. I force it to a stop, smiling at him as my cheeks heat up.

"Sorry." After a lingering look at me, like he couldn't decide what to think, he goes back to watching Harry at the zoo.

Minutes of chewing on my bottom lip pass until a sudden warmth settles just above my knee. I look down in awe at Elija's hand covering my clothed thigh, his long fingers spanning a wide breadth, before turning to face him.

"Better," he says softly, and I notice the bouncing has finally stopped. "Are you going to tell me why you're so fidgety all of the sudden?" Magically, Harry Potter is reduced to nothing more than background noise, and I focus on the guy on my bed.

"I really like the movies," I tell him slowly. He looks at me as if that explains nothing, which I guess it does. "You're going to think I'm the biggest nerd," I groan.

"Yeah? Try me," he mocks in a horrible British accent. My jaw drops.

"Was that just? Did you just quote Harry?" I ask, baffled. Elija simply smiles at me, a dimple appearing on his right cheek while I compose myself. "I'm trying not to spoil the movie with my babbling," I finally admit.

"So what you're saying is that you're trying not to behave like a babbling, bumbling band of baboons?" I can't help it, I burst out laughing. After softly laughing along, he adds, "What babbling, Florence?"

"I usually speak along," I say silently, hoping he won't hear. He does hear. And he chuckles.

"Speak along all you want. In case you haven't noticed, this isn't my first time watching the movies. Besides, I'd love nothing more than to see you recite Hermione's lines."

"Why hers?" I ask easily. Elija simply studies me for a beat, smile still in place, before he shakes his head and looks back to the movie.

"I'm eager for the show now. Go on."

And so I stop holding back.

Chapter 5

Elija

I need to get a grip on it or I'll scare Florence off. Seriously, when she asked why I'd like to hear her recite Hermione's lines, I nearly told her it was because they're both pretty smart girls. How horribly basic would that have sounded?

Furthermore, my hand is still resting on the soft, flower-patterned fabric of her skirt. It was meant to be an innocent touch based on good intentions but now I'm painfully aware of it. Does her skin tingle like mine does or am I just losing my mind? At least she seems less fidgety now that she's talking to the TV.

It's quite impressive to watch. Florence knows nearly every word spoken by every character. I wonder how many times she's watched the movies.

Probably too many. I'm guessing there's only so much you can do to occupy yourself when you're home alone as much as she is. If her parents leave for several days each month, Florence would be home alone almost every other week. The thought shouldn't bother me as much as it does.

My life's pretty much the opposite. With two adults and four children, barely an hour goes by when I'm awake and alone. It can be a bit much, but I'd rather be surrounded by people that love me too much instead of too little. I get the feeling Florence is more used to the latter.

As the movie plays on, I play around with the idea of taking the girl beside me to my place sometime. I know my family would love her. Who wouldn't? Even without having spoken to her much, I noticed how nice she is to everyone around her. She seems so genuine and precious, at times, it makes me want to wrap her up in bubble wrap to make sure nothing can ever hurt her.

I sound like a crazy person, having thoughts like that about a girl I barely know. Something about her just evokes a protectiveness I don't feel toward anyone else. Besides, it doesn't feel like I don't know her.

Perhaps she's easy to read to everyone or I simply watch her too often. Truth is, the small glances we exchange at school every day are kind of the reason I look forward to getting up early every morning.

I groan inwardly. I sound so crazy to myself that the thought of ever letting anyone know my thoughts makes me want to rip out my tongue as insurance.

"Elija?" Florence's voice breaks me out of my thoughts. I look at her just as she turns a bit more my way, making my hand move further to the inside of her lower thigh. Not wanting to make her uncomfortable and seeing her red cheeks, I pull my hand away.

Her reaction to such a simple contact makes me wonder if anyone has ever touched her in a more-than-friendly way. The thought of another person's hands on her doesn't sit right with me, even though I'm not entitled to feel that way. More than that, it makes me want to keep touching her. I love seeing her blush and smile because of me.

"Did you hear what I said?" she asks so damn softly my chest squeezes a little tighter. She is so close right now and it's all I can do not to pull her into a hug. Or a kiss.

Most mornings I see Benji embrace her and it's so tempting to follow his example. I'd do it properly though, unlike my friend. No one-armed side hug BS.

I wonder how her body would fit against mine. If she'd smell of sandalwood like the scented candles in her room.

I think the fumes are getting to my head.

Realizing Florence is still looking at me expectantly, I pull myself together. "No, sorry. I zoned out there for a bit." I can see her smile growing a little smaller and mentally kick myself. It's obvious Florence is very unsure about certain things, like inviting me over, and whatever reason she came up with for my zoning out, I can tell it makes her uncomfortable.

I hope she came to the wrong conclusion so my thinking about touching her isn't the reason for her dimming smile. I can learn expressing myself in a way that banishes all her insecurities, but if she's not interested in me romantically, I'm fighting a losing battle.

It would be disappointing, but it wouldn't make me respect her any less. I'm not entitled to her attraction or emotions, after all.

"I asked what bus you want to take," she repeats patiently. Right, I was supposed to hang around here until my next bus arrived. Here I am, overstaying my welcome by suggesting we watch a two-and-a-half-hour movie. I'm an idiot for forgetting this wasn't a date but probably just Florence being too nice to kick me out.

"Right, sorry." I laugh and check the time. "The next one leaves in twenty minutes. I should be able to make it if I leave soon," I tell her even though leaving sounds less than tempting.

"I could give you a ride to the bus stop," she offers but I shake my head. She doesn't mean that, she's just too nice for her own good.

"I really appreciate it, but you've already done enough. It's a short walk, and I don't want you going further out of your way. Thanks for humoring me."

A slightly awkward goodbye and thirty-five minutes later, I enter my home. The first thing I'm greeted by is the familiar scent of my stepfather's cooking. Judging by the date, he's making lasagna. Hell yeah.

The next thing I know, two little demons try to tackle me. I laugh and ruffle their hair as the twins bombard me with questions about where I've been.

"Dad said you didn't call," May complains.

"Were you with Ricky?" Daniel asks hopefully.

"No, little dude. I told you I'm not seeing her anymore." His smile falls a bit, making it hard for me to keep my anger toward that girl at bay. I used to hang out with her and eventually made the mistake of introducing her to my family. We dated for a long time, after all, so I thought nothing of it when I brought her over.

Little did I know it wasn't going to last. The twins got attached, so I didn't have the heart to tell them what went down between us, but it's for sure that she won't ever come over again.

"Glad to see you're not dead in a bush," my stepfather says as he walks out of the kitchen. He's a big bald guy with huge hands but the warm smile on his face makes it impossible for him to seem intimidating. He finishes the distance between us and pulls me into a hug by the back of my neck as if we hadn't seen each other this morning.

"I missed my bus, so a friend offered me to stay with her. We watched a movie, and I forgot the time. I'm sorry I didn't call." There's no need to lie to my stepfather. He can read me like a book either way.

"Anyone I should know of?" he asks with slightly narrowed eyes. He and my older brother are the only ones I told the full story of what Ricky did, and ever since, he's been more protective of me. The sentiment is appreciated, but there's still a bout of discomfort at his apparent distrust towards Florence even though he doesn't know her. She's so sweet, I wouldn't want him to judge her unfairly because of my ex-girlfriend's faults.

He's been around since I was little and cares for me just as much as he does for May and Daniel. I've always known it and didn't feel threatened even when the twins came along, but ever since, he had these moments where it felt like he was going all out to reassure me I was his son as much as his biological kids are. Quite frankly, he's more of a father to me than my biological one ever was.

"She's a friend, dad. I barely know her," I tell him.

Somehow, reducing Florence to that feels wrong but I couldn't tell my dad anything else. Not yet and definitely not surrounded by two curious little kids who will demand answers I do not have.

Seeming to follow my train of thought, my dad nods in a way that tells me we'll talk later before he heads back to the kitchen.

Chapter 6

Florence

I narrow my eyes, trying to figure out what's wrong with the portrait I'm working on. I keep adding and deleting layers, adjusting shadows and highlights but it's still missing something. I'm losing my mind.

Just when I'm about to snap and smack my iPad against the wall behind me, a startling sound cuts through the silence. My phone's ringing, and I turn to see Benji's name on my screen. It's surprising enough since I don't remember this having occurred before. We're not the type of friends that call each other. We get along well but our relationship is usually tied to our time at school.

With every second I stare at his name on my screen, I grow more anxious. What if he's hurt? He wouldn't call *me*, then, though. It's probably a butt dial.

When my brain finally snaps out of the loop, I pick up the phone.

"Benji?" I ask slowly.

"Get your ass out here, we're going to the movies," he simply replies.

"This is Florence," I clarify only for him to laugh at me.

"I am not that high, Flo. I know who I called. Now quit letting me wait. The movie starts in twenty minutes." I check the time, still dumbfounded. It's four pm and Benji wants to go to the movies.

"Did I miss something? What movie? Did we make plans?" I'm about to feel really bad if I forgot about plans with him. I'm supposed to be organized.

"Nah. I just felt like watching the new Marvel movie and none of the guys have time for me. Don't tell me you'll make me go alone. I'd offer to pay for your popcorn, but I'm broke so all I have to offer is my dashing company. I'm not above begging," my friend warns.

I groan inwardly, having wanted to finish the piece I'm working on, but agree nonetheless. Maybe taking a break from drawing will enable me to look at the portrait from a new perspective later. Besides, going out with a friend on the weekend could be a nice change.

A rather foreign concept, but nice.

I promise Benji I'll be down in a minute and hang up on him. I change out of my pajamas at lightning speed, throwing on a sage skirt and white top before brushing my hair, rinsing my mouth, and washing my face.

I started drawing right after I woke up and haven't set it aside to get ready since. I'm just glad I took a shower and brushed my teeth this morning. Morning breath makes me uncomfortable, so at least my anxiety is good for my hygiene.

Not wanting to let Benji wait any longer, I apply a bit of mascara and rush to the door.

"Took you long enough," my friend teases, not seeming very bothered.

"You wouldn't have had to wait if I had known I was going to leave the house earlier," I counter a bit out of breath. "Sorry," I mumble as an afterthought. First, I leave him waiting. Then, I snap at him. Looks like I'm on a roll.

"Why do you always do that?" When I look at my friend questioningly instead of answering, he elaborates. "Apologize for every little thing."

"Are you high?" I ask him with a laugh. I just now noticed his red eyes, but I might be trying to change the topic as well.

Truth is, many people have asked me the same question. I just never know how to respond.

My friend smiles goofily. "Maybe a little," he admits.

"Change seats with me then. I won't let you drive while you're under the influence."

"I drove here," he reminds me even as he unbuckles his seatbelt.

"Only because I wasn't there to stop it."

I refrain from giving him a lecture about how he's being irresponsible and a possible danger to himself and others and silently get in the driver's seat instead. At least today, I can make sure he's safe.

"That was awesome," Benji exclaims as we leave the cinema. I nod my head in agreement, trying hard to keep up with my friend's long strides. Then, his whole demeanor changes, his expression becoming serious. "I'm hungry. How do you feel about pizza?" His eyes narrow as he sizes me up and I nearly burst out laughing.

"We just ate popcorn," I remind him though I could go for some greasy, cheesy pizza right now. I accidentally skipped breakfast and lunch, too focused on the portrait.

"Your point, woman?"

"Absolutely nothing. Lead the way." I'm not very familiar with the district we're in, but Benji tells me there's a pizza place nearby. We sit in a cozy little restaurant less than ten minutes later, tucked in a booth in the back of the dimly lit space. With anyone else, it would almost seem romantic.

"The guys are on their way over. Apparently, they'll show up as long as there's food. Traitors. Not that I blame them, the pizza here is to die for," he gushes, stopping my eyes' perusal of the place to look at him. "You keep saying that but where is the actual proof? The smell alone in this place makes my mouth water," I whine.

We laugh and order the food only for Benji's friends to join us right when I'm supposed to take my first bite. The first thing I notice is that Elija is not with them. That triggers some disappointment but at least he won't see me eat like a starving pig.

"Hey flower girl," Jamie says. He sits on the bench next to me, throws one of his arms over my shoulders, and helps himself to a slice of my food. Before I realize what's happening, the blonde guy has his phone held up in front of our faces Facebook-mom style.

"Say cheese!" is the only warning I get before he snaps the picture. All I have time to do is lift my own slice of pizza in front of my face so my startled expression is partially hidden.

Jamie looks at the picture he took, obviously satisfied.

"It's cute. Look, guys." He shows the picture around, and I realize the rest of his friends are making faces in the background. Good to know I'm the only one with a slow ass reaction. Then again, his friends are probably used to his impromptu photos while it was a first for me, so I should cut myself some slack.

"I'll put it on my story, righty?" he asks, and I see him upload it before I've even had time to answer. Maybe I should be bothered but all it does is make me smile. I've never been posted before.

"Late night yesterday?" Liam asks, referring to my lack of concealer. I turn my attention to him, reminding myself he's just a brat and that I don't care about his opinion. So what if I look tired without concealer? At least I don't deal with back-handed questions to bring others down.

I roll my shoulders back when I feel them trying to droop in an attempt to hide myself. This isn't the place for me to cower. Not for him. I build myself back up with that mantra.

"Sure," I reply with a smile.

"What'd you do? Talk to your many friends? Tell me, do your books talk back? Is it more like a puppet show or a monologue?" Orion throws in there. I keep my back straight to refrain from sinking further into my seat. When did we vote on playing all-against-Florence?

"At least she knows how to read," Jamie tells his friend, receiving another glare. I'm just glad they don't start chasing each other again.

I look at the rest of the guys to gauge their reactions. Marcus has a rather stoic expression, but I see the hint of amusement playing behind those hazel eyes as he watches his buddies. Jamie looks perfectly content as he eats my food and teases his friend. Orion is glaring at Jamie, Liam is on his phone, the newest model, of course, and Benji is devouring his pizza as if it were a matter of life and death.

Though considering the rate at which my slices are vanishing, it might as well be.

Chapter 7

Elija

They're with her. Literally, my whole friend group apart from me is with the girl I haven't been able to get out of my head since I left her house yesterday.

After my mom got home last evening and we ate dinner, my dad pulled me aside to speak to me. I tried to explain what was going on between Florence and me as well as I could. Not that there was much to tell. The more I tried to insist she was a sweet girl and nothing to worry about, the more suspicious he got, and it only got worse when I gushed about her good qualities.

Eventually, the interrogation stopped and I was left to stew over my words and the girl they revolved around.

Now, I'm in the car with the twins. I took them to the zoo so my parents could sleep in and we're currently looking for a place to get dinner.

I saw Jamie's picture right before getting into the car and have been conflicted ever since. I know it would be a bad idea to go to the pizza place my friends are at because one, I'd look like an obsessive stalker, and two, the twins shouldn't meet Florence.

The chances of them liking her and getting attached are too high. Besides, they're little kids with no filter which could get me into trouble or end very embarrassingly.

On the other hand, I really want to see her. And my friends, of course. It definitely has nothing to do with jealousy, I simply miss my friends.

"Hey guys, you in the mood for pizza?" I ask over my shoulder.

"Yeah!" they agree quickly. I love how excitable they are even though they're tired after the long day. At least the house will be calm tonight for once.

It takes us twenty minutes to arrive at Paolo's, and I have my fingers crossed that my friends are still here. As soon as we enter the restaurant, familiar laughter hits my ears like music and I know we aren't too late.

She's sitting in a booth in the far corner, her head thrown back while her hand covers her face. The way she hides herself when I'm sure she looks best when she's laughing sits slightly wrong with me. How such a stunning girl can be so insecure is a mystery to me.

I walk over, one sibling at each hand, and try to divide my attention between my friends rather than just stare at the girl amidst them. It takes a lot of effort.

"Thought you couldn't make it today?" Liam asks once I'm close, and while I'm not usually a violent person, a few words from him are enough to make tension rise within me.

That guy really pushes my buttons. The way he speaks with his nose pointing to the ceiling. Like, relax, you're not better than us because you're coming from old money.

"Change of plans, these two were hungry," I tell the group as I desperately try not to look at Florence. I can feel her watching me and it's making me nervous. If I meet those pretty emerald eyes now, I won't be able to look away and my friends will make a comment.

"Heyy, where are my favorite twins?" Jamie asks playfully. In the bat of an eye, my hands are no longer being held and my two little companions jump at my friend. They adore him just like he seems to do in return. They're little kids, they're obsessed with all of my friends – Liam not included, I said friends – but they have the strongest bond with Jamie.

"Who is she?" Daniel suddenly asks, apparently just now noticing Florence. Her cheeks grow red and she sinks further into her seat, apparently uncomfortable even under the attention of a five-year-old.

"That, my friend, is Florence," Jamie explains. Florence gives the twins a little wave and smiles at them. It does something weird to my chest, seeing them together.

"She's pretty," May announces and I can't help but chuckle along with my friends. I'm about to agree with her when Florence speaks up first.

"That coming from you is the best compliment I've ever received. I don't think I've ever seen a face as cute as yours," she replies, and now it's my sister's turn to shily turn her face into Jamie's chest.

"What about me?" Daniel demands, evoking a few more laughs.

"Don't worry, buddy. You'll grow up to be the most handsome man anyone has ever seen," Marcus promises, causing Florence's head to snap his way. I guess she's never heard him this affectionate or seen such a warm smile on his face. She should see the way he acts toward his own sister.

"Even more handsome than Elija?" my brother asks, making my heart swell to the size of a football.

"That ogre? Of course!" replies blondie.

Both of my siblings look like they've just been told that it's Christmas. I'm glad I took them here tonight.

"Is she your girlfriend?" Daniel whispers to Jamie loud enough for the whole table to hear, obviously referring to Florence. For the first time, she meets my eyes only to look away hurriedly. I'm just trying to stay quiet and let my friend answer.

"No, little dude, sadly not," he says playfully.

"Why not? Is she not nice?" May asks.

"Ricky was nice. Right Eli?" my brother adds. Thereby, he successfully causes a tense moment of silence. My friends might not know all the details about my breakup with Ricky, but they know enough for the air to turn stifling.

"Sure," I say with an attempted smile.

"And no, May, Florence is very nice," Jamie swoops in.

"Then why-" my brother cuts my sister off.

"Because he's into guys! We've been over this," he declares, copying parental exasperation he surely picked up from my mother and causing the whole table to erupt with laughter. In the corner of my eye, I see Florence.

Her laugh's different from the one before, and I can't help but feel it's because of the Ricky comment. I doubt she knows my ex since she doesn't go to our school, but she must have picked up on the change of atmosphere.

Our group orders another three pizzas to share. Throughout the meal, everyone, even Florence, seems to be in a good and relaxed mood.

"We're hanging out afterward, you coming too? Maybe your brother can pick the twins up," Marcus asks.

"We want to come!" May protests.

"You've had a long day and it's time for bed soon. You'll go home with Kai," I tell them. Maybe they know how tired they really are since they don't try to protest and in other circumstances, I'm sure they would have turned into pests real quick about being denied. I text my brother, glad he has his own car since I took my parents' this morning.

Ten minutes later, I've said goodbye to my siblings and am on my way to Liam's shed. It's not an actual shed but it's what we call it for the lack of a better word. The "shed" is bigger than my room and secluded from the rest of his parents' estate. Therefore, a good place to hang out without anyone calling the cops or being disturbed.

I'm in the car with Jamie since Florence drives Benji's car and the other guys came together.

"About that Ricky comment, you good?" he asks me carefully. Like I was still beat up about it after all this time.

I don't argue with him about his tone, worried he'll see a retaliation as my being defensive. Instead, I brush him off to move on, "Yeah, whatever. Thanks for the safe, though. The moment could have dragged on horribly." He nods as if it were no big deal. It is to me.

"What's going on between Flo and you, by the way? The tension between you two could have been cut by a knife this evening." Is that so? I hadn't really noticed. We barely interacted with so much going on at all times. In my friend group, everyone has a lot to say, so it can happen that a shy person like Florence would struggle to get a word in.

"There's nothing going on," I insist. After all, there really isn't anything worth telling, and I don't want to be the kind of person that starts rumors. Nope, I'm going to keep whatever thoughts I might have about it to myself until there's more to tell. Not that my friend seems to believe me, but he doesn't pry.

Chapter 8

Florence

"Flo?" Benji asks, holding his J out to me. I shake my head with a smile. The guys should do whatever they feel like doing but I've never tried any drugs and I don't plan on starting now.

Marcus takes a hit before handing it to Elija. He declines, earning surprised glances from his friends and a knowing smile from Jamie.

"So, flower girl. Tell us something about yourself."

"What do you want to know?" I feel comfortable enough right now, even as everyone is looking at me. I don't get the sense that they're trying to judge or criticize me, which puts my anxiety at ease. I don't know why I'm so sensitive to that, but I'm glad it isn't the case.

So far, the day was nice even though I've been feeling like an outsider since the rest of the group joined Benji and me. I'd hate for the night to be ruined now by my sensitivity.

But with their expectant gazes so bare of malicious intent, I feel at ease and ready to share whatever they want to know. Besides, the room is quite dark, illuminated by some colorful LEDs along the top of one wall. I'm always more comfortable when the lights are dimmed. It feels a bit less like family meals.

"Mhm, something juicy but we'll start off nice. Any partners we should know about? Present or past," Jamie asks.

"Lorence? Come on, we know she's never been in a relationship. Have you even had a kiss before? Buses not included," Orion interjects. Somehow, even his comment feels friendlier than usual. Like it's all good-natured fun.

"No relationships. Yes to a kiss," I correct him before immediately blushing. What I'm talking about barely classifies as a kiss, but mentioning it in front of Elija still makes me nervous. Especially since I can't see his eyes from where he's standing on the other side of the room, grabbing a bottle of water.

Not that I think he cares. Why would he? It was a long time ago and he and I are not even a thing. I need to stop driving myself crazy over this.

The sound of Jamie gasping dramatically pulls my attention back. "You have? Who? When? Where? Was it good? Was it juicy? Tell me!"

"Okay, let's calm down a tad. The unspoken rule says she gets to ask a question for each one she answers," Marcus says. Thank him for that. I was about to run for my life to escape Jamie.

"I like the sound of that, but I'm bad at thinking of things to ask. How about someone asks a question and everyone just answers?" I propose. I'm relieved to see some nodding going on. Good, I want to get to know them better.

"I've had one boyfriend, but he dumped me for a chick after four months," Jamie says to which Orion mumbles, "Hated that douchebag anyway."

"I've dated a few people," Marcus says.

"*Dated* a *few* people? Oh, shut up! Don't you dare act like you're innocent like that now," Jamie exclaims. Marcus flips him off.

"I don't do relationships. Can't be tied down, you know? Never seems to keep the ladies away though if you know what I mean." Liam winks at me and I nearly recoil.

"Excuse me, I have to go and vomit," Elija mutters from where he sits, his eyes trained on me. While his friends seem confused, I can't help but break into a grin that makes my cheeks hurt.

"I thought Hermione's lines were mine," I tease him, ignoring our company.

"You wouldn't have said it. You're too nice." He makes it sound like I'm some lame, stuck-up goody two shoes. Not that he's wrong. I may have vomited a bit in my mouth, but I never would have said it out loud. Dammit, do they all think I'm boring?

"I won't even ask what just happened. Orion, your turn," Jamie moves the conversation along.

"No relationships. Enough kisses for you to judge me," Orion tells me. I think he might actually be waiting for me to comment on it, but I have to disappoint him.

"As long as everything was consensual, I have nothing to say about it but good for you." That didn't help the whole coming-across-as-lame thing, did it? "Elija?" I ask. He's the only one who hasn't answered and I'm desperate to put an end to the silence.

"One past relationship," he says curtly. I don't like it. He's never spoken to me like that, and it makes my mind wander back to Paolo's. I'm guessing he's talking about Ricky again.

"What about currently?" I ask, trying to act leisurely. Now that he's settled and my eyes have adjusted to the light, I can see him arching an eyebrow. By his amused expression, I'd say he sees right through my act. Embarrassment worms its way through me for being dumb enough to even ask something like that.

"Sorry, could you elaborate?" he asks politely. He's toying with me. Even worse, I like it no matter that my cheeks burn up hotter.

"Do you have a partner, uh, currently?" Please ground, if you can hear me, swallow me whole. The guys surrounding us are watching Elija's and my conversation as if it were their favorite show, so I lower my gaze to my hands, which have started drumming my rhythm on my leg softly.

"Nope, no partner," Elija tells me quickly as if he noticed I was getting uncomfortable. "My turn. Hobbies?"

"That's a boring question," Liam whines. "We're not five."

"Too bad you don't like it. Mine's playing the guitar or anything that has to do with music," Elija tells us, keeping his eyes strictly on me.

"We all know that," Orion adds.

"I didn't," I add. No idea why but I felt the need to defend Elija. It's useless since these are his friends and he's more than capable of standing up for himself, but the urge was too quick to quench.

In this round I find out that Liam plays tennis, Benji pretty much spends his time taking walks in the woods and smoking weed, Marcus plays soccer or goes to the gym, Orion skates, and Jamie does nothing but inhale anything Netflix throws his way.

"We know your hobby, Lorence. You take your books everywhere you go," Orion cuts me off before I can even say a note. I clamp my mouth shut and laugh to seem unbothered. I hate being interrupted or cut off. It's rude and makes me feel silly. Like my words aren't worthy to be heard and I was presumptuous to think otherwise.

"Shut up, Orion and let her speak," Elija snaps before he turns to me, his voice immediately softer. "Go on, Florence."

"I do like to read." I let Orion look around triumphantly before going on. "Other than that, I draw or visit nice places with my baby."

"You have a child?" Liam all but cries out.

"So you have had a bit more than a kiss," Orion mutters at the same time. I smile but it's Elija who answers for me.

"It's her Vespa. Right?" He looks at me for approval.

"Ten points to – hang on, what's your house?" I ask him.

"Equal parts Gryffindor and Hufflepuff every time I take a quiz. You?"

"Ravenclaw," I respond without hesitation. "But Gryffindor's a close second. I have to admit those quizzes make me anxious. I always feel like none of the replies are completely me so my result will be inaccurate." Elija just laughs and shakes his head as if nothing I said surprised him.

"Sorry to interrupt the dorkention but how about we talk about something more interesting," Orion offers.

"More interesting than Harry Potter?" I ask, unable to help myself, at the same time as Jamie says, "Dorkention?"

"Dork and convention," Orion tries to reason but Jamie just bursts out laughing. "Shut up! I was trying something." He pouts so unlike himself I snort. Then immediately bury my face in my hands to hide my no-doubt tomato-looking face.

Chapter 9

Elija

We keep asking questions and it's going surprisingly well. That is until we talk about favorite colors. A seemingly harmless topic, I thought. I forgot to consider the lengths Liam will go to be insufferable.

"Mine's green," Florence tells us, earning a few "No shit"s and "We know"s.

"Wasn't Ricky's favorite color green?" Liam, the idiot, interrupts.

"Dude?" Even Jamie seems ridiculously close to snapping at him, and he's the only reason we're friends with Liam in the first place. He and Jamie grew up together and my friend insists Liam didn't use to be such a prick. The rest of us simply try to tolerate him, even after what went down.

"What? I just remembered it. Why am I not allowed to bring her up? She used to hang out with us all the time back when Elija was doing her."

"Wow!" a few of my friends say in outrage but Liam decides to keep playing dumb. I have my fists balled and teeth gritted at how he makes me sound. Ricky and I dated for a month before we ever shared a kiss and now my "friend" is here, making it sound like she was some sort of booty call.

Not that that's necessarily a bad thing, I just don't want Florence to get the wrong impression about me.

"Okay, okay, I get it. We're playing innocent for his new chick now," he adds with an infuriating smile.

"If I were you, I'd really shut the fuck up now," I advise him. I don't even have to look at Florence to know she's probably regretting making every choice that led her here.

"Geez, all right," Liam says as if I was the annoying one. I look to my right to see Benji holding another J my way but I shake my head. I want to stay sober so I can leave when things go south and preferably take Florence with me. I'm sure as fuck not going to drive under the influence, much less with her in the car.

Jamie is quick to start up a new conversation and once I took a few deep breaths to calm down, I risk a glance at the girl next to him. She's drumming something on her leg again, something I've noticed her doing whenever she's stressed. It makes my blood boil all over again.

I hate that we've made her uncomfortable when it's been so much fun to have her around. I was hoping it might turn into a more regular thing, but the chances of that seem slim with how much Liam is running his mouth.

For the next twenty minutes, Liam keeps making subtle comments everyone picks up on. Most of them include a certain girl that isn't present.

"Is it too late to try your weed?" Florence asks Benji at some point, making everyone's heads turn her way.

"No," Benji tells her at the same time as I say, "Yes."

"Dude?" Benji asks me.

"She's not smoking weed," I say firmly. My behavior is only one more thing to scare her off, I guess, but there's nothing left to lose anyway. I'm sure as soon as she's away from us she'll stay gone. I hate that thought but I don't blame her.

"It's my weed. If she wants to try it, she can."

"No, she can't," I force through gritted teeth, hating the way I must come across. I don't want her to think I'm a controlling ass, but I know she'd regret it if she smoked now. This is not the right environment to be high for the first time and I don't want her to end up having a bad trip.

"I'm right here," Florence speaks up softly. Something like pride settles in my chest as I hear the slight edge in her voice. I want her to stand up for herself.

"Have you ever tried it before?" I ask her, knowing the answer even before she shakes her head.

"See? Benji, you know how strong your stuff is."
"Maybe he's right," Benji tells Florence softly. Even in the dark, I see the way her chest falls with a shaky breath. It's a slight change but it tells me all I need to know. I'm taking her home now.

Just as I'm about to offer her a ride, Liam opens his mouth again.

"Ricky told me she smoked for the first time with you."

Yeah, that does it for me. I was already too agitated but that was just one comment too much.

"Yeah? Was that before or after you fucked her on my birthday?" I snap. The jerk has the *audacity* to laugh.

"Chill, bro. I told you I didn't know you two were dating." Such a filthy liar.

"The party was at my house. There was a picture of us on my bedside table."

"To be fair, I wasn't looking at your furniture." He still has that smug expression on his face and the last of my restrain slips through my fingers. I try to jump at him, my arm cocked for a hit, but Orion and Marcus are holding me back before I can do any damage. They speak softly to me, trying to get me to calm down, but I can hardly hear them over the blood rushing in my ears.

"Elija, you're scaring Flo," Orion finally whispers. I drop my hand, the words sobering me up. Maybe it was the fact that he called her Flo and not Lorence, or perhaps her name is enough for me to get a grip on it.

Either way, I take three deep breaths before looking at her. She's staring at the floor, her leg jumping, her hands drumming, and her chest falling and rising with too quick breaths.

"I'm taking you home," I tell her, hating the way it comes out as a demand rather than an offer. This whole situation is messed up.

"You don't have to do that," she answers softly, not meeting my eyes. Meanwhile, it's all I can do not to start cursing myself for stressing her out.

"Please, Florence. Let me take you home," I try again, more gently. This time, she nods a few times before getting up. All without meeting my eyes.

"Bye guys," she says when we reach the door of the shed.

"Goodnight, Flower girl," Jamie says with a warm smile. She smiles back as the other say goodbye only for the façade to drop as soon as the door closes behind us.

"Sorry that I snapped like that in there. For Liam's behavior too but mostly for mine. Are you okay?" I ask her on our way to my car. The cool air is really helping me to calm down, clearing my mind enough to make me feel even worse.

"Yeah, don't worry about it." She's less than convincing and I hate the fake smile she tries to sell me. I'm sure I've done enough tonight, though, so I won't call her out on it.

While I'm driving to her place, I rack my brain for some topic to break the tense silence. I come up empty-handed and insanely frustrated.

"I'm sorry about Ricky. I don't know anything about it but her sleeping with one of your best friends is really shitty. From both of them," Florence says quietly. She's still drumming her fingers against her thigh, and I'm starting to notice it's always the same rhythm.

"Liam's not my friend. I try to tolerate him because he and Jamie used to be close but we're not friends," I clarify.

"Well, either way. I'm sorry." I'd tell her not to apologize again but I'm done ordering her around for the night. "When's your birthday?" she asks after a moment of silence.

"November 14th. Yours?"

"April 30th."

"A Taurus, then." I chuckle but it's mainly so she finally looks at me. It works. She turns my way with a slight blush on her cheeks and a curious expression.

"You're into astrology?" she asks me.

"A bit. I kind of grew up with it because of my mom so I know the basics. Don't ask me what the combination of your different planets and the signs they were in when you were born mean, though. You'd have to ask my mom about stuff like that." I risk another quick glance at her and instantly know she didn't understand a single thing I said. She's looking at me as if I spoke French or something.

"Right, I'll keep it in mind. Wait you said November? That's Sagittarius, right? My aunt's birthday was in November and she used to joke about shooting me with an arrow if I didn't eat my vegetables," she says with a faraway look in her eyes. I didn't miss the fact that she spoke of her aunt in the past tense.

"Her birthday must've been after the 21st. I'm a Scorpio," I tell her softly.

Florence simply nods absently, and although I'm disappointed to have lost her there, I'm glad she's calmed down a bit.

Chapter 10

Florence

I need to get out of this car.

First off, I'm confused about my feelings about earlier tonight. Or more precisely about Elija's behavior. I know I should be mad at him for telling me what I could and couldn't do and maybe even intimidated by how he was about to attack Liam.

I don't think I'm either.

I think Elija was trying to look out for me. He probably would have said it differently if Liam hadn't tried to get a rise out of him all evening. Therefore, his little outburst was understandable.

Also, the way his two friends had to hold him back was somehow attractive to my hormone-riddled brain. Then he told me he was taking me home in that rough voice I can't stop thinking about. What kind of person does that make me? Liking it when someone tells me what to do.

I'm glad Elija went back to normal quickly. However hot his moment of anger might've been, I love that he is well-mannered. Plus, I was getting flustered.

The second reason why I need to get out of the car is that I need a moment of quiet to think about all the things I learned this evening. I want to remember everything important about Elija and his friends, and I'd like to sort out my thoughts about the whole Ricky thing.

It has nothing to do with me and I shouldn't think about someone else's business but I can't help it. Liam was comparing me to her all evening. Not that it means much coming from him. He called me Elija's new chick, for Pete's sake.

Was it just part of making Elija mad or does he honestly think there's something between his not-friend and me?

And lastly, now that I mentioned my aunt, I can't stop thinking about her. She and I used to be really close back when my parents were always busy at work. I probably spent more time and laughter with her than with my mom and dad combined. She got sick when I was about ten, but it didn't get bad for two years. In the end, it was a good thing when she could let go after a year of fighting for every breath.

I was thirteen and devastated when she died, and my parents thought that the right time to start taking more vacations. To this day I'm pretty sure them leaving me so often is because I reminded my mother too much of her dead sister.

That was probably the source, at least. Now, they might just enjoy the changes of scenery.

"Florence? We're here." I startle at the male voice beside me but am quick to recover. I set a smile in place, knowing it's less than convincing. Maybe he won't notice and if he does, maybe he'll believe I'm just tired.

"Right! Thank you for the ride home and for letting me tag along tonight. I had a great time. Goodnight." The words escape me thoughtlessly as I reach for the door handle and escape the car as if my ass was on fire. I rush to my house before he can say something in return and unlock my door with numb fingers.

I don't know why I'm feeling so overwhelmed right now. It's not like anything happened. It's just those stupid memories and painful thoughts I always try hard to stay away from. Is it normal to still struggle with the loss of a person this much after more than four years?

She was the only person to ever accept and love me unconditionally.

There was no need for good grades to get some affection in return and there were no uncomfortable clothes I had to fit in to look how she perceived my perfect version of myself to appear. Maybe it still hurts this much because I know I'll never get that sort of relationship back.

I shut my front door behind me and lean my back against it. With my eyes closed, I take deep breaths and tap my rhythm on the solid material of the door. I try to tell myself I'm fine, that there's enough air in the room.

It doesn't feel that way.

Slowly, I slide down until I sit on the floor. I pull my legs toward my chest, trying to feel any sort of comfort while still tapping the rhythm on my knees. In an attempt to think of happy things, I envision sunflowers in a wide, green field. I think of my books, my drawings, and even school. It hardly does anything against the bitter hopelessness clawing at my chest.

My skin feels too tight, my clothes suffocating. I grip at the hem of my shirt, then the skin underneath it. Feeling my protruding ribs is what finally pulls the first sob from me. I hate how they feel. They're too prominent, too tight around my lungs, and too pointy beneath my fingertips.

I try to get a good grip on one of them so I can pull it away. They're squeezing me. They're the reason I can't get enough air.

Another sob cuts through the silent house but I can't hear it. I can't hear a single thing other than my heart's frantic beat. It's trapped behind my ribs and doesn't have enough space. It's suffocating in its tight cage.

I give up on trying to pull them away. It never works. Instead, I start running my nails over every inch of skin I can reach. It's my skin's fault for being this tight. It doesn't fit me. I don't want it anymore.

When even that doesn't help I resort to curling into a ball on the floor. I run my hands into my hair and try to pull on it. It looks like hers. It's another reason my parents left. Another thing reminding them painfully of what they lost. It's my fault for being so much like her. Or maybe not enough.

Too much to let them forget about my aunt, too little to fill the void she left.

I'm too lost in my frenzy to notice the warm hands wrapped around my wrists until my fingers can no longer grasp my brown strands. I open my eyes, trying to scramble away from the intruder but my vision is too blurry and the grip on me too tight to allow an escape.

I hastily blink away my tears, my heart going a hundred miles per hour. Finally, I'm able to make out a pair of wild, dark eyes, wide with panic. Elija's lips are moving. I think he's talking to me, but I can't process the words.

What is he doing here? I'm home alone. I was supposed to be alone so why is he here? And what is he saying? The confusion and frustration cause fresh tears to blur my vision and wet my cheeks. He's not supposed to be here. No one's supposed to see me this way.

I try to pull away from him again and he finally lets go of my wrists. I scoot back, wanting to feel something solid at my back again only to be greeted by a fresh breeze. Elija must have left the door open when he entered. It takes everything in me to realize I need to move to my right or I'll fall down a few steps.

When my back is up against a wall, I can finally pull my legs back toward me and tap my rhythm. Elija is no longer speaking. I'm not looking at him, but I can hear his heavy breathing.

I don't know what to do as my own heartbeat calms a bit. I start feeling the effect of what I did to my body. My head and lungs hurt, my throat is dry, and my skin feels raw where I clawed at it. I must look like a lunatic.

I'll really have to change schools now because there's no way I'll be able to face Elija again.

As if hearing my thought, the guy in my house gets to his feet and walks away from me.

Chapter 11

Elija

I could tell something was wrong with Florence when she kept staring out of the window of my car with unfocused eyes after I pulled into her driveway. I knew her smile was anything but genuine and I only got more worried when she slammed my door shut before I could say so much as a quick goodnight.

Despite all that, I let her go without asking if she needed anything. I couldn't bring myself to drive off either, so I ended up sitting in my car in her driveway like a creep. I told myself I just wanted to make sure she got inside safely but I stayed even after she shut her front door.

I got a bad feeling when none of the lights turned on inside. I entertained the possibility that she was trying not to wake her parents but she's home alone so it made no sense.

Finally, after seeing her phone on my passenger seat, I had an excuse to go after her. I rang the doorbell and waited patiently. When nothing happened, I rang it again. And again. I eventually pressed my ears against the door only to hear concerning noises. It sounded like someone was crying. Scratch that, it sounded like someone was full-on sobbing inside.

I hated the way the knot in my stomach twisted. I wasn't particularly proud of breaking into her home either, but any guilt vanished when I found her curled up in a ball mid-panic attack.

It was horrible. She looked so broken, rocking slightly and pulling at her hair while pained sobs racked her body. I went into panic mode myself, frantically calling her name and trying to stop her from hurting herself.

Now I'm standing in her kitchen, searching for water to give her while a voice in the back of my head is calling me an intruder. The shock reflected in her eyes when she recognized me told me Florence didn't want me here, but how could I possibly leave? It's a rhetorical question, I can't.

When I go back to the entrance, Florence is in the same position she was in when I left, silently staring ahead of her. I hand her the glass of water, which she accepts without looking at me.

I feel like the most useless little shit alive, standing here with no idea what to say or do. And I hate knowing the silence is probably making Florence nervous all over again.

It's a desperate attempt but I end up reaching for my phone and playing the song she showed me two weeks ago. When that doesn't seem to upset her further, I carefully reach out to grab one of her hands. She doesn't protest and goes along when I pull her to her feet and drag her into her room. She's shaky on her legs but she follows me.

I'm freestyling this as I go but considering how she hugged her own legs so tightly to herself; I take a leap of faith. I lead her onto her bed, kick my shoes off, and pull her into my arms on top of the sheets. The music is still playing. Now, it's the song Florence showed me last week that's filling the heavy silence between us.

She seems a bit unsure in my arms; as if she didn't quite understand what was going on.

Her skin is cool to the touch and she's shaking slightly so I try to pull her a little closer and start rubbing circles on her back. Her face is buried in the crook of my neck, her body curled towards mine. It's how my mom used to comfort me whenever I felt bad as a kid, so with that as my only reference, I just keep going.

I hate to think about what would have happened if I hadn't found her. Would she still be in the position and state I found her in, or would she have passed out by now?

My irritation toward her parents spikes again. They shouldn't leave her alone as much as they do.

"You don't have to stay," Florence whispers hoarsely after several minutes.

"Please don't ask me to leave you alone right now. I'm afraid I won't be able to respect your wishes," I tell her softly. I'd hate it if my presence made her uncomfortable, and if she asks me to, I'll let go of her in a heartbeat. So far, it seems I might've been helping though, so I won't move away just yet. I really believe she needs some comfort right now.

For a while, the music is the only sound in the room. Then, "Thank you." It comes out so quietly I'm barely able to make out the words.

"Don't thank me," I reply, matching my voice to hers. Really, she shouldn't thank me. If I hadn't let her leave or waited for less time, she probably wouldn't have had a panic attack in the first place. It my and my friends' fault for making her spiral, and my fault for not helping sooner. It's the least I can do to try and help in whatever small way I can.

No idea how long it takes, but I eventually feel the girl in my arms slowly drifting off to sleep. I can hear the change in her breathing and feel it in the way her body relaxes fully against mine.

My thoughts are still a jumbled mess, and I don't think I'll be able to fall asleep in this position, but I'm more than glad to stay awake all night if it makes Florence feel better.

I shut my eyes and listen to her even breathing, letting it calm my fraying mind.

I blink groggily at the daylight streaming through the windows in Florence's room, clearly off with my earlier assessment of my incapability to fall asleep. I slowly take stock of my surroundings, surprised to find Florence still in my arms.

It seems last night has taken its toll on her since she's still fast asleep.

I look down at her, my chest growing warm as I take in the way she's curled up against me. I'd love to stay in this position for longer. I truly would. If only my body wasn't such a damn traitor and demanded I use the bathroom soon. Florence's arm pressing on my bladder isn't helping either.

I carefully untangle my limps from hers and try to sneak out without waking her up, but I'd say I failed since she speaks softly when I'm just about to exit her room.

"Thanks again," she mumbles. I realize she thinks I was about to sneak out on her and that thought sits very wrong with me. Considering the way her back is now turned to me and the tension in her shoulders, I'm guessing she doesn't want me to.

"I was just trying to go to the bathroom. I'm sorry I woke you," I tell her, taking a step back toward the bed.

"You really don't need to stay," she insists. She sounds better than last night, but her voice is still a bit hoarse.

"Can I get-" I break off after taking another step toward her. From this angle, I'm able to see her arms. More precisely the red, angry trails along her skin and the hint of blood adorning some of them. "Holy shit," I mumble. Then I curse myself for it because Florence visibly winces, curling up further to hide her arms from my view.

"Florence, please look at me." I kneel on the bed as she slowly turns to me. She sits up, her posture on point as always but doesn't look at me. I gently take her hands in mine.

"Has this happened before?" I ask. No idea where I'm going with these questions, but I really want to understand. Her silence is answer enough.

"Is there something you need? Some way I can help?" I scan her body for more injuries, pausing on the sliver of skin that peaks out between the bottom of her shirt and the top of her skirt. The skin there is even more irritated, and I'm sure if she pulled her shirt up a bit, more marks would be revealed.

"No thanks. I'm fine." She gives me one of those fake-ass smiles I hate so much but I don't call her out on it. "You should probably get going. I'm sure your family is asking themselves where you're at," she goes on.

I'd like to tell her that they don't matter right now. That I don't want to leave her alone and that she might feel better if she talked to me. I want to hold her again. To comfort her and feel the way her body fits so perfectly with mine.

I say and do none of those things, not wanting to force my proximity on her when we're barely more than strangers. "Are you sure?" Florence nods, much to my dismay. It's fine if she doesn't want to talk to me, though. I just hope she can confide in someone.

"Mind telling me where you've been all night, young man?" my mother asks as soon as I step inside the house. She pulls me into a hug, telling me she was worried sick, and then takes a step back to take a better look at me. As always, it seems she can read me like a book.

"What's wrong? Does it have anything to do with that girl the twins wouldn't shut up about? Is that where you were until now?" Of course, my whole family knows about Florence by now. News spread like wildfire in this nosy family, and for once, I'm not too happy about it.

"It does and it is but it's not what you think. Nothing happened. Well, something did but it's not what you think." I exhale roughly and run a hand through my hair. I just want to take a shower and sleep. "I'm tired, mom. I'll talk to you later, okay?"

My mom's a short lady, but she's far from harmless. She used to scare the shit out of me when I was younger. I was never scared she'd actually hurt me but god knows I didn't want to test her by not eating my vegetables.

Right now, her eyes are filled with sympathy and worry. Thankfully, she doesn't try to push. Instead, she ruffles my hair and starts shoving me toward my room herself.

I'm eighteen after all, and even though I know she'd prefer to keep tabs on me at all times, she respects my boundaries and tries to treat me like an adult when she can. That means giving me the right to stay the night where I want to, although I should let her know where for her own peace of mind.

I feel a lot better after my shower and nap, so I join my family for lunch. My parents seem to hold back whatever questions about Florence they might have, and my brother keeps glancing at me curiously. When May finally drops her name, it's like a dam breaks.

"Florence, that's a nice name. Isn't it, Robert?" my mom asks. I hide a smile by taking a bite out of my toast. I love her name. It suits her really well, which is why I insist on using it rather than call her by a nickname.

"It is, Amelia. So, Eli, how do you know her?" my dad replies in an act that belongs to a bad tv show.

"She's a classmate and Benji's friend," I tell them, not sure how else to explain it. Especially in front of the twins.

"And she's Jamie's girlfriend," May announces loudly, making everyone's heads turn her way. My family knows very well that Jamie does not have a girlfriend.

"No, she's not. He's gay, May!" Daniel says as if he's had enough of this conversation already, and I bite back a smile. It's funny seeing him mimic my parents' behavior.

"It's not normal!" my sister whines.

"May!" her father snaps.

"Don't *May* me! I just don't understand why anyone would like men when there are women!" With that, the tension bleeds out of the room.

I should have known that something like that was about to come, but the little girl had me scared for a second.

But really, May hasn't been able to shut up about Astrid from *How to train your dragons*. Not that I blame her. Astrid and Hiccup could both gladly run me over.

Moving on. The laughter going around the table dies down a bit, which my older brother takes advantage of as he speaks up.

"She's pretty. I saw her when I picked up the twins." My dad raises an eyebrow at me, but Daniel beats me to answer.

"She looks like Ricky. Ricky was pretty." I groan, knowing exactly that my parents will now think I'm using Florence as a rebound. Even more than a year after the incident, my parents still don't believe that I'm over Ricky, which I am.

"She's nothing like Ricky and the only thing their appearances have in common is their brown hair. Although, Florence's is darker, shinier, and way longer. Besides, she always wears it up while Ricky left it down. They're not even the same height. Ricky was like two inches taller."

I smile a bit. Florence is ridiculously short. 5.5 Maybe? Just tall enough to reach my chin, though I get the feeling I shouldn't point that out to her.

"Florence's eyes are green, not blue. They might look brown from afar but when the sun hits them right, you can see they're really not." I trail off, finally realizing that I'm still talking about Florence in front of my whole family.

Shoot me now.

Everyone is staring at me like I just broke out into a song or something. Meanwhile, I just know my cheeks are burning up, which is really not helping right now.

"And you spent the night with her? Benji's friend?" my dad asks slowly.

"She hung out with us last night and I dropped her off at home, but she wasn't feeling well, and her parents weren't at home so I kept her company. That's all," I insist. I can tell they still have questions but telling them more about what happened last night would feel wrong. It's something between Florence and me.

"So you two are not a thing?" Kai asks, grinning like an idiot.

"No," I say, though my teeth might be slightly gritted.

"Good to know. It's all right if I shoot my shot then, right?" he goes on, still smiling. I know he's just trying to get a reaction, and I try to reason with myself that he has no point. That he's in a relationship, for Christ's sake.

Still, it seems I'm unable to act rationally when it comes to her, and even the thought of him with Florence makes my blood boil. I know how he used to treat girls before he got into a relationship.

It's not like he led them on, he told them what his intentions were from the start. They just seemed to fall for his stupid, cocky smile and the confident way he behaves either way and ended up getting hurt.

I don't think I could look him in the eyes if he hurt Florence. It's that stupid urge to protect what isn't mine again but I can't help it when it comes to her.

"She'd never go for you," I tell him, trying to find comfort in the thought. I truly don't believe he's her type, but I also can't imagine her rejecting someone either. She's too nice for her own good.

"Mhm. That reminds me, my friends keep telling me how much you resemble me. Same hair, eyes, you get the point," he says thoughtfully. I ball my hands into fists. I haven't physically fought my brother in years but nothing lasts forever, right?

"Boys, that's enough," our mom interjects. "Elija, you said she was home alone? Where are her parents?"

"On vacation," I grit out a little too harshly. I don't think they should leave her by herself. Not after last night, at least. "Sorry," I mumble. Great, my family will think me a psychopath now. I need to work on my filter.

"And they just left her here?" my mom asks, clearly outraged. I'm guessing it's hard for her to put herself into her mother's shoes since she feels bad for so much as taking a weekend trip with dad every once in again.

Seeing her become outraged on Florence's behalf, a girl she's never met, does something to soothe my irritation.

"You should invite her over for dinner. She shouldn't be alone all the time. Does she have siblings?" my dad asks.

Honestly, I'd really like to invite her over to meet my family, and I hate that because I know it won't happen. It's most likely that Florence would be really uncomfortable, and I don't want her or my family to get the wrong idea. Especially the twins.

"She doesn't, but I'm sure her parents will be back soon."

I hope they will, and I am glad the discussion ends at that.

Chapter 12

Florence

"Flo, you coming?" Benji asks, stopping on his way out of the classroom and looking at me expectantly. It's Monday and most of the students have already left for lunch. I was just about to reach for my current read when my friend interrupted.

"Yeah, flower girl. Quit letting us wait!" Jamie calls from somewhere outside the room.

"What are you talking about?" I ask, puzzled. I don't remember having made any plans with them.

"Lunch, Lorence. Ever heard of it? You're coming with us," Orion adds helpfully.

"I am?" When blondie just arches an eyebrow, my brain finally catches up and I scramble out of my seat. I have nothing better to do, so why not grab a bite?

In my hurry, I manage to hit my knee on a chair, causing me to stumble a few feet away from Orion. He, to no one's surprise, seems rather amused by my clumsiness but he refrains from making a comment. It's a good thing too, since my throbbing knee is punishment enough. Either way, at least I made Elsa smile.

Oh, hang on.

Did I just come up with the perfect nickname for Orion? Hair color, check. Cold attitude, check. I must admit, I'm rather proud of myself for that.

"What are you grinning about?" Orion asks suspiciously.

"I just found the perfect nickname for you," I tell him sweetly as I walk out of the classroom with him on my trail.

On my way, I lock eyes with Elija, and it's enough to make butterflies come to life in my stomach. As quickly as they came, they shrivel and die again while I remember the way he saw me last Saturday. I avert my gaze quickly, not managing to return his smile for once.

I hate that I no longer know how to act toward the guy I kind of like, but kind of don't know, but who has also kind of held me through the night after helping me deal with a panic attack. The internet doesn't have a clear reply, and I've checked.

Without anyone to talk to about the dilemma, I'm stuck reeling and uncomfortable.

"What's that?" Orion asks, bringing my attention back to the announcement I made. Right, I'm still speaking to Orion.

"Elsa," I announce proudly, shooting him a megawatt smile. Jamie bursts out laughing and throws an arm around my shoulders as the group walks through the halls of the academy. Orion simply mutters something behind my back but I'm not about to worry about it.

Happiness is blooming in my chest as we pass some curious onlookers. This is my first time being paraded around as someone's friend, and it's nice.

The guys and I end up getting Chinese takeaway and settle in the grass of the academy's campus park. I love our school's premises. They're stupidly enormous but most of the space is taken up by the park. There are a few trees to sit beneath in summer and otherwise just a lot of mowed grass. All of that is surrounded by beige buildings, where our classes take place.

The more time that passes, the more relaxed I become. Even whatever awkwardness I feel toward a certain black-haired guy is vanishing by the time Jamie finally manages to flip his chopsticks with his elbow, a challenge he spent the better part of the break on. All because Benji said he couldn't do it, clearly awakening Jamie's competitive side.

Surprisingly, Liam hasn't made a single inappropriate or rude comment. Nor has he mentioned a certain girl that used to go out with Elija.

I suspect Jamie talked to him, but whatever the cause of Liam's change in behavior, I appreciate it. He went so far in his attempt to redeem himself, he even told me he liked my shoes. His tone was grumbly and he looked unsure of his words, but he still tried.

My heart swelled a bit at the compliment. It has nothing to do with who said it, rather than the fact that I spend a lot of time picking out outfits. Therefore, whenever someone notices it or says something positive, it makes my day.

Our break is over way too quickly, and I'm soon back in a stuffy classroom, daydreaming about the park outside and the ways I'll spend my last day home alone.

"Florence, we're home. Help your mother with her bags, please." That's the greeting I get from my father after ten days of not seeing or hearing from him. I shouldn't have expected anything else, but the bitter taste of rejection settles in my throat like a lump of cotton.

Nevertheless, I get up from my bed and go to help my mother.

"Hey honey, take these for me, will you? Thank you," she says, shoving all sorts of things into my hands. Only when I'm barely able to see past the bags stacked on my arms does she lead me back toward the house with only her purse in her hands.

Whatever, I tell myself. They had a long trip home and must be exhausted. The thought makes me feel a little better, the same as every excuse I've ever made up for them has. *I'm not the problem, they just had a rough day at work.* Or, *it's not my fault, they just didn't get much sleep.*

I set everything down as soon as I'm through the door, unable to keep up the weight any longer. My mother makes a disapproving sound behind me, reminding me uncomfortably of Ms. Umbridge from *Harry Potter and the Order of the Phoenix*. I ignore that too.

"I guess they're fine there," she says stiffly before looking over me once with pursed lips. "Have you been eating enough, sweetie? You're starting to look a little boney."

Gritting my teeth together painfully is all I can do not to stare at the woman open-mouthed. I'm hurt more than I am surprised, though. There's never been a time when my mother didn't comment on my appearance. It was either *"Florence, sweetie, are you sure you want another plate?"* or *"Honey, these aren't the nineties. We don't need to be able to count your bones."*

Whatever, I repeat to myself stubbornly. She just wants me to be healthy.

I have my smile back in place in no time. "I missed you guys. Do you want to get dinner at that Italian place you like so much?" I ask when my dad is in the corridor with us. It's eight pm and I'm starving but I wanted to wait for them so we could eat together again.

My parents have this obsession with having dinner together. They say families share meals but since they work all day, dinner is all we get. Besides, I'm sick of eating whatever snack I can find alone at that big dinner table of ours. Why we have it? No idea. It's always just the three of us.

I snap out of my thoughts and take in the way my dad keeps an appropriate distance from my mom like he always does. Their postures are both straight to the tee and they smile pleasantly. It might not be a warm family reunion but at least it's familiar.

"I'm sorry honey but we grabbed a bite at the airport," my mom tells me, her smile turning sympathetic.

"I'll call the restaurant to get us a table for tomorrow," my dad promises.

"Right. Of course." I try to shoo the oncoming feeling of rejection away by reminding myself that it's late and traveling makes hungry.

I tell them a quick excuse and head to my room before my smile falls. Just when the door is shut firmly behind me and the lights in my room are off, do I let the first tear fall. I curl in on myself on my bed, trying to be quiet as I cry.

Five more minutes left until this hellish period finally ends. No offense to Mr. Hank but we've been discussing the annual camping trip for over thirty minutes, and I'm about to fall asleep. Some of the students definitely are sleeping and I'm sure if our teacher hadn't asked me personally about my tent and so on then so would I be.

"Remember, eight am in the parking lot. Whoever is late will have to find another way to the campsite. Well then, enjoy your weekend. Class dismissed."

Finally!

My classmates start rushing out the door but despite having eaten lunch with the guys all week, I don't make a move to follow them, seeing as Elija isn't moving either. When we're alone in the room, he pulls out a container from his bag and starts eating.

Looks like leftover pizza. The homemade kind. Is it sad that my mouth waters at the sight of cold pizza? To be honest, it's been a while since I ate something I made myself.

My parents took me out for dinner on Wednesday as planned and we ordered something in on Thursday, and as much as I appreciate it, it's not the same as devouring something homemade. Something a person you know and care about put in the time to make for you.

I've probably been staring for too long since Elija looks up from his phone to meet my eyes. He pats the desk beside his as if I were a dog to call over. I should hate it more than I do. Since I don't – and generally lack any restraint when it comes to staying away from him-, I walk over, holding his gaze if not a little defiantly. Not knowing where else to go once I reach his side of the room, I sit down on the desk.

It's too late to change it by the time I realize that the way he's looking up at me seems ridiculously enticing and slightly inappropriate. Knowing I shouldn't feel this way, I look away to decide where to place my feet.

As if reading my mind, Elija gently grabs my calves and sets my feet down at the edge of his chair. *Between* his spread legs.

My cheeks heat up involuntarily, the defiance I felt a moment ago gone as my heart starts racing and my head starts spinning. Yeah, it's been reestablished who holds the control here, and it isn't me.

I don't pull my feet away after Elija has let go. There's a good distance between his legs and mine so this really isn't as inappropriate as it may feel to me. I kind of like it.

"Here," Elija says, holding out a slice of pizza.

"No, thanks. That's okay. I don't want to steal your food," I assure him, laughing a bit to lighten the mood and hide my unease.

"Please take it. I prefer not eating by myself." He's smiling so genuinely – almost hopefully, that I can't possibly deny him. It feels too nice to see a real smile after all the pretended ones I'm faced with at home.

"Thanks," I tell him, earning a nod in return. Then, we fall into a comfortable silence as we eat and listen to music individually.

"May I?" the guy in front of me asks after I've swallowed my last bite. He's pointing at my phone, causing my heart to skip a beat. He wants to show me a song.

I unlock it for him, anticipating what I'll hear next. When the first note of FRIENDS by Marshmallow registers, I burst out laughing.

"Very funny," I tell Elija, who's just grinning at me. Idiot.

"Just kidding. Here you go." Something I don't recognize starts playing, and I find myself hanging onto every key. There's no singing but the way the guitar harmonizes with the beat is seriously impressive.

"I love it, really. Who's it from? Do they have any more?" I ask. Elija's eyes seem to shine a little brighter, and I love the thought that my liking a song he showed me makes him happy. It's what I feel whenever he tells me my music is nice.

"Something like that," he tells me. I'm not sure what that means, but Elija distracts me from asking anything else when he lays his arms on my knees. He places his head on top of them before I can even form a solid thought.

Meanwhile, my heart is going a mile a minute and my muscles tense. He's not making me uncomfortable, quite the contrary. I just don't want to move because I'm scared he'll go away again.

As if hearing my thoughts, the boy lifts his head slightly and smiles up at me, his dimples showing. "That's better," he says before lying back down.

"Huh?" I ask dumbly.

"Your legs. They're not bouncing anymore," he mumbles against his arms. I barely register his words, too busy reeling over the fact that he's touching me so casually. My stomach is swooping in the best way, my hands itching to dive into his thick dark hair to touch him back.

I don't, too unsure whether that would be the right thing to do since he's just touching me to stop my knees from bouncing. He's being nice, and I don't want to ruin it by touching him against his will.

In the silence, more thoughts and worries about his motives assault my head. Sure, he seems relaxed as can be where he's lounging with his head on my legs – or rather on his arms, which are spanning over my thighs. It's surprising how simple things seem with him.

I usually get along with people, but that's mostly just me being friendly and them extending the same courtesy in return. I'm inconspicuous, not bold enough to threaten anyone in any way shape or form, so they have no reason not to like me. I tend to keep things that way for that exact reason, because if I stay in my little bubble and don't get too close to anyone, they can't reject me.

With Elija, I'm actually comfortable. I feel like he – well maybe *cares* is a bit of a stretch – but maybe he enjoys my presence.

Or he's just a good person and I'm his charity case, a treacherous voice whispers in the back of my mind. After all, he never showed this much interest in me before he witnessed my panic attack.

Is it selfish of me that I don't care? Am I ignorant for wanting moments like this to keep happening regardless of his motives?

I think forward to where I'll be in a few hours. The cold home where all the comfort I get comes from my own arms. Suddenly, I don't care whether I'm ignorant or selfish. Spending time with Elija, with any of the guys, makes me happy. I'm not ready to give up on that just yet.

As our lunch break comes closer to an end, the guys are the first to return to the classroom, finding Elija and me in the same position we were in all break. With me sitting on top of the desk next to his, my feet on his chair as he looks up at me, one arm still casually laid over my thigh.

Much to my surprise, none of them make a teasing joke. Sure, they're all looking between their friend and me funnily, but everyone keeps their mouth shut. As they settle down around us and I catch a glimpse of the look Elija is sending Jamie, whose grin is a tad too big, I realize why. The boy who shared his lunch with me is glaring at his friends.

Figuring it's for my sake rather than his, I smile to myself. It's small moments like this when I feel like this thing between us isn't just conjured up from my wishful thinking. It feels like he notices things about me, and that must mean something.

I brace myself for embarrassment when Jamie opens his mouth, expecting him to ignore his friend's silent warning and make a comment about our proximity.

Instead, he sighs heavily. "I can't believe we have to go to this thing today. Miss Yeng usually hates staying longer at school, but she's fine with going to court for an hour, the way there and back not included? It's so unfair!"

"I'm sure it won't be so bad. Depending on what the case is about, it might be interesting to watch," I try to reason. My voice lacks any conviction, though. It's not like I'm enthused over the special program of this afternoon.

While usually, I'd be at home and enjoying the beginning of my weekend after one more lesson, today, that won't be the case for a few more hours. All because our law teacher thinks it'll be of educational value to make us witness a real trial.

From what I've heard from other classes, it's not likely to be as interesting as I just promised Jamie, seeing as most trials are about trivial crimes.

"Either way, we don't have a choice but to go. I don't know about you guys, but I don't want another lecture from Miss Yeng on how disrespectful it is to be late, so what do you say we get moving to meet the rest of the class in time?" Marcus interjects, already getting to his feet.

Benji groans as the rest of us move after him. Meanwhile, Jamie has rediscovered his cheer, practically skipping next to Orion as his friend grumbles at him to stop messing around.

As I trail after the bunch, Elija slows his steps just subtly enough for me to realize he's waiting for me to catch up. With a few long strides, I'm at his side, trying my best to appear to be focusing on our friends ahead when really, all I want to do is turn my head to look at him.

We're too close for me to watch him now, though. Practically shoulder to shoulder. Or, well, my shoulder to his arm.

Neither of us says anything, and it's starting to put me on edge. Finally, I try to sound as casual as possible as I ask, "So, do you have any plans for the weekend?"

I turn my head just in time to see him blink as if ripped out of deep thoughts. He catches himself, smiles at me, and throws an arm over my shoulder.

I nearly miss a step as he leans in, his face coming closer to mine. *What the hell is he doing?* Not that I mind. I just wish my heart would stop racing so much so I could stop staring at him dumbly.

"Sorry, what was that?" he asks easily.

I clear my throat. "I asked whether you had plans for the weekend," I repeat, finally able to put my smile back in place.

The boy straightens again but keeps his arm around my shoulder. "Just looking after the twins since Kai isn't around. What about you?"

"Well, the books I ordered a few weeks ago finally arrived yesterday, so I can tell you what I won't be doing; sleep," I say, attempting a joke even as heat blooms in my cheeks. Yeah, that was a lame try. I know.

Still, Elija chuckles and shakes his head, looking rather amused. It's enough to soothe my nerves a little. "I'm somehow not surprised at all." Then, he proceeds to ask me about my next read. What really gets to me is that he sounds interested, asking follow-up questions after every reply I provide, no matter how brief.

I don't mean to sound dismissive with my short answers. I'm just not used to people showing interest in the books I like, so this is new territory. I don't want to bore him.

Usually, whenever I burst at the seams and can't help myself but tell my parents about a story I read, they're quick to tell me they don't care in more flowery words. Either way, they always dismiss me or fail to acknowledge my words at all, and my track record with those interactions has dimmed my excitement to talk about books.

But even though Elija might not read for fun, there's something about the way he speaks to me that makes me feel like he is invested and truly cares about my replies. It's a foreign, fuzzy feeling.

Too soon, we meet our gathered classmates in the parking lot outside the school, and I subtly step out of Elija's hold. Not because I want to, but rather because I feel like he was just about to take his arm off my shoulders, and I'd rather avoid the sting of rejection that would evoke.

If he's bothered by it, he doesn't show it. No, we join his friends and everything remains as easy as before.

The trial turns out to be just as boring as expected. Honestly, why was a teenager dragged in front of a judge for shoplifting? Just let her pay for the item and be done with it.

Jamie seems to agree with me, though he is much more verbal with his disapproval of this drama, turning his face into Orion's shoulder as he laughs quietly at some joke he made.

For once, I'm glad I'm not sitting next to him. Miss Yeng's chiding glances would have made me itch. Orion seems unbothered by them, despite the faint blush I can make out on his fair skin. Yeah, that's not likely to have anything to do with our teacher and everything with Jamie slapping his thigh as he laughs silently.

I glance away when Elsa's eyes meet mine and his expression shutters, feeling like I interrupted in a moment I don't quite understand. I think back to how Orion scowled at the mention of Jamie's ex-boyfriend and suddenly wonder if the cold man has a thing for his best friend.

By the time the third short trial is over and most of the class looks half-asleep, Miss Yeng finally announces that we're free to leave now if we wish.

It's safe to say that I've never seen my classmates move so hurriedly. It's as if they are scared Miss Yeng is about to change her mind and force them to stay.

"Oh, my bus actually takes off in a few minutes. I have to run. Bye, guys," Marcus says once we're out, barely looking up from his phone. The rest of us check for connections and one after the other, our group decimalizes.

"You have to go back to school, right? Do you want me to come with you?" Elija asks me when only he, Benji, and I are left.

Before I can tell him that he doesn't have to do that, Benji chimes in, "What are you talking about? We need to go on the same bus. If you go back to school, it'll take you an hour to get home."

Elija looks anything but happy at his friend's point. I try to ease the tension. "It's a nice offer, but he's right, it would take you a lot longer to get home if you took that detour. Besides, I have a book with me that I've been eager to start," I tell him.

He smiles knowingly. "All right, then. I wouldn't dare interrupt such an important date. Have fun and don't miss your stop."

"I'll do my best. Bye, you two," I say, even as my eyes mostly stay locked on just one of the two guys.

"Bye, Flo," Benji tells me, patting my arm affectionately as he passes me. I make sure to send him a smile then.

"See you on Monday, Florence. Get home safely," Elija says, walking after his friend.

Chapter 13

Elija

"Have you seen Florence anywhere?" I ask my friends as the other students start getting on the buses.

"Nope. Maybe she's already inside." Jamie shrugs and follows Orion into the vehicle closest to us.

"You coming, Eli?" Marcus asks, stopping in the doorway, thereby effectively keeping anyone else from entering. I'm convinced he's the only person going to this academy who can do that without getting yelled at.

"Save Florence and me a seat," I tell him. I know she's not in any of the other buses since I've been scanning the crowd for her since I got here. Besides, I think she'd come to find us if she was here. Just to make sure, I send her a quick text asking where she was.

"Five more minutes 'till take off, kids! Everyone get on the buses!" Mr. Hank yells. Not many students are still outside but I don't make a move to join my friends in the vehicle. I simply stand next to one of the doors so I can stall a bit.

They can't leave if I keep the door open and I won't let it close until Florence walked through it.

"Elija! Stop messing around and take a seat!" my teacher snaps at me, leaning out of the window of a bus nearby. The ones surrounding the vehicle my friends are in start filing out of the parking lot, but I refuse to get inside. Florence hasn't answered me which means she's probably on her way. It's unlike her to be late. I'd bet my right foot she is freaking out about it.

"Florence isn't here yet," I tell him calmly.

"Florence?" The red-faced man groans, looking skywards as if asking for strength. Then he mutters something under his breath and glares back at me. "If your ass isn't placed on one of those seats in the next five seconds, I'll come out there and drag you inside. Don't make my job any harder than it already is."

I'd feel bad for him if a new voice didn't reach my ear at the exact same moment.

"I'm here! Don't drive!" I see Florence running across the parking lot to reach us, nearly falling over her suitcase in the process. I try my best to stifle a laugh.

"Oh, thank god. I thought we were about to have a tent shortage situation like last year," Mr. Hank mutters.

A very out-of-breath Florence finally stops in front of me, bending over with her hands on her knees as she wheezes slightly.

"You good?" I ask, still trying not to smile. The girl is many things, but athletic clearly isn't one of them. Intelligent, caring, adorable, yes. Into sports? Maybe less so judging by the way her arms were flailing as she ran and tripped over her feet with every step.

"Yeah. Totally. Just need to – catch my breath. Ran – all the way," Florence tells me between breaths.

"You take a second. I'll just put your Suitcase away." My fingers gently pry hers from the handle of her luggage so I can take it from her. I'm already opening the storage area on the bus when she tries to tell me I don't have to do that. "Florence, it's already done," I tell her. She finally stands up, wipes her forehead with the back of her hand, and smiles shyly at me.

"Thanks." Her cheeks are really red but I'm not sure if it's just Florence blushing like she often does or because of the heat. Either way, our teacher interrupts our little moment.

"Both of you, INSIDE THE BUS!" Florence flinches and apologizes profusely while I shoo her into the vehicle, no longer hiding my laughter.

Inside, Jamie waves us over. My friends are taking up two four-seater booths if you will, and I see they've saved us two seats. Florence damn-near slumps in the one beside Benji who's quick to hold out a bottle of water for her.

"How did you manage to be late? You're always on time," her friend asks while she drinks up.

"Yeah, Lorence, don't you live like right next to the school?" Orion adds.

"My parents-" she breaks off and her eyes find mine for a quick second. "I slept in." she laughs a bit. Yeah, that really wasn't a good safe. I'm curious to know how her being late is connected to her parents but I won't ask her now. Not when it's clear she doesn't want to tell us.

I take a seat opposite her, leaving the window seat empty next to me. Marcus, Liam, Jamie, and Orion are sitting in the booth next to us but it's a long ride, so we'll probably end up changing seating arrangements at some point.

Probably when someone from the other booth gets too sick of Liam. Full offense.

A few hours in, the semi peaceful ambiance is shattered by Jamie's whining, "I am bored!" He's sprawled over two seats, his back on Orion's legs while his head hangs down over the edge of the seat and his feet are up against the windows. I can see Elsa, how Florence so helpfully named him, is trying his best to look annoyed. Meanwhile, his hands are absently playing with the hem of the other boy's shirt, so I don't know whom he thinks he's fooling. Orion has been pining after Jamie for years, but I'm pretty sure Jamie is the only one in a ten mile radius that has no clue.

"If you don't stop whining, I'll kick you so hard you won't be making any sounds other than squeals for a week," Marcus threatens. I don't doubt he could make that happen. I've seen him score a goal. I wouldn't want to be in the football's place.

"You'd have to catch me first," Jamie challenges him but I think it might be due to Orion's death glare that Marcus doesn't say anything else. Instead, he chuckles and raises his hands in surrender.

Yep, Elsa has it bad.

"Well, if you guys are really bored, we could always take the Pottermore sorting quiz," Florence suggests. "I can't believe you've never taken it," she adds. I smile to myself and shake my head.

This girl.

"We're talking about Harry Potter again, right?" Benji asks tiredly. We've been on this trip for about three hours and that might be the longest my friend has gone without smoking in months. Orion seems a bit edgy too. Edgier than usual, that is. Though, he's longing for cigarettes rather than weed.

Only the guy on his lap seems to be holding on to his good mood.

"I'm down. Though we all know I'm Gryffindor," Jamie announces loudly. Then he asks Florence more quietly, "They're the funny ones, right? I remember liking some twins in the movies and they had red hair. Red's Gryffindor."

"First off, *some* twins? You are breaking my heart. Second, hair color has nothing to do with your house. But yeah, the twins were in Gryffindor."

With that clarified, the discussion is over, and my friends take the house sorting quiz. Every once in a while, one of the guys asks what a certain word or question means but other than that, they seem quite focused.

I think I can guess who's in which house, but I'll wait for the test results to confirm my hypotheses.

"I got Hufflepuff," Benji announces finally.

"Duh," Florence and I reply at the same time, and my heart skips a beat at the smile she sends my way. She's achingly beautiful when she smiles.

Ugh, what is happening to me? This shit is getting to my head.

"Why are you guys not surprised?" Benji asks.

"Let's just say Hufflepuff is often associated with herbology," I tell him, earning a stifled laugh from Florence.

"Mine says I'm Slytherin," Liam announces. Again, I knew that. Even though I think Liam offers a really bad representative of that house. As a Hufflepuff, I feel the need to defend our friends in green. They deserve better than someone like Liam.

"Bam, check it out! Gryffindor! I told ya!" Jamie yells loud enough to cause many annoyed faces to turn our way.

So far, I'm going three for three.

"They put me in the same house as *him*? I don't think I like that old hat or whatever it's called," Orion mutters. I'm going to guess he's referring to Liam which would make him a Slytherin as well. I can see that, though he wouldn't have been completely misplaced in Gryffindor with how fiercely loyal he is.

"What about you?" I ask Marcus.

"Gryffindor." Florence raises an eyebrow at him, quietly sizing him up. When he notices, he asks her what she's thinking.

"Nothing. Just didn't know where to place you. You know, with that whole "guarded and mysterious" vibe you've got going on," she mocks him slightly. She's smiling as she speaks, not at all coming across as mean as Orion would, and Marcus clearly finds it amusing. He returns the smile, which makes her beam in return.

I expect to sense the usual twist of jealousy, but it doesn't come. I feel like Florence just likes to make people smile.

Either way, I have no claim on her. She's free to beam at whomever she wants.

Doesn't mean I'd have to like it.

Chapter 14

Florence

I've never appreciated fresh air as much as when I got off that stupid bus. I've never appreciated the quiet as much as when I finally collapsed on my sleeping bag after spending half an hour setting up my tent. The girls I share the tent with all seem to have other plans than taking a nap at 5 pm but that won't stop me. Being surrounded by people all day has really drained me.

"Flo?" I hear someone say from outside my tent.

"Are you sure this is hers? Seems empty," I recognize Orion's voice and nearly groan out loud. While I appreciated the guys' presence on the ride here, my social battery is down.

"Maybe she's not in there," Liam says boredly. For once, I hope the other guys listen to him and decide to leave.

"Let's go find a place to hang out first. Then we can look for her again," Marcus proposes. Hearing that makes me feel bad. They want to hang out and I'm basically hiding.

"Jamie, what are you-? Hey, don't!" Elija yells right before the flap of my tent bursts open.

"See, she's here. You good, flower girl?" I turn my head to see Jamie standing in the tent, shoes and all. Even from where I'm lying, I can see the dirt that now stains the previously clean floor and my irritation spikes.

"Your shoes are dirty," I mumble. When the boy's face loses some of its cheer, I instantly feel bad. "Sorry. Yeah, I'm fine.

Just a little tired. You need anything?" I ask with a smile, not wanting to be the kind of person that kills a friend's mood.

"The guys and I are about to look for a place in the woods where we can hang out without Marcus' groupies ganging up on us. We were wondering if you wanted to come."

"Dude, she just said she was tired. You don't have to come, Florence. I'm sure the marathon you completed this morning knocked you out." Elija pulls the tent doors to the side enough for me to see him. He starts pulling Jamie outside by the back of his shirt and smiles at me.

Who said anything about being tired? Never heard of it. I'm wide awake.

"You know what, some fresh air might be just what I need," I tell him as I get to my feet.

"You sure? We can come to get you a bit later if you want," he offers, but I'm already putting on my shoes.

"Careful, Elija, or I might think you don't want me to tag along," I tease him as I walk out of my tent. I intend to look really cool doing that, unbothered in a way I never am. Instead, I end up standing inches away from Elija's chest since he doesn't step away from the door.

He seems to enjoy this position profusely judging by the smirk that's playing on his lips as he looks down at me. Meanwhile, I have my head tilted back so I can meet his eyes in the first place.

My cheeks are heating up further with every second we spend in this position, and my heart is beating so furiously I'm scared he can hear it.

When I finally can't take it anymore, I gently lay my hand on his chest to push him away. Only that as soon as I make contact with his body, I can't seem to move at all. He is radiating heat even through the fabric of his hoodie, and I can feel the soft beat of his heart against the palm of my hand. My body locks up.

Elija looks down at where we're touching, and when he meets my eyes again, he's not smiling anymore. The look he gives me now only makes me burn up hotter.

For a quick beat, I could have sworn his eyes dropped to my lips, but they're back on my eyes too fast for me to be sure. I hope my mind isn't playing tricks on me.

"So, should we leave or..." Benji breaks the silence. I forgot the others were still surrounding us and the sudden reminder makes me jerk my hand back so quickly I lose my balance. It only gets worse when I take a step back to regain composure and my foot hits the side of the tent instead. I'm about to topple the whole thing when a pair of strong hands steady me by the elbows.

"Easy there," Elija says with a smile so bright it nearly makes my knees buckle.

Dammit, I need to get a grip on it.

"Right, sorry." I laugh awkwardly, finally push past him, and only stop walking when I'm next to Benji. We're now standing a few feet away from the others.

"Not a word," I tell my friend, who's smiling suggestively.

"Not saying anything." He shrugs and walks toward the forest after Marcus and Liam. I look over my shoulder to see Jamie whispering something to Elija, both of them grinning goofily. That's my cue to follow the others.

It turns out that finding a place to hang out away from others is harder than one might think. Especially when it has to meet the princess', aka Liam's standards. While Benji seems to be fine accepting any fallen log or even just a patch of grass, Liam keeps finding something unacceptable about the suggestions.

After walking for an hour, we just settle on a cozy-looking patch with two fallen logs and the others tell Liam to suck it up and bring a towel to sit on if his pants are that important to him. We mark one of the trees by tying a bright red shirt from Marcus to a low-hanging branch, take a picture, and head back to the camp to eat dinner. Just for insurance, I saved the location on my phone. Benji might be good at finding his way in the woods, but I don't like taking chances.

By the time we sit down to eat, I'm starving. Honestly, my stomach has been growling like crazy the whole way back and it's all I could do not to die of embarrassment. Especially when Elija pulled a granola bar from his pocket and held it out to me. I just wanted one of the trees to swallow me whole.

As it turns out, Mr. Hank, or whoever was responsible for the meals, decided on serving us one of my favorite foods tonight. I could kiss them.

I don't even care what I look like as I dig into my food. I can even ignore the embarrassment of moaning slightly when I take my first bite.

Only after finishing half of my meal in a short amount of time do I look up at the rest of the guys. Benji seems focused on his own plate, Orion is staring at Jamie who's creating some kind of art with his rice, and Marcus is having a conversation with Elija. Only Liam is staring at me funnily.

I decide to ignore him and prepare my next bite. My fork can barely handle it, but I'm determined to make it work. It's not every day I feel up to eating this much, after all. That is, until Liam speaks up. "Easy, girl. No one's going to steal your food," he tells me with a soft laugh.

The comment is innocent enough, but my mind snags on it, twisting and turning the words until they sound like a replica of my mother's backhanded remarks. All my life, she's been pestering me about my eating habits or my body, making me dread mealtimes more than anything before my age hit the double digits. She had the inexplicable power to make me feel small and worthless with a single comment, leaving me to question and doubt every bite until my appetite left for days on end.

It's a habit I'm unable to shake but manage to sometimes forget when I'm far away enough from home or losing myself in the distraction of watching tv or reading while I eat, like today. Until now.

My stomach churns as I look down at my food, my hunger and appetite snuffed out like a dead candle. All the sight of it does now is make me want to cry while the weight of my last bite clogs my throat. It looks like a lot more than it did before, making me wonder how I could stomach so much of it already.

Like a greedy pig. Scarfing down a plate too big for a woman my size.

The iron fist around my stomach clamps tight and I cringe at the feeling of the waistband of my high waisted jeans brushing against my ribs as I slouch. The trigger is immediate, and suddenly, the feeling of my lowest ribs feeling too tight and suffocating is all I can focus on. It makes me want to crawl out of my skin.

I raise my eyes to see all the guys staring at me, raising my anxiety. Everyone but Elija, who is glaring daggers at Liam.

"Yeah, right." I laugh it off, desperate to escape their attention. It seems to be convincing enough since everyone returns to their previous activities. I pretend to listen to the others while trying hard to quell my rising nausea. It would be rude to leave the table before everyone is done eating, not to mention suspicious if I just left now to run to the bathroom.

Elija keeps glancing my way as I push my food around on my plate, trying not to be too obvious about not eating. I feel like he sees right through me, same as he seems to do so often. That's why I'm extra careful to smile convincingly and seem unbothered.

"If everyone's done, how about we go back to the woods? Mr. Hank said we were free to do whatever we want to tonight," Marcus says.

"As long as no one gets pregnant, I think were his exact words," Jamie adds with his signature grin.

"You guys go ahead. I'll be right behind you," I tell them.

"I'll wait for you," Elija is quick to offer, and while it's a sweet gesture, the thought of him nearby while I throw up the contents of my stomach only makes me feel worse. A conflict is raging within me, warring between the knowledge that I shouldn't waste food this way and the need to stop feeling like a bloated pig. I ate too much, and the reminder of it sits in my stomach like a boulder.

In the back of my mind, I hear my mother scolding me. Telling me to know better than to stuff my face. Telling me I'm letting myself go eating like that. Telling me no one will love me if I look disgusting.

"It's fine. Thanks for the offer, though," I push the words past trembling lips. He frowns, a line appearing between his brows, but he doesn't fight me on it. Perhaps he knows I can't handle arguing right now. Or maybe he's sick of my theatrics and is glad I gave him a way out.

"You sure you can find us again? It'll be dark soon," he says as a last effort.

"I have the location on my phone."

"Smart girl." Elija smiles an unconvincing smile before the group finally leaves.

I head to the camp's bathrooms instead, more self-hatred cursing through me with every step I take.

Half an hour later, I reach the hidden spot where the guys are already hanging out. I take a seat along their circle without a word, a smile plastered on my numb features as I try to pick out their conversation.

"Flo? You look like you could use it," Orion points out, handing me a beer as he opens one for himself.

So much for keeping the facade up.

"Yeah, why not? Thanks." I smile softly but I'm more focused on someone else's attention. I turn my head slightly to meet Elija's eyes. He takes that as an invitation to come closer to me.

"You sure that's a good idea?" he asks, though it sounds less demanding than it did when we were talking about the weed in the shed. This time, I think he might genuinely be asking, not trying to tell me what to do. I appreciate it.

"One won't hurt, right?" I tell him with a smile.

"I'll ask you again in the morning." I glance down at the bottle in his own hand.

"How exactly are you the right person to talk right now?" I challenge him playfully.

"Just expressing concern for an inexperienced friend. You look like you'd be a lightweight." My mouth drops at his audacity.

"What did you call me?" He simply laughs at me, bumping his shoulder against mine before taking another sip of his drink.

"I'm joking. Cheers," he says expectantly. I clink my bottle against his, only to stare down at it after. "Changed your mind?" Elija asks with a slight smirk.

"It's closed. I don't have anything to open it with," I tell him all the while thinking I really must seem inexperienced.

Without a word, Elija places his bottle between his legs, reaches for mine, and opens it. Like, with his bare hands. *HOW*?

"Here you go," he tells me. Then he chuckles, finding my apparent shock amusing. "You should close your mouth before you catch a fly."

"Very funny," I tell him, though the smile on my lips is genuine. I guess I might not need alcohol to make me feel better after all but it's too late to turn back now.

The other guys, led by a clearly drunk Jamie, come closer to us so we sit in a circle. Benji plays some music and we all start having conversations as we hang out. I keep sipping at my beer. And then the next one that is handed to me. I don't particularly like the taste but the more I drink, the better it gets. Or the less I taste.

"Can I get another beer?" I ask Elija, leaning onto his shoulder a bit more than I might should. It's not my fault my body wants to be closer to his. I feel like tension has been brewing between us for a while now, and I can barely take it anymore.

Maybe alcohol doesn't have a good effect on me. I've been dangerously close to asking Elija what we are all evening. Like, are we friends? Our relationship doesn't feel the same as the one I have with Benji. Strictly speaking, we haven't kissed or anything so we're not more than friends either. But we're spending a lot of time together so we can't be nothing.

"I think you've had enough for tonight," he tells me with a chuckle. The world is still tilting slightly so I bury my face in his shoulder and groan. Damn, he smells good. "You okay?" Elija asks.

I nod against him. "A little tired." Before I can process what is happening, my head is no longer on the guy's shoulder but on his lap instead.

"What?" I ask dizzily.

"I don't think the guys are ready to leave and I need to make sure everyone gets back to the tents safely. Just rest a little," he tells me, and whatever protests I might have had vanish the moment Elija takes the clip out of my hair and starts playing with it. The last thing I remember thinking is; best hair treatment ever.

"Is she okay?" I hear a voice say from a distance. Who the hell is speaking? I could have sworn I was riding a hippogriff just a moment ago.

"Yes. Now shut up or you'll wake her," another voice replies. The words hardly register but I slowly become aware of the rocking ground beneath me. That's enough to make my eyes snap open, only to realize I'm being carried.

In a moment's panic about being kidnapped, I push at whoever's arms I'm in. My attempt at freeing myself nearly succeeds as the person stumbles.

"Whoa, it's me, Florence. I'll set you down, hang on." I recognize that voice. *Elija*. Damn me! If I had known it was him, I would have pretended to be asleep.

As it is, I enjoy the way his strong arms tighten around me as he regains his balance. Then, he slowly sets me down, keeping a hold of my waist as the world around me tilts.

I laugh, unable to help myself. "I think I like beer," I tell no one in particular.

"I think I like having you sleep on my lap. Though, I'd prefer it if you were sober the next time," Elija tells me. That finally makes my eyes rise to meet his.

"You're really tall," I remark stupidly. Then, I cover my mouth with a hand as if I'd said a slur. Finally, I feel silly for both actions. "Sorry, something seems to be wrong with my filter. You know you're tall. Not freakishly so, of course. In a good way. I'm not saying short people are unattractive. You'd definitely be good-looking either way. I mean-"

"Florence." Elija stops my rambling by gently placing a hand on my cheek. My mouth clams shut and my cheeks burn up, tingling where his skin meets mine.

"Sorry," I say, wishing for the second time today that the trees would swallow me whole. *Remind me to never drink again.*

"No need to apologize. You're cute when you ramble." His compliment does nothing to ease the frantic beat of my heart. The unhealthy one that pounds so loudly I can hear it in my head, that is. This boy's going to be the death of me.

"You can't say things like that," I tell him, making him laugh.

"I can't?"

"No."

"Why's that?" he asks, still smiling so sinfully handsomely.

"You're confusing me," I admit stupidly, watching his smile droop a little.

"I am?" he whispers, searching my face closely. I simply nod, holding his gaze. I get the feeling I shouldn't have said that and I'll regret it in the morning but what's there to do about it now?

Seriously, what is? I need suggestions.

"Where's that little head of yours drifting off to again?" he breaks the silence.

"Just wondering if I need to flee the country tomorrow." That earns me one of those laughs I love to hear so much. It also makes me more aware of the position we're in right now. Elija's hands are still on either side of my waist and our chests are nearly touching. If he looked down, I'd only have to get on my tiptoes and our lips-

"I told you not to drink that last beer. Eli, I need your help carrying Jamie!" Orion yells from wherever he's standing. Elija groans and shrugs apologetically, releasing me from his gentle hold.

He takes my hand instead and starts pulling me to the rest of his friends. There, he pretty much hands me over to Marcus before he jogs off to help Jamie.

I'd expect it to be awkward, holding hands with Marcus but he's actually really sweet about it. He doesn't sound sober either but it's not stopping him from telling me when to pay attention to the uneven ground.

I lose sight of where Elija and Orion went with Jamie but Marcus makes sure I get to my tent safely.

"Thanks," I tell him as I pull my hand from his.

"Of course. Drink some water before going to bed. You'll thank me tomorrow." With one last smile, he stumbles off to wherever his tent is.

"Be down at the lake in ten minutes, everyone!" Mr. Hank yells for the third time. Meanwhile, I'm contemplating just hiding in the woods to get away from all the noise and light.

"Remind me not to drink again. Ever," I tell the guys at the table.

"How are you feeling this bad after only having had two beers? As long as you don't drink on an empty stomach, you should be fine," Liam tells me. I guess I know why I'm not feeling well, then, don't I? The warning with the empty stomach comes a little late now.

"Did you drink water before going to sleep like I told you?" Marcus asks me.

"I did." Then I had to get up a few hours later to pee. That wasn't fun, crawling out of my tent in the middle of the night, trying to navigate the dark ground clustered with my sleeping tentmates without stomping on them.

"Either way, we need to go to the docks. The first challenge will start soon and I'm not trying to get behind already," Marcus says.

Right, the first challenge. Dear Mr. Hank has decided that the trip would be unbearably boring without any activities. What was his solution to that? A sports tournament. That means there'll be a challenge every day. The bright side is that you get disqualified and don't have to go through with the rest of the tournament as soon as you did badly enough at one.

I'll be in the audience soon enough.

I feel the change of atmosphere as soon as we reach the docks. The air's more charged and people are running around, yelling at their partners. I watch my classmates, marveling at how serious they take this.

Then I realize I don't even have a partner. When I intend to tell the guys as much, I realize they no longer surround me. Orion and Jamie are bickering as they tie two of their legs together. It's adorable. Further ahead in the mass of people are Marcus and Elija. I only manage to see them because their heads tower over the people around them. I guess they're ready to take off already. Liam's standing next to Benji, who looks about ready to go back to sleep. That leaves me to fend for myself. Damn.

I scan my surroundings a bit more thoroughly until my eyes settle on a lost-looking girl. I hesitantly make my way over, setting my winning smile in place.

"Hey there. Are you by chance missing a partner too?" I inquire. As I do so, I realize how much I've missed making friends casually. The guys are great and it's nice to be part of an actual friend group, but this is what I'm used to. Getting to know and getting along with strangers is my thing.

"Yes," she breathes in relief. There's a nervous air around her that does nothing to hide the underlying sweetness. I vow to put her at ease all the way.

"That's lucky. How about we help each other out and suffer through this together. I'm Florence but you can call me Flo," I cut right to the chase since the race is about to start, all people gathering at the starting line. If we want to do this, which I don't but need to, we have to get ready.

"Yes, please." She snorts in a sound of relief induced hysteria, then catches herself. "I mean, nice to meet you, Flo. I'm Sarah, and I'll gladly be your partner." I smile to myself. It's the kind of awkward backtrack I'd do.

The two of us grab an elastic rope and tie one ankle each together. Then, we try to take a first step and nearly faceplant. Sarah's taller than me and I'm pretty sure she's used to making longer steps. She's only barely able to hold me up by the shoulder before I can fall.

"Good safe. Thanks," I tell her before we both burst out laughing.

"Start in five seconds!" Mr. Hank announces.

"We're not going to make it, are we?" Sarah asks dramatically. I eye the distance between us and the crowd.

"Listen to me, I'm not letting you give up. We need to keep fighting!" I tell her dramatically, trying to match her energy.

"But there's no time!" she protests.

"It's not over until it is," I say. The girl bound to me blinks a few times, then bursts out laughing. "That made no sense, did it?" I ask, biting back a grin of my own. She simply shakes her head, unable to catch her breath. Meanwhile, a shrill sound cuts through the air, announcing the start of the race.

"You want to try it, don't you?" my new friend asks.

"Not a sore loser but definitely not a quitter," I tell her with a shrug. She smiles, nods, puts an arm around my shoulders, and starts counting steps with me.

By the time we reach the start line, I can barely see the other students in the distance.

"You really want to walk around that whole lake?" Sarah asks one last time.

"Sure. Looks barely bigger than a water whole, doesn't it?" I ask her playfully.

"It really does."

"Please, Flo. Let's just take that stupid elastic rope off. I can't stand being this close to you any longer. The heat is killing me!" Sarah whines about thirty minutes later. It's definitely a lake. Not a waterhole.

"Are you calling me hot?" I tease her.

"Flo!"

"We're almost done. Look, I can see the finish line." Truth is, it feels like I'm dying. I haven't sweated this much in years if ever, and neither of us has brought water. That means I've spent the last half an hour trying to motivate a stranger while losing a lot of body fluids. It's been delightful.

At least I got to know Sarah a bit better. I know she has a younger sibling who always steals her clothes. Their name is Micky, and they just started their first year at the academy. We've already sent them a selfie of the two of us since Sarah told me her sibling demands to know everything about this trip. The first-years' trip is a month after ours.

"Look who's finally coming! We thought you were dead. Go, go, Flower girl!" Jamie starts screaming from where he's sitting next to the finish line.

"Friend of yours?" Sarah asks.

"Yep," I pant.

"What about the one staring at you without blinking?" she asks, a smile playing on her lips. Of course, this will get her to stop whining. Gossip and a crowd of attractive men.

"I don't know whom you're talking about," I tell her. It's a lie. I know it's Elija staring at me, but he *is* blinking, in my defense.

"Yeah?" Sarah asks me. Before I can reply, she raises her voice and yells at the guys. "Hey, you! Black shirt, black hair guy. Take a picture, it'll last longer!"

Oh god.

Kill me.

"Sarah!" I hiss, mortified. I can hear the other guys laugh from where they stand while Elija tries to tell them something, swatting at the back of their heads in reproach. "You know what, you're right. Let's just give up." I make a move to bend down to untie us, but my friend keeps me from doing so.

"With that hot band of cheerleaders waiting for you? Don't you even think about it, Sunshine. We are finishing this race!" Sarah insists. Then, seemingly getting distracted by something else, she lowers her voice. "Who's that?" she asks, nudging her head in the general direction of the guys.

"How, dear friend, am I supposed to know who you're talking about?"

"Brown hair," she tells me.

"Marcus? Blue shirt?"

"No, the other one. White shirt." It takes me a second to realize she's actually talking about Liam.

"Oh, eww. That's Liam but he's not really nice. He kind of has the idea he's better than the rest, you know? Besides, with the way he talks about women, I'd stay away."

I chew on my bottom lip, worried I came across as mean. Liam is all those things, in my opinion, but I should probably let her make her own impression. On the other hand, I feel like warning her is appropriate thinking back to his referral of all woman being unable to stay away from him.

"If you want, I'll introduce you," I add halfheartedly.

"Nah, I'm good. If something's supposed to happen, it will. I'll sit back and see where things go in the meantime."

Now that's an attitude I could get behind.

Chapter 15

Elija

"Shh! They're coming. Shut the hell up, I swear to god!" I hiss at my friends. They haven't stopped teasing me about the comment the girl next to Florence said and I don't want her to hear it. She told me that I was confusing her last night, and I'm pretty sure the guys making comments about how whipped I am won't help that.

The last thing I want is to lead Florence on when I'm not sure what I want in the first place.

"Almost done, guys. Come on!" Marcus cheers for the two girls as they get closer. He's really warmed up to Florence but I guess she just has that effect. Even on a guarded person like Marcus.

The girls pretty much collapse as soon as they cross the finish line while I and the guys start whooping for them as if they'd won. The race ended like fifteen minutes ago, but it's a really Florence thing to do to finish it either way.

"I will never move again," she announces, finishing untying the rope binding her to her new friend before she lies down on her back.

"Remind me to think twice before agreeing to one of your ideas the next time," the other girl says. "I'm Sarah, by the way," she adds as an afterthought, not sitting up to look at us.

"Nice to meet you. Now, Lorence, you do know that it was a race, right? You were supposed to run," Orion teases her.

"It's impossible to run while being bound to another person!" Florence protests.

"Is it, Elija?" At my name, Florence raises her head softly. Her eyes find mine in a second, and even though she looks exhausted, my heart skips a beat knowing she put in an effort to steal a glance.

"You guys won?" she asks, sounding like she already knows the answer. I smile at her and nod. "How long?"

"Six minutes," I tell her, trying not to sound too smug. Truth is, Marcus and I totally rocked this task.

"Six?" Florence exclaims while her friend groans. "It's so unfair! Of course, you finish four times faster with legs as long as yours!"

"Five," Benji chimes in.

"What?" Florence officially looks lost and it's freaking adorable.

"They finished five times faster," my friend clarifies.

She huffs in exasperation and rolls into an exclamation, "Sure! Now you can do math! If I were able to get up, I'd totally hit you!"

I try my hardest to bite back a grin. Who would have thought that it only took little sleep, a hangover, and thirty minutes of exercise to turn Florence feisty.

"You wouldn't hurt a fly, Flo. Your threat would have been more believable if you had mentioned a flying bigfoot," Benji retorts good naturedly.

"You are the worst friend," she pouts, lying back down like a deflated balloon.

"You want a hug?" he offers in return. I can see her smiling but she shakes her head.

"I'm sweaty and gross."

"Well, I know one way to fix that." In a heartbeat, Benji picks her up while she voices loud protests and more threats. I consider coming to her rescue, but she seems to be enjoying herself even as she kicks her feet and pounds her little fist against my friend's chest.

Jamie has already pulled out his phone by the time our friend reaches the end of the docks.

"Benji, I swear-" Before Florence can finish her sentence, she's thrown toward the water and her words turn into a shriek. That ends with a loud splash and a lot of cheers from my friends.

The rest of our group, including Sarah who seems to be wide awake now that there's drama, has gathered on the docks as well. Jamie pushes Orion into the water to my right, only to be pulled in alongside him. While the others laugh, I pull off my shirt and sprint toward Benji.

"No! Elija, don't you dare!" Too late does he see my attack coming. I duck to wrap my arms around his waist and tackle him off the dock, going in with him.

The water feels like heaven on my hot skin, enveloping me wholly in a gentle hug and cooling me down. I linger, suspended in the weightless feeling of being underwater until my lungs start straining for breath. Then, I drag myself up with a stroke of my arms and break the surface once more.

"Not cool, dude!" Benji protests before splashing water in my face.

"Oh, you don't get to speak," Florence appears behind my friend, placing her hands on his shoulders before she pushes him beneath the water.

"If you're not careful, we're going to have a Regulus situation on our hands," I tell her as my friend weakly thrashes underwater, causing her jaw to drop.

"You did not say that!" she exclaims before letting go of Benji to swim closer to me.

"Oh but I did."

"From all the jokes!" she goes on, her outrage apparent. Meanwhile, I'm a bit distracted by the way her eyes pop now that her hair seems almost black. It's usually pulled back but now it's framing her face and it makes her look painfully beautiful, even as she's glaring at me.

"Sorry, Love. Won't happen again," I tease her. She freezes mid-stroke and I realize what I just called her.

Shit, shit, shit! Damnit Elija, what about not confusing her? Okay, we're fine. Just gotta play it off before it settles in.

I laugh and splash some water on her, trying to seem as relaxed as possible. She breaks out of her stupor, *thank god,* though my heart is still doing cartwheels.

I want a nickname for her like the others do but it won't be Love. It's a cute name but I'd want something more personal. Every person can be called Love. Florence deserves something as extraordinary as she is.

I'm not talking about her bubbly attitude or everlasting happiness that's a façade half of the time. I'm talking about the unnecessary apologies, the too-long stares, the tapping rhythm, hell, even the flower patterns and hair clips she wears every day.

Speaking of which.

"When'd you let your hair down?" I muse, twirling the wet ends of it between my fingers. I faintly wonder if the change of topic seems weird to her, but I'll try not to overthink it. That's her job, anyway.

"My hair?" she trails off, reaching for the brown strands over her shoulder. Realization dawns on her and her face falls drastically, her smile replaced by apparent panic. "My clip!"

Her eyes leave mine to search the dark teal water around us while her hands frantically try to swipe it away to get a better view. The sight of her freaking out over an accessory confuses me at first but then my brain catches up that it must've had some sentimental value.

I want to help Florence with the search but she needs to calm down first because right now she's just making waves. Literally.

"Florence," I call her softly.

"No, no, no! I need to find it," she mutters but I get the feeling the words aren't really meant for me. After trying to call her name one more time, I swim over and gently place my hands on her shoulders.

The act brings me really close to drowning now that I have to keep myself afloat with my legs only while taking care not to kick Florence in front of me, but I'll have to make it work.

"Florence, we'll find it. Deep breaths, okay?" She finally meets my eyes, letting me see the unshed tears inside them.

"I can't lose it," she tells me.

"We'll find it but you need to calm down first. Can you do that?" She takes a deep breath and nods slowly. "Good," I tell her before turning in the general direction my friends are in. "Guys! Get your asses over here, we have a hairclip to find!"

My friends don't question it but silently get to work, diving into the area I assigned them. Liam's the only one still on the dock rather than in the water. It's probably better this way though. All that hair product can't be good for the water.

After about twenty minutes of holding my breath dangerously long and making my eyes burn from the exposure to the murky water, my hands finally find the familiar plastic. I grab the clip and push myself up toward the surface for what's hopefully the last time. I blink away the burn in my eyes and heave a sigh of relief when I recognize the sage clip.

"Got it!" I announce, receiving some tired whoops from my friends. They haven't left any more than I and Florence have, and even Liam joined the search after some convincing on Jamie's part.

"You found it! Holy shit, thank you so much!" Florence exclaims before throwing her arms around my shoulders. This is probably the first time I've heard her swear. She must really love that hairclip.

"Florence, as much as I'd love to hug you for longer, my legs are about to give up on me and no matter how poetic it sounds, I don't feel like dying a hero," I tell her. She lets go of me, apologizes, and blushes profusely.

That's my Florence.

I mean – The Florence I know.

Chapter 16

Florence

After Elija found my hairclip, I was quick to retire to my tent. It was barely after 4 pm but I was more than drained. The race alone was enough to knock me out, but what really got me was losing that damn clip. It was my aunt's favorite accessory, and she specifically told me to take good care of it in her goodbye note. What do I do? Lose it in a damn lake.

Thank god the water wasn't that deep. I don't know what I would have done if it had been lost for good. I really owe Elija and the guys for their help. Even in the frantic state I was in, he managed to calm me and make me see reason. I cringe at the memory of how I panicked. He must think I'm real shallow for worrying so much about a piece of plastic.

Before I can spiral down the rabbit hole of my regrets, sleep drags me under. Alone in my tent, surrounded by the faint noises of other students and the nature around me, the toll of the day is enough to shut even my masochistic brain off.

I don't know for how long I'm asleep, but when I open my eyes once more, I'm no longer alone. The sight of a broad frame hovering not too far away from me nearly gives me a damn heart attack, and I jump awkwardly inside my sleeping bag. Not funny.

"What are you doing here?" I ask Elija, my voice a pitch too high. He's sitting on the ground near my sleeping bag, twirling something between his fingers. At my outburst, he looks up from his hands and smiles softly at me. Damn, that smile almost makes me forget he broke into my tent while I was sleeping.

"Saved you some dinner and thought I'd bring it here before it got cold." He nods his head to the side, and I follow the movement to a plate next to him. I can't help but laugh.

"Are the other guys coming?" I tease him as I sit up, but he doesn't seem to understand. I shoot the plate a meaningful glance. "Elija, how am I supposed to eat all that?" Seriously, the plate is filled to the brim with mac n cheese.

"You walked around the whole lake. I figured you'd be hungry." He shrugs but I don't miss the pink splotches that creep up his neck. I like to see *him* blush for a change.

"Hungry, maybe, but not on the verge of starving." When I keep laughing at him, he raises his hands and chuckles as well.

"Fair, so I might've been a bit optimistic. How about we share?" he asks. My heart has the audacity to beat faster as I keep looking into those brown eyes of his and I find myself nodding even as I know it's not a good idea.

As romantic as a dinner date might sound, I struggle with eating even when I'm alone. Seeing or hearing someone chew, or worse, being watched as I eat only makes it worse. People have all sorts of weird eating habits, and with my sensitivity on the topic, I pick up on all of them.

Since I can't tell Elija that, though, I take a fork out of my backpack and watch him place the food between us.

"I should have known you brought your own cutlery," he tells me with a smile. I take I look at the plastic fork in his hand, which must've been intended for me to use.

"Plastic kills our planet," I tell him, only half joking so I don't come across as judgmental. It's not like I think my using my reusable fork will save the planet just like I know the other students using the one-way ones aren't destroying it. He should do what he wants, it just makes me feel a little better about myself to do small things like this.

Elija looks slightly sheepish as he glances at the plastic in his hand. "Right, sorry. Boy scout's promise I'll remember to bring my own fork next time. Deal?"

I laugh. "Deal." With that, we start digging into the mushy macaroni. Or better, he digs in while I try to do the same, faking enthusiasm where I feel none.

The more I chew to prolong the time where I actually have to swallow a bite, the more my stomach clamps down. I can hardly keep the food down, and I hate that today has to be a bad day. I've been doing better recently, even though I skip meals. At least I didn't get sick as often as I used to.

With Liam's comment still fresh in my memory, it's hard to remember what that's like though. I feel like a pig for eating, stupid for thinking that, weak for struggling with something as vital as nutrition, and yet still disgusted with myself for every forkful I stuff into my mouth. *I need to eat.* Is quickly followed by *But do I need so much?*

One's the voice of reason, the other one sounds suspiciously like my mother feeding into my insecurities.

What is wrong with me? My frustration only adds to the stifling pressure on my chest.

"You know I can't finish this by myself either. Technically, I already ate," Elija tells me, and I realize I've stopped eating when I zoned out, my mind racing. *Shit.* Way to lose it twice in front of the same man in one day. I force a laugh that sounds unnatural to my own ears.

"Sorry. In my defense, I just woke up. I don't usually feel much of an apatite two minutes after leaving the dream station." I shrug, trying to appear sheepish even as I cringe at my awkward wording. Elija studies me for a moment before smiling back.

"Right. I didn't know if I should come wake you when they announced dinner, but I'm sorry if you'd rather have eaten with us." Great, now I made him think he did something wrong when he's been so thoughtful to even save me dinner. I rush to reassure him.

"Not at all. I mean, it was really nice of you to think of me at all. I'm just not that hungry, sorry," I try to explain.

"Please, Florence, you seriously need to stop apologizing so much to me," he tells me. The problem is that he's not smiling anymore and the sincerity in his voice makes me want to apologize again. "Don't," he says as if reading my mind. At least he tunes in when I laugh about it.

I force myself to keep eating, even if I just take one bite for every five Elija does. He doesn't comment on it and eventually turns on music to play in the background. I don't know if he does it because he finds the silence awkward, to drown out our chewing sounds which were all I could focus on, or because he seems to have this intuition when it comes to tending to my needs. I just know that eating gets slightly easier from there on.

"Now, what's the story behind the hairclip? Don't tell me if you don't want to but I haven't been able to stop thinking about it," he says after swallowing the last bite. I force my glance away from the empty dish, unsure how to feel about having finished it. How much of that plate landed in my stomach?

"It's a long story," I tell him automatically. When Elija nods as if accepting defeat, I feel surprisingly disappointed. I know he might be trying not to be pushy, and while I appreciate it, part of me wants to turn his reaction into something ugly. Part of my mind is whispering that he doesn't care, or wants to leave.

I hate my brain sometimes.

I don't even hate the idea of telling him. I answered that way out of habit, not used to people expecting an actual answer to cordial questions, but it might be nice to talk to Elija. I get the feeling he'd be a good listener.

Can I still answer or would that come across as weird now? Maybe I should just drop the topic and ask him something about himself. Maybe whether or not he had an aunt. Is that a weird thing to ask? Probably, since I haven't mentioned mine yet.

"Florence? I'm losing you again," Elija interrupts my spiraling thoughts softly.

"Oh, sorry. I can tell you the story if you want," I tell him. He chuckles before telling me to go on. "The aunt I told you about, you remember her?" I ask.

"The Sagittarius," he supplies in place of confirmation.

"Exactly. Well, she died a few years back." I try to let the words sink in but when I wait for a reaction, I get nothing.

"Yeah, I figured that when you spoke of her in the past tense the last time," he tells me, and I swear his voice somehow got softer. It makes the lump in my throat tighten but I will myself to keep it together. I'm almost an adult, I can't keep falling apart at the mere thought of my dead aunt.

"Always so observant." I chuckle but I'm sure he sees through it. Before I can go on with my story, Elija tells me to hold on for a second. He reaches for his phone and the bitter taste of rejection sours my mouth. So much for talking about this to someone for the first time since she died.

I must have misjudged him. He didn't sign up to hear a sob story. I'm sure there are more interesting things happening in his phone.

I feel my eyes prick and blink more furiously. I will not let myself fall apart in front of him. Not again. It would be like guilting him into paying attention to me, and I hate that thought.

Then, a familiar melody hits my ears and I raise my eyes back to Elija's. There's a small crease between his brows and I can see worry written all over his face as he studies me. He's worried *about me*, I realize with a start. It only makes me want to cry more.

I hate being emotional.

"What's that?" I smile slightly when I notice that it's not the song I thought was playing.

"Do you recognize the beat?" Elija asks me. It only takes me a second to understand what he's talking about.

"Wait, that's my rhythm. How?" I ask and it's all I can do not to stare at the guy in front of me with my mouth agape.

"I made it. It wasn't that hard, I just took the song you liked, recorded your rhythm, and put them together. I hope I got it right," he tells me and shrugs. Like it's no big deal. Like this isn't the most attentive, mind-boggling action anyone has ever done for me.

"I- Elija, I don't know what to say." My voice is barely louder than a whisper.

"Well, did I get it right?" he prompts but I'm still at a loss for words. I simply nod as I collect myself. This boy is unbelievable.

"Well good then. Just go on whenever you're ready," he tells me patiently. Meanwhile, I almost forgot what we were talking about.

"Right, sorry. There's not much to tell. We used to be really close and she left me that hairclip." I hate how stupid I feel when my eyes start filling with tears, so in a desperate attempt to keep from crying, I chuckle and stare at the ceiling.

"Florence," Elija says softly.

"It's nothing." I take a deep breath and pull my eyes back to his with a smile. He swears under his breath.

"I hate it when you do that," he mumbles roughly.

"What?" I ask, not having expected such a reaction.

"That fake smile. I don't know why you do it and I won't tell you to stop if it makes you feel better, but I hate it when you look at me like that. It feels like you're hiding. Lying to me. I don't like lies."

"I'm sorry. Agh, sorry, I'm not supposed to apologize. Ah, damn it," I ramble yet again. At least it seems to lighten Elija's mood a tad.

"Don't worry about it." Both of us are quiet for a beat but Elija speaks up again. "I have a question." He suddenly seems uncharacteristically unsure of himself. Truth be told, it makes me kind of nervous.

"Go on." Here goes nothing.

"Well, that night – when you had the panic attack – was that because of your aunt? Or because of how I acted that night? You became kind of quiet after mentioning her but I still worried," he asks.

"Oh," I chuckle since I need a moment to think about my answer. "It had nothing to do with you, don't worry. I guess it was connected to my aunt. Less about her than what happened after her death, but that's a long and boring story. I'd rather talk about something else," I tell him honestly.

It's good he asked so I could at least put his worries to rest. I'd hate to think he was beating himself up over my fragile mind when it wasn't his fault, but that's about as much as I'm willing to disclose right now.

If I got into all the issues I have with my parents and so on, I'd just bore him to sleep. Not to mention I'd sound like an absolute brat. After all, my parents raised me in a nice house in a good neighborhood and always bought me whatever I could wish for. I was never forced to get a job or worry about my next meal, so I don't think I should complain. I'm just being silly.

"All right. What do you want to talk about?" Elija asks me as he gets a bit more comfortable on the floor of my tent.

"Well first off, feel free to get over here. I imagine my sleeping bag's a bit more comfortable than the floor, and we've probably been as close as humanly possible before, either way," I tell him and pat the space next to me.

His sharp inhale of breath is my first indicator that I misspoke. "Florence, you should be careful around whom you say things like that. They might get the wrong idea," he explains, the look in his eyes telling me a lot more than his words. It takes me a beat to understand what he's saying. When realization dawns, my cheeks heat up.

Yeah, it's a good thing Jamie wasn't here to witness those words. He'd surely tease me about it for an eternity. And I couldn't even correct him since telling him I have panic attacks would be worse than letting him think I slept with Elija.

Oh god, danger zone. Abort mission. Backtrack right now. Steer conversation to safer topics.

"Right, I'll keep it in mind. Now, tell me about your family. Or, hang on, your music. You said you liked anything connected to it, but I didn't know you made your own remixes.

Hang on! That song you showed me last week, that wasn't – I mean, you didn't – I don't care if I'm rambling, I need answers," I finally burst theatrically as the pieces connect in my mind. Thankfully, he looks amused rather than intimidated by my lunatic behavior.

"So let me help you get them. Yes, the other beats were by me. Like I said, I play the guitar, have tried my luck with the piano a few years back but never really got into it, and I like making remixes or creating songs myself. What else was there?" He takes a moment to let the information sink in, watching me as it does. "My family?" he recalls.

"First off, I'll need a private concert at some point. Also, you're really talented, honestly. Now, yes. Please proceed." Finally, I can announce that my smile feels natural.

"I told you about my siblings already and you've met the twins. We all live at home with our mother and the twins' father. Don't be confused but I call him dad since he's been around for a long time. He and my mom both work but at least one is home most of the time. If they're not, it's either my brother, me, or my grandparents who take care of the twins. My mom's parents live about thirty minutes from our place, so we see them fairly often.

"Kai's and my dad wasn't around when we were younger and my mom used to work a lot so our grandparents pretty much raised us. I'd say I get my sense of humor from my grandpa but I'm not sure I deserve that much credit. He's hands down the most effortlessly comical person I know. Whenever I had questions about school, I could always ask my grandma, so growing up with them was quite the win. That's it, I'd say." By the time he's finished, I'm grinning at the image of a younger Elija studying with his grandma.

"They all sound awesome," I tell him wistfully. I imagine for a beat what it might be like to grow up surrounded by so many people that truly love you. He might have been dealt a bad hand with his biological father, but it seems the other adults in his life worked hard to make up for his failure.

I'm glad to hear his stepfather was there for him from such a young age. While I don't know the circumstances around his biological father, I can't imagine what it would be like to be abandoned by a parent. It must have been so confusing for him when he was little. My chest aches for young Elija, but I reassure myself that he's fine now.

His tone held no anger or resentment when he mentioned his father's absence. Just a whole lot of admiration and love for the people who were there.

Some of my thoughts must have bled into my expression because when Elija meets my eyes, he looks contemplative. Without saying a word, he reaches out and opens his arms invitingly. I don't question it but hesitantly crawl closer to him to hug him.

I kneel between his legs, trying to keep enough distance between us so I don't make him uncomfortable especially since I'm pretty sure this is for my sake. When my arms wrap around his middle and my head rests on his chest, his own arms pull me closer, allowing me to melt into the embrace and soak up the rare comfort of physical touch.

It's a good hug, I'm not going to lie.

I may or may not have sighed against him as I softly breathed the air doused in his scent in. I let his body heat stream into me, warming places I didn't know were cold in the first place. His thumb caresses me, one on my back where his harm is banded around me and one over my shoulder. If I could, I'd stay like this forever.

Too soon, Elija starts pulling back slightly. His hands drop until they lazily rest on my hips while I keep mine around his waist. Maybe we're both not willing to let go quite yet. I know I'm not.

My skin buzzes where he's touching me, awareness rising as the moment seems to shift. Elija is just staring at me, his face still only inches away from mine in out half-embrace. The custom-made song is playing on repeat, nothing more than background noise barely audible over the blood rushing in my ears.

Is it abnormal that I can hear my pounding heart? Can he hear it too? What is happening?

Elija has never looked at me like this before, his features solemn but his eyes alive with the kind of heat I'm unfamiliar with. His thumb starts moving over me but he doesn't pull away. Is he getting distracted by this strange pull between us as well? It feels like a physical thing, silently urging me to get closer to him. To close the distance between our bodies once more, maybe not to hug this time but kiss.

The thought makes my eyes drop to his full lips like a command. *Yep, tempting as always.*

Will I get to taste them finally? I raise my eyes back to Elija's and feel like I know my answer. His eyes are jumping back and forth between mine, a silent question burning within them, and then, they eventually drop to my lips. He stares at them for a few beats, making them tingle as awareness rises within me.

They part on their own accord as if readying for his attention, but he doesn't lean in. Just takes in my lips with a thorough intensity.

Does he like what he sees? Is his heart racing like mine? Does he want to kiss me? How far would I let this go if he did?

The questions come to a sudden halt when his eyes meet mine again, any hope vanishing. The heat they were displaying just a moment ago seems to have turned into indecision and maybe even regret. Slowly, painfully slowly, and gently, he pulls his arms away from mine and gets to his feet.

All without saying anything, the silence stretching to the point of suffocation.

All without taking those regretful, apologetic eyes off me. Or maybe it's pity I see within them. That's even worse.

I let it happen, staying seated as if in a trance, all the while wondering what the hell just happened. Only after I hear the tent's flaps close do I slump on my sleeping bag. He just left?

Here I was thinking the two of us would finally become something more than friends, and he just left.

An uncomfortable knot tightens in my stomach. I'm an idiot. Honestly, why would Elija want to kiss me? I'm sure he has many girls swooning over him. Funnier girls, less damaged girls. They probably don't whine about their dead aunts to him, and it most likely didn't take them a year to speak to him in the first place.

I curl up in a ball, wrapping my sleeping bag tightly around me to replace the heat he provided me with just a moment ago.

I'm stupid. This is my fault for getting carried away in what was supposed to be a friendly hug. I'm his charity case, not the girl he wants to kiss. It's nothing to be upset about. Knowing him, he'll have the decency to pretend this never happened and things will go back to normal with minimal embarrassment on my part. I repeat that to myself as I try not to cry.

Anyone could come into the tent at any given moment and the last thing I need is to cause a scene. No, I'm fine. It doesn't matter. I don't care anyway.

Chapter 17

Elija

I've never wanted to murder anyone as much as I do now, staring at the mirror. Such a fucking moron!

"Dude, you okay?" Jamie asks as he enters our tent.

"Just hit me. I deserve it," I groan pathetically.

"Okay, normally I'd gladly take you up on the offer but considering you look like shit, I feel obliged to ask what happened."

"I didn't kiss her. Well, that's not the dumb part. I almost kissed her, that's the problem. It's not like I didn't want to. Fuck, I've never wanted to kiss anyone more, but she seemed so sad and she's tired and I didn't want to take advantage of that. I wanted to settle on a hug but got carried away and I was so close to finally giving in to that stupid urge.

"Instead, my dumbass decided to leave. I just got up and left without a word, Jamie. What kind of jerk does that? Ugh! She must be fucking confused now." I groan and drop my head against the cool surface of the mirror. My thoughts are all over the place, too quick to morph to put into words for Jamie. I wonder if this is what Florence feels like whenever she rambles. I hope not since this sucks.

"Wow. I have no idea what to say to that other than that you should just go back and explain," my friend tells me seriously. So damn rationally. Why can't he make a dumb joke the one time I need him to? Nope, of course, this is when he decides to be wise or whatever.

"I can't. I wouldn't know what to say, and I don't think she wants to see me right now. Can you check up on her for me? I'll stay outside the tent and decide how badly I fucked up after hearing her talk," I ask my friend. That seems like a solid plan, right?

"I could do that, I guess. What's my excuse to bother her?" Jamie replies hesitantly. Thank god for friends.

"Just ask her if she wants to hang out," I offer, not entirely sold on the idea. I don't want to bother her again, even if it's Jamie doing the actual bothering, but I'll die of a stroke if I can't calm my worries.

Maybe I imagined the hurt look on her face when I left. Maybe she didn't even realize I was about to kiss her and things aren't as ruined as they feel. Or things are worse, but at least knowing where she stands will allow me a plan to make it up to her.

"Yeah, good enough. Now get your sorry ass out of that sleeping bag and follow me to her tent," Jamie jabs, kicking my form on the floor.

I don't protest since I need his help right now. Instead, I follow after my friend like a beaten dog.

Our tent's not far from Florence's so it takes us mere minutes to reach it. Jamie uselessly knocks on the fabric of the tent before entering while I stay outside, trying not to look like a creep.

"Hey, Flower girl," I hear Jamie say as he steps inside.

"I'm sorry, Jamie, but I'm kind of tired right now." Her slow, measured words are like a knife to the chest. She sounds sad. So genuinely sad that I doubt she's going through the trouble of smiling that fake smile for Jamie. It's worrisome. She never drops her smile.

"I was just wondering if you wanted to hang out a bit?" Jamie goes on, and I cringe a bit. I know I made him go in there, but she's made it clear that she wasn't interested in any company. I wish he'd just step out and leave her be while I figure out how to make it up to her.

"I think I'll just sleep," Florence replies, sounding positively drained. And no wonder after the day she's had.

If only Jamie could take a hint. I know he can tell she's upset, but instead of leaving her like she asked, he does what he does best; he tries to cheer her up with his persistent go-lucky attitude. "Come on! I'm sure you'll feel better once you get some fresh air. You've been holed up in here for hours."

If I could, I'd pull Jamie out of there myself and save her the trouble of shaking him off. He can be rather pushy when he set his mind to something, and Florence is known for putting her needs last to accommodate others. She's historically bad at standing up for herself.

It's a token of her state that she doesn't give in to his demand. "Just leave, Jamie. I mean it. Please." Her voice breaks softly on the last syllable, and the blade in my gut twists further. I didn't kiss her to prevent any further confusion and possible regret on her part, but hearing how beaten she sounds right now makes me seriously question my choice.

What's going on in that overactive head of hers? What explanation for my sudden exit did she come up with? I have a feeling I wouldn't like whatever it is. It probably couldn't be further from the truth, either. I know she's insecure and the way she rambles tells me she's an overthinker. It's why I've been trying to be so careful with her.

Trying and failing after today's events.

"Right. Sweet dreams, then. See you at breakfast," Jamie says, failing at hiding his disappointment but still aiming for a cheery voice. He and Florence are similar in that way, I guess.

When my friend comes out of her tent, he passes me wordlessly, slapping me over the back of my head as he does. I don't protest, following him back to our tent where we end up sitting in silence.

"So, what do I do now?" I finally ask.

"I don't think there's much to do. She's clearly disappointed and all up in her head about it right now but she'll probably sleep it off. If something still seems wrong tomorrow, you'll figure something out. For now, we respect her wishes and leave her alone," my friend replies. I nod. That sounds reasonable enough.

"Don't beat yourself up over it," Jamie adds, sounding more serious than I've heard him in some time.

"Right, because you already did it for me?" I mock half-heartedly. He gives me a flat look.

"I forget that you grew up in a soft ass home sometimes. I basically caressed the back of your head."

"I know, I know. Thanks for your help, anyway," I add.

"Sure thing. Now, let's go meet the guys in the woods. They must be wondering what's keeping us." I don't feel like going out right now, but hanging out with my friends might be just what I need. A little distraction has never hurt anyone. Especially when I've settled on not harassing Florence any more tonight.

Since Benji apparently demanded Jamie got him some skittles for his munchies, my friend and I get to walk through the whole campsite. Halfway on our way to the vending machine two girls corner us. Well, they don't corner us but it kind of feels like an attack with the way they're eying us.

"Hey, I'm Joe. You're Elija, right? I heard you won the race today," one of the girls says, basically preening when my eyes briefly sway in her direction. I frown at the unfamiliar reaction. I'm not usually approached by girls unless Marcus is around and I'm the friend for the friend. In those situations, I usually stay friendly while I wait for Marcus to shoot his girl down, which he always does. They luckily always leave then.

Marcus isn't here right now, but if she heard I won the race, she probably knows who my partner was. The thought settles my nerves slightly. I don't like the thought of this girl hitting on me or having to reject her. It's easier when Marcus gets them off our backs.

"Yeah. It was nice meeting you, Joe," I tell her, hoping that's the end of it. It's getting late and we still have to walk through the woods to get to our friends. I'm not in the mood to entertain a jersey chaser that's only paying attention to me because of who my friend is. *I'm not interested in entertaining any girl apart from the one I can't talk to tonight.*

So many girls are doing their best to lock in the future pro player, and that's exactly what Marcus is. Judging by his stats and performance, he'll sign a contract before he's done with college.

"Of course. I imagine you are really busy. Where are you guys going?" Joe asks, not taking the hint as she keeps up with my and Jamie's quick pace. Her friend is too busy ogling Jamie, who seems oblivious to it, to even engage in the conversation. Poor girl doesn't know how hopeless that chase is.

"Vending machine," I tell her, my voice gruffer than planned. I don't mean to sound like an abrupt jerk and usually, I'd be more amicable, but right now I am tired and fed up and entirely not in the mood for this interaction and her blatant show of interest in me. I mean, is it too much to ask of her to quit staring without blinking. She's making a move, I get it.

Maybe I'm being overly sensitive. On other occasions, I might've enjoyed the stroke to my ego, but now, all I can think about is Florence lying alone in her tent while this girl makes a move on me. It's not like I owe Florence any sort of commitment. Thinking so when we never so much as kissed would be nuts.

And yet I don't want to touch another girl with a ten-foot pole. Probably why I'm reacting to intensely to Joe's advances.

"That's where we're heading too. We don't have any plans for later though, do you know if anything fun is happening around here?" Joe keeps pushing as she trails me toward the vending machine. Today really is the day of people not taking hints.

"Nope," I pop the p.

"Oh, come on, Eli! Don't be so mean! We're just hanging out with our friends but you could tag along, I guess. It's nothing wild, just some music," Jamie interjects, making me groan inwardly. No one's supposed to know of our little hangout-hideout. These girls will probably tell all their friends where to find Marcus now, forcing us to find a new place.

That'll be fun with Liam's constant nagging.

Joe's face lights up like the sun, but it's her friend that speaks. "It sounds like fun, but are you sure we're not intruding?" She seems genuine, so I decide my exasperation towards her friend doesn't extend to her. At least she's not practically undressing us with her eyes.

"Yeah, absolutely. Though, from an outsider's view, you probably shouldn't follow two guys out into the middle of the woods. At night. To meet more guys. You've never talked to. Oh, yes, that sounds really bad," Jamie thinks out loud. The girls don't seem put off by it. If anything, Joe's answering laugh makes it sound like he made a joke. It makes me consider two explanations. They're either stupidly trusting and might've heard of us before, or they're plain stupid and don't value their lives.

I hope it's the first one.

Never mind that, I hope they change their minds and decide it's not worth the risk.

"What's life without a little adventure?" Joe teases right as we reach the vending machine. As if I wasn't already cringing, she tops the statement off with a wink in my direction. I wince and focus on getting Benji's skittles before leading our little group toward the forest wordlessly.

My hurried steps are less of a token of my enthusiasm but rather an attempt to put some distance between me and the blonde still eyeing me. Jamie hangs back with the girls, chatting away happily.

"Fancy seeing you alive. Where's Flo? And who are those?" Benji asks when we finally reach them, his eyes squinting at the girls appearing behind me. I ignore him and drop myself to the ground near the others.

"Flo's tired but these are Joe and Miley. We found them on the way here," Jamie explains lightly, gesturing to each of the girls as he makes the introduction. I guess he got to know them

Jarah Aurel

a bit better while I was running away. I hope he managed to mention he's not into girls before Miley gets her hopes up any further.

Knowing him, he would have easily done it *if* he noticed she was making gooey eyes at him at all. He's not all that perceptive to women's attention. They're so long written off in the romantic part of his brain that he forgets his sexuality isn't tattooed on his forehead so he very often seems like an option to straight women.

Miley's more like Benji's type anyway, with those almond eyes and her rich dark skin. Yeah, she could have him kneeling in a heartbeat if she fluttered those long eyelashes in his direction.

To my surprise – and dismay – Joe doesn't ditch me to talk to Marcus. Instead, she plops down on the grass to my right and stares at me. This time, her gaze contains careful contemplation rather than desire. It's a welcome change.

"Why do I get the feeling you don't like me?" she finally asks when I do my best not to meet her eyes. *Shit.* She really hit the nail on the head with no hesitation. I can't very well ignore that. I look at her and sigh.

"I'm sorry. It's been a day, but I shouldn't have been a jerk. I just," I trail off. I what? *I'm not available?* Not strictly true. *Not interested?* True but harsh. *Just can't stop thinking about another girl?* True but not her problem.

"I was just a bit put off because I thought you were expressing interest, but I should have just said I'm not on the market to be anything other than a buddy rather than try to freeze you out," I finally settle on. I know I'd feel like a douchebag if I didn't remedy my gruffness somehow, so in the name of not having later regrets, here we are. Being cordial.

"It's fine. I'm sorry if I came on to you a bit too strong. I just heard things about you all day, how you won the race with Marcus. You're kind of the talk of the camp if I'm being honest. Plus, it probably didn't help that I read some smut right before

Miley and I saw you guys. Either way, I'm sorry if I made you uncomfortable."

She read *smut?* I thought that was a nicer word for porn. And she's telling me that because...? *It made her horny and that's why she came onto me?* I stifle a shiver. Why would she openly discuss something like that? I'm pretty sure if I walked around talking about watching porn, I'd be a certifiable pervert.

Be nice. Shake it off. Focus on the good thing.

She apologized for coming on to me and is now strictly keeping her eyes on appropriate zones and her hands to herself. I can work with that. Buddy territory. I'll treat her like any guy acquaintance of mine.

"It's all right. I know better than anyone how one can get carried away in a moment," I tell her, then groan when flashes of my moment with Florence in the tent return to the forefront of my mind.

There's a soft puff of laughter that probably belongs to my new friend. "I sense a story is coming."

I keep my face buried in my hands and nod, my shoulders hunched. "Yeah, one I don't even know the outcome of yet." My head snaps up suddenly, looking at Joe in a whole new way as some hope sparks in my gut. "But you're a girl. Maybe you can help."

And so, I get into the tale of a pretty girl decked in flowers who I'm doing a very bad job with not confusing.

Chapter 18

Florence

Before our group's hideout comes into view, a foreign voice makes me stop in my tracks. A loud, shrill, very female voice, which was the last thing I expected to hear.

After convincing myself I was fine and taking some time to collect myself in my tent, I decided to stop wallowing in self-pity and pick Jamie up on his offer to hang out. I also felt like I owed him an apology for my rude behavior earlier. It was unlike myself and he didn't deserve it. Besides, I kind of wanted to check up on Elija, make sure I didn't make him uncomfortable or anything, and see if we were okay.

Now here I am, spying past a tree to see who's at our place. After all, we did choose it to be away from others, right? Not that I mind hanging out with strangers, but the guys said it was for Marcus' sake. I hope no one followed them here to harass him with fangirl behavior. Marcus would probably be upset, and I'm sure no one wants to look for a new spot to hang out the last two nights. Not with Liam in tow.

But I don't find a crowd of groupies swarming an uncomfortable Marcus. Instead, I see the guys all hanging around a girl I've never seen before while Elija sits apart from them, laughing with another girl. I hate the way my stomach tightens at the sight. I have no right to feel jealous. Elija is my friend, so I should be happy to see him have fun, even when it's not with me.

Even if it's with another girl. A very pretty girl, all voluptuous and soft angles. The perfect picture of soft femininity.

With that in mind, I slowly turn back to where I came from. I can accept that Elija doesn't see me as more than a friend or that he has a date or whatever with another girl, but I won't force myself to witness it first-hand unless I have to. Nope, I'll just go back to my tent and call it a night. Might be best to just go to sleep.

Taking the first step away from the guys, I curse myself when a twig snaps beneath my boot.

"Hey, who's there?" I hear Orion demand, his voice dangerously low. They clearly haven't been able to make me out in the dark, and I seriously consider making a run for it. "Show yourself, Creep!" Elsa adds.

With no doubt flaming red cheeks, I turn once more and finally walk up to my friends. Although, I do take care not to look at Elija, even as I feel his eyes on me.

"Hi," I say sheepishly. "Sorry, I didn't mean to scare you. I changed my mind about coming but I think it was a mistake. I'm kind of tired," I tell them with a smile.

For the first time ever, I hate it. I hate the stupid smile on my face because with every second I avoid meeting Elija's eyes, my heart seems to sink a little more. I felt better before coming here, but now I feel about two feet tall. Especially knowing Elija can tell I'm wearing a mask. It's useless and certainly adds to his impression of me. That I'm a sensitive, ingenuine wimp. A liar, even.

Everyone is staring at me.

"Nonsense, Flo. You're here now, stay a little," Benji tells me, patting the ground next to him. Groaning inwardly, I sit down next to him.

"Hi, I'm Florence," I finally introduce myself, looking at the girl closest to me before quickly glancing at the blonde girl next to Elija. Even in the dark and with the short second I look at her,

I can tell her face is gorgeous. Full cheeks and awake, upturned eyes framed by golden curtain bangs.

Comparing myself to her I can't help but notice we're opposites. Her features are soft and easy on the eyes while mine are sharp. Too sharp.

No wonder Elija fled my tent.

"I'm Miley. Nice to meet you," the brown-skinned girl tells me, a warm smile lighting up her whole face. She's just as beautiful as her friend, but it helps that she's sitting with her back to the happy couple. It's petty and silly, but I like her a little more just for not looking so chummy with Eli.

Without trying, she makes me feel welcome in my own friend group. It doesn't matter what I look like, these are my friends. They've seen me before and obviously don't care. So what If I'm drowning in the hoody I'm wearing with dark circles underneath my eyes. We're camping. I'm just tired, that's why I'm acting so unlike myself.

"I'm Joe," the other girl says. I smile at her too, straining to make it look sincere. Then, Benji picks up a conversation with me and everyone starts doing their own thing. The tension leaves my shoulder immediately once everyone's attention disperses, and I settle into my position.

As the night drags on, my comfort drags into drowsiness. Honestly, it's more exhausting than you'd think to ignore a person you've gotten used to paying constant attention to. Especially when his loud laughter mocks me every time I try to relax, reminding me I'm not the cause of it.

"Flo, did you hear what I said?" Jamie asks. I smile at him apologetically and shake my head.

At some point, my friend sat down on the other side of me and started talking. I'm sure I engaged in it, but I can't remember what topic we were on about.

"I was just telling you about the time I stuck a bright pink Hello Kitty sticker on Orion's gloomy skateboard. It stuck out like a sore thumb, but I superglued it on there so short of sanding it off, it stuck. He chased me with it afterward, threatening to smash it over my head," he tells me wistfully before zoning back. "Come here, why don't you lay down?" he asks, motioning to his legs expectantly.

"That honestly does sound nice. I'm sorry I didn't pay attention. I'm sad I missed it, I would have liked to see his reaction to the sticker," I assure him, getting ready to lie down even though I'd rather go back to camp.

"There's no need for that," a voice interrupts me, successfully making me meet the dark eyes I've been avoiding all night. "I'm walking Joe back to camp. Come on, Flo, you can come too," Elija says.

My heart twists a little, his words hitting me like a brick in the face. *Flo*. He called me Flo, not Florence.

It's my nickname, I know. It really shouldn't bother me, but my tired mind and exhausted heart both protest at the sound of it from his lips. The grim expression on his face doesn't help either.

Averting my eyes, I get up and mutter a quick goodbye to Miley and the guys.

Joe's already a few feet ahead and Elija catches up with her effortlessly, leaving me to trail behind them like a beaten dog. The two of them have a fluent conversation, but I'm too tired to listen to it, much less engage in it.

They seem so comfortable together, I wonder if they've hung out before. Are they a thing? Was I so oblivious I missed the signs that Elija is not available?

They're not touchy or particularly close, but I can't help but notice that neither is stuttering or rambling. Their conversation flows smoothly. Without me. Neither tries to include me in the talk or even looks over their shoulder to check if I'm still following.

Halfway back, I decide I've had enough. This isn't me. I'm not some pushover to order around and treat like dirt. I'm Florence fucking Lite and even though I'm tired, I won't let myself sink that low. With that in mind, I stop in my tracks in my first act of rebellion. It's anticlimactic since the two people in front of me keep walking, unaware of my change in attitude, but I gladly watch them go.

I don't need an audience as I silently rebuild my pride. I just watch them go.

It's best they don't turn to talk to me since I'm sure I would regret speaking my mind right now. Elija might have been rude tonight but that's not a reason for me to be as well. So, I need to cool off. Alone.

Chapter 19

Elija

"My tent's just over there. Thanks for walking me back. Goodnight, Elija," Joe says when we reach the edge of the camp.

"Night, Joe. It was nice meeting you," I tell her, surprised to find it ringing true. Despite my first impression, she ended up making my night marginally better with her steadfast humor and no short list of random questions to keep a conversation going. It's what kept me from snapping all night.

Why would I snap?

That's easy. It's because a certain brown-haired girl wouldn't acknowledge me, only looking at and talking to my friends and the two girls instead. At first, I was glad when she came since I thought it meant she was feeling better and might even have come to talk to me. I wanted to apologize, but then she seemed so determined to ignore me that I threw those plans out of the window.

I get that I acted strange tonight with the way I left things, but I didn't think she'd give me the cold shoulder. It's Florence, after all. I'd have hoped she'd at least allow me to make things up to her before writing me off so completely.

Joe told me I should give her space or wait until she wasn't tired, and since I didn't know what to do, another woman's opinion was really appreciated. It's all we talked about at first, my situation with Florence, that is, but as soon as Florence arrived, we had to find other things to talk about. It was mostly Joe trying to cheer me up.

When I heard Jamie offering Florence to sleep on his lap, I couldn't keep myself from going over there. It's completely irrational to be jealous of my gay friend but I couldn't help it. He was getting her attention, and I wasn't. You'd think I was an only child with that line of thinking.

I talked myself into believing taking her back to camp was the right thing to do because I'm pretty sure Florence didn't want to be there in the first place. She tried to leave right when she came, and she did seem really tired when I asked her to come with us. I was giving her an out.

Sure, you were being rational.

But now that Joe is gone, I'm mustering up the courage to finally turn to Florence. Even if it's just to say goodnight. Bad enough that she didn't get a single word in on the way back. My gut clenches at the realization. Shit.

I turn around in the silent night, finding myself standing alone for as far as the eye can see.

When did she leave? Was I really so focused on giving her space that I tuned out the sound of her steps? When did she fall silent?

"Florence?" I speak toward the tree line. Even as I say, I know it's no use. She clearly isn't here.

I know I was an idiot tonight. I was rude and bossy and ignored her all the way back here, the last part without really noticing. I know she followed me away from the guys since I was hyper-aware of her footsteps behind me for the first ten minutes of the walk.

I thought she was quiet because she was tired but eventually relaxed a bit more, knowing she'll sleep soon. Apparently, I relaxed too much because I have no idea when she stopped being behind me.

Trying to be reasonable and not lose my shit, I head toward her tent. She probably left when Joe did, right? I lift my hand to knock on the tent or something but stop. Should I do this? If she fled without saying goodnight, shouldn't I take that as a hint that she doesn't want to talk to me? Joe told me to give her space. Besides, most of her tentmates are probably asleep, and I'd just wake them.

Sighing, I leave and don't stop walking until I plop down on my own sleeping bag. *She's fine*, I repeat to myself. Florence is a smart girl, I'm sure she's sleeping safely in her tent.

"I can't wait for this trip to be over. I miss my four-poster bed," Liam whines at breakfast. He's been making similar remarks for the entirety of the trip, but since I'm also sleeping in his huge ass tent, I can't ream into him about it. Instead, I speak as if he hadn't said a word.

"Has anyone seen Florence?" I ask. Liam huffs but no one pays him any attention. Nope, they zero in on me with varying degrees of interest at my words.

"Not since you guys left last night, why?" Benji questions, suspicion coating his words. I curse under my breath, worry rushing through me in waves once more. I was barely able to close my eyes all night because stupid images of Florence dead or hurt in the woods kept torturing me. I told myself it was irrational, but the second challenge should start soon and I have yet to catch a glimpse of her.

"What's up?" Marcus inquires cautiously, noticing my unease.

"Well, last night I kind of lost her. Well, I didn't *lose* her. I just didn't particularly see her enter her tent, you know?"

"I don't think we do. What happened?" Jamie prompts. My friends are now officially staring at me, the tense set of their shoulders telling me I'm in trouble. I rub my hands over my face and mumble into them.

"Florence kind of walked behind Joe and me and when I turned around to tell her goodnight after reaching the camp, she wasn't there. I figured she just went to her tent already." When everyone's quiet, I slowly lower my hands to look at my friends.

They're just staring at me, but I can tell they're pissed. Marcus has his jaw clenched, Jamie's not smiling, Orion glares at me more than usual, and Benji has his hands balled into fists. Even Liam seems mad, though I don't know why he would be. It's not like he cares about anyone but himself.

"I'm sure she's fine," I add weakly, unable to stand the silence. "Please say something." "You'd think one whack over the head would teach you?" Jamie mutters roughly, and I realize it's the first time he's ever been mad at me. It's a strange realization after years of friendship and only solidifies what I already know. I'm an idiot. I used to think I was good at reading Florence's silent moods and realizing what she needs, but this trip is proving me wrong.

I'm a fucking disaster, and now anxiety that I fucked it all to hell with her joins the knot of tension in my gut. I tried to be good and gentle and calm around her, and yesterday I was rude and gruff instead.

And I lost her.

Literally, physically lost her.

In the woods.

"I swear to god, if she's hurt, I'm going to break your fingers," Benji adds. Knowing I play the guitar, this really means something. Especially because he's the peaceful one.

"Okay, why are you all so mad? I didn't tell Florence to walk off without saying a word," I protest, feeling slightly indignant.

"You didn't tell her anything else, either, did you?" Marcus offers neutrally. While I can tell he's put off by this situation like the rest, he's keeping himself in check. Not that I'd understand any other reaction since I don't think I've seen him so much as talk to the girl.

"Marcus," Jamie warns him and when their eyes meet, something passes silently between them. It makes me wonder what the hell I missed and since when I'm out of the loop.

"No, don't you *Marcus* me. Honestly, Eli, you're one of my closest friends but I can't say I like you a whole lot right now.

No idea what's going on between Flo and you, but it was clear to everyone that you were acting like a jerk last night."

"You're right about one thing, you don't know what's going on," I snap. The fact that I'm feeling defensive just says that they're right and I know it. Maybe the lack of sleep is getting to me. I don't think I like myself a whole lot either at this moment.

"I know that Flo didn't deserve to be treated by you the way she was yesterday. I didn't say anything last night because I didn't want to cause a scene but the way you ordered her to go back to camp was just weird. You two are friends or whatever the hell you want me to call it, but you acted like she was some kind of burden," Marcus goes on.

I have a snappy reply on my lips but swallow it with a single pleading look from Jamie. "Was it really that bad?" I ask, deflating. My heartbeat slows as my chest tightens. I know the answer before he says it.

"You called her Flo, dude. You never do that. It's a thing between you two. I definitely know she noticed if I did," Benji tells me, though the anger bleeds from his expression at the sight of my apparent remorse. *Shit, did I?*

"I'm sorry. I don't know what the hell was wrong with me."

"You're an idiot, that's what's wrong," Liam adds unnecessarily, making me turn to him.

"Why do you care?" I snap. He huffs but doesn't answer.

"Both of you just shut up. Let's find Flo," Benji interjects. At the same time, a girl passes our table and Orion speaks up.

"Hey, you! You're staying in Florence's tent, right? Did you see her last night or this morning?" he asks her.

She looks like he just jumped her with a gun. "Uhm, no. I don't think so." The second the shaky words leave her lips, she hurries off. I don't blame her. Our group doesn't look particularly friendly right now.

"Everyone, down to the lake! The second challenge starts in ten minutes. The twenty students that passed the first challenge need to be ready in their swimming suits, the rest is obliged to come to cheer them on!" Mr. Hank yells right as I was about to ask what we should do about Florence.

"You guys need to get ready. I'm calling her and we'll check the crowd at the lake. If we don't find her, Liam and I search the woods. I'm sure she's fine," Benji offers. He and Liam were the only pair in our group that didn't finish in the top ten at the last challenge, so they're not part of today's.

I hate the idea of doing basically nothing but oblige begrudgingly, forcing myself to get ready and meet my friends at the lake lest I get an earful of my teacher on top of things.

Time passes in a blur as we hurry to get to the lake in time.

"Five minutes! Participants, get into the water!" Mr. Hank yells.

"I haven't seen her," I tell my friends. This has gone too far. I haven't seen Florence in ten hours and here I am, expected to take part in some stupid challenge.

I don't care about this game. Not as long as my mind is busy making up worst-case scenarios about her whereabouts.

"She hasn't picked up her phone," Benji tells me, running a hand through his fiery curls.

"Who hasn't? Shouldn't you guys be in the water already?" a new voice speaks up from behind me. I whip around, startled to see Florence looking up at me, appearing perfectly fine.

"Where the hell have you been?" the words tear out of me in a rough demand, my pent-up worry seeking release. I feel a rough hand on my shoulder a second later and quickly apologize. Not that she seems affected by my tone. She's still smiling unperturbedly.

"I felt like sleeping under the stars." She shrugs.

"You couldn't have told us that? We thought you were dead or something," Orion pushes in a rare show of emotion. Or at least an emotion other than anger.

"I'm really sorry. I thought I'd be back at camp before anyone would notice but I kind of slept in. My phone died so my alarm didn't go off," she explains. Meanwhile, I'm just glad she's here and looking better than I've seen her in days. I don't mean her looks, she's always stunning. Nope, it's her smile, a genuine smile that calms me down. This is the Florence I've grown used to.

"Well, it was really irresponsible," Marcus says before I cut in.

"Either way, you're fine which is all that counts. I'm sure we'd all love to hear about your adventure, Snow White, but we really have a challenge to get to," I tell her, trying to contort my face into a matching grin. She smiles at me while my friends make approving noises behind my back.

Marcus, Orion, Jamie, and I join the other swimmers while our friends search for a good spot to watch.

Yeah, this super fun challenge is swimming. There's a small island in the middle of the lake and Mr. Hank thought it a good idea to make 20 people swim around it at the same time. Of course, the island is more of a big rock, so this is about to be tight.

Our teacher starts counting back from three and right before he blows his whistle, I spot Florence in the crowd. Figures that she managed to sneak past everyone and ended up with the best viewing place.

The sound of the whistle rips me from my thoughts, and as the spectators start cheering, I start swimming. I don't usually take sports that seriously but with Florence watching, I feel the need to prove myself. That's why I push my arms and legs to the max until I'm almost tied with Marcus. We swim around the rock, and only then do I risk a glance back.

We're a comfortable distance ahead of the others so I allow myself to slow down a tad. Just enough to be able to breathe. After all, the top ten make it to the next and last challenge which means I'm in no hurry.

Ahead of me, I see Marcus come to a sudden stop mid stroke.

"You okay?" I ask as I swim up to him. The closer I get, the clearer it becomes that he's not. His face is pulled in a grimace and he seems to be clutching one of his legs while keeping himself afloat with his free arm.

"Fucking cramp!" he swears.

"Shit. Come on, hold on to me. We'll swim back together," I offer, trying awkwardly to get close to him with our combined flaying limbs around us.

"Hell no. Just finish it, I'll get there myself. At least one of us should finish as part of the fastest ten," my friend insists. I glance over my shoulder to see the other swimmers catching up fast. Marcus is right, if I help him, we're both out.

I let my eyes wander to the people standing at the shore. I can't see Florence from here but just knowing she's there is enough. Marcus chuckles.

"Just go, you idiot."

"Don't drown," I tell him before leaving him behind to finish the race.

By the time I finally reach the shore, my legs and arms feel like pudding and my lungs burn.

"First swimmer is back!" Mr. Hank announces while I simply lay in the sand like a stranded whale. Oh well.

"You did it!" I recognize Florence's voice amongst all the yelling and cheering and slightly turn my head to look at her. She kneels down beside me, beaming brighter than the sun, and gently wipes my hair from my forehead. I enjoy the movement, but when she catches herself, she pulls back and chuckles awkwardly.

"What's wrong with Marcus? I thought he'd win for sure," Liam says from where he stands next to Florence.

"He got a cramp." I'm faintly aware of our teacher announcing more arrivals, but my focus remains on the emerald eyes keeping me captive.

"That sucks," Benji mutters.

"I could give him a massage later. My mom taught me how to do it so I could help her relax in the evenings," Florence tells us.

"You definitely won't do that," I argue before chuckling it off. Smooth, really. What is it with me and acting like a neanderthal whenever it comes to this girl? Telling her what to do, snapping clipped sentences. My parents would smack me over the head if they caught wind of this.

"Is that so?" she challenges me, raising an eyebrow. "In that case, you don't want one either? I thought you could use it after doing such a good job on the race but if you don't think I can do it," she trails off with a shrug.

"Oh, I don't doubt your skills, Florence. I simply don't think Marcus deserves your services. If you want to prove a point, I guess I'd be willing to be your subject though," I tease her. There's a nagging voice in my head saying that this isn't right. That I don't deserve her banter and smiles when I haven't had to apologize for yesterday.

I need to get her alone sometime so we can talk. I don't like leaving things unspoken. It's a surefire way to make me anxious, and I can only imagine it's the same for Florence and her overactive mind.

"I'm sure you would be." She breaks off with a squeal, getting to her feet and turning around at the same time in an awkwardly twitchy dance.

"Sorry, Flower girl. I meant to get Liam," Jamie apologizes hastily, backing away from her.

"You're lucky you missed. If you'd gotten that nasty water all over me, I would have sued you," Liam announces.

"Naww, you'd do that to your oldest friend?" Jamie pouts playfully.

"Only friend," I hear Orion mutter, making me chuckle.

The guys keep up their banter but I zone out and watch Florence instead. She's bending over, shaking her hair in an attempt to get all the seaweed out. Her dark strands shine in the sunlight before she stands back up. Her eyes meet mine and she smiles as she pulls her hair back as always, securing it with a clip.

Just why does she have to be so achingly pretty?

Chapter 20

Florence

"So, Snow White, how was your night beneath the stars?"

"Liam, shut the fuck up and get your own nickname," Elija snaps. I stifle a laugh before it can break free. Liam might not be my favorite person but I don't want to make him feel bad. Or at least not because of me. Elija and he have their own issues.

The guys and I are at our hangout again. Benji, Liam, and I came here after the race, not before they forced me to get a late breakfast though, and the others just joined. They wanted to take showers first, which I more than appreciate as the scent of Elija's body wash wafts over me.

All the guys look at me expectantly, so I disclose the tale. I'm sure they all remember the last trip and how some had to sleep outside because there weren't enough tents, so I just tell them I wanted to do that again. It's partially true since I do enjoy sleeping under the stars. Of course, I'd have enjoyed it more if I had a sleeping bag or a blanket, but the damp grass did just fine as a bed.

Mostly though, I stayed outside all night because the thought of going to camp and so close to Elija was stifling. I didn't want to be mad at him, but his behavior stung too deeply for me to shake easily, so I stayed out until sleep eventually claimed me.

It's a trigger point of mine, being dismissed and treated as a nuisance. It's how my parents so often act towards me, so last night, experiencing the same behavior from a guy I think so highly of was like picking at a scabbing wound.

I don't tell the guys any of that though, and they don't question my short explanation. Still, they frown at me.

"You should have just told us. We totally would have been down to join," Benji tells me.

"Speak for yourself," Liam mutters, though he gets ignored as usual. I flash him a quick smile since I feel bad before turning to Benji.

"I didn't plan on doing it and you guys were busy." I shrug but don't miss the looks the guys share. *Love to feel excluded.*

"Next time, no matter how busy we seem, you tell us where you're going or at least make sure your phone is on," Orion tells me. I smirk at that.

"I knew you guys loved me," I tease them. "Especially you, Elsa. There's a soft heart hidden beneath all that ice, isn't there?" I add toward Orion. The guy's just a big softie using some strong sarcasm to keep people from coming too close.

"You wish, Lorence," he mutters indignantly, but I'm already on my feet. "What are you doing?" he questions, his eyes narrowing.

I head towards him as if he were a cute fluffy pet rather than a six-plus foot tall grump of a man. "You just need a hug to melt away some of that ice, don't you?" I tease him playfully, enjoying the way his eyes widen slightly.

"Lorence, if you hug me-" I don't give him time to finish his empty threat but wrap my arms around his neck in a tight embrace.

"Don't worry, Elsa, it's okay to care about others." I stroke his hair in a jokingly comforting manner.

"Don't touch my hair, you hag! Guys, help me!" he yells even as his arms gently stay on my back. They're barely there, the touch both unsure and hesitant. Despite that, it warms my heart. I really am a sucker for physical touch.

After a few seconds of the awkward embrace, I decide I've tortured him enough and release him.

"Anyone else?" I joke with my arms opened invitingly. Jamie's the first to react, swooping me up into a bear hug that nearly brings us both to the ground.

"Ha! My flower girl, I got her first!" he announces proudly, squeezing me tight enough to make it hard to breathe. I won't complain though, not when he's acting like "having" me is the equivalent of winning a precious prize.

"Actually, she was my friend first! Give her back!" Benji protests. Soon, all of them start bickering like little boys, and I stop being the topic of conversation. With the easy out presented, I move over to sit next to Elija, who's watching his friends with a bemused expression on his face.

"I swear sometimes it feels like we're ten again," he utters, not taking his eyes off them. And there's so much affection in his gaze, my chest aches with envy.

"You're lucky to have each other," I say a little wistfully, the words slipping out without my permission. *Shit.* Elija obviously heard it since he turns to look at me, his relaxed demeanor tensing like he's preparing for something. I guess this is the part where we talk about yesterday.

"I'm pretty sure they like you more than me," he starts, making me chuckle half-heartedly. "I'm serious. You should have seen them when they found out I lost you last night." He lets that sink in for a beat, searching my face as if he was waiting for physical confirmation that I accept his words. When I keep my expression carefully blank, he sighs and goes on.

"I'm sorry for the way I acted last night. Both in the tent and later that night. I have no real excuse other than my brain seems to short-circuit around you, leaving behind a senseless bundle of immature emotions and half-formed thoughts. I didn't mean to make things weird in your tent. I don't know what's gotten into me but I promise I'll do better. I shouldn't have left without a word.

"And by the time we walked back to camp, I was convinced you didn't want me to speak to you, so I kept my distance." He picks at the grass near his feet.

"Why would you think that?" I prompt, frowning.

His eyes briefly find mine. "Why wouldn't I? You seemed rather determined not to look at me all night, so I figured you were mad about I left things with you. Understandably so, don't get me wrong. I don't blame you for it, I just want you to know that I was trying to respect what I thought were your wishes by keeping my distance. I'm sorry if I seemed abrupt and harsh as a result of it."

"Oh, I didn't realize that. I'm sorry for making you think I was mad. I was just feeling awkward after whatever happened in the tent, to be honest." I laugh off my embarrassment as my cheeks heat. "Not that I know what exactly happened, but I got the sense it was something to be embarrassed about. I should've handled it more maturely. I hate leaving things unsaid like last night. Makes for a lot of reeling thoughts." It's about has honest about my feelings as I've ever been. Around anyone. It's both frightening and exhilarating.

"Yeah, I get that, and I agree. But at least we're talking now, right? And we can settle whatever happened is nothing to be embarrassed for. Does that sound good?" he offers, some of the humor returning to his voice.

I smile, relieved that we got this entire mess of miscommunication out of the way. "Sounds good."

I might've been hurt and mad at him last night, but in the light of day and after hearing his side of the story, it doesn't sound all that bad anymore. He didn't mean to dismiss me if nothing else. Knowing that helps.

Sure, we neither cleared up what really happened, or nearly happened in my tent or what's going on with him and Joe, but since he thought I initiated the radio silence between us, I guess I can't fault him for not speaking to me on the way back to the tents.

He's proven he's good at taking silent hints and respecting my boundaries. That's what he tried to do yesterday.

I sense that there might be something more to his side of the story – something that would explain why he called me Flo all of the sudden or why he seemed mad when he did – just like there are things I'm not bringing up. Things like a certain girl he walked back to her tent...

He must have reasons of his own to deflect from it, and I'm all too happy to join that train of action.

"What I'm saying is, you can count on us too. They're just as much your friends as they are mine," Elija adds, his gaze returning to them as our conversation loops back to where we started.

I'm sure the statement is supposed to be comforting, but it opens the lid to a whole lot of questions in my frantic mind. I turn my gaze away, worrying my bottom lip as I ponder my next words. He said *they* are my friends, not "we".

Did he just not think about it or does it really mean something? He said I could count on them using *us,* so including him, but then said *they* are my friends. Does that mean he doesn't think we're friends or that we're more than friends and he doesn't want to friendzone me.

After the circus yesterday with Joe, I kind of abandoned the idea that he was romantically interested in me. It seemed out of the realm of possibilities seeing him with a girl so effortlessly charming and pretty, but maybe my insecurities jumped the gun there. His words ignite a spark of new hope in my chest, silly and fragile. I probably shouldn't read so much into it, but I can't help it.

I must read too much romance if I see potential in a small slip of his tongue. Romanticizing life at its finest.

"What about you?" I ask, unable to stop myself.

"Me?" he repeats, clearly thrown for a loop.

"Well, I mean. Are we friends?" I clarify, crossing my fingers behind my back. Honestly, I'm not sure what I want him to say, but my heart is still racing with anticipation.

Elija searches my face, dark eyes holding a whole dictionary of unspoken words and emotions I can't place. It's the first time he's looked at me like that, and it has my breath catching. He's beautiful when he's unguarded.

Before I can get lost in the moment, he looks away and nods to himself. "Sure, Florence. We're friends." Simple words, and yet the statement sounds so loaded, I don't know what it means.

I stop trying to figure it out. At least we're back to *Florence*.

"Are you ready for the last challenge?" I ask Elija as he prepares to get into his canoe. The last challenge is another race. This time, the last ten students in the competition need to row one length of the lake and back. Fastest one wins before we go home tomorrow.

"As ready as I'll ever be. Not sure how well I'll do but whatever," Elija tells me with a hesitant smile. He disclosed earlier that while he wasn't afraid of water, he's feeling irrationally nervous about being in a canoe so far from the shore. Something about him seeing two people get trapped in an upturned canoe when he went for a ride with his dad as a kid.

"I'm sure you'll do great. Either way, I'll cheer for you."

His face lights up at that statement, and although he looks like he wants to say something, Mr. Hank interrupts before he can, counting down from twenty. "Go. And win." I wink at him, hoping it doesn't look awkward.

Elija blushes – for the first time since I've known him, he blushes. I can only hope it's not from second hand embarrassment. "Well now I have to, Snow White," he teases, his smile so wide his teeth show. The flash of white is enough to drag my eyes to the straight row of teeth uncovered by his full top lip. Just for a split second.

We're standing close together, people closing in on every side in anticipation of the third race. All the other contestants are already in their canoes, but Elija keeps staring at me.

"Kiss her already!" Someone yells nearby. I try to laugh it off even as Elija glances at my lips, seeming to seriously consider it.

Do it, I'd like to urge him. Of course, I stay silent.

"Elija!" Mr. Hank finally snaps.

"You need to get into the canoe," I tell him softly. He nods, looking less than eager for someone who claims he wants to win. When he finally gets into the water, I release a steadying breath. Then, the race starts and the ten students push themselves away from the docks, providing me with the perfect distraction from my racing heart.

The viewers break out in cheers and I join them happily. Despite my first thoughts, this competition is actually fun. Now that I don't have to participate, that is.

The rest of the guys find me and help me yell Elija's name as he gets further and further away. None of them qualified for this round, but it makes it all the more fun for me. At least I only have to yell one name now.

"He's doing really well!" I say even as the others see it themselves.

"I bet he won't win," Liam huffs.

"Bet against you. Fifty bucks," Orion challenges him. Liam agrees but only after making a comment about how fifty bucks wouldn't hurt him as much as they would Orion.

Meanwhile, I make a bet with myself, of sorts. If Elija wins, I stop being a coward and kiss him. If he pushes me away, I'll know where we stand, and even though I'd be disappointed, at least I could be done with it and get over this crush. Or try to.

The crowd grows painfully loud with every foot Elija gets closer, taking the lead. The fact that he's done this before with his father clearly gives him an edge despite his inhibitions. The crowd gets rowdy. Behind me, more people start pushing forward as they try to see who's winning, causing me to nearly fall into the water.

"Hey, back off!" Marcus barks at a few people, but for once, no one seems to listen to him.

"Come on, Flo, let's get away before they throw us off the dock," Benji says. He gently takes me by the elbow and steers me away from the edge. I frown since I'm no longer able to see Elija but don't fight him. It would be awkward for me to try to kiss him looking like a swamp monster after being thrown off the deck.

Suddenly, a whistle goes off and more whoops and cheers erupt. I hear his name being cheered so I turn around.

The guys and I are on the beach next to the lake and I see Elija fighting his way through the crowd, getting patted on the back on his way.

His head swivels around, clearly looking for his friends, so I wave at him. When he sees me, his smile seems to brighten and his steps grow more determined. I'd like to meet him halfway, but I need to muster up my courage. He won. Elija actually won. That means I need to kiss him.

Is it too late to take it back?

Yes. I'm doing this.

Florence, you're doing this.

Elija isn't very far anymore so I start walking as well, taking hesitant steps. The guys are cheering as they follow me but the champion's eyes stay on me. As if he could see my thoughts, his tongue darts out to wet his lips. I track the movement with my eyes, nearly groaning. Now that I'm this close, I can't wait to finally taste them.

It might be awkward and clumsy and I'd rather enjoy what could be our only ever kiss in private, but if I don't go through with it now, I never will. I'm too chicken shit unless I have a reason, like the bet with myself. Going back on my word now would be bad Karma after all.

Right, we're doing this.

But before I can reach him, a girl appears by Elija's side as if our of thin air. She grabs his shoulders and turns him roughly. Then, without another warning, she slams her lips on his.

With a start, I realize the girl is Joe from the other night.

My steps falter and I feel the smile freeze on my lips.

Typical Florence, this close but still not managing to pull it off.

Chapter 21

Elija

My body goes as stiff as a board as soon as Joe's lips meet mine, my body aware that it's an unwelcome touch but my mind too slow to catch up and order my limbs into action.

A moment ago, I was staring at Florence, mentally preparing myself to finally kiss her. I made a promise to myself to finally do it. If she had rejected me, I could have just brushed it off and told her that it was all the emotions running high after my win.

I had it all planned out, a safety net in place to ensure I don't ruin our friendship if she doesn't return the kiss. An excuse to let her think it didn't hurt if she rejected me so she wouldn't overthink it afterwards for my sake. It was a foolproof plan designed specifically to work on my snow white.

But even if I hadn't thought up this plan during the race, she looked so pretty as she waited for me, her eyes big and happy, I don't think I could have stopped myself if I tried. Not when the happiness in them was for *me*. Because she was excited that I won the race for her like I promised.

But here I am now, the lips of a different girl assaulting mine. *Shit.* Before I can finally push Joe off, she pulls back by herself, probably realizing she's not getting the reaction she wants. I don't spare her another glace as soon as she's out of my face, looking up to see how much damage control I need to do. Kissing me after I told her all about how torn apart over another girl I am officially puts her into the unredeemable category of a homewrecker in my book. She doesn't deserve my time or attention when Florence is waiting for me.

Did Florence see that? What am I thinking, of course she did. Her eyes were locked onto mine when it happened.

What could have only been less than a second after Joe pulled away, I locate Florence where she was before, frozen in place. Her smile is already fading but when her eyes meet mine, I can tell she tries her best to hide it.

Does that mean she's disappointed? Did she know I was about to kiss her? Did she want me to?

Am I projecting?

Hands start pulling at me, and more people gather around to say congrats. In no time, the only person I want to see is blocked from my view and I am unable to get to her.

Shit! Maybe I'm wrong, but if this thing between Florence and me isn't one-sided, she'll probably feel bad right now. I know I'd snap if I saw her kiss someone else. I need to get to her and clear this up. She must know I didn't want Joe to kiss me. She saw what happened. I didn't kiss her back. *You also didn't push her.* But just because I locked up. Was that not obvious?

From somewhere in the crowd I hear her say, "I knew you'd win," but it's quickly lost in a chorus of voices. I'm sure it's her and that means she's nearby, but I still can't see her. Panic starts clawing at my chest at the tightening circle of people around me and no visible way out. What is up with my classmates? It's not like I won the Olympics, it was just a mock race.

"Good job, dude. You just won me fifty bucks," Orion tells me, clapping me on the back. I nearly slump in relief at the familiar sight of him. It assures me that I'm not about to be suffocated by a bunch of near strangers, irrational as the fear is.

"Great," I reply absently, trying to push past him with the intent to get some air. I'm feeling fucking crowded and he's my way out. Unlike the others, he quickly steps out of my way and allows me to resume my mission of finding Florence.

But instead, the first thing I see outside the crowd are angry eyes. Figures that Benji would glare at me. Leave it to him to make me the bad guy when I was just jumped by a crazy woman. I don't pay him much mind since the girl to his right is whom I'm looking for. She's smiling convincingly, making me think I might've imagined her reaction. Maybe I was wrong? Was it just wishful thinking?

"Hey," I say. For some reason, I feel weirdly awkward as I step up to their private corner. It feels like I'm the odd one out, missing something vital only kept between them. Behind me, I faintly hear Marcus tell our peers to get off my back, and I remind myself to thank him for that later.

"Hi. Good job with the race," Florence tells me. Then, she elbows Benji.

"Yeah. Congrats," he mutters glumly. One would think I peed in his cereal with the way he eyes me.

"Thanks." As I contemplate saying something about the kiss, a group of girls passes us. They're whispering something while looking at me before they start giggling obnoxiously. Oh, the world's really playing with me now. Never have I gotten this much attention, but now, everyone seems to be attracted to me. Now when I certainly don't want it.

My heart goes out to Marcus for dealing with this on the daily.

"So, I heard there'll be a party tonight since we go back tomorrow. I think I'll go and get ready," Florence tells me, ruining my chance to bring it up.

"You're going?" I ask instead. She doesn't seem the type to go to actual parties.

"Oh, well. You won the competition so I figured I'd go with you guys." As her cheeks burn up a bright crimson, I realize my question came out all wrong.

"I didn't know we were going but if you're there, then so will I," I tell her, trying to clear things up. It would be nice if there wasn't any further miscommunication between us today. To my relief, Florence laughs.

"Good to know. I'll see you later." With that, she's gone, and I'm forced to turn to Benji.

"What are you playing at?" he asks me, his expression grim.

"Excuse me?"

"You're toying with Flo. First, you act all nice and mysterious. Then, you're possessive. You almost kiss her before ignoring her completely. Today, I saw you two at the docks, almost kissing again, only for you to shove your tongue down that other chick's throat. Now, you tell her you'll be wherever she is!"

"Shove my- It's not my fault Joe attacked me like that. Besides, I certainly did not shove my tongue down her throat! I didn't kiss her back. And I don't mean to toy with Florence, I'm just having the most rotten luck all of the sudden.

"I've been pining for nearly a year, and now that I'm finally getting closer to her, there are suddenly weird girls interested and my temper decides to act up out of line at the worst time. I don't want to hurt Florence. You know that's not me," I snap back.

"Coincidence or not, fact is you're confusing her and she deserves better than that," he persists. I throw my hands up in the air, suspicion curdling my gut.

"Better, is that right? Fucking hell, don't tell me you mean yourself. Is that why you're trying to swoop in now, telling me to stay away from her so you can go from loyal confidant to the one that wins her over? Is that why you're so pressed?" I challenge him only for him to laugh at me like I'm an idiot.

And maybe I am.

"Me? You're delusional, Elija. She is my friend and I don't want her to get hurt," he argues.

"Neither do I," I concede, but he merely shoots me an unimpressed look.

"Then stay away from her," he says like it's so easy. Like that's not what I'd been doing for an entire year before he forced her deeper into my orbit.

I work my jaw. "I can't do that."

"Why not? Honestly, Eli, what are your intentions here?" My friend's eyes soften before he goes on, and I just know I won't like his next words before they leave his lips. "Is this because of Ricky? I know the two girls might have a few things in common, but Florence isn't like Ricky. She isn't Ricky. It's not fair to use her as a rebound."

It's a wonder I stop my jaw from clattering to the floor. From all the turns this conversation could have taken, this was the last one I expected short of Benji telling me he's from Mars.

Scratch that, I would've been less surprised – and annoyed – at that. But no such luck. Instead, here we go again with the same old farce. Poor Elija got himself cheated on and even more than a year later, he's desperate to replace the girl.

Heavens forbid he moves on and actually wants someone else. Least of all, a really awesome girl he's been mooning over for months.

"I'm saying this one last time so listen carefully. I am over Ricky. She is not what I think about or see when I'm with Florence. I have no bad intentions with Florence, I just can't seem to do anything right with her this week. Now, please, get your nose out of my business and stop trying to turn my attraction to this girl into something ugly when it's not."

After studying me for a beat, Benji chuckles and raises his hands in surrender. "You're serious, aren't you? You really have it bad," he jaunts, back to teasing me in the face of my more than serious little speech. Little turncoat.

I grab him by the neck and steer him to walk ahead in the direction of the tents, making him stumble a step when I give him a small shove. "Shut up. Let's get ready for the party," I grumble even as my scorn towards him quickly fades.

"Why, sure. Loverboy needs to make himself pretty for his girl, doesn't he?" he teases me, so I punch him. Just softly. For now. But only because I'm glad that the air between us has been cleared.

"You're annoying when your mouth isn't busy taking drags. Besides, I'm always pretty." Both chuckling, we go to our tent.

Chapter 22

Florence

I'm talking to Benji, surrounded by a crowd of students. The guys and I came here as a group over two hours ago but more and more of them have dispersed over time. Jamie and Orion were with us a moment ago, but Jamie dragged his friend off to dance. Elsa was not delighted, or at least he acted like he wasn't. I'd imagine he secretly enjoyed any excuse to be close to Jamie. Marcus keeps getting trapped in conversations with people I've never talked to, so Benji and I stopped trying to tag along and have since lost track of his whereabouts. Elija and Liam left a moment ago to grab some drinks.

"Here you go," Liam says as he hands Benji a drink. Then, to my surprise, he turns toward me. "I got you one as well. It's non-alcoholic since you've proven to be unable to handle your liquor," he tells me, and it comes across as friendly teasing rather than an attempt to put me down. Speaking of surprises.

"Piss off, Liam." Elija pushes past him and holds out another drink to me. "Here you go, Florence."

After a lifetime of hearing that I shouldn't accept any open beverages at parties, here I am, faced with two options. It's not like I think any of the guys would intentionally drug me or anything of the sort, and yet the warning's been drilled into my mind so insistently, I feel wary.

But I guess if I do have to bite the bullet, I'd rather accept Elija's concoction. Besides, maybe my accepting his offer will trigger some long-forgotten animal instinct in him and he'll suddenly think of me as his. Wouldn't that be something.

Smiling at Liam apologetically, I take the drink from Elija. "Thanks. Both of you," I say, mostly looking at Liam even though he's not the one I want attention from in the first place. Still, I feel bad for rejecting a kind offer on his part, and unless my mind is playing tricks on me, he actually seems upset at my quick dismissal. As quickly as the emotion entered his expression though, it's gone and he's back to looking his usual, snotty self.

He downs the drink he offered me before throwing the cup to the ground and storming off. Was it to prove a point that nothing was wrong with it? It's not like I really thought he'd have tempered with it, but the options were him and the guy I'm into. Isn't it kind of foreseeable that I'd have to take Elija's?

"I didn't mean to offend him," I tell the others quietly as I stare at Liam's discarded cup. He's already so often shot down by his friends, I didn't want him to feel like I was doing the same. Especially since he was being nice.

"Nah, his fragile ego is probably just hurt. Don't feel bad, though, I wouldn't accept a drink from him either," Elija offers, eying the cup as if it were something disgusting. Knowing the history between the two guys, I get where his disdain is coming from. I mean, Liam committed the worst kind of betrayal against him. Still, being trapped in the middle of their power plays isn't nice.

"Nothing was wrong with it. He drank it himself," I argue half-heartedly, glancing at Benji.

"Flo, don't worry about it. It's good to be cautious at parties. Besides, Liam has probably forgotten all about it and is already busy making slimy moves on some poor girl," he assures me.

Imagining that with the reminder of how cockily he described his love life, I try to shake the lingering guilt. It's not like he likes me or really cares what I think anyway. Benji is right, it wouldn't have mattered to Liam for long that I refused his drink.

When Jamie and Elsa finally return, Orion actually has a smile on his face he can't suppress. His cheeks are a little flushed, standing out drastically against his white hair even in the dark.

"Well, well. What did we miss?" Elija drawls, looking between his friends.

"Nothing," Orion tries to brush him off, but Jamie shoots him a funny look.

"Nothing? You call that kiss nothing? If you were planning on keeping me a secret, think again." With so much theatrical flair it's a wonder he isn't the lead in a telenovela, he turns his back to Orion and addresses the rest of us. "To clear things up for you guys, I finally kissed Elsa since he was taking too long to take the hint and make a move." He looks so pleased with himself, and it only amounts when Elija whoops while Benji looks anything but surprised.

I bite back a knowing grin of my own. Yeah, this isn't a surprise, but I'm still happy one of them was brave enough to make a move. I can't blame Orion for wanting to take it easy and play it safe. Having feelings for your lifelong friend, especially when he hasn't always proven to feel the same way can't be easy. There's so much on the line.

"That's awesome, you two. I was wondering when you'd finally get there," I tease.

"Look who's talking," Orion retorts, still smiling. It suits him, unfamiliar as the happy expression is on his face. Without my permission, my eyes move to Elija but instead of meeting my gaze, he's focused on something behind me. I turn to see Joe talking to a few friends a few feet away, Miley amongst others.

Oh, that's so awkward. Here Orion is, making hints that one of his friends hasn't had the guts to go after who they wanted, and my silly ass thought he meant me. Me and Elija, while his mind clearly first went to Joe.

I shouldn't be surprised. She's the girl he kissed, after all. Not me.

"Sorry, I'll be right back," Elija mutters before walking off without a glance at me. I catch myself staring after him and quickly redirect my gaze to the other guys, though that sight might be even worse than watching Elija walk off to another girl. I'm met with a sympathetic look from Jamie while the other two guys are glaring after their friend.

They quickly snap out of it and try to distract me as well as possible. It's a nice effort but my mind keeps wandering to Elija. Am I the problem? Is there something wrong with me or am I just that delusional? Honestly, I have no clue at this point.

I keep getting my hopes up with him only to be let down again. I don't blame him. After all, he's never told me he wanted us to be anything other than friends. Only last night he said we were just that. Friends. I think it's time for me to take the hint. My refusal to do so up until now just keeps making room for disappointment.

Besides, Joe is really cute. If she and Elija are a thing, I'll stay away. You could call me a lot of things, but I won't be a homewrecker.

The two of them fit together, don't they? Joe with her blonde hair and golden skin the perfect contrast to Elija. After all, opposites attract. I can see that. And they're both so pretty, like the sun and the moon finally meeting on earth.

"Sorry for that." The voice drags me back to reality when I hadn't even realized I zoned out. But now Elija is back, without Joe, as I notice. *Weird*, I think, but it's none of my business.

I'm getting over this silly crush of mine once and for all, and I'll start doing that by keeping my distance.

"Right, I'll go look for Sarah now. She's the one that told me about the party, so I should probably say hello," I lie easily. I don't really plan on finding Sarah, as much as I like the girl. I've had enough excitement for one day, and she's a firecracker.

"We'll help you look. That way, we'll find her faster," Benji is quick to offer but I shake my head.

"It's fine, I can just text her."

"Tell her to come here, then," Orion says as if it were the obvious solution. What smarty-pants doesn't know is that I'm trying to get away from here. Or more precisely a certain person present.

"Florence, we're not letting you walk around alone, at night, near the woods, surrounded by drunk people," Elija reasons. He smiles as he says it, but I feel like he just does that to soften the blow when he tries to tell me what to do.

"I can take care of myself," I state firmly, in no mood to be bossed around. In the dim lighting, it looks like Orion's mouth twitches.

My hunch is only confirmed when the guy leans over to whisper something to Jamie. Apparently, he's had a beer too much, though, since he's speaking loud enough for the rest of us to hear. "She definitely gets that from me. The sass. I feel like a proud parent."

I try to stifle my smile, but when my eyes meet Benji, we both burst out laughing.

"Tell you what, I'll call her and stay on the phone until we're together. If you're really that worried, I can text you once I find her," I suggest. I don't owe them anything, but I'd be lying if I said it wasn't nice to feel cared about.

The guys grumble some unconvincing agreements, so I dial my friend's number. Since we didn't actually make plans to meet up, my intending to sneak off to my tent instead, I'm not surprised when she doesn't pick up. Good thing I used to dream of being an actress.

I wave at the guys with a smile and walk off into the crowd while pretending to talk to Sarah. When I'm far enough, I take my phone away from my ear and head for my tent.

Honestly, it's been too long since I read, and the camp should be blissfully silent now so far away from the ongoing party.

Chapter 23

Elija

"That was weird," Orion says while Benji turns to me. I brace myself for whatever he might have to say, knowing it can't be good with the scowl he's sporting.

"After the talk we like just had before the party, why'd you ditch us for Joe? Unless you're trying to seem uninterested in Florence, you're failing miserably," he exclaims.

"Yeah, that was weird. And horrible in terms of timing, bro, " Jamie adds, ganging up on me.

"Not as weird as Lorence's disappearance," Orion mutters under his breath.

"I just went over to tell Joe to stay the hell away from me. I know that if I actually want to do this the right way with Florence moving forward, I can't have any other girls sniffing around me," I clarify, confused about this renewed outburst.

"Wasn't that a bit harsh?" Jamie contemplates.

I rear back. I thought he'd love hearing I closed that door once and for all. "After I spent a whole evening talking about Florence to her? Nah. She knows I'm interested in someone else, so kissing me was completely unnecessary and provocative."

Slowly, Jamie nods in agreement. "Fair. You still chose shitty timing though. Orion gave you such an easy in to prove to her that you're interested. You could have done the whole *Oh no, we got called out. Let's act all shy and flustered and brush the claim off defensively* spiel. She was ready to do her part, and you walked off to find another woman."

Wait. What?

"What do you mean we got called out?" I ask no one in particular, frowning.

"She said something about *them* finally getting there," Benji gestures between Jamie and Orion, then goes on, "And Orion said *Look who's talking.*"

Wait, they did? "I stopped listening after hearing about the kiss because Joe blew me an air kiss and it pissed me off. That's why I left so suddenly. I got sick of her games." I groan and tip my head back, realizing that must have seemed like really bad timing to the rest, including Florence. And after the kiss today on top of things. "Was it obvious who I was walking towards?" My only hope is that Florence didn't see that and came up with her own reasons as to why she'd have my attention during that conversation.

"Obvious as her ensuing disappointment," Orion supplies, unfiltered as always.

"Oh, fuck it all to hell," I mutter, in disbelief at my horrendous luck. Even when I'm trying to get a clean slate and do things right, I give her the wrong hints.

Jamie slaps me onto the shoulder and shrugs. "I know just what you need."

Doubtful, but it's not like I'm having any bright ideas so let's hear it. "What's that?"

"To get fucking shitfaced. All this standing around and talking, when have we gotten so boring? You have the rest of your life to mull your course of action over, but this is supposed to be a party so let loose. What's done is done," his voice is loud like he's trying to rally the masses. Not like any of us seem particularly moved his speech.

He notices too and shrugs. "Y'all do as you please, I'm getting drunk. Come on." He grabs Orion by the hand, and he follows like an eager puppy, scowling at everyone else that turns to look at Jamie as they push thought the crowd.

"Where's Florence?" I ask once the guys and I have finished putting our luggage in the trunk of the bus. I'm surprisingly glad to finally go home. This trip was a mess and after hearing Jamie retch all night and making sure he doesn't hurt himself or someone else, I'm worn out.

"Maybe she's running late again," Marcus says. But really, how late can anyone possibly be when we're five minutes away from the camping place?

"Relax, Loverboy. She's coming right there," Jamie tells us, motioning behind me. For someone that seemed to be on the highway to hell last night, he's surprisingly well this morning.

I turn when I hear her approaching steps, my worry easing and my mood brightening just because she's nearby. She stops a few feet away, her voice chipper even though her words feel like a sucker punch of disappointment to me. "Hey, guys. I just thought I'd let you know I'm sitting with Sarah. She asked me to keep her company last night since she doesn't have anyone else to sit with."

She meets everyone's eyes but mine, only making my discomfort rise. I fucked up again yesterday and this is my rightful punishment.

"Damn, Flower girl. You're really ditching us? Why don't you invite her to sit with us?" Jamie protests.

"Oh, I guess I could have done that. I'm sorry. Either way, we're already settled on the other bus now. I had a lot of fun with you guys the last few days," she says, making this interaction feel a whole lot like goodbye. Especially when she smiles apologetically.

"Right. Well, you two have fun," I tell her even though those are the last words I want to say. She nods and walks off toward another bus while the guys and I find ourselves somewhere to sit.

To say this new development is a downer would be an understatement. Last night before I went to sleep, I specifically looked up BuzzFeed quizzes I thought Florence might like. Most are Harry Potter related but I found one that should tell you what flower you are. It was supposed to be a way to make last night up to her. Or a first step at least, but I guess it would have been trivial either way. Now, I have them saved for no reason. Fun.

I have no one to blame for that but me, which makes this even worse. I gave her every reason to want to sit far away from me throughout the trip.

I sit mostly silently through the drive, listening to music and watching the landscape change continuously.

When the buses finally stop at the school parking lot, I get out quickly. I love my friends but their constant teasing, shouting, and laughing have given me a massive headache, despite the music I was trying to listen to. I just long for some alone time.

Not that I'm really getting that at home, considering my whole family is there. I just hope it will be a quiet day.

But my penance resumes and I have no such luck. After a quick welcome and a brief summary of the trip on my part, the twins quickly got into a fight. No idea what started it this time. Now, my brother wants my attention since his twin isn't entertaining him.

"Eli, will you play with me? May is ignoring me," Daniel asks. I groan inwardly since I just finished unpacking and all I want to do right now is lie in my bed and maybe make a few beats.

"Sorry, little guy. Not right now," I try to let him down easily, but as soon as the boy's ears turn pink, I know I'm in trouble.

"You're just as mean as May! None of you care about me! No one ever wants to play! All you ever do is make your stupid music!" the little guy yells, throwing his hands around wildly. Meanwhile, I'm trying to breathe through the pain pulsing at my temples.

"How about we play later? I'm tired and I think I'll nap for an hour, okay?" I try.

"No! I want to play now! But you only play with your stupid friends and your stupid guitar!" he goes on. Okay, ouch. My guitar is not stupid. It's my most prized possession. I spent two summers earning enough money to buy it, working at McDonald's on weekends, and picking up whatever other job I could find. But Daniel is too young to understand that, so I pull myself together and try to be patient.

"First, you love my friends. Second, my guitar is not stupid, and third, I said I'll play with you later."

"You're so mean!" my little brother continues yelling as if I hadn't said a thing. Then, he turns toward my guitar and before I can react, he rips it off the wall. Time seems to slow as it nears the ground. It lands with a crash, and I see a few strings rip while two of the turning pegs fly elsewhere.

I curse under my breath as I rush toward my instrument. When I take in the damage, all I see is red. It's broken. My brother ruined my fucking guitar.

"Get out," I tell my brother, my voice deadly quiet.

"See, all you care about is music!" he protests but I've had enough of his tantrum.

"Out! Now!" I yell, looking him dead in the eye. He has the audacity to cry out loudly, effectively making my mother appear in my doorway.

"What's going on here?" she asks.

"Elija doesn't want to play with me!" Daniel complains.

I grit my teeth against the aching tightness in my chest. "What happened is that this brat ruined my fucking guitar!" I say as I get to my feet. Daniel buries his face in my mother's side and cries out loudly, but I don't care. I could honestly cry myself since I know I don't have enough money to get my baby fixed or replaced anytime soon.

"Elija," my mother scolds and my mouth nearly drops. Now *I'm* the bad guy?

"You know what, I can't deal with this right now," I snap, pushing past her and leaving my ruined guitar on the floor.

"Where are you going?" my mom demands as I put on my shoes.

"Somewhere to cool off! Somewhere where privacy exists!" I yell before slamming our front door shut behind me.

Chapter 24

Florence

It's a little after 8 pm and I'm lost in my book when the doorbell rings.

"Sweetie, can you get that?" my mother yells. I'm already on my way to the door, though, knowing the drill.

I don't know whom to expect at this hour, so I peek through the spy hole in the door just to give me a heads up. It could always be a very uncreative axe murderer, after all. That's not who it is, though judging by the way my heart starts pounding, it might as well be. I take a deep breath, open the door just enough to slip outside, and turn to face Elija once the door is almost fully closed again.

"Hey, what are you doing here?" I ask in a hushed voice, knowing my parents wouldn't appreciate me being visited by a guy this late.

"I – my brother –" he breaks off a second time and gathers his bearing with a deep breath. "Home was too loud. Is this a bad time?" he asks. Taking a closer look at him, I realize he looks unlike himself. His eyes are red and tired, and his hair is messier than usual, his shoulders seem to sag into himself, and his head hangs in defeat. Has he been crying?

I'm almost tempted to ask him why he didn't go to his girlfriend, but I can't bring myself to do it when he looks like a lost puppy. It would be petty and misplaced at a time like this.

"No, of course not. My parents are home, though, so maybe come in through the window?" I ask quietly. What am I doing? If I get caught, I'll be in so much trouble.

But then Elija smiles weakly at me, clouding my judgment further. I give him directions before going back inside my house.

"Who was it?" my dad asks.

"A friend of Mila. You know how they always switch up our houses, so I gave her directions," I tell him, throwing my neighbor under the bus. She's a girl two years older than me, and to be fair, her friends often do mistake our home for hers.

With my parents still unsuspicious of me and my cover, I quickly head into my room. There, I open my window to see Elija already waiting. It's a good day to live on the ground level because he can easily climb inside without endangering himself.

Once he's in, he takes off his shoes hurriedly, apologizing for making a mess of my room when his shoes literally seem clean to me. He's uncharacteristically fussy, so unlike the first time he was in my room cool as a cucumber. I brush him off and tell him not to worry about it.

"So, want to talk about what happened?" I muse once we've both settled down on opposite sides of my bed. I'm whispering while music is playing in the background, but I've locked my door just in case. I don't think my parents would be thrilled to walk into my room and find a boy they've never met sitting on my bed when they thought I was alone.

They could think this was a regular occurrence, and that would certainly not go over well.

"Not really," Elija tells me, settling further onto my bed and getting comfortable. When he notices the book I was reading before he came, he picks it up.

"Well, this cover looks interesting. What's it about?" he asks, studying the shirtless guy on the cover. I can feel my cheeks heating up but try to play it off. This is exactly why I hate it when authors put real people on their covers. Especially half-naked ones. I only ever buy them if they sound too good to miss out on and exclusively read them at home where no one sees.

Where usually, no one sees.

"A romance story. He's, uhm, her boss, I guess. She's his best friend's little sister so he was forced to give her the job as his assistant as a favor to his friend. They can't stand each other, though, so they're set on making the other's life a living hell. It's enemies to lovers, I guess," I ramble, trying to keep it short.

I tend to lose myself when I speak about books and end up annoying whomever I'm talking to. I always catch myself when my mom and dad reach for their wine and take a long sip during dinner. It's my cue to stop talking for the rest of the night.

"Sounds good," Elija muses, not seeming bored by my ramble in the least. He merely studies me when I don't add anything, then glances back at the cover, and I know my cheeks heat up further. That makes him smirk. "Tell me, is there smut in this?" he taunts.

"You know that word?" I exclaim instead of replying. Seriously, I thought only book people understood.

"I'll take that as a yes. Well, well, I really didn't peg you as the type," he teases me. At least he no longer seems upset now that he's torturing me. Feels good to be of use, but I'd take a change of topic any second now.

"It's just a really good book," I mumble in my defense. When Elija starts flipping through the pages, trying to open an annotated passage, my heartbeat picks up.

I reach over to grab the book from him but he's too fast. He pulls away with a chuckle, so I scoot closer. Since he's lying and I'm sitting, I should be able to get my book back. I reach over Elija, trying to get it but I end up losing my balance.

My hand drops to the mattress at his side to support myself. When he laughs again, I turn to look at him. My cheeks heat up as I realize we're way too close. Like, about to hug or kiss kind of close. I mean to pull away before he notices and an awkward moment ensues, but I'm too slow.

Elija opens his eyes and looks at me, his laugh breaking off. I'm hyper-aware of his reaction, noting the slight arch of his eyebrows, the narrowing of his eyes, and the pink tint crawling up his neck. When my attention returns to his dark eyes, I see him scanning me the same way. When his gaze drops to my lips, I practically feel my heartbeat quickening.

Then his tongue darts out slightly to wet his bottom lip and I think, this is it. Then, some sense returns like a bucket of cold water over my anticipation, and I pull back instead.

What am I doing? How could I just forget about him and Joe like that? Even though I'm not sure what they are, Elija's obviously off-limits.

Trying to defuse the awkward tension in the room, I chuckle lightly, then say about the worst thing I could have said. "So, how's it going with Joe?" I hear it as I speak and mentally headbutt myself for being so transparent. Oh, this would be a good time to crawl out of my skin and hide forever.

Elija raises himself up on his arms and looks at me all serious. Doing nothing to ease my flaring anxiety for once with a bit of humor or the grace to ignore my slip up. Finally, he sighs and explains, "Florence, there's nothing between her and me."

Okay, I guess we're doing this. There's no turning back now anyways, so I decide to speak my mind for once. "It didn't look that way when you guys hung out. Or when she kissed you." Kissed him like I planned on kissing him.

"The night she and Miley hung out with us, we only talked about you. I was feeling bad for having fled out of your tent without a word and I thought another woman's opinion might help me find a way to make it up to you. I thought we might be friends, that I made it clear I was not interested in her by telling her so several times. I hate that she kissed me, Florence," he finishes, sounding sincere. I guess that would explain why he didn't go to her tonight.

I mull his words over and get stuck on a particular part. He was talking to her about me? It's so tempting to believe him,

Jarah Aurel

the butterflies in my stomach taking flight, but what if I'm just being naïve?

"What about the party?" I ask, looking anywhere but at him.

"I told her to stay away from me. I swear. I didn't even hear what Orion said about us." *Us.* So there is an us? His hand gently cups my face, turning it his way before he goes on. I'm forced to meet his eyes as he adds, "It really wasn't her I wanted to kiss after the last challenge."

Oh.

Oh!

This is happening. Did he just say what I think he did? He can't have meant anything else. Me. He wanted to kiss me. And now he's here, in my bed, alone with me in my room –

"Florence? Are you talking to anyone in there?" my mom's voice breaks me out of my trance. I jump and get off the bed as if my ass had caught on fire. "Why's the door locked?" she adds, yelling against the wood.

"Just on the phone, mom," I tell her while trying to make Elija understand he needs to hide. Thankfully, he catches on quickly and hurries to get beneath my bed. No points for creativity but my parents have never searched my room and I doubt they'll start now. I throw his shoes under there with him, biting back a laugh when he hisses like one might've hit him.

"Open the door, Florence." I can always tell that I'm in trouble when she uses my full name. Still, I unlock the door and let her enter my room, head ducked and braced for an outburst.

"Who were you on the phone with?" my mother asks while looking around my room skeptically.

"A classmate, she had a question about our history homework," I lie smoothly. That's the thing about strict parents, it teaches you how to be a good liar. It becomes a necessity when confining to their rules is too stifling.

"Mh. I could have sworn I heard a male voice. And what's that smell? It smells like cologne." Damn that woman and her good nose.

"Mom, I think I'd know if I had a guy in my room. Maybe Lynn's voice just sounds masculine to you, or perhaps you've mistaken it for the songs I'm listening to. As for the scent, I tried a new perfume I found in the back of a drawer but I guess it doesn't suit me." I say all that with a smile plastered on my lips, and my mother's stance relaxes.

She pats my head like I'm an endearing pet rather than her nearly adult daughter. "Of course. I forgot who I was talking to for a second. Just sleep now, honey. You look deadly tired." She smiles a saccharine smile as she leaves, and I blow out a breath as soon as I've closed the door behind her.

"That was way too close. Let's not talk anymore. Are you tired?" I ask Elija as he crawls from beneath my bed. That's certainly not an image I thought I'd ever see. It's a wonder his big frame even got under there so quickly.

"Sure, I could sleep. But I don't want to get you into trouble so I think I better leave," he suggests.

"Are you sure? It's really no big deal if you need a place to stay," I assure him. We've spent a night together before, and I cling to that knowledge as my nerves try to rise at my offer. He stayed the last time to make sure I was fine after my panic attack. Now, he just kind of told me he's thought about kissing me and there would be nothing to keep him from trying it again.

Hell, I'd probably try it again if he gave me any indication he'd be up for it.

"I really appreciate the offer, and that you took me in tonight in the first place, but I think we shouldn't test our luck after such a close call. I'll see you on Monday though, right?" he asks, already putting his shoes on as he stands next to my window.

Not sure whether to be disappointed or glad he's trying not to get me into trouble, I merely nod. And so he climbs out of the window the same way he came in, and before he turns to leave, he adds, "And by the way, your mom was wrong. You look beautiful, Florence. You always do."

Before I can muster a reply, still dumbfounded by the unexpected compliment, he vanishes into the night.

At school on Monday, I feel like I'm missing something. The same girls that usually greet me with a smile now ignore me, their stares following me only until I wave. When I do, some just look away, some return the greeting though without their usual cheer, and others even scoff.

Maybe my mind is playing tricks on me. It's probably just Monday gruffness. Everyone's displeasure at being back at school after the trip. There'd be no reason for them to be mad at me specifically. Most of them don't even really know me beyond my name and vice versa.

By the time my third period, art, rolls around, I've managed to brush the strange notions off and convince myself everything was fine. At least until someone taps my shoulder as I'm cleaning my paintbrushes over the sink, I did.

I turn around to see Lynn, who's got an expression on her face I'm not used to. Somehow both upset and angry. She's usually such a sweet, upbeat girl, and I'm about to ask her what's wrong when she pushes her paint pallet forward, smearing the acrylic paint all over my shirt.

I'm stunned as the cold, wet stains bleed onto my skin, chilling me in an uncomfortable way that has goosebumps erupting all over.

I look down at my ruined shirt, then back at Lynn's triumphant expression, sure my face mirrors my confusion. My shock. Some distant chuckling and faint whispers reach my ear, solidifying the knowledge that I didn't imagine everyone's strange behavior this morning.

Somehow, it seems the school has simultaneously decided to hate me when I've worked so hard all my years here to stay under the radar and be passably nice. Likeable but nothing more.

Blood rushes in my ears, so loudly it makes it harder for my head to catch up with what just happened. I'm not used to confrontation and I'm sure as hell not used to being meangirled. I ball my hands into fists, trying to blink back tears. I need to get away. I want to run away from here, but I'm frozen in place.

Lynn mocks me at the sight of my watery eyes, her voice taking on a tone so sickly sweet it's giving me whiplash. "Oh no, is poor Florence going to cry? It's not nice when someone else ruins something important to you, is it?" she taunts. My mind reels with confusion, but my instincts finally kick in. Unable to stand being publicly humiliated any longer, I push past her and rush out of the room.

I only stop my hurried steps when I reach the girls' bathroom. While I'm deciding whether I want to curl up and cry in self-pity or try to wash my top, the door creaks as it opens. *They followed me?* My heart starts pounding. Fight or flight, those are supposed to be my options, right? I chose flight, so why isn't it over?

I turn away from the door, bracing myself for more taunting even as my hands start shaking. I'm not made for fighting. The thought of needing to stand up for myself in the face of a bully leaves me tongue-tied.

Strong hands settle on my shoulders, too strong to be Lynn's, and the feeling of them interrupts my mini breakdown. For a second, time stands still with my facing the wall and the person that followed me grounding me with their touch. Then, they use their grip on me to turn me around. I'm met with the blurry silhouette of Elija, the last person I'd have expected in a girls' bathroom.

He studies me for a second, a frown tugging at his full lips. "Hey, don't let her get to you," he whispers even as I feel the first tear dropping. I cringe when it spills over my lashes and leaves a wet trail down my cheek, but my attempt at turning away from Elija is quickly halted when his hands cup my face. "Please don't cry. Tell me what I can do," His thumb wipes away my tear so gently, it's like I'm made out of sugar. Really though, I might as well be as easily as I was just rattled. I laugh a bit, mostly at myself.

"It's fine. Sorry, I'm being dramatic. I was just surprised because Lynn and I are usually friends but it's not that serious." I take a deep breath. "Dang, I really don't know what's wrong with me. I feel a lot better already," I tell him truthfully. Then, realizing my sudden change in mood might very well have to do with his presence, I add, "Thank you."

"Of course. Are you sure you're all right? Do you want to try to clean the shirt?" he asks as he eyes the damage skeptically.

I follow his gaze and shake my head. "Nah, forget it. It's ruined, I'll see what I can do with it at home later."

"You don't know why she did it, do you?" he asks, clearly agreeing the shirt is nothing to argue about. I shake my head, and he sighs. "You really should check your phone more often."

"Why, what's wrong?" I ask, making a grab for said gadget only to come up empty-handed. Shit. I guess I left it in the classroom.

Reluctantly, Elija takes out his own phone before showing me a post. It's a picture of Marcus and me holding hands near my tent on the trip. I remember that night, he walked me back since the others were busy taking care of Jamie. It's a cute picture, we're both smiling. I don't understand how this explains anything.

Apparently noticing my reaction, or lack thereof, Elija clarifies things for me. "Lynn has been hanging out with Marcus. It's nothing serious but she obviously wants it to be. I don't know who took or shared the picture, but it somehow landed on our school's gossip page. Everyone's talking about how you're trying to worm your way into our friend group, intending to break us apart or get with one of us.

"Honestly, they're nothing but weird rumors made up by bored students. Everyone with half a brain would know not to jump to conclusions based on one picture, but Lynn must've seen this and thought you and Marcus are becoming a thing. She's crazy for attacking you."

I nod, not sure what to think. On one hand, I feel bad for Lynn since her situation seems a bit too familiar. It sucks being interested in someone when everything is still unspoken and unsure. She probably knows about as much where she stands with Marcus as I did with Elija on the trip, and seeing him with me, if only on one misleading picture, must have hurt her like Joe kissing Elija did.

On the other hand, I'm really disappointed in the way she reacted. She's known me for two years... What made her think I'd go after a guy she's interested in? And more importantly, what made her think she had the right to attack me, publicly no less. From what Elija just said, she has no claim over Marcus so even if we were as close as the picture suggests, she'd be in no position to lash out.

What happened to handling rejection like a grownup?

I guess I'll talk to her after we've both cooled down.

"Florence? Where are you again?" Elija interrupts my train of thought. I don't know how he does it, catching me whenever I zone out, but I find myself smiling at him.

"Sorry, I'm back. So, want to talk about what happened on Friday?" I ask him. I haven't heard from him since he left my place, but my mind spent hours thinking up why he came over.

"Oh, right. Daniel had a tantrum and broke my guitar. I worked my ass off to be able to afford it in the first place so it was best that I left instead of doing something I would have regretted in the heat of the moment. I know he's just a kid, but god, he can be a brat. When I came back home, he apologized and my parents said they'll help me get a new one but, I don't know. I don't want them to spend their savings on something so unimportant when there are so many bills to pay. I'll try to get a job soon and work things out myself. It's fine," he tries to shrug it off, but despite his nonchalant act, I can tell he's still upset about it.

I get it. If I'd suddenly be unable to draw or read for whatever reasons, I'd be crushed too. We all need some sort of reprieve every now and again, and Elija can't have that now that he has no guitar. At least until he's saved up for a replacement. My chest aches at the thought of him having to work on top of going to school when it sounds like he already does so much at home when it comes to taking care of the twins.

"I know it's not the same as a new one, but if you don't mind, we have an old guitar in our basement somewhere. I could lend it to you until you have the money to buy one yourself. That way, you could wait to get a job until the next break," I offer. He smiles a smile that lets me know he'll decline even before he says the words.

"I couldn't accept that, Florence. I'll be fine," he argues.

But I think about the beat he created just for me and the hours he spent diving in the lake to find my hairclip. He's too selfless for his own good, and maybe this can be my way of thanking him. Of giving something back. "It's collecting dust in some dark corner, Elija. I mean it, please," I insist. I haven't seen the thing in years, but I know we kept it. It belonged to my aunt, and we never threw her stuff away.

"Are you sure?" Elija asks slowly.

"Yes. I can take it to school tomorrow, does that work?" I offer, relieved when his face breaks out in a grin. Clearly, he hated the idea of not being able to play more than he let on.

"You're the best!" he exclaims before trying to pull me into a hug. As tempting as that is, I push him away before our chests can touch.

"I'm covered in paint," I remind him quickly, and his gaze drops to the mess covering me once more. He smiles sheepishly and takes half a step back.

"Right, my bad." His hand finds mine and gives it a squeeze, his eyes earnest. "Thank you, Florence."

Three days later, I'm home alone again. Not that that's the unusual part. The unusual part is that I'm home alone when I should be at school.

I'm not one for breaking the rules, any rules, including skipping school, but in this case, it's all part of a tradition.

My birthday is the one day a year where my parents allow me not to go to school so we can spend it together. For as long as I can remember, we've done it this way. They took a day off work and took me on some sort of adventure. It's the one ritual I could count on even after my aunt died, the one day where the strain in our relationship seemed to disappear. It was like entering a time machine every year and going back to before the loss of my aunt tore us apart.

Until this year, only that I didn't get the memo beforehand.

This morning, when I happily emerged from my room, expecting to see my mom make us pancakes – all part of the birthday ritual – I was met with an empty house. I was surprised enough to call my dad, which turned out to be a huge mistake since he was busy at work.

"What is it?" he asked, his voice clipped. "I'm about to go into a meeting. Shouldn't you be at school?" His harsh tone startled me enough to lie and tell him I was at school and that I had a free period.

I knew then, my parents forgot my birthday. Or maybe they didn't even forget but just decided I should be over something as silly as a birthday ritual when I'm legally an adult.

The sad part is, I can't even say I'm shocked this happened. I only regret having found out after school has already started since I'll now be spending all day by myself. I texted my teacher last night already to let him know I'm sick and won't be at school today. I can't exactly take it back and go anyway.

Now, here I am lounging on my bed and opening Instagram after hours of drawing because I just got a notification. It's pathetic how desperate I am for anyone whatsoever to have thought of me today. Not that it's likely to be a message anyway. Not many people know when my birthday is, and even less would remember it unprompted.

As it turns out, it is in fact *not* a message but a story notification. Someone *tagged me* in a story. I don't think anyone has ever tagged me on social media.

My heart skips a beat when I see Elija's user at the top of the notification, and I press onto his story trembling with excitement.

I'm greeted by a meme, presumably self-made. It's a viral picture of some guy appearing highly offended with the caption "**When you made plans to use her birthday as an excuse to hug her but she doesn't show up at school**" To which he added the comment *"Yeah, fr"* as if he hadn't created the entire thing himself.

It's so silly, so goofy in its nature that it draws a laugh of pure disbelieve from me. The first sliver of happiness today shoots through me, and after the morning I've had, it feels amazing. He wanted to hug me, and for me to know it too. For all his followers to know it... Is it too late to go to school? I still have thirty minutes until the last period ends.

No, wait, that would be crazy.

I decide to simply text him instead.

Me: Oops, my baaad...

To make sure I don't come across as too dry, I add the extra letters. Though as I send it and reread the message on our thread, it looks weird.

Elija: You should be.

He replies before I can worry about my reply too much. Then, he quickly follows it up with another text.

Elija: Just kidding, of course. Why aren't you here, though? The guys missed you.

Even though he's probably lying about the last part, the thought that the guys noticed my absence makes me smile. Benji did text me a simple happy birthday this morning when it became clear I wasn't going to school and he attached a picture of him and Jamie, saying he wanted to congratulate me as well.

Me: I usually spend my bdays with my parents
Elija: Okay, I can accept that… makes sense
Elija: How's it been so far?
Me: Fun

It's just a partial lie. One that allows me to not go into detail about today's disappointment.

Elija: What are you doing?

Me: You know, I'm pretty sure you're not supposed to be on your phone during class...

Elija: why do I feel like you're avoiding my question? What's going on?

Elija: And don't think about lying, Florence. It's bad karma

He added a period. Now it's serious. Damn bloodhound that he is, of course he noticed something was off.

Me: Okay, technically, my parents aren't here

I confess. No use in testing fate by lying outright when he just warned me.

Elija: Where are they?

Me: at work hahha

Oh, texting is so cringe. Why am I so cringe? The stupid laugh sounds fake even over text, like I can mentally hear my most awkward chuckle by reading the letters. I'm crazy, but I'm scared he can hear the same.

Elija: no offense but that sounds like a boring tradition.

That at least makes me grin. He's right.

Me: It's not part of it. I guess we're not doing anything this year, but I didn't realize until school had already started so I couldn't come anymore.

This time, Elija takes longer to reply. He keeps typing something only to delete it. Finally, a message comes through.

Elija: Can you pick me up after school?

Elija: Nvm, can you come straight away? No one needs school

Me: yeah, sure. Where do you need to go?

Elija: home

Elija: well, with you

Elija: if you want, of course

Me: my parents will be home in two hours. You sure you want to hide again?

Elija: Not your home, Florence, mine.

Me: you want me to come to your place?

Elija: Yep. Or we can go somewhere else, your pick. I'm not letting you spend your birthday alone.

Me: Oh, that's nice but you really don't have to do that, it's fine.

Elija: Florence, don't fight me on this. If you don't want to spend time with me, that's totally okay but don't try to be selfless. I'll make another meme complaining about how you never understand that I want to spend time with you.

Me: hahah all right but won't your parents say something? You said there's always someone at home and I don't want to cause you any troubles

Elija: I'm allowed to have girls over, Florence

Elija: besides, my family's been dying to meet you

My heart skips a beat at that. He's told his family about me?

Elija: the twins couldn't shut up about you after they met you

Oh well, good enough.

Me: All right, but I won't let you skip school. I'll be in the parking lot after school

Elija: Look who's talking about skipping school

Elija: but fine. Only because it's your birthday. See you later:)

I spend the next thirty minutes stressing over what to wear. I got ready this morning since my parents wouldn't allow me to look like a zombie at breakfast but now, all my clothes seem inappropriate. It's horribly warm outside so I'd like to wear a crochet top but the ones I own all seem too revealing. In the end, I decide to wear my favorite one even though it stops above my navel and has a V-neckline.

It's colorful and with my lack of boobs, it's not like I look sexy. It seems like a good mix between looking nice for Elija and not appearing like a tramp in front of his family.

I throw on a thin white jacket, which makes the green and pink of the shirt pop more, and pair it up with some white linen pants. Finishing it off with some gold accessories and my flower converse, I get going.

At school, Elija's already waiting for me. He smiles warmly before pulling me into a hug.

"Happy birthday. Welcome to the world of adults," he says. I'm too busy inhaling his scent and enjoying the close contact to reply, but he doesn't seem to be in a rush. He just keeps holding me, caressing my back until I pull away.

"Ready to go into the lion's den?" he jokes as I hand him the spare helmet.

"I hope so. I don't know where you live though so I'll need directions." Focusing on finding the way there will hopefully also keep my mind from spiraling and my anxiety from rising. *I'm meeting Elija's parents. His whole family.* I've never met anyone's parents, which should be obvious since I've also not dated anyone in my eighteen years of living.

Not that Elija and I are dating.

Come to think of it, I have no idea what we are. Since his possible confession that he wanted to kiss me on the camping trip, he's given me no other indication that he was romantically interested in me. If anything, things have seemed rather amicable between us.

"I'll do my best. It's not hard to find," he replies, reminding me he's still waiting for us to leave. Right. I start my Vespa, tell him to hold on, and with his help, we reach his home in less than thirty minutes.

Elija heads for the door the second I'm parked but I shake out my hair first. I'm sure it looks all messy after the wind's torture but I try my best to comb it through with my fingers before reattaching my clip at the back of my head. Then, I smile at Elija, who's, as always, staring at me. When I tell him I'm ready, we enter his home.

The first thing I notice is all the noise. I'm not accustomed to it since my parents are always quiet eve if they're at home but it's reassuring, somehow. Lively, unlike the cold silence that lingers in my place.

"Home sweet home," Elija tells me spreading his arms in front of him.

Before I can reply, two weights throw themselves at my legs. I look down to see the twins smiling up.

"Flower girl is here!"

"Happy birthday, Flower girl!" they sing. They're quickly followed by a plump woman with the kindest eyes I've ever seen, who also pulls me into a full body hug.

"You must be Florence. I'm Amelia, it's nice to finally meet you," she tells me. I'm beyond startled by the affectionate greeting, but I snap out of it and hug her back. She smells of vanilla, sweet and familiar. Warm and homey. I quickly blink back a rush of sudden tears before she pulls away. Shit, not the place to cry, Florence. I guess I never noticed until now how much I missed a mother's embrace.

"The pleasure's all mine," I tell her, glad when my vision clears and my voice doesn't sound choked. She pulls away and hugs her son next, squeezing him even tighter than me. Is this what Elija always comes home to? To so much love and affection? The thought sends a pang of regret and unwanted envy straight to my heart.

"Elija, you're home!" says a deeper voice. I step away as the next person pushes his way up to us. It's a bald, tall man who I'm guessing is Eli's stepfather. He looks just as sweet as his wife as he welcomes Elija, but I notice the shift in his demeanor when he looks at me. His eyes become more guarded and calculating, his smile more hesitant.

"I'm Robert," he tells me, holding out his hand for me to shake. I try not to be intimidated as I smile at him.

"Florence. Thank you for having me," I tell him.

"Of course, Sweetie, and happy birthday," Amelia says. Somehow, the nickname sounds different coming from her than my own mother. More genuine, maybe.

I thank the woman and follow Eli to his room as he excuses us.

"You survived the first test with flying colors. Honestly, I think my mother loves you more than me already," Elija jokes as he sits down on his desk chair. He tells me to sit down on his bed which I happily do. Even though my brain is in a haze, being surrounded by so many new things, I recognize his bed is smaller than mine. That's probably why he isn't on here with me. Stupid gentleman.

His room is exactly what I envisioned it to be like. It's mostly black and grey with a few blue accents. There are no clothes strewn across the floor, but boxes filled with various things are set in the corners. My aunt's guitar is hanging from his wall right across the bed.

"Are there any more tests?" I ask absently, still taking in the room. Pictures are hung up on a wall along with a few records. It all screams Elija.

"Well, there's dinner if you're up for it," he offers. That gets my attention.

"Are you sure it would be okay for me to stay?" I wonder while running the scenarios through my head. Would I be able to stomach anything surrounded by so many strangers? Kids without any real table manners on top of it. I've been having a few good days recently so I might. I'm just scared it'll get worse again. I don't want to come across as impolite because I can't finish my plate.

"Of course, Florence," Elija assures me, oblivious to my inner conflict. It would be so much easier if my body wasn't constantly fighting a battle against me. Or maybe it's all in my head and that's the source of it. Wherever my problems with food stem from, I wish I could just erase them. Ignore it and just be normal.

In the name of that wish, I accept the kind invitation. "All right, then I'd love to stay. Thank you," I tell him. While he puts on music, my eyes go back to the guitar on the wall. I still remember when my aunt used to play for me. I loved her playing almost as much as I loved her singing voice.

"Who's is it, anyway? I forgot to ask you the last time," Elija asks, following my gaze.

"My aunt's," I tell him with a wistful smile. For once, it feels nice to mention her.

Chapter 25

Elija

Her admission makes me whirl to face her, already shaking my head. "Wait really? Florence you shouldn't have lent it to me." I felt bad for accepting it in the first place, but now knowing that it has such sentimental value, it feels even more inappropriate. It makes the guitar even more precious than the fine craftsmanship of the wood.

But she doesn't seem to think the same. Instead, she brushes me off, "It's fine. As I said, no one uses it anymore. I haven't even seen it in years before I got it out for you."

"But what if one of the twins throws a fit again and it gets damaged? Or what if I accidentally destroy it." I've never even slightly damaged an instrument of mine, but maybe the pressure will make me crack, knowing this one belonged to someone Florence cared so much about.

She just smiles patiently. "Elija, relax. If it gets destroyed, which I don't think is likely to happen, then it'll at least have been played again before. My aunt would have hated to see it boxed up in our garage." I search her face, trying to find an indication that she's just being nice for my sake, but she seems genuine.

I like the way she talks about the guitar being played, and it has been a huge relief to tug at the cords again... "I'll take the best care of it," I promise. "And you're getting it back as soon as I can get my own."

"You're welcome to keep it for as long as you'll play for me," she counters hopefully, making me grin.

"You want to hear me play?" I ask, to which she nods. "Very well, any wishes?" I let her consider it while I get the instrument off the wall.

"Play your favorite," she tells me. Then, she pats my bed next to where she's sitting, telling me to come over. I comply happily. Any excuse to be close to her is welcome, especially when she's the one initiating it.

I don't have to think about what to play. A year or so ago, shortly after my breakup with Ricky, I composed my own song. I've played it at least a hundred times but I can't seem to get sick of it. It's not about my ex or what happened between us, but I think her betrayal just unlocked a new depth of my connection to music and that's why I started creating songs then.

I start playing the intro softly, trying to calm my nerves before singing the first note. I haven't shown this song to anyone, and I rarely sing in front of people. My family members are the only ones that have heard me before. My family and now Florence. I like that.

I lose myself as the song goes on and only snap out of it after the last note rings out.

"I don't know what to say. That was beautiful, Elija. Did you make it yourself?" she asks quietly, as if she might've been swept away by the soft melody. I like the thought that something I made could have an influence on her, so I mirror the soft tone of her voice, happy to linger in this moment.

"Yeah, I did. I'm glad you like it," I respond, feeling uncharacteristically nervous.

"You should post or publish it somehow. I'm sure people would love your music," she goes on, and I can see in her eyes that she's already got it all planned out. It's like when she talks about her books or Harry Potter. She loses herself in it, and honestly, I think it's when she's most beautiful. Full of passion and filled to the brim with her creativity.

That's why my heart is skipping beats like crazy and my skin is heating up as I watch her. I'm painfully aware of her knee touching my thigh and her proximity overall.

I slowly put the guitar down, trying to chuckle it off. When I come back up, her smile is slowly fading, and I can tell the wheels are turning behind those pretty emerald eyes. Her eyes drop to my lips before quickly snapping back to mine. By now, her cheeks have turned a bright pink, making me wonder what she's thinking about.

"You and Joe are really nothing?" she asks.

"Nothing," I reassure her as I did last week.

"So, you're totally single?" she asks hesitantly, chewing on her bottom lip. And now I'm staring at her lips... I nod since my voice is positively gone. Then, I drag my eyes back to hers.

Okay, I'm doing this.

Leaning in, I cup her face and wait for a second, trying to give her a way out just in case. When she leans into my touch, holding my gaze steadily, it's like a barrier is shattered and I finally close the distance between our lips. There's no way I could have resisted if I tried.

She sighs against me at the initial contact and I nearly groan in response. It's those little reactions I get from her that make my blood run hotter. And right now, my heart can't handle anything more. Not when I'm finally kissing her.

Florence pulls back a little and I miss the contact instantly. But then her hands find my neck and her lips are on mine, this time more surely than before. Her hands slip up into my hair, burying into the wayward curls gently. My hand on her cheek flexes, a possessive gesture I can't stop.

I run my tongue along the seam of her lips, burning to taste her. To feel her closer. To ravish her until she forgets her own name.

She opens readily, and when my tongue darts out the next time, hers is there to hesitantly meet it. I let my groan run free as I get my first taste of my new favorite drug. My free hand finds her side, running down alongside the slope of it until it's placed on her waist. I hold her in place and lean closer, nearly going mad when she pushes right back, connecting our upper bodies.

It's reassuring to know I'm not the only one craving more contact. I need to know she's with me on this.

She shifts again, and just when I think she's trying to pull away and plan on letting her go, she surprises me by climbing into my lap, straddling me without ever breaking the kiss. She settles down softly, barely putting any weight on my lap, but I still can't suppress my groan at her taking the initiative.

The amount of times I've thought about this is lowkey embarrassing, but it still didn't prepare me for the real thing. Having Florence in my arms, *kissing* her. It feels better than I could have imagined.

I wrap my arms around her until they're spanning over her entire back, enveloping her as much as I can in this position. She sighs softly against me, a sign of approval, and I tuck that piece of information away for later.

"Is this okay?" she asks softly, her eyes barely focusing on me they're so glazed.

I smile at her show of concern for my sake. "More than okay, Florence," I assure her. She nods to herself and scoots a little closer. Now we're almost chest to chest, her ass nearly nestled on top of my straining dick. "How about this?" she asks.

"Still good," I repeat, my voice low and guttural. His brows raise at the sound of my voice, so I clear my throat. "Sorry bout that."

Blushing, she shakes her head. "No need to apologize. I was just surprised your voice could get so deep." Her fingers are absently playing with my hair, her short nails scraping over my scalp with heavenly pressure. She shifts again, holding my gaze as she sits down as far up on my lap as she can. She sucks in a breath when she feels my growing erection against her center and I curse myself, blushing ferociously.

"Sorry, I can't really – " she cuts my apology off by capturing my lips in another kiss, her entire body moving against mine until we're plastered together. I groan against her lips, tightening my arms around her. One of my hands moves to the nape of her neck, holding her head in place as I meet her kiss for kiss. The other moves down until it's wrapped around her waist and I'm gripping the opposite slope.

My fingers slip underneath the hem of her shirt so my entire palm can feel the heat radiating from her skin, but I don't move up to grope her or reveal more skin.

She pulls at my hair, deepening the kiss and making me moan in surprise. Fuck, I didn't expect Florence to have a slight violent streak. It's fucking hot.

As if my noise of pleasure spurs her on, she starts moving her hips, surprising me as she grinds against my erection. The movement is shy and exploratory in a way that only Florence could muster, and it's enough to make my head spin. What is it with this girl and having such an effect on me? I tighten my grip on her waist, intending to keep her from torturing me any further, but she moans softly against my lips rather than stilling on top of me.

"Fuck, Florence, I'm trying really hard to take this slow," I breathe against her. She pulls back a little more to look at me.

"Just don't," she retorts, looking like she means it too. My brave girls. I smile and brush a stray strand of her maroon hair behind her ear, taking in her red lips. I can't wait to see more marks of mine on her but not yet. Not today.

"Don't tempt me. Besides my whole family is home," I remind her gently.

"Oh shit." I can tell she's forgotten all about that, especially when she tries to scramble off my lap. I shake my head with a chuckle and hug her around the waist to hold her in place.

"They won't come in here. Not without knocking, at least. Besides we're both adults, so no one would be upset about us kissing."

She settles back against me and laughs softly as she mumbles, "Your dad already hates me, though."

"What are you talking about? Of course, he doesn't." She just shrugs and smiles some more. "Florence, my dad doesn't hate you. He's just a bit protective. Give him a chance to get to know you and he'll warm up a bit. He won't be able to help it," I assure her. I mean, really, who wouldn't like her. She's like a ray of sunshine wrapped in spring flowers. Sweet and smart, inherently kind and selfless.

She leans against me, her forehead on my chest as I lie down on my back, relaxing with her in my arms. Man, I could get used to this. Having her cuddle up to me feels like heaven.

I draw circles on her back as we talk, drifting over all sorts of topics.

When it's time for dinner, May and Daniel pound on my door like two bloodhounds.

"Kai said to tell you to get dressed. We're eating in five minutes!" May yells. I can hear her and Daniel giggle while the girl on top of me stiffens.

"Oh god, is that what your family thinks we were doing? I'll never be able to face them again," she groans into my chest, and I laugh.

"Don't worry about it. It's just Kai being Kai, and the kids wouldn't get the insinuation anyway," I assure her.

"Your parents better not have heard it. The twins might not understand but they definitely would." She cringes visibly but doesn't fight me as I pull her to her feet.

"If they did, they'd know it's just Kai teasing me. Don't lose your mind over it, really. It's all friendly fire here." From what I've seen so far, it seems Florence's family deals more in backhanded comments than friendly jokes so I don't blame her for worrying. It might take time for her to get used to the status quo around here, all the noise and constant excitement, but luckily, I plan on giving her a lot of it. She deserves to be surrounded by good vibes when her own family is lacking in exuding them.

I keep her cool hand in mine and lead her back to the living room. I can tell she's nervous, her steps unsteady and slow so she falls slightly behind me. I give her hand a squeeze and smile reassuringly over my shoulder. She returns the gesture and visibly build herself up, gathering her courage with a deep breath. When she smiles back, I believe she feels it. We step into the living room side by side, hands still connected.

My entire family notices the gesture and react to varying degrees. Kai winks at me, my mom smiles to herself as she averts her gaze, and my dad still has that stupid tough-guy act going on. The twins with their non-existent filter don't let me off so easily.

May starts off strong by making a gagging noise. Then, Daniel hits the spot with, "Is she your girlfriend?" Before things can get awkward over *that*, May swoops back in with the final blow, "Like Ricky?" I stiffen, trying to think up a way to fix this situation right this very moment before Florence gets up in her head about it. My body goes through the motion of pulling back Florence's chair and then my own on autopilot as my mind whirrs.

But the double trouble team has one more ace up their sleeve, and they reveal it when Daniel adds, "I liked Ricky. She always played with me. Flower girl went straight to your room."

I dare glance at Florence on my right to see a frozen smile on her face. Before I can speak up in her defense, she takes a deep breath and tells the twins, "I'd love to play with you guys. Maybe next time, your brother won't drag me off to his room as soon as I arrive." She even eyes me playfully, and I relax a little. She can gladly throw me under the bus as long as she's not uncomfortable.

I throw an arm over her shoulders and shrug at the twins. "Can't help it. I want her all to myself," I tease them, and their eyes immediately light up. Of course they do, knowing I have something I don't want to share. Brats.

"But she said she'd rather play with us!" "Yeah, she likes us better!" their triumphant protests fill the air, seeming to relax everyone as we recover from the short-lived awkwardness. Finally, my mom gently gets the twins to shut up so she can redirect the conversation to what they've been dying to ask about. Florence.

Throughout the meal, my family interrogates her and she handles it like a pro. She laughs and smiles as they talk, exchanging anecdotes, and the sight of it all makes my chest feel fuzzy. I like that she gets along with the people that mean the most to me.

Her left hand stays in mine beneath the table at all times, which might complicate it for me to eat but I won't complain. Not when she's looking at me for comfort, taking what she needs to feel at ease.

When I notice her taking smaller bites and eying the rest of her food skeptically, I squeeze my fingers against hers.

"You don't need to finish it," I assure her. That has never been a rule at our table. Whatever wasn't eaten could just be reheated the next day. Honestly, who wins when someone has to force themselves to eat more than they want? I don't want her ending up feeling sick.

Florence smiles gratefully at me and sets her fork down.

"You can give it to me, I still need to grow!" May says proudly.

"So does she," Daniel protests instantly. "She doesn't look tall and strong. Her arms are thinner than mine!" He flexes his nonexistent bicep like he's seen being done in the movies, looking proud of the unnecessary observation he made. This is the downside of having young siblings that can't take social cues. I try to subtly kick him under the table as my warning glances go unnoticed but can't reach him. Unaware of the rising tension and the fact that he's crossing all sorts of lines, he squints at Florence and adds, "Her stomach is skinny too. I can see her ribs."

By the time he's done, Florence has pulled her hand from mine as if she was physically hit by the words. When I look at her, her smile looks ingenuine and stiff. She chuckles uncomfortably and subtly rearranges her jacket so it fully covers her body, a gesture that sits entirely wrong with me. I hate that Daniel's words made her uncomfortable and that she now feels like hiding herself. The outfit she's now covering was so *Florence*, colorful and upbeat. I really liked seeing her wear it, and I'm only now realizing I didn't even tell her so.

I think she could have used the reminder of a truthful compliment when Daniel just bulldozed all over her confidence.

Thankfully, Kai starts up a completely new conversation as if Daniel had never spoken, diverting the attention away from Florence. I could kiss him for that. Metaphorically speaking, of course. We're not that kind of family.

Meanwhile, I have no idea how to cheer the girl next to me up. She's relaxing a bit more as the minutes tick by, but I can tell my little brother's comment really got to her. If he wasn't so young, I'd start a fight. Maybe not at the table but certainly later.

"You said that?" Florence asks me, clutching her stomach as she laughs. Kai just told her a story from when I proposed to my old history teacher because he looked like professor Lupin. I can't even complain about the subtle humiliation. Not when she's finally genuinely laughing again.

"Are you guys ready for cake? Elija didn't give me much of a heads up so it's store-bought. I hope you like lemon, Florence," my mom interjects, looking at her hopefully.

Florence visibly startles, and a blush tinges her cheeks as she stutters, "I- yeah, of course. I love it but you really didn't have to do that. You already let me stay for dinner."

"But, Sweetie, it's not your birthday without cake," my mom insists. I carefully watch Florence as the words hit her, and the visible emotion on her face makes my chest clench. I'm sure she appreciates my family's impromptu invitation, but it should be her parents to buy her a cake and pay attention to her. I wonder if she's thinking the same thing when her phone goes off loudly.

She checks her screen and I have a first row seat of the color draining from her face. She grimaces in her attempt to smile. "So sorry. It's my mom, I should take it," she apologizes as she gets up from the table. She walks a few feet away and answers the phone.

"Hi. Yeah, I'm at a friend's house," she says quietly. Meanwhile, my noisy family is unnaturally silent for the first time tonight, clearly eavesdropping. I don't have the strength to tell them to stop, especially when I'm doing the same thing.

"I'll come after we ate the cake, okay? Well, because it's my birthday, I guess," she says shyly into the phone, making me narrow my eyes. "Yeah, that's today. I understand, no worries. Thanks, see you later." As soon as the phone call ends, my mom walks to the kitchen before Florence can catch sight of her pursed lips and pinched brows.

I share the sentiment, it's obvious her mom forgot about her daughter's birthday. That's why Florence was home alone. I clench my fists but force myself to smile when my girl comes back.

"Here it comes," my mom announces extra cheerily, coming back carrying a cake decorated with eighteen candles. We all sing happy birthday diligently even as Florence flushes beet red under the attention. May reminds her to make a wish before she can blow out the candles and when she manages to distinguish them all in one calculated blow, we clap. Florence is practically glowing, but she does seem glad when the conversation sways from her.

Nearly an hour after that, Florence finally gets to her feet and starts her rant of profuse gratitude towards my parents, especially my mom for organizing tonight. My mother hugs her again. "Of course, honey. I was happy to do it. Don't be a stranger, okay?" she asks during the tight squeeze.

She tells the others goodbye until I finally steer her towards the front door, leaving the two of us alone for the first time in hours. She turns to me with a more subdued, calm smile. Like she's happy but also a little tired and she just now feels comfortable to admit the latter. "Thank you for today. It was probably the best birthday I've ever had. I love your family," she tells me.

"They loved you too and I'm really glad you had a great time. Drive safely and text me when you're home, okay?"

"Will do," she says. I lean down to kiss her goodbye just because I can't help myself and I've been wanting to do that again all evening. My lips brush over hers in a gentle caress that makes her sigh wistfully. When she pulls back, her cheeks are rosy and she's grinning.

"Bye," she says shily, stepping through the door. Then, she's gone.

As soon as the door closes behind me, Kai jumps me, shattering the lingering peace I just felt with Florence.

"So, is she your girl or what?" he asks. I just laugh at him and shake my head. I've had too great a night to be mad at him for snooping. When I settle down on the couch in the living room, I find my mom already waiting. "Don't get me wrong, I like her. She's really sweet, probably good for you," my brother goes on. Then, my dad joins us.

"Twins are in bed, what did I miss?" he asks.

"They kissed," my mom bursts cheekily.

"Not surprised. Eli's been mooning over her throughout the whole dinner," my dad adds.

"Longer than that. Remember when he told us all about how shiny her hair was?" Kai laughs.

"I hate you guys," I grumble playfully.

"Florence loves us, though," my mom adds, revealing she really did listen in on our goodbye. At my pointed look, she seems mildly chastised. "Sorry, couldn't help it."

Ignoring his wife's antics, my dad's face morphs into a thoughtful frown. "I can't believe her own parents forgot about her birthday. She doesn't even have siblings, you said. Who can't remember a single date?" he mutters in apparent disapproval. No one said anything to her after the phone call, but I already knew what my family was thinking. Her parents are jerks. It's ironic that Florence thought my dad didn't like her and here he is, angry on her behalf.

Chapter 26

Florence

She's sorry, it *slipped her mind?* They were *busy with work?* That's the excuse they give me for ditching me on my eighteenth birthday?

I'd usually just accept that and make up a better excuse for them myself but after spending the evening with a proper family, I don't feel like doing that. Sure, people forget things sometimes, and that's okay but my parents didn't even seem to care.

Honestly, what have I done to make them lose interest in me so thoroughly? How come everyone seems to like me more than my own family? Even a group of strangers I met today went out of their way to buy me a cake! I don't expect that from my mom and dad, I don't care about it, but is a little affection too much to ask for? Some curiosity about my life, maybe a hug?

Nope, nothing.

I park my Vespa in our garage and wipe away my tears, furious to have let it get to me as much. With Elija, it's fine to feel whatever I do but here, it's different. All this will get me here is a comment about how puffy my eyes are and maybe a lecture.

The worst part is, I've never even noticed how messed up my family was until now. I always thought it was fine. So what if I'm alone more than I'm not? Who cares if they're emotionally a little detached and distant at times? They're good parents, aren't they? They make sure I have access to all sorts of necessities and privileges that go beyond that.

But they don't make me feel like they love me, care what happens to me or even like me. All my mother does is criticize me and tear me down while my father watches. They treat me like a servant in the odd cases that they are at home and the older I get, the less they seem willing to even pretend to care about what happens to me.

I'm not sure I still think they're good parents. Not as I step into the silent, cold house I grew up in.

Elija's home might not be as big or tidy as this but at least it's lively and full of laughter. It feels like a home. This feels like an open house up for sale.

"I'm home," I announce, frowning when there's no reply. Confused, I check my phone.

Dad: *Went to bed. Lock the door when you're home, please. Happy birthday*

I bite down on the inside of my cheek and blink back tears. *It's fine*, I repeat. *They had a long day and were tired. I didn't tell them when exactly I'd be home so they were unaware of how long to wait up.* I know it's a shitty excuse, but I don't want to deal with anything else right now. Don't want to face the fact that my parents went to sleep in the less than two hours since I reminded them it was my birthday and told them I'd be home soon. It wasn't worth it to them to try and stay awake even though they might've been tired, not even to wish me a happy birthday to my face.

Growing up, people always say adulthood is nothing to look forward too, full of disappointments. I just wasn't prepared for that to become true the day of my birthday like a slap to the face.

I lock the front door, trudge towards my room as if a physical weight was dragging me back, and finally do the same to the door separating my personal space to the rest of this shitty house. There, I cry silently, allowing myself to feel bad about it for one evening. Spending the last few hours of my birthday crying, why not?

I don't bother checking the notifications that keep lighting up my phone, sure it's just Pinterest sending me emails because no one else ever tries to reach me. It's only when it starts ringing, telling me it's definitely not Pinterest, that I pick it up.

"Florence? Are you home? You haven't answered my texts, I was worried," Elija starts ranting the second I accept his call. My body quickly rebels against my tightly held restraint, eager to keep crying even knowing he'd hear it since I'm sure he would make it better.

Dang it. I thickly swallow a sob. Why does he have to be so sweet? It only adds to the ache in my chest. I wish I hadn't come home. It's not like my parents would have noticed.

"Florence?" Elija prompts when I don't answer for a while. Knowing he'd hear that I've been crying, I end the call and text him. It's definitely suspicious but having him suspect something is wrong and confirming it by sobbing over the phone are two different things.

Me: *I'm home.*

He reads my message and calls me again. I press decline, wincing at the loud, intrusive ringtone set on my phone. I quickly switch it to silent mode, scared to get my parents' attention. I couldn't hide that I was crying after being at it for so long and talking to them when I'm already sad is like begging to be emotionally flogged.

Me: *I don't want to wake my parents*

I double text, hoping he'll believe the excuse and let it be. He wanted me to text him when I got home – not that I thought he was so serious about it – but I did now so why is he insisting on speaking to me.

He clearly doesn't care about my reasons behind not picking up because his name flashes on my screen again as he calls me. I let it ring out now that there's no sound to it and he finally texts me in response.

Elija: Pick up, Florence.

So demanding… I swallow around the lump in my throat and answer the next time he calls.

"Talk to me," he says softly. I shake my head even though he can't see me. I don't want him to know I'm crying again. Not after he's done everything to make sure I had a great birthday. "Florence, say something, please."

I clear my throat roughly before whispering, "Hi." The line's silent for a beat.

"Do you want me to come over?" he finally asks, his voice set somewhere between anger and determination.

"It's fine, really. Just go to sleep, we have school tomorrow," I tell him, hating how hoarse and fragile my voice sounds.

"I honestly don't give a shit about school, Florence. It's you I care about, and I can't do nothing when you're crying on your birthday because your parents are idiots," he argues. His interest in the entire situation and the fact that he seems upset on my behalf helps soothe the ache in my chest. Even though my parents might not be there for me, I'm not alone. He's been proving that all day.

It's why I try even harder to reassure him that I'm fine. I don't want him worrying when he should go to bed. "It's fine, they were just tired." I wince as the words leave my lips. The excuse sounds lame even to me. I can hear Elija huff before he takes a deep breath.

"Is there anything I can do?" he finally asks, resignation tinting his voice.

"You did so much today. Thank you. And thank your family from me, please," I brush him off.

"If I tell them that one more time, they'll stop believing that you mean it, Florence," his half-hearted teasing startles a wobbly huff of a laugh out of me, and I can hear his sigh of relief in response. It's like I can imagine him perfectly in this moment, lounging on his bed, finally allowing his muscles to relax now that he's made sure I was fine.

The bed I was on with him only hours before. Kissing him. Moving on his lap. I blush as I imagine those long fingers that touched me so reverently now idly playing with his rings. Is his black hair all mussed and messy because he ran his hands through it waiting for my response? Are the veins on his forearms still bulging like I've noticed before when he rolled up the sleeves of his hoodies?

"It's good to hear you laugh. Much better than hearing you upset," he speaks quietly as silence descends between us. My heart stutters a beat.

"You have that effect on me. Good night now, Elija. I'll see you tomorrow."

"I'm glad. Sleep tight, snow white, and 'till tomorrow."

With that, I try to sleep, thinking about the good parts of today and a certain tattooed guy I owe them to.

"Good morning, Sweetie," my mom greets me the next day, acting as though nothing was amiss. As if she didn't avoid me for the whole day yesterday. We're ignoring all of it as per usual.

"Morning. Why aren't you at work?" I ask her, not quite managing to sound cheery. I needed her here yesterday, not now when my hurt over last night is still fresh in my mind.

"Careful, you almost sound like you're not glad I'm home," she teases sweetly with a smile. *That's because I'm not,* I think. I'd never say something like that to her, though.

"I'm just wondering."

"I know, Honey. I'm just here to pack your father's and my things up while he finishes some last-minute work in the office. We're leaving for a business trip and won't be back until next Tuesday."

Business trip my ass. I keep my quiet, used to it by now. She wants to call her vacations business trips? I let her. She wants to pretend my birthday didn't happen? Fine by me.

Who am I to make waves? Demure little Florence. I let her get away with everything with a fake smile on my lips and my jaw aching from how hard it's clenched.

"Okay," is all I say before I head back to my room, ignoring that I meant to grab breakfast. I really don't feel like talking any longer, and the thought of having her scrutinize my every bite and spew her venomous remarks already has my guts in knots. My apatite is gone. I'll just wait until lunch.

I get ready, make sure to pack my book, and head off to school.

"Flower girl! How was your birthday?" Jamie asks, pulling me into a bone-crushing hug as soon as I enter the classroom.

"It was really nice, thanks," I reply automatically. When Jamie lets me go, the other guys each take their turn hugging me. My cheeks heat as they overwhelm me with questions and their unexpected attention, but I'm not one to complain. Hugs are my biggest life source at this point, and now that I'm being spoiled like never before, I can feel myself only getting greedier. What would it have been like to be at school yesterday? Would they have been so nice too?

I regret having skipped class once more.

When it's Liam's turn to hug me, it's a bit awkward. "Hey," he says, scratching the back of his neck rather than making a move to greet me as the others did. Trying to diffuse the tension, I decide to hug him as well. He might not make it easy to like him and I get why the guys hold a grudge against him, but I shouldn't add insult to injury. The guys are making me feel so cheery, I wouldn't want to bring anyone around me down.

At first, his arms are stiff and unsure around my back, but after a second, he pulls me tighter. It's all fine by me up until the moment I feel his nose graze the top of my head as he breathes me in.

I look at Elija over Liam's shoulder to see his jaw clenched. Attempting to ease the tension, I smile at him, but he's too busy glaring at his non-friend's back to see. I feel like I'm missing something again.

When I'm finally able to free myself from Liam, Elija steps forward. Without a warning, he cups my face and presses his lips to mine, dragging my body close by my waist. It's not as gentle as the goodbye I got yesterday. No, this time, I can feel the tension humming in his body and the possessiveness in his grip.

It makes my mind go blank and my body melt to his will. It's a good kiss, one that feels straight out of the movies. Possessive and consuming, though his hands on me stay gentle. I wrap my hands around his neck and arch into his touch, happy to have his lips back on mine. It's all it takes for me to stop overanalyzing and just –

"Get a room!" Orion's comment rips me from my trance, and I realize we're still at school. Not that many students are already in the classroom but still. With an embarrassed chuckle, I take a step back and touch my fingers to my throbbing lips.

"Good to know you two finally grew some balls," Benji approves with a smile.

As more students start filling the room, Elija gently pulls me into the chair next to his instead of my usual place opposite him. I smile, happy with the new seating arrangement even though I already know it'll be a lot harder to focus with his hand on my thigh.

Who cares about school, though, when I can revel in the sweet ecstasy of having Elija caress me like I mean something.

Chapter 27

Elija

Now that the weather is thawing, our group is back to spending our lunch break outside to soak up the sun. It used to be the source for my serotonin reserve, but now I feel happy for a different reason. Florence is sitting between my legs, leaning against my chest as I play with the ends of her hair. I took out her clip and intended to figure out how she pulls her hair back, but it turns out I'm a disaster.

I've given up out of fear to hurt her and with her hair down, I at least have the liberty to caress her as I please. She's made no attempt to scold me or put her hair back up, rather leaning back with a content smile on her lips as she faces the sun. With her eyes closed, her cheeks rosy and her hair gleaming copper in the sun, she's a sight I can't take my eyes off of.

"What are we doing tonight?" Marcus asks.

"Shed?" Liam's idea comes in the form of a grumble. He's been extra moody recently, and I can't shake the feeling that it's especially directed at me. Not that I care much. Whatever has got his panties in a twist is his problem, and if he irrationally takes it out on me... well I've been waiting for an excuse to fight him for a while. Just not in front of Florence this time. I don't ever want her to look at me, or rather not look at all, like she did that night when I lunged at Liam in the shed.

"Sure, I'll get my sister to buy some beer," Jamie adds, clearly up for a party. We barely have time to hash out the rest of the details before the bell rings in warning that our break is almost over.

Oh so reluctantly, I let Florence go and get to her feet, then follow the rest of the group inside the building reaching for her hand. These last few days have been a blur of sweet kisses and good vibes, but since we've only seen each other at school or surrounded by the guys, I can't kiss her like I really want to. I make up for it by keeping some sort of physical connection between us at all times,

After class, I can't muster the memory of a single thing my history teacher said. It's been this way ever since Florence started sitting next to me. I'm so aware of her proximity that I can barely think about anything else and I don't even mind.

I always keep one hand on her thigh, stroking my thumb over the fabric covering her skin in an innocent, nearly unconscious habit by now, but today, my mind kept wandering off. There was no fabric between my fingers and her smooth skin because she's wearing a skirt, and my hormonal mind kept thinking about what would happen if my hand just slipped beneath it. I'd never do it, of course. I think Florence would have a heart attack if I tried anything of the sort in public. Still, my mind wandered so the old lady standing at the front of the classroom has never seemed less interesting.

Now that we're done with school, Florence leans in as we trail after the others. "You know, my parents aren't at home. If you want, we could hang out at my place before we meet up with the guys. Only if you don't want to go home first or anything, of course. I understand if you have other things to do as well," she dissolves back into the rambling girl she was when we first started talking and I can't quite hide my grin.

She's so endearing.

But I still don't want her to be uncomfortable so I squeeze her hand in a sign that she can stop talking.

"I'd love to come, Florence," I assure her.

We tell our friends goodbye as they head for the bus stop or their car, and on the back of her Vespa, we head to her place. The second we get inside, she asks if I mind if she takes a super quick shower. "Not at all. Take your time, I'll just be snooping," I tease her.

She smiles and in a rare show of taking the lead, she surprises me by pressing a tender kiss to my lips. "Snoop away. I'll be right back."

So here I am, taking in Florence's bookshelf while she takes a shower. I recognize the book she wouldn't let me read the last time. She doesn't know it yet, but I actually read it myself after having seen it in her room. I wanted to know what kind of books my girl spends all her time reading. To say that I was surprised when the main characters outright started going at it, the entire ordeal described very explicitly, would be an understatement.

After that, I bought myself another book from the same author since I lowkey enjoyed it after I got over my initial astonishment and slight embarrassment. I asked the lady in the bookstore for a suggestion, and now, a week later, I'm almost done with it. Who would have thought I'd enjoy reading?

"What should I wear?" Florence's voice breaks through my thoughts, dragging me back to the present. She's standing in front of her dresser dressed in nothing more than two towels. One in her hair and one around her body.

My heart stutters a beat as I blink at her. Oh shit.

My greedy eyes rove over the length of her, taking in her long, smooth legs, still glistening with droplets of water, the sinful curve of her neck, and the swing of her collarbones. They fly over the towel covering her middle, but I force myself to look away before my mind can drift too far off.

I'd like to answer her, but I think there might not be enough blood left in my brain to form a coherent sentence. I try to hide my reaction to Florence subtly so I don't make her uncomfortable, but she seems sweetly oblivious. Does she know what she's doing, standing a few feet away, *naked*? Well, naked under those towels. Like a present barely wrapped, the most enticing parts already on show as if to beckon you to see more.

"Whatever you're most comfortable in," I tell her, averting my eyes to my feet. She turns around, and when I feel her gaze land on me, I look up to see her frown.

"I'm giving you a choice here. Be helpful," she demands exasperatedly. It brings a small smile to my lips.

"You look good in everything you wear," I assure her with a chuckle. To that, my girl tips her head back and groans, putting her throat to show. I watch as a drop of water slides down her skin, taunting me. Come on! She must know what she's doing.

"Don't look at me like that," she breathes, making me realize I've been staring at the expanse of skin of her neck. *Caught red-handed...*

I study her for a second, not moving closer out of fear some strange urge will arise and shut my brain down. "Am I making you uncomfortable?" I ask her. Her cheeks tint pink.

"No. You're making me want to be late or simply ditch the others completely," she admits, making my eyebrows rise instantly on my forehead, a clear display of my surprise. Is she suggesting she likes it when I look at her? Really look at her? Enough to get her mind to wander down the same slippery slope as mine constantly tries to when she's around.

At the sight of my new, puzzled expression, she nods, pleased. "That's better. Now tell me what to wear," she adds.

"Fine." I get off her bed, holding onto my restraint with an iron fist as I get close enough to smell her shampoo, and take a look at her closet. Unsurprisingly, everything is folded neatly and sorted by color. "Do you have any more skirts?" I ask her, to which she smiles. She silently opens another drawer, revealing about a billion skirts. I study them before choosing a brown one with a flower pattern. Now that we got the flower part down, I can choose the top freely. *See that, smart*!

"Is this comfortable?" I ask her, taking out said skirt.

"Absolutely," she says with a smile. *Fuck* it's so tempting to reach out and touch her, to kiss her maybe, but I wouldn't dare in her current state of undress. Instead, I look away and I take a glance at her shirts, settling on a beige one that ties at the back and handing it to her.

Thinking we're done with it at that, I try to turn to put some distance between me and her addictive scent, only for Florence to place a firm hand on my shoulder. I halt and look at the hand currently burning through the layers of my skin with how viscerally my body reacts to her touch. Before I can question what she's doing touching me right now, her hand is gone and she opens another drawer. I do a double take when I see it's all underwear before whipping my gaze toward her, feeling like this is a trap.

Something seems too good to be true? Then it probably is. And the idea that Florence, shy, rambling Florence is asking me to pick out her *underwear* for the evening we're about to spend together when she's already standing naked next to me seems unreal.

That doesn't stop my blood from rushing right south as images of Florence wearing the few scraps of lace I saw in the second I looked at the drawer's insides. My imagination is both a blessing and a pain in my ass because what the hell happened to being a gentleman?

"Really?" I ask her, inwardly feeling like a little child on Christmas.

"Well, I'm not going without panties," she tells me as if that had been what I was talking about. And goddamn, now it's what I'm *thinking* about. After reading exactly the type of content she's been reading for who knows how long, I really shouldn't be surprised by this openly seductive side of Florence. I guess there's nothing for me to do than to embrace the change in her. After all, it does hint at her growing to trust me, and that's a huge win in my book.

I shake some of my nerves and grin back at her. "That's not what I thought before but it's where my mind's at now. We'll do that next time, I guess." I wink and turn to choose underwear, judging my options by sight only. I wouldn't dare just touch her delicates like some weirdo. Instead, I try to assess what could be comfortable by just looking at the fabrics.

"Do I get to see it on you?" I tease, unable to help myself. Her cheeks flame up and she smiles shily. Ah, there she is, back to being shy. She doesn't answer me, but that's fine. I'm ready to work for more scraps of the more hidden aspects of her character.

"So, do you want something natural or should we go with that one?" I ask, motioning to the bright red lace. With the shirt I chose, I'm guessing she won't wear a bra, though there would be a matching one, I see. "I think I'd enjoy knowing you're wearing something the guys would never guess," I add, smirking.

"Yeah," Florence agrees almost wistfully before clearing her throat. "I mean, it's entirely your pick. Everything I have is comfortable."

Well, if that's the case... "Let's go with that, then. If you're sure that's alright. By the way, why do you have so much lingerie?" I wonder, looking at all the lace in the drawer. She tries to avert her eyes as she blushes, but I gently cup her face and smile at her. "There's nothing to be ashamed of, Florence."

"First off, it's not lingerie, just matching sets. And secondly, it's fun to shop for them. They make me feel," she breaks off, swallowing and smiling shily. For a second, she seems to mull over the right word to use. Then, she settles on, "Hot, I guess. Even if no one sees it."

"Oh I believe that. Then again, I think you're mind-numbingly beautiful in whatever you wear, so I might be biased. Either way, I'll let you change now." I turn around but stay in the room, unsure of where else to go because I've only ever really been in here. I hear the towels drop and the sound of rustling clothes, and it takes my all not to let my mind wander.

"All done," she tells me finally. I allow my eyes to briefly travel over her, trying not to linger where the skirt ends mid-thighs and her shirt's V lands. "Happy with your choices?" she asks, seeming more confident now that she's dressed.

"Very. You look stunning, Florence" I tell her before pulling her close enough to kiss. Finally, finally, I get to kiss her.

It's meant to be a quick peck, but Florence quickly deepens the kiss, liking along the seam of my lips and driving me fucking crazy. I like it, though. Like that she's gradually becoming more sure of herself to the point where she's not scared to ask for what she wants. And right now, she seems to want a proper kiss. The same kind I've been starving to get as well.

Her hands find mine on her hips, and she gently pulls them further down toward where I know I want them but wasn't sure it was the right time to place them. Once I'm cupping her ass, pulling her further against me, she tangles her fingers in my hair and releases a soft hum of approval.

"Let's tell the others we won't make it. You can be the first one to ever see my pretty underwear," she tempts me against my lips. I laugh at that because seriously considering what she's offering would bring me to my knees, ready to beg her to do what she promised. Who would've thought the shy girl I knew for two years would suggest things like this?

"As much as I'd love that, they'd probably take it as far as coming here to get us themselves," I tell her, smiling at the thought. I wouldn't put it past my friends to interrupt our private evening if we ditched them without reason, and as much as I truly would like to stay here with Florence, I'm scared of what we might be tempted to do.

I know that I'm tempted to do certain things as it is, and I have no intentions of going through with them just yet. I want to take my time getting to know Florence. Really know her. All the physical stuff can be explored together later. We're in no hurry.

After a second of consideration, my girl nods if not a little reluctantly. "I can see that. Fine, let's go to your place."

Chapter 28

Florence

After letting me decide what he's wearing tonight in return, Elija takes me to the shed in his family's car. Before we left, I made sure to play with the twins for a good thirty minutes, though, making us the last ones to arrive at Liam's. I can't say I regret it. I want Elija's siblings to like me like they did with *Ricky.* Actually, some small petty part of me wants them to like me more, which is why I enjoyed it so much when Kai said, "See, Daniel? No one else has ever had the patience to play with you as long as Florence."

As we get out of the car, I walk behind Elija to take in his outfit once more. Black cargo pants with two chains at the side and a black, fitted shirt. It might be basic, but he looks sinfully handsome, those tattooed, trained arms of his showing off for a change.

"Done staring at my ass?" he teases, glancing over his shoulder.

I catch up with him and wink, "Not even close." He shakes his head at me as he laughs and opens the door for me to join his friends. When I enter the shed, I make sure to get my face back in check and smile at the guys.

"I wonder why you guys are late," Jamie taunts, wiggling his eyebrows. Elija flips him off, walking past me with a subtle brush of his hand against my back. The touch is enough to make my blood hum sweetly but not visible enough for his friends to tease us for.

He takes the last available seat on the couch on Benji's right and I hesitate, not sure where to go. Luckily, Elija notices and pats his thigh in silent invitation. That stupid, satisfied grin of his remains steadfast on his lips as I make my way over, horribly aware of the others' attention.

When I slowly sit down, the worry of squashing him is added to my nerves about the guys' reactions. I hate sitting on people's laps simply because I'm scared I'm either too heavy or my bones too pointy. My cheeks flare and I start fidgeting with the hair tie around my wrist.

Elija doesn't seem to share my doubts and pulls me all the way against him, so my feet are off the ground and my back is against his front. I notice Liam eying us before he diverts his attention and starts talking to Jamie. Looking around, I realize they're not watching us with avid curiosity, acting like this is completely normal. And maybe it is since we have been a bit touchy at school around them. It allows me to relax against Elija right up until doing so makes me realize how close we are. Then, my heart starts racing for a whole no reason.

It doesn't take long until Benji offers me a beer and I start sipping it. Everyone apart from Elija is drinking, and I'm guessing that's because he's the designated driver tonight. It's not like my last beer had a particularly great effect on me but I guess it's a good idea to try it one more time if only to see if not drinking on an empty stomach makes it better.

"Do you want me to drive today? You did it the last time," I offer after a few sips, realizing maybe Elija doesn't want to be the drive us home again. If I don't drink anymore, it'll definitely all be out of my system by the time we leave, so I could trade places with him. I definitely wouldn't mind.

"Oh, no, that's fine. But thank you," he tells the side of my neck, making me shudder slightly. The way his breath fans against my sensitive skin ignites every last cell in my body. "Are you cold?" Elija asks, clearly noting my reaction. I shake my head and clench my legs as inconspicuously as possible, trying to stop my body from reacting any further. The movement has the guy behind me chuckling, though.

I can tell I'm in trouble even before he whispers, "Are you turned on?" His mouth brushes against the shell of my ear with every syllable so I know the others can't possibly have heard it, but my eyes still scan the room frantically. We're not even doing anything wrong but somehow, I don't want the others to notice. When everyone seems to be busy in some other way, I shake my head in silent denial.

"I see. So if my hand moved up beneath that cute skirt of yours, I wouldn't find you wet for me?" he asks softly, teasingly letting his hand slide further up my inner thigh. I lock my legs together, biting back a sound at the friction the move provides.

My heart is thumping like a violent creature trapped behind my ribcage. Honestly, what is wrong with me? I can read smut at school without being affected but a few whispered words from Elija and I'm nearly a moaning mess?

I shake my head one more time to answer his last question, my voice positively gone. He chuckles behind me, and with a soft kiss to my neck, he puts his hand back to my knee.

"If you say so," he muses and I can just hear the satisfied grin he's surely wearing on his handsome face. I release a breath and slump against him, finishing my beer in the minutes to come. This evening is turning out to be very strenuous for my heart.

"I think we're going now," Jamie announces a few hours later.

"Already?" I ask. My words are slightly fuzzy, but I don't think I'm feeling much of an effect from the beers I've had otherwise. I feel cozy, not dizzy. It's actually kind of nice.

"Yeah, I'm a bit tired," my friend replies, making Benji laugh.

"Mhm, tired of not having Orion's tongue down your throat," he teases the couple.

"Or elsewhere," Elija adds.

"Okay, enough! Bye, guys," Orion snaps, his voice rough but his touch infinitely gentle as he takes Jamie's hand to drag him outside. I'm not sure how they plan on getting home, but they'll figure it out. I know Orion would sooner die than let anything happen to Jamie, and while the latter might not act it as openly, he definitely feels the same. Hence, I smile and wave a grinning Jamie off.

"Do you want to leave?" I ask Elija over my shoulder, readjusting myself on his lap a little to face him. Perhaps I accidentally and totally coincidentally rub myself against him a tad, hoping to tease him like he did to me earlier. I'm pretty sure he's been hard all evening, and I might have played into that a bit. I do like knowing he's as into me as much as I am into him.

"Absolutely," he replies, holding me by the waist as he gets up. "Bye guys!" he says a tad too urgently, pulling me toward the door. I laugh as we speed walk to his car.

"Why in such a hurry?"

"I need a moment, Florence. You've been teasing me all night and I need to get a grip on my self-control before locking us into the small, private space of my car," he says. I laugh some more and get into the vehicle, undeterred by his warning.

"You teased me first," I remind him helpfully as he starts driving.

"Really? Was I the one wearing nothing more than a towel earlier today?" he retorts, raising a brow at the road ahead as he pulls out of the driveway.

"So you didn't like that?" I challenge.

He huffs a laugh. "Hey there, no don't go putting words into my mouth. Feel free to parade around me mostly naked anytime you want. Fully naked too." He shrugs, oblivious to my rising blush even knowing he's only teasing. Now, do you want to go to my place or yours?" he asks.

"Mine, if that's okay. You could stay over if you want," I tell him. Maybe it's the booze granting me some extra confidence, but I'll gladly take advantage of it either way. If I could, I'd always be bold and go after what I want without doubting myself. Tonight, I don't want to part ways with Elija.

"Of course, if that's what you want." A silent beat passes before he groans. "Tell me something random," he demands. Sounding suddenly anguished.

"Why?" I chuckle.

"Because the silence leaves too much room for my mind to wander so I need a distraction. Just do it, please."

I take a bit of pity in him at the pleading note in his voice. Grinning to myself, I consider my next revelation. "Do you remember the time I was hit by a bus right before school?"

"How could I forget? What about it?"

"That was totally your fault," I muse. His head snaps to mine, his mouth slightly open in surprise and confusion. "Watch the road," I remind him, making him look ahead once more.

Hesitantly, he asks, "It was? I'm not following."

"I bet you aren't. The thing is, I was too busy ogling you as you sat in that other bus to realize the one ahead of yours was driving. Hence, it's your fault."

Elija laughs, shaking his head. "You're serious? You're not just making this up now that we're together?" he asks. I ignore the heat that blooms in my chest at his saying we're together and trudge on. With no label slapped onto our situation so far, hearing him say even something that could be open for interpretation feels nice.

Not that I questioned him and his intentions. I know he wants to do things right by me.

"As a heart attack," I confirm, sharing his smile.

The rest of the ride flies by quickly. As soon as we're in my room, though, I don't waste time to kiss Elija. Honestly, I've been watching his hands all ride, and to say that put some unholy thoughts in my mind would be an understatement. It's definitely all the smutty reading I do. It's got me thinking all those unhinged thoughts at the sight of something as innocent as *hands*.

Elija reacts instantly, drawing me in by the waist with ever so gentle hands. Even after I've been teasing him all night, he's gentle and patient as he explores my lips. Everything I don't want him to be right now. I tug on his hair the way I know he likes, then bite on his lower lip to finally get him to retaliate. The consequences are heavenly, coming in the shape of his tightening grip on my waist and a warning growl that only turns me on more. He does deepen the kiss, and I'm not sure he even notices I'm dragging him backwards until I collide with my bed, falling and taking him down on top of me.

He catches himself quickly, heaving most of his weight off me so I'm not crushed against the mattress, but I don't let him pull away. My arms tighten around his neck, kissing him once more until he catches up and kisses me back. He helps easing me further on the mattress so we're both on all the way, with him nestled between my open thighs and his arms framing my head as he keeps himself up.

I run my hands up his muscled arms and over his shoulders, then the length of his back until they reach the hem of his shirt. Greedy, I tug at it and he leans back, lifting his arms to help me take it off.

I hold his heated gaze before slowly letting my eyes trail down his chest and abs, the golden skin peppered with various tattoos. Here I thought books were exaggerating. I was wrong. This is a sight for sore eyes. His skin is taunt and smooth over his defined muscles, a smattering of hair trailing from below his navel towards the waistband of his pants.

I must be losing my mind because my first thought is that I want to lick him all over.

"Done staring?" Elija asks, his voice rough.

"I don't think I'll ever be, but you're lucky I want to feel you more than I want to see you right now" I lean up to get closer, so close that my heaving chest is pressed against his naked one and I can brush my lips over his jaw. His eyes get hooded as he watches me, pressing kiss upon kiss to his skin.

When my lips brush against his, he's the one that captures me and deepens the connection. He moves us back down, arching his back into me so I can feel the heat of his skin through the thin material of my shirt. I feel my nipples pebble as they press against him, eager for friction. I can tell by the low groan reverberating in his chest he feels it too.

He bites down on my bottom lip, and in return, I tug harder on his hair. He pulls away long enough to place his lips on my neck instead. He kisses his way along my jaw, down to my collar bone, nibbling and teasing until I'm breathless with the need to feel more of him. All of him.

My mind doesn't even process the words before I ask, "Do you have a condom?" Elija reels back as if a jack in the box had replaced my head, dousing my lust with a cold bucket of embarrassment. With the distance between us, he studies me closely, making my cheeks flush and my nerves rise. *Backtrack. Backtrack now. Wrong move. Rejection incoming.* My heart starts pounding as the silence stretches. *Isn't this what people our age who* are together, *do?* Jamie was rather vocal about his experience in the department, so I figured – it doesn't matter. I clearly figured wrong.

And when Elija's eyes soften as if addressing a child, I feel it like a punch to the gut. "You're drunk," he concludes instead of outright turning me down.

Something inside me rejects the notion. His assessment is patronizing, not to mention wrong. "I'm not. I'm nowhere near drunk, just more confident." Confident to know what I want and ask for it, or so I thought. The idea was quickly shattered with his apparent appalment at my suggestion. Fact remains, I'm sober enough to make decisions.

And sadly sober enough to remember this. The mortification will no doubt stick to me like a second skin from now on, tainting every second I spend in Elija's presence and never allowing me to sleep again. I cringe.

"Florence, I don't want you to regret anything in the morning. When we get to that point, it'll be with both of us sober and sure it's the right thing to do," he insists, leaning back a bit further.

I chuckle half-heartedly, trying to play down the gut-churning embarrassment. With every inch he pulls away, my brain seems to wake up more from its lust-induced slumber, and it's making me feel stupid. I finally scoot away and sit up against my headboard. "I'm sorry. I shouldn't have said anything," I tell him, crossing my arms over my chest even as I force a smile.

I can't believe I just threw myself at him like this. And now my cheeks are heating up uncomfortably, making it impossible for me to look at him.

"Florence, you don't have to apologize. I'd just like to take you on an actual date before I sleep with you." I resist the urge to bury my face in my hands and nod to my bed. It's even worse when he says it like that. Maybe it's a good thing he stopped this, though, because if I can't even talk about it, I definitely shouldn't do it.

"Yeah, totally. So, do you want to leave or?" I trail off, mortified.

"Was sleeping with you a condition to stay over?" he asks, and the distinguishable disappointment in his voice is enough to make me suck it up and meet his eyes.

"No! Of course not. I just thought you'd want –" He cuts me off before I can finish the sentence.

"Stop thinking about what I might desire for once, and tell me what *you* want," he counters. That makes my frantic thoughts come to a halt. Him, I want him. But he rejected me already and I'm not going to try to convince him, so I bite my tongue.

"I can see the wheels turning in your head. Speak your mind," he adds, seeing through me like he so often does.

Without granting myself time to second guess it, I tell him, "I don't want to go to bed all hot and bothered." The words leave me in barely more than a whisper, feeling forbidden on my tongue, but I can sense they're true as they pass my lips.

Instead of laughing or rejecting me like I was afraid, Elija looks surprised. Then, something darker, more desperate flashes over his features and he looks down at my lips. With a muttered a curse under his breath, he crosses the distance between us and slams his lips to mine.

I'm confused and unsure about his intentions, too stunned to kiss him back, and when he realizes that, he bites down on my bottom lip harder than before, demanding my participation. I gasp, giving him the opportunity to slip his tongue into my mouth.

I stop trying to anticipate his next move and decide to trust him, giving myself over to his control.

When he starts kissing his way down my neck, I don't try to stifle my moan. Who would have thought that such a simple touch could set my whole body on fire? A simple but skilled touch, I think to myself as he gently starts sucking on the place just below my ear, making my toes curl. It's different from his teasing before, the touches more intently placed. I tighten my hold on his hair and try to cross my thighs, wanting some kind of release from the pressure building between my legs.

Elija chuckles but doesn't let me move my legs. Instead, he pushes his hips harder against me, making me suck in a silent breath. "So needy," he tuts playfully, kissing the corner of my lips. The sudden one-eighty of his demeanor, going from rejecting me to *this,* gives me whiplash and makes me wet at the same time.

Is this him listening to what I said I wanted? If so, what happens next? My skin is buzzing with anticipation.

He continues kissing his way down my body, pressing his lips onto the fabric of my shirt. He stops when he reaches the waistline of my skirt, looking up as if seeking confirmation.

"Can I take this off?" he asks softly. I nod mindlessly, too far gone to feel insecure. When the skirt is off, he doesn't give me time to feel ashamed. Not with the way his eyes roam my body.

"I definitely made a good choice with these," he murmurs, slipping a finger beneath the lace hugging my hips, pulling it back, and letting it snap against my skin.

He kneels between my knees and his eyes hold mine as he leans down, pressing a kiss to the inside of my thigh. He spreads my legs wider and softly bites down on my other thigh. I close my eyes, trying to take in all the sensations.

"Tell me if you want me to stop, okay?" he asks against my skin. I nod.

Chapter 29

Elija

My heart is racing and my mind reeling as I try to decide what to do with Florence. I meant what I said about wanting to take her on a date before we have sex, but who am I to deny her an orgasm when she asked so nicely? I'm still reeling because she asked in the first place. I really thought we'd take things a lot slower, that we'd spend a few months dating before she ever felt comfortable enough to let me touch her. I would have waited gladly, but this... Well, it's a surprise but not one I can say I mind.

I really want to do this right with her.

I press a kiss to her skin again, this time just below her navel, and Florence whines nearly inaudible. Gooseflesh blooms in the wake of my touch, making me smile against her skin. I take the sound as a sign she's getting impatient and decide tonight won't be the night I show her how good endless teasing can feel.

No, tonight, I'll give her what she asks for.

I slip my hands beneath her lace underwear, waiting for a second to see if she wants to stop me before pulling it down. After kissing her thigh one last time, reveling in how smooth her skin is, I spread her legs wider for me to finally put my lips where she wants them.

Florence's hips buck at the first touch of my lips against her clit, and she buries one of her hands in my hair while the other one takes hold of her sheets. The contact was barely more than a whisper of a touch, just a gentle first kiss to her exposed skin. The fact that she's already so responsive has my blood rushing south, making my dick so hard it aches. It only makes me crave her more.

I flatten my tongue against her and lick her from top to bottom, groaning at the taste before I move my tongue to circle her most sensitive bundle of nerves. Today is as much about her getting to know what she likes as making her come, so I'll try to give her a variety of new sensations that she can give me feedback on later.

Looking up at her, I take in her closed eyes and the uneven rise and fall of her chest. A pang of regret hits at not having taken off her shirt earlier, but I was worried she might feel too exposed. Now, I get the feeling it wouldn't have been a problem. Not with how lost she seems, how comfortable in her skin and with this entire situation.

As I keep playing with her, exploring her skin eagerly, I pay close attention to every little reaction she has. The more she relaxes underneath my mouth and hands, her face twisting with pleasure, the more I allow myself to let go of my worries and enjoy it to. I savor her taste, revel in her approving moans.

When I suck her clit into my mouth, sliding one of my fingers through her folds to wet it, she curses under her breath. That's the final indication that she's letting herself go; when she stops being the perfectly polite girl and starts swearing. If only a little. It's unusual for her, but I'm satisfied to know I can make her stop thinking.

I slide one finger inside of her without any resistance, curling it against her G-spot. That grants me the pleasure of feeling her walls tighten against me, and it's me that groans this time. Is that how she would squeeze my dick if I were fucking her? Holding on so tightly it's like her body wants to keep me close. The thought is maddeningly arousing, so much so that I press my hips against the mattress to alleviates some of the ache in my balls.

When I find a rhythm with both my hand and my mouth that she seems to enjoy, I stick to it. She's so swollen and dripping, her moans growing desperate and needy, I think it's time I try to really get her there. Keeping up a steady rhythm, I flatten my free arm against her stomach to hold her down. She's shifting more and more relentlessly as she grows closer to coming, her fingers in my hair tightening and releasing my strands repeatedly. "Elija," my name falls from her lips like a prayer, making me groan against her wet pussy. Her walls tighten around me in response.

When her legs start shaking and her hips roll to grind against my face, I suck her clit into my mouth again, grazing my teeth over the bundle of nerves. That does the trick, and I feel her come apart with a low moan.

She clenches so tightly around my finger that I'm forced to keep it in place, so I just gently lick her through her release. Only when she slumps against the bed, her hand pushing my head away almost too softly to feel, do I rise from between her legs and kiss her lips instead.

"Damn, that was," she trails off, her eyes still shut, despite my silent pleading that she'll look at me. She looks happy, though, relaxed and sated as she melts into her mattress.

"Glad you approve," I tease her with a kiss on the tip of her nose. She smiles tiredly and nuzzles herself further against the bed.

"Where are your PJs?" I ask since she seems rather unwilling to move. It's kind of cute to see her shrug tiredly, and I improvise, grabbing my shirt from the ground and handing it to her. She's got a closet full of her clothes right next to me and thanks to earlier tonight, I do know which drawers contain her stuff. Still, I like the idea of seeing her in something of mine too much to pass up on the opportunity. Especially when I can still taste her on my lips.

I help her pull it over her head, drag it down until it falls mid-thigh, and then untie the shirt she's wearing beneath it. She shrugs out of it and closes her eyes again, smiling to herself. Meanwhile, I'm trying to get over how good she looks in my shirt. Better than I even hoped. I could seriously get used to this.

I get on the bed next to her and pull her against my chest, sighing at the way we fit together.

"Wait, what about you," Florence mutters, presumably feeling my hard-on against her back.

"Just ignore it, it'll go away," I tell her, but she turns around to look at my face, blinking those big, dazed eyes at me.

"Isn't it uncomfortable? I can help you, you just need to tell me what to do," she says even as her eyes start drooping. I laugh softly and cup her cheek, running my thumb back and forth. She leans into it as always, and my heart skips a beat.

"I'm perfectly content. Just sleep," I tell her. It's a testament of how tired she is that she agrees so readily, nodding and scooting a little closer. I keep caressing her skin as my other arm wraps around her waist to keep her close. When her head is tucked underneath my chin and her clean scent invades my nose, I take an unintentional deep breath.

I realize I'm falling hard and fast, and the fact doesn't even scare me. She feels safe in my arms, so good I know it's how things are supposed to be.

"Thanks," she mutters against my chest, her lips brushing the skin right above my heart.

I wake up to an empty bed. It makes my stomach tighten with worry, all sorts of doubts infiltrating my mind. Where did Florence go? Why did she leave? Does she regret what happened last night?

The last one makes me freak out the most. She *asked* me to finish her off, but maybe she really was drunk despite her insistence and it was the beer talking? Worry tightens my gut. I shouldn't have taken her up on the offer. I should have –

"Morning," her voice interrupts my jumbled thoughts. She's smiling, wearing nothing more than a towel again. "Sorry for sneaking out on you but I felt sweaty and nasty," she adds, perhaps taking notice of my worried expression. I sigh in relief, glad that she didn't change her mind about what we did last night.

"Geez, leave a note next time. Or even better, wake me," I say on a laugh.

"Will do," she promises over her shoulder, walking over to the dresser.

I push up on my elbows to see her better and ask, "So, do you have any plans for today?" I'd like to spend more time with her, but I don't want to intrude on her existing plans if she has any.

I'm pondering all the dates I could possibly take her on so last minute when the towel drops. My smile freezes on my face, shock and surprise warring through my system as I try to process what I'm looking at. Florence, her backside to me as she faces the drawer... Naked as the day she was born. Naked and glowing from her shower. I can't do anything but stare at her naked backside, groaning inwardly. She's fucking stunning.

"Take a picture, it'll last longer," she teases me, smiling over her shoulder before putting on her underwear. She only turns to me when she's wearing a matching set of white lace.

My poor dick starts throbbing again as I take in her subtle curves. It took a while for me to fall asleep last night, and this is reminding me why.

"A warning next time," I tell her, averting my eyes before I take her right back to bed and go against my word from last night. First date who? Never heard of it. Florence is mine anyway, who cares about the order of things.

I do. Shit.

"Sure." She brushes me off, completely unconcerned about how she's torturing me. "So, today? I don't have any plans," she tells me, throwing on an oversized shirt before climbing back into bed with me. "What about you?"

"I thought I might ask a beautiful girl out on a date. Do you think she'll say yes?" I muse, running the back of my hand up her arm.

"Mhm, who knows," she teases me, leaning over to kiss me. She lingers for a few seconds. "I think she might," she hums.

"Later tonight, Jamie's throwing a party. We could grab lunch, maybe go to the park for a while, and swing by at his if you're down," I propose. It's probably a lot to ask of her, spending two entire days in a row with me and parts of it with my friends, non-stop with no chance to recharge her social battery. If she's feeling anything like me, it might not drain her as much to be around me, but I still wouldn't blame her if she declined or made another offer.

But if anything, her smile grows. "That sounds great. You need to take your guitar with you, though."

"Only if you bring your iPad. I want to see your drawings." Florence blushes shily but agrees.

I soon head home to get ready, looking forward to the day we have planned.

Chapter 30

Florence

"Where do you want to go for lunch? I'm thinking Thai, maybe," Elija asks, holding my hand as he leads me to his car. He picked me up a few minutes ago, coming to my door like a true gentleman, and now, we're trying to figure out what to eat.

"That works for me. I'm not a picky eater," I reply, knowing it's a rich comment coming from me. Strictly speaking, I really am not a picky eater. I just can't eat. But he wants to grab lunch, so I'll have to figure something out and do it fast. I don't want another embarrassing breakdown like I did the first night on the camping trip, knowing when it's just the two of us he'll be even more aware of my mood changes.

Half an hour later, he and I are sitting on a blanket in the park, eating our takeout. I'm playing music in the background, and there are a lot of distractions around, making it easier for me to stomach my food.

Right now, I almost manage to forget that I have silly eating issues. It makes me feel blissfully normal, sitting here with Elija under the sun with so many strangers around doing the same. It's nice.

When the song that's currently playing is interrupted by the ding of a message, I risk a glance at my screen to see who it's from, the reaction an instinct by now. I don't get a lot of messages, ever, so on the rare occasions that I do, my curiosity quickly makes me cave.

This time, my curiosity only grows at the sight of the banner. My mom replied to my Instagram story.

I'm surprised enough to open the message. After all, it's not usual for my mother to text me. Much less on my socials.

I posted a picture of my food and the park on my story a few minutes ago, to which my mother said.

Her: Are you sure you want to eat that? I saw your picture from last night, Honey. Your clothes were struggling to keep it together.

I stare at my phone, rereading the message until my disbelieving confusion morphs into hurt. Like always, her words make my insecurities rear their ugly heads as if on demand, making me feel about two inches tall. A lump tightens in my throat, the bliss from a few moments before evaporating. Why does she have to do this? Now, of all times. Sure, I've noticed that my parents have started being less discrete about their dislike of me, less eager to keep up their façade, but this? This was so uncalled for.

I can't help myself, I go to my account to see my most recent post. It's a picture I took of the outfit Elija chose for me. It was risky to post since I was in his room, using his mirror for the selfie, but apparently, my parents are more concerned about my figure than my whereabouts.

I delete the picture, blinking back tears. I honestly really liked it and was proud to show off what Elija dressed me in, but it's ruined. My often has the ability to do that. Before, I saw myself smiling happily. Now it's a girl with clothes that can barely keep it together. I don't recognize myself, it's just a distorted body, revolting and dirty.

I can feel the blood draining from my face as my stomach churns with nausea. I hate it. This familiar self-loathing at the thought that I just ate something when I didn't even have to. I wasn't that hungry. I shouldn't have stuffed my face. I could have waited until dinner, or longer even. I don't need to eat twice a day. I could have put this feeling off if I hadn't tried to seem normal when I'm not. I'm broken and weak and all wrong for feeling so different from everyone else.

Waves of hot and cold wreck my body in turn, and I can feel a cool sweat break out on my skin. I tighten my fists, letting my nails dig into the flesh of my palms as I try to ground myself and breathe through this moment.

A warm hand touches my arm, making me aware that I'm shaking. I look up to see Elija's worried expression, but I don't hear him speak. I can't hear the chirping birds, my music, or the screaming kids in the background. It's all tuned out by the self-loathing pulsing through me.

When I feel a familiar rhythm against my skin, I realize Elija's tapping it. I close my eyes and force myself to breathe, focusing on the beat. I'm fine. It's fine. It's just words, they can't hurt me. They don't mean anything. Food is necessary. It's not as bad as it feels.

"Thanks," I murmur finally, keeping my eyes shut. I don't want to look at Elija. I don't want to see the pity or confusion on his beautiful features.

"What just happened, Florence?" he asks softly. I chuckle watery, shrugging.

"Nothing." When Elija doesn't speak up again, I decide to look at him. He's staring at his hand on my arm but, noticing my eyes on him, looks up. His jaw is clenched, and I can tell he has things to say but tries to hold them back. Sighing, I hand him my phone without a word.

He reads the message from my mom before looking at me with furrowed eyebrows. "What is this?" he asks.

"Mom being mom." I shrug.

"She's kidding, right? Florence, she's talking absolute shit. Your last post is beautiful, and your clothes fit perfectly," he protests. I merely shrug one more time as I lie down on my back. If we're really having this conversation, I'd rather look at the sky than him.

"Wait, where did it go? Did you take it down?" he asks a few beats later. I nod. His voice softens. "You can't let her get to you, Florence. I think your picture was perfect."

"Whatever," I tell him.

"Come on, don't shut me out." He tugs at my arm until I'm sitting upright again. Then, he nods to my food, attempting a smile. "Your food's getting cold. Let's eat," he suggests. Clearly, it's his attempt to change the topic because he can tell I don't want to talk about it. He doesn't know it only makes me feel worse, this reminder that I'm all wrong.

I can't help it. I bite down on my bottom lip to stop it from quivering as my eyes fill with tears. I shake my head, not wanting to do this in front of him, trying to deny myself from doing this. It doesn't work and Elija notices.

"Hey, don't cry. What's wrong? What did I do?" Elija asks, hastily pulling me into a hug. It's the straw that breaks the camel's back, his kindness breaking my heart and making me feel undeserving.

I start shaking and he pulls back, cupping my face to wipe away my tears.

"Talk to me," he pleads with me, his tone sincere in his worry.

"I can't," I whisper hoarsely. My throat hurts from how much the lump in my throat is growing. That, and the effort to keep down the few bites I've already eaten. The sour taste in the back of my tongue makes me know I'm fighting a losing battle, but I'm forcing myself not to heave with single-minded determination.

"You can't what?" Elija probes gently, still caressing me. I wish it were enough to flood my frozen limbs with warmth.

"Eat," I clarify, looking anywhere but at him. This is the first time I've said it out loud, the first time I've admitted it to anyone but myself.

"What are you talking about? You just have to calm down a bit and it'll be fine. Tell me how to help," he argues, oblivious to the true meaning of my words. Swallowing hard, I try again.

"That's not what I mean. Elija, I can't eat. I have an eating disorder." The words taste bitter in my mouth, and I feel like taking them back as soon as they're out. There's a reason why I've never told anyone. It's no one else's problem, and I regret my decision of speaking up when Elija's face falls. The crease between his brow deepens as he searches my face, and I feel him pulling back further. All the while my heart drops to my stomach like a cold rock, landing right on top of my food. Fuck, I'm tired of this.

"I-" Elija breaks off, shaking his head. "I don't know what to say," he finally admits, looking lost. It twists the knife in my stomach. I'm stupid! So stupid for telling him! Of course he doesn't know what to say. This isn't normal. I'm not normal. He shouldn't have to deal with my weird issues, not when he's just looking for a good time. It's my happy, optimistic exterior that he's interested in, not this ugly distorted version of me that only I can see.

I wish I could take it back. It doesn't matter, anyway. I'm fine. He shouldn't know. No one should.

My forced chuckle is watery even as I feel like breaking down or running away. In a desperate attempt to make him look at me the way he did before, I grab my food and start loading up the next bite.

"I'm just kidding." I laugh again, sounding almost frantic to my own ears. I must look like a lunatic as I shove the food into my mouth, chewing as if it was sawdust. "It's fine," I add after swallowing. I don't dare to look at Elija again before I force down the next bite. I nearly gag, but I don't dare stop. *Just keep eating. Take it back. Make it go away.*

"Florence," I hear him protest softly, but I don't turn. I just prepare my next bite, even as tears flow down my cheeks.

"Florence, hey, stop!" Elija says more forcefully, taking hold of my arm again.

I shake my head, crying harder and finally meeting his eyes. "It's fine." I attempt a weak smile.

"Fuck. Stop saying that when it's not. Now, calm down and tell me how I can help. Please," he sounds as frantic as I feel, clearly out of his depth and while I feel the same, I feel the need to soothe him. It's my fault he's feeling like this now. I have to take it back and make it all fine again.

I try to do as he ordered, taking deep breaths to calm down. As soon as my frenzy wears off, I can feel the food I've eaten worm its way down my esophagus like a lump of lead. I clamp my mouth shut against the bile crawling up my throat and clutch my stomach, digging my nails into my skin to feel anything but that. Anything but disgusting.

"Don't do that. You're fine, Florence. It's fine," Elija says desperately, placing his hands over mine again. He taps my rhythm softly.

"You don't have to stay," I tell him quietly. This must suck for him. He wanted to have a nice date, and I ruined it by acting like a nutcase. Even worse, I can't seem to pull myself together.

"I'm not going anywhere, okay? Let's just calm down and talk," he repeats.

"Why are you doing this?" I ask, blinking back a new wave of tears.

"Florence, I care about you. I hate to see you cry, but I'm certainly not going to leave you when you're feeling bad."

"You're being too nice," I argue, shaking my head.

"Please don't say that," he mutters.

"Why?"

"Because it seriously makes me wonder how you've been treated by others up to now, and I don't think I'd like the answer."

"I've never been treated poorly," I protest.

"Florence, if you think me sticking around in a moment like this is some heroic behavior, you haven't been treated the way you deserved."

Chapter 31

Elija

I hope I look good in orange because if I ever meet this girl's parents, so help me god, it'll be my daily clothes' color for a while.

Florence is taking a nap on my chest right now while I'm glaring at the sky. We talked some more after she calmed down, but the whole interaction must've drained her because she passed out as soon as we lay down. She didn't say much, just that it's sometimes hard for her to eat and that it gets worse when someone makes a comment about her appearance. Which, with the way her mom texted her, I'm guessing isn't too rare.

I can hardly wrap my head around it. To me, Florence is such an awesome person with a beautiful soul and body. There's nothing wrong with her, there never could be, but she somehow can't see that. I hate that for her, and I hate her parents for reinforcing her insecurities with their remarks, maybe even for being the source of it. This is the second time I witnessed this kind of behavior of her mother, and it makes me seethe. To *bully* your own child. What kind of monster do you have to be to stoop to such levels? Florence deserves the world and here she is, stuck with neglecting, dispassionate, hateful parents.

And to think she's never told anyone about that or her eating disorder. She's been dealing with it by herself for who knows how long, and here I was, reacting like a total jerk when I found out.

I didn't mean to be so stupid, but her admission took me by surprise. I'm not well-informed about ed's and didn't know what to say, and it only upset her more as a result when the admission must have been hard either way. The second I'm alone, I'll do my due diligence and figure out how I can help her. She deserves nothing less than to have someone fight for her.

Florence stirs in my arms, taking a few moments before she slowly sits up. "How long was I asleep for?" she mumbles.

"Only about thirty minutes. Are you feeling better?" I ask, gently brushing a loose strand from her face. My need to take care of her, to protect her and somehow make sure she's happy is at an all-time high. She feels fragile in my arms, like so many precious things are.

"Yeah, I am. I'm sorry about before," she apologizes for the thousandth time. I've told her not to apologize before, but I'll keep saying it until she understands that she did nothing wrong.

"You have no reason to be, Florence. What do you say you show me your drawings now? I've been dying to see them since you first said you liked drawing," I ask, feeling that it's time to change the topic and talk about something happier.

"Oh, right. They're not that good. It's just a way to pass the time," she rambles, her cheeks heating up.

"She said before showing me some first-class art, I bet," I tease her.

"Don't get your expectations up, it's not fair," she complains. Meanwhile, I'm just glad I managed to coax a smile out of her. She unlocks her iPad and hands it to me. Seeing as I have access to all her works, I start off by checking out the most recent one. I can't help but gape at it.

"Florence, that's incredible. It's Lina and Mattheo, right? The time they're locked in a staring contest after she splashed the coffee she was supposed to get him all over his shirt," I say, referring to the characters of the book she wouldn't let me flip through.

"Yeah," she says shily. Then, as if stumbling over the realization, her gaze snaps to me. "Wait, how do you know that?"

Oops. Guess the cat is out of the bag now. "Right, I meant to tell you. Since you didn't let me read your annotated book, I bought a copy myself. It was really nice, but I think I prefer the first book of the author's new series. I just finished it today and the ending was perfect." When she just stares at me, I laugh. "Don't look so surprised."

"I- You read one of my books?" she asks.

"Yeah. You really sold it to me with that little summary," I tell her. Slowly, she breaks out into the biggest grin. Then, she throws her arms around my neck and hugs me.

"Thank you," she whispers, making it sound like it's for a lot more than just reading one silly book. I hug her back, not sure why I deserve such a reaction for such a simple act but happy I clearly pleased her.

"It's no big deal. I enjoyed it. Besides, now we have another thing to talk about," I say. And we do. For about an hour, we talk about the book we now have in common and whatever other books I need to read. I make a list out of them, putting her favorites at the top. After that, I play a few songs for her to which she pulls out a whole planner. Yep, she made a planner on how to get me famous, full of research of other indie musicians and how they established a name for themselves. That and so much more. She must have spent hours on this, just for me. My heart swells as I listen to her presenting all the information, looking so invested.

This girl is really something else.

"So, are you still up for the party?" I ask her as the sun sets.

"Yeah, can we swing by my place first, though? I'd like to change."

I don't question it, rather agreeing easily. It's not like there's an exact time when we should be at the party and even if that were the case, I wouldn't care. The lady gets what she wants. "Sure thing," I tell her. The two of us pack up our things and go back to Florence's place. She tells me to wait in the car since she won't be long, and I don't question it when she comes back wearing an oversized hoodie. It's windy tonight so at least she'll be warm. Other than that, I see she's wearing her hair down. It's different than usual but no less beautiful.

"Yay, look who made it!" Jamie squeals excitedly, throwing his arms around mine and Florence's necks and situating himself between us. Apparently, the party has been going on for a while, judging by the state some of these kids are in.

"Would you mind if we ubered home tonight? I'd like to drink a bit myself and I'm not going to drive under the influence," I tell Florence, ignoring Jamie when he already moves onto another side quest. He can be a real whirlwind of excitement when he's in his element, and socializing is just that.

"Yeah, sure. If you don't want to leave your car here, I can stay sober," she offers, but I brush her off.

"It's fine, really. Besides, if you drove me home, my car would just be at your place instead, so it doesn't make much of a difference. We can share an uber so you don't have to get into a stranger's car by yourself, don't worry," I assure her. No way I'm letting her do that. I've seen the news.

Benji appears out of nowhere, and he must have known we had arrived because he immediately hands us two beers. We've only just made it into the living room where most of the guests are. How fast do news here travel? I accept my beer, getting a good whiff of Benji's last joint, the scent still clinging to his clothes in the most familiar way. I smelled it in the air the moment we got inside the mansion since Jamie isn't bothered when people smoke inside, but the smell isn't oppressive yet. With so much air in the giant building, it's not like a few people sharing some weed will have a huge impact but this close to Benji, it's more pronounced.

Man has made it into a real habit, though he insists it's all chill. His parents smoke the same shit, it's where he got it from, and that reassures him that it's not a habit he needs to quit.

Seeing his puffy eyes and noting the vacant look in his eyes, not to mention the fact that he doesn't try to initiate a conversation, I nudge Florence. "Do you want to dance?" I ask over the music, knowing Benji would rather be alone right now anyway than forced into talking to us.

"Sure!" she yells back after a quick glance at Benji. I'm sure she knows as much as I do that he'll be just fine on his own. I pull her into the living room, where the music is the loudest, and as more bodies press in around us and our beers get lighter in our hands, Florence gradually dances more openly.

Laughing and dancing wildly as she is now, it's all I can do to stare at her. She throws her head around, unbothered by the long strands falling into her face, and jumps along with the people around us. I don't even have it in me to care that I must seem lame as hell, standing here and swaying slightly rather than going wild.

I've never seen Florence act like this before, and after seeing that sad, defeated look on her face earlier, it makes me all the more desperate to soak this moment up and let it calm my lingering worry. *She's going to be okay.*

"I'm going to grab another drink. Do you want something?" I ask her after a solid half an hour. I'd rather not leave her side, but if I already decided on not driving, I might as well indulge in more than one beer. Otherwise it's wasted calories, seeing as I can hardly feel an effect from the first one.

"Yes, sure. Thank you," she replies, heaving a breath and wiping her hair from her forehead. Her face is glowing and she looks elated.

"I'll be right back, stay here," I instruct. I don't like leaving here alone but we're at Jamie's place so there won't be any weirdos around, and I don't want to kill her vibe by dragging her after me like a controlling ass. Either way, I'll try to get back fast.

When I enter the kitchen, I nearly groan. There are a ton of people standing in line for a beer since Jamie insists on having someone hand them out instead of letting people get them themselves. That way, he wants to make sure no one knocks themselves out too badly or whatever. It's a bad time for him to be cautious.

I could try to get to his private stash in his room, but then I'd risk interrupting him and Orion... I haven't seen either in a while, not that I've been looking, but it leaves me hesitant to go upstairs.

I'll be here for a while.

Chapter 32

Florence

I'm vibing by myself after Elija leaves, only interacting with the near strangers around me when a few nice girls see me standing alone and encourage me to keep going. Their exaggerated whooping makes me both blush and feel happy. Confident even, if such a thing is possible after the day I had.

One thing soon becomes clear though; dancing and jumping wearing a hoodie is not appropriate unless the goal is to sweat excessively. It's sad that one part of my mind thinks that at least I'm burning off the calories of my lunch...

"Oh, shit! I'm so sorry," someone says as they stumble into me, and I feel his drink soak through my hoodie the next second. I hiss and arch my back away from the cold liquid, then turn around to come face to face with Liam. He looks unsteady on his feet and his expression is so stricken, I wholeheartedly believe he tripped and spilled his drink on accident. The relief that I'm not experiencing another Lynn situation is enough for me to smile at him.

"Don't worry about it," I brush him off. Who cares if it's my second clothing item in a short while that gets ruined? First, my favorite shirt. Now, this. I'm on a roll. At least this time, I'm sure it'll wash out and if I can look past how sticky it is, I can almost pretend the spilled drink is just what I needed against my feverish skin.

"I'll help you soak it. It'll stain if you wait," he offers, his words just slightly uneven. "Come on." He takes my wrist gently and starts pulling me through the crowd. I look over my shoulder, hoping to see Elija somewhere already. I don't want him to think I ditched him and he has my phone since I don't have pockets so I can't text him.

"It's no big deal, really. I told Elija I'd wait here," I tell my friend over the music.

"He'll be fine, Florence. Besides, I kind of wanted to talk to you so will you please follow me? I don't want to add ruining your sweater to the list of things I have to apologize for," he mumbles, stopping to look at me. I sigh and nod. He wants to *apologize*? I guess I should at least hear him out then. I follow him up the stairs until he pushes open an empty room.

"All right, this is Jamie's room. Take off your hoodie, I'll wash it in the sink of his bathroom," Liam says as soon as he closed the door behind us. I'm too busy taking in my friend's room to follow his orders, though.

I figured his family might have money, as most people at our school do, but I didn't know he was rich. I mean, a TV the size of a projection screen and speakers behind his bed kind of rich. Other than that, his room is rather basic. Everything is grey and the LEDs behind his TV are set on yellow. A fluffy carpet takes up most of the floor. It's comfortable and clean.

"Flo?" Liam interrupts my marveling.

"Right, sorry," I say, quickly shrugging my hoodie off and throwing it at him.

"Woah, girl. A warning would have been nice," Liam says after catching it, averting his gaze to the floor. I realize I'm in nothing but my white bra now, which my intoxicated mind seems strangely okay with. *Not much more revealing than some of the crochet tops I've worn to school. Got no boobs to show off anyway.*

I giggle as I ask him, "Never seen a girl in a bra before?" I walk past him into the ensuite bathroom. It's open to the rest of the room. Fancy.

Liam follows me, his cheeks slightly red and I have to stifle a laugh. He gets to work with the cleaning, avoiding looking at me at all costs. It's nice of him. I'm sure I'll appreciate it tomorrow and with that in mind, I turn slightly so it's mostly my back facing him.

I don't want to make him uncomfortable but my inhibitions just really aren't that high when it comes to what others might consider revealing clothes. I doubt anyone but Elija has ever seen me as a sexual being, including myself most of the time. All my important parts are covered like they would be in a bikini and this moment isn't anything more than him cleaning up a mess he made. And apparently, his sudden growing of a conscience.

"So, what did you want to talk about?" I prompt.

"Oh, right. I don't know where to start so I'll just say it. I'm sorry. For more than the hoodie, though I'm not proud of that either," he starts. Then, he looks at me expectantly while I have no idea what he's talking about. I must be wearing my thoughts on my face since he chuckles. "I've been rude to you when you didn't deserve it, Flo. That's what I'm apologizing for."

"Oh," I say. I can't argue with him there, I guess. When the silence stretches on for too long, I ask, "Why'd you do it?"

"Well, I guess you could say I had a crush on you. Had, being the keyword since I'm over it now. You and Elija are good together, and I won't repeat a past mistake and try to destroy that for him. Or you. I'm actually here with Sarah. She's the one that told me to apologize to you or she won't consider going on a date with me." He chuckles, smiling brighter than I've ever seen. "She's waiting downstairs somewhere. I really like her, and I guess I have you to thank for that," he adds with a sheepish smile.

"That's great! I'm really happy for you," I tell him honestly. Who would have thought that he'd be the one to apologize so sincerely for a shot with another girl? It's pretty romantic considering I never took him as someone who'd admit his faults.

Liam turns off the water and lays my wet hoodie on the edge of the sink before turning to me, standing just a few feet away.

"Only needs to dry now," he says.

I pat his arm and squeeze it in a friendly gesture, trying to convey there's no bad blood. I'd hug him if it weren't for my current state of undress. Not that I think it would be anything else than two friends hugging, but the thought of Elija and his feelings toward that stops me. With any of the other guys, I wouldn't worry about him being upset, but Liam's a whole different story so a bicep squeeze it is.

"Thanks." He places a hand atop mine and squeezes it back. It's an innocent touch, and I'm teasing when I bring a warning finger up in the air and say, "You better be good to Sarah." He grins down at me, and just when he opens his mouth to retort something else, the door swings open.

I turn my head to find Elija staring at me, standing in the doorway with his hands clenched and an expression of disbelief on his face. His brows furrow, his hands unclenching and then clenching again as anger replaces the confusion. Anger and betrayal. For half a second, I'm scared he'll attack Liam. If looks could kill, the man still touching my hand on his arm would be dead on the floor.

My hand on his arm. Me in a bra. Shit!

I hastily step back from Liam but even though I want to explain, the fire in Elija's eyes makes it impossible for me to speak. My tongue is a useless, stunned deadweight in my mouth, words evading me. What can I say knowing their history that wouldn't set him off? *It's not what it looks like? Let me explain?*

Elija's gaze goes back and forth between Liam and me until he finally settles on me. His chest heaves, and the look of scorn with underlying disgust is like a punch to the gut. He's *disgusted* with me. He thinks I came up here with Liam to take off my clothes, to stab him in the back like Ricky did. Before my panic can take root, I tell myself it's fine. It's a misunderstanding. He is reading this situation completely wrong but it's fixable.

I open my mouth to start explaining, but Elija cuts me off.

"Don't!" is all he grits before storming out of the room. I snap out of my daze, running after him and pushing past drunk people to catch up. I finally manage to grab his wrist when we're on the lawn, making him whip around.

"Really? Fucking *Liam*?" he yells in my face, looking down at me with enough distaste to make me want to cower. He looks unlike himself, his eyes a little bloodshot and his expression wild. I don't think he'd hurt me, but I still take a step back.

"We were just talking," I tell him, pleading with him with my eyes to believe me.

"Fuck, Florence, that is exactly what she said!" he yells, running his hands through his hair and tugging at his roots. It's like he's at war with himself, wanting to believe me but thinking he cannot. He looks so lost that my heart aches for him.

"Elija, do you honestly think I'd cheat on you?" We're not officially together but we're clearly something. We're *together*. That means everyone else is off-limits.

The accusation in his gaze makes my stomach twist, but I know he's not thinking clear. That he trusted a girl before and it backfired so he's wary. So instead of being offended, I try to reassure him. "I am not Ricky," I add softly.

Elija stares at me, still breathing heavily, but he seems to be calming down. Like my words might actually have gotten through to him enough to remind him to stay in the presence rather than letting what happened in the past cloud his judgement. I take a step toward him, reaching out to touch his chest when a voice stops me.

"Flo, you left your hoodie," Liam yells from somewhere behind me. I don't turn around, but Elija's eyes move past me. His gaze hardens as he looks at the other guy, and I know I'm losing him again. He starts shaking his head to himself before striding off without another glance at me.

This time, I don't follow. I tried to remedy this immediately, but maybe he needs to cool down before we can have an actual conversation. For a change, I'll be the one trying to help him however I can. That includes giving him space when he needs it.

I walk back to Liam defeatedly, taking my hoodie from him without a word.

"I'm really sorry. I know what he must be thinking," he trails off, looking positively chastised about what he did with Ricky for the first time since I met him. If I weren't feeling like such a dirty idiot, I'd finally ask him about his side of that story, about what compelled him to betray his friend. There's no excuse, but I feel like there has to be something else no one knows about. I don't think Liam is a horrible person.

"It'll be fine. He just needs to cool down," I tell him, trying to reassure myself more than him. He nods slightly, though his features remain strained as he looks at the corner Elija disappeared around.

When his eyes return to me, shivering in my wet hoodie, he asks, "Do you need a ride home?"

"You drank tonight. Besides, Sarah is waiting for you. I'll just call an uber," I reassure him. Just because I ruined my night with Elija doesn't mean he has to fuck up things with Sarah when he seems to really like her. He insists on at least paying for the ride, so he calls an uber from his phone and waits with me until it arrives.

By the time we say our goodbyes, I'm shaking from the cold. It might be spring but the nights are still bitingly fresh.

I get in the backseat and confirm with the driver that I'm the one who called him. Then, I look out of the window and try to think of a way to make it up to Elija. I was stupid to get so close to Liam with my top off, but it's not like I meant anything by it. I just need to get Eli to listen to me. I know he trusts me, deep down, I'm sure he does. It's just the heat of the moment that made him snap.

About thirty minutes into my pondering, my eyes refocus on the window and I realize that I don't recognize my surroundings. My heartbeat spikes and my blood grows cold. The street we're on is abandoned and lined with small houses and apartment complexes. I can't see a single light on, and I curse myself for not having paid more attention.

I lean over to look at the driver's phone in the front. I saw when I got in that he had my, or rather Liam's request open on it, but that's gone now, the screen black. *What the hell.* Isn't uber supposed to be safe? Did Liam notice that I'm being taken off course? Or did the driver cancel the ride after I got in?

Is this the part where I die? I can hear the blood rushing in my ears but I force my fear to stay down. I'm not having a panic attack right now. The last thing I need is to be completely at the driver's mercy, unable to control my own limbs or even breathe.

I reach for my phone, intending to call Elija or send him my location. I know he's mad at me right now and there's the possibility he'll ignore me but someone has to pick up eventually. I hope it's him. The other guys are probably all completely out of control by now and there's no way my parents would care enough to take my call even if they were home.

My hand finds the seam of my skirt and with a start, I realize Elija still has my phone because I have no pockets Oh no. No, no, no! Please, this can't be happening. Forcing myself to take subtle, deep breaths, I try to find my voice.

Before I can say anything, the car comes to a halt. With a short look in the rearview mirror, where his eyes lock on my wide ones, the driver gets out and walks around the car. My instincts take over as I unbuckle my seatbelt with shaky fingers, throwing the door open. The driver was about to open it himself, which means the door effectively hits him in the gut. He doubles over and I rush out of the vehicle, sprinting toward the houses nearby.

The man recovers quickly from my surprise attack and I can soon hear his heavy footsteps slapping against the pavement behind me. He's yelling something as his steps grow louder, but I can't distinguish his words over the blood rushing in my ears. I push my body, trying to outrun him even though I know it's no use. I don't exercise, barely feed my body enough to get through a tame day, and men are made to be faster. Stronger too. When I finally feel his hands wrap around my arm in a death grip, I don't scream. I was mentally preparing for this the last few steps, assuring I won't freeze up like I so often do now that it really counts.

I remember what I once learned in a self-defense seminar and thrust the palm of my hand into his throat. His grip on me loosens as he gasps for air, clearly caught off guard, and I use the momentum to grip his shoulders and bring my knee up to his crown jewels.

He howls in pain, dropping to his knees. I push him once more before turning and running again. I don't hear his heavy steps follow my retreat but still don't allow myself to stop. Not until I finally see a house with some lights on several streets down, my heart racing and lungs burning from running so much.

I ring the doorbell, trying to get my breathing under control and to keep myself from ringing the bell repeatedly as I obsessively look over my shoulder. This might be a bad idea considering it's the middle of the night, but I don't have much of a choice. I need a phone.

Besides, one of the house's windows is lit up blue with LEDs, so I pray a child or teenager lives here. Please just let it be someone friendly. Someone female.

When the door finally opens slowly, revealing a young woman, it's all I can do not to start crying in relief. The woman takes me in once, maybe assessing the danger she's in herself. After a few seconds of taking in my shivering, out-of-breath form, her gaze softens.

"How can I help you?" she asks.

"Can I use your phone, please?" My voice cracks, and I can't help but look over my shoulder again. It's a compulsion too strong to deny right now. I feel like someone's watching me, like the uber driver is about to jump out of the bushes and attack me again. I feel violated and scared.

I think the woman realizes the same thing because against all odds and the fact that I'm a stranger at her door in the middle of the night, she offers, "Sure. Do you want to come inside? You look cold."

I shake my head, the idea of being confined in another stranger's space stifling. Even though it's another woman, I'm too shaky to try and trust her enough for that. "Thank you but it's all right. I just need to make a call." She nods in understanding, unlocks her phone, and hands it to me.

I silently thank my parents for forcing me to do memory practice when I was younger as I type in Elija's number. The line rings twice, setting my nerves on edge with each passing second. Then, he finally picks up.

"Elija Mongrow."

Chapter 33

Elija

"Elija." My blood freezes at the sound of my name. She said a single word, but it hits me like a whole damn bullet train. Florence's voice sounds shaky and so genuinely scared it makes my stomach clench. I can't hear the sound of Jamie's party in the background and it's not her phone she's calling me from, so where on earth is she? And what scared her so much if she really is alone, somewhere, in the middle of the night.

I was staring at my ceiling just a moment ago, thinking about what happened tonight and wondering whether I overreacted. Then, my phone went off and seeing as it was an unknown number, I was curious enough to pick it up. Thank god I did.

"Florence, what's wrong? Where are you?" I press, getting to my feet.

"I don't know," she tells me before taking a shallow breath. I'm already at my front door, putting on my shoes and grabbing my brother's car keys. Good thing he's home.

"It's okay, deep breaths, okay? Are you hurt? Whose phone are you calling me from?" I ask, trying not to freak out too badly myself. Meanwhile, inwardly, I'm losing my mind, making up scenarios of what might have happened. If she was jumped or hurt herself it's my fault. I was supposed to make sure she got home safe. My heart seizes with guilt and worry.

"No, and a woman's that lives near the street." *Street*? What street?

"Ask her for the address, I'm coming," I tell her as I start my car.

"You can't, you drank tonight," she protests.

"One beer over an hour ago, Florence. I want that address," I repeat.

I hear her talking to someone else in the background while I nervously tap my fingers on the steering wheel. I shouldn't have left her at the party. I should have let her speak, *fucking idiot*. I told her I'd make sure she got home safely but was so pissed and hurt, I completely forgot to worry about her.

I just knew I had to get away from Florence before I said something I might have regretted. Look where that got us. I really need to know what the fuck happened before I lose my mind.

Finally, Florence tells me the address and I race off, going over the speed limit. The streets are empty at this time of night, so I honestly don't give a shit.

I make her stay on the line with me, even though we don't speak. When I finally pull up to a small house in one of the rougher neighborhoods, I slump against my seat when I see her. She talks to another woman, probably thanking her and apologizing for the inconvenience. Then, she gets in my car without looking at me.

"What happened?" I ask desperately as I start the car back up, cranking up the heat at the sight of her blue lips.

"I don't know. I got an uber and didn't pay attention. I realized we weren't going to my place too late, and I don't have my phone. We stopped and I ran away from the driver," she explains, her voice growing smaller the more she speaks. I glance at her to find a vacant expression on her face while she holds her left arm above the elbow.

"Did he touch you?" I ask slowly. If he did, I'll never fucking forgive myself. Florence shakes her head, releasing the smallest amount of pressure in my chest.

I sight. "I'm so sorry. I shouldn't have left," I tell her. I walked home from Jamie's place since it wasn't too far, and I can't believe I didn't think of how Florence might get home.

"It's not your fault. I know what you walked into looked bad, but I promise nothing like that happened between Liam and me. He spilled his drink on my hoodie and told me he wanted to speak to me. He cleaned my hoodie and apologized for being a jerk. He was at the party with Sarah, Elija. And I want no one else," she tells me, finally meeting my eyes. "Thanks for picking me up," she adds softly, making my heart crack in my chest.

Of course, she wasn't trying to cheat on me with Liam. This is *Florence.* Sweet, precious, selfless Florence, and she nearly got hurt tonight because of me. Because I lost my temper with her and shut her out like a child when I should have let her explain right when I found them. "Don't thank me. I really can't stand myself right now. I don't know how you're not angry." My temples are throbbing, and I just wish I could pull the girl next to me into my arms until she stopped shivering. "You're cold. Turn on the seat heating," I say instead.

"Of course, I'm not angry at you. Your reaction was justified. You're allowed to need time to cool off when I do something to upset you, and you couldn't have known I'd get so unlucky tonight. It's fine, really. Nothing happened," she tells me, wrapping her arms more tightly around herself.

"But it almost did. What if you hadn't gotten away? This could have been so much worse and it's all my fault. I messed up, Florence, and you nearly paid the price. You're allowed to be angry at me for that, for not taking care of you when I promised I would. You don't have to be so perfectly collected and reasonable all the time," I snap. Then, seeing she's already crying silently to my right, I curse. "Hey, no, I'm not trying to raise my voice. I'm sorry. Shit. My heart is still racing so much, but that's no excuse. I shouldn't have yelled."

"It's fine. The night was a mess and we're both tired," she says silently even as more tears stream down her face. She's still making excuses for me, and I hate it. She should just be angry and get it out of her system before it eventually overwhelms her.

Deciding it might be best if I didn't say anything more, I turn on the radio for the rest of the ride. By the time we arrive at her house, she's stopped crying. I get out of the car and follow her to her door only for her to hesitate. "What are you doing?"

"I thought I'd stay here tonight. With you," I half propose half plead. She looks at me for a beat before silently unlocking the door and going inside. I'm too selfish to ask her if she wants me to leave. There's no way I could sleep knowing she's alone after what happened. It must have been so scary, realizing some strange man was taking her somewhere she didn't recognize. To a neighborhood where no lights were on and no one was out on the street to help if things got out of hand.

I take off my shoes and get onto her bed as she changes out of her wet clothes. She puts on a big shirt, long pants, and fuzzy socks before sliding beneath the covers herself. I might smile at her get-up if it were a different day. As it is, I recognize the comfort clothes for what they are.

When she turns so her back is to me, I feel like someone just punched me. I lean over and gently lay my hand on her arm, intending to get her to speak to me, but she winces and then stiffens. I pull my hand back, my mind coming to a halt. *Did she just flinch at my touch?* I sit up and scoot further away.

"I'm sorry. I'll just sleep on the floor," I rasp, unable to keep the emotion from my voice. *She's uncomfortable with my touch. I lost her trust.* I throw my legs over the edge of the bed and get to my feet.

"You don't have to do that," she protests, but I'm already shaking my head.

"It's fine. I don't want to make you uncomfortable."

"You don't," she insists, sitting up herself.

"Florence, you flinched. I understand tonight must've taken its toll on you and I'm just here to help you. If you don't want me to touch you, that's okay, just please don't ask me to leave." I'm wearing my heart on my sleeve at this point, for her to take and do with whatever she wants.

Florence sighs, looking skyward before meeting my gaze. Then, she silently pulls up the sleeve of her shirt, waiting for me to look at her arm. I walk closer, turn the bedside lamp on, and what I see in the low light makes my jaw clench. There's a bruise in the unmistakable shape of a hand forming on her arm.

"That's why I winced, Elija. Not because I don't want you close to me. Now, please come back to bed," she sighs, letting her sleeve drop.

"I thought he didn't touch you," I ask, my words rough and low. The image of the bruise on her perfect skin burns into the back of my eyes, adding to the headache building there. *He got his hands on her. He* hurt *her.* I swallow thickly.

"Only there," she reassures me, but it doesn't alleviate the oppressive weight of my guilt. I get in the bed next to her and this time, she lays her head down on my chest and snuggles close. I don't know if she does it for my sake or hers and I hate to think she's thinking about comforting *me* in a moment like this, but I lack the strength to fight her. To remind her she can be selfish in moments like these and put herself first.

Instead, with a resigned voice, I ask, "How'd you get away?"

"I took a self-defense seminar a few years back," she says before yawning against me. *Right, she's tired. No more time for my questions. No matter how many are running through my mind.* I cup the back of her head and hold her close, caressing her hair in a way that hopefully soothes her. Feeling her body pressed to mine, her chest brushing against me with each breath is the reassurance I need that she's okay. Everything else can wait.

"My sweet girlfriend is secretly a ninja?" I tease half-heartedly.

"I'm your girlfriend?" she asks rather than engaging in the banter.

Honestly, I didn't even realize that's what I called her. It's what she feels like, but we never actually talked about it.

"Do you want to be?" I ask. My heart's racing as I wait for her response but then she smiles at me and nods. Another weight lifts off my shoulder. "Then, yes, you are my girlfriend. So, do I have anything to worry about?"

"Not unless you mess up," she jokes, some lightness returning to her voice. It allows me to take my first deep breath in over an hour.

"Goodnight, my little ninja," I tell her, kissing the top of her head as she settles down again.

"Goodnight, Eli."

Chapter 34

Florence

Run!

My lungs are screaming and my legs burning but I keep running because I know if the man behind me gets me, it'll be so much worse. I see Elija's silhouette in the distance so I scream his name. I just need to reach him. Just a little more and I'll be safe. He'll help me.

But when he turns to look at me, he's not himself. His face is wrinkled, his eyebrows bushy, his lips thin and cracked and his eyes a cold blue instead of the warm dark brown I'm used to. I take a startled step back, covering my mouth with my hands so I don't scream or throw up. Maybe both.

A set of hands grabs me from behind, twisting me around by my arm. I can't move, pain burning up where the stranger is touching me like a paralyzing venom. Tears stream down my face but I can't fight the stranger off, my limbs entirely useless and uncooperative. I'm helpless as his hands start roaming my body and he leans closer so his lips almost touch mine. Instead of kissing me, he talks though.

"Florence," is all he says, but the voice doesn't suit him. It's too young, too smooth. Too nice for a man this disgusting.

"Florence," he repeats, this time against my neck. I can feel his wet breath on the curve of my shoulder and bite back bile.

"Florence!" My eyes snap open, but I still can't move. Elija's looking at me, seeming relieved to see me awake, but I'm still panicking. Why can't I move? Why can't I speak?

"Woah, hey, breathe," Elija adds, noticing something is wrong. He cups my face with his hands, and as the warmth of his skin registers, I snap out of my frozen state. I fill my lungs with a deep breath, the organ burning with the strain of it. My hands fly up to wrap around his wrists to make sure he's really here, that he's not about to turn into the cab driver of yesterday and assault me.

"Fuck," I breathe. "I couldn't move."

His hand on my cheek flexes. "Sleep paralysis. You were having a nightmare and wouldn't wake up," he says, sitting back on his knees. "Was it about last night?"

"Yeah," I admit, focusing on the way his thumb is stroking my cheek instead of the lingering unease my nightmare left behind. Is that what would have happened if I hadn't gotten away? Not the part with Elija, of course, but the other aspects. The driver's unwanted touch, his sticky breath on me. I shudder at the thought.

I'm safe now, I remind myself. The what if's aren't important.

"Do you want to talk about it?" Elija asks patiently.

"I think it's okay. Probably just my brain trying to cope with what happened, but I'm sure it won't happen again. Now, I don't want to throw you out, but I really need to catch up on some reading. You can stay, of course. Just don't try to talk to me because I will ignore you," I tell him sweetly, not really joking. Honestly, my escapism has been feeling neglected. Besides, I could use a break from this reality right about now.

"Bold of you to assume I won't read something of yours myself. You told me about one of your favorite Y/As. I think I'm in the mood for that. After we ate breakfast, of course," he proposes. I groan comically.

"But if I eat then I won't be able to lie down to read," I complain, turning on my bed until I'm sprawled over him. Elija said he'd like me to tell him about my ed so he can understand it better and try to help as long as I'm comfortable with it. I'm not going to sit him down and give him a lecture, though. It's either dealing with it with sarcasm and humor or not at all.

The guy beneath me muses. "Sitting's really good for you. Or so I've heard. Besides, I'm starving, and eating alone is just sad. Your pick, though, since I'm feeling generous," he teases me. I sit up, still pouting, and hit his shoulder. "Don't look at me like that. Your brain needs something to work off if it's going to spend the next few hours creating different worlds and characters."

"Fine. I like apples, they're easy to stomach. Fruit and vegetables work best on bad days, generally. Not bananas though."

"Is today a bad day?" he asks, sitting up himself. His hair is all tousled from sleep and I itch to lean over and run my fingers through it. I remind myself that we're having a conversation and that'd be very inappropriate just in time.

"I don't know. I don't feel sick thinking about it right now, so it's not terrible," I tell him with a smile.

"What do you do on the days that are terrible?"

"Well, sometimes I don't eat. Or I eat multiple small meals but it's complicated." I think about my next words before deciding to take the leap and really let him in.

"It's like this, I don't really like food but at the same time, I know I need it. Especially if I don't want to lose weight, which I really don't. Whatever." I chuckle. "Generally, it's easier for me to eat small meals because I feel less bad about it. But eating smaller meals means eating more often and that brings its own problems," I stop there, trying to give Elija some time to think about it. If he wants me to go on, he can tell me. If not, that's fine too. I don't want to force this on him.

"Which are?" he prompts readily.

"Every time I eat, I feel bad about it afterward. Like my body's too heavy and not mine at all. Especially lying down doesn't work then. I always imagine the food being pulled down against my ribs by gravity, gathering on the inside of my stomach even though I know it's ridiculous. I've grown used to it, though, so it's just a bit uncomfortable. When I eat many small meals, I just feel bad all day."

"That happens every time you eat?" he asks, his eyebrows furrowed. I really wish I knew what he was thinking.

"I guess. The feeling definitely, but on good days, I don't get sick because of my food. Sometimes I even want to eat, though that's mostly confusing," I say. I can't believe I'm actually talking about this. More than that, I can't believe Elija seems this interested.

Some doubt creeps up on me. What if he feels bad and that's why he sticks around? After all, this side of me is so different from the Florence he got to know up until now.

But it's hard to distrust him when he seems so genuine in his pursual of answers. "How come?"

"We don't have to keep talking about it if you don't want to. You said you were hungry," I remind him, to which he takes my hand in his.

"Well, since I'm a big boy, I think I can manage to wait a little longer," he teases me.

"If you're sure. But I'm telling you now, I won't take the blame if you pass of starvation."

"I'd never ask you to. Now, go on, how is it confusing?"

"I guess it makes me feel like I'm faking it. Like the bad days are just in my head and that I really don't have a problem. I think it's called imposter syndrome or something," I say honestly. Elija blows out a breath.

"So you feel bad when you can't eat and you feel bad when you can. You also don't like to eat but you feel bad when you do like it," he repeats.

I chuckle at the assessment. "Sums it up nicely, I'd say."

"That sucks. Is there anything else?"

"While we're at it, I might as well mention that water's a problem too. Or just drinking in general," I tell him.

"So basically, whenever you consume anything at all, you feel bad?"

"It sounds worse than it is. You kind of get used to it, you know. And water by itself is the easiest, I guess. It's never made me sick so that's something. It just feels like another meal minus the nausea.

"And then there's the sudden urge to throw up that's the worst. I don't get it often, but you'll definitely notice when I do. It can come after a single bite or a whole meal. Without warning, my stomach clenches, and it's nearly impossible to keep my meal down." I clap my hands. "Oh well, let's go find some food."

I jump off the bed and head to the kitchen. Honestly, I expected to feel bad after talking about all of this, but weirdly enough, I don't. No sickness at the thought of food yet. Yay.

"Have you ever thrown up? Like purposefully?" Elija asks from behind me.

"I've tried. No matter what life hack I used, it didn't work so I eventually gave up. Does that bother you?" I ask without turning around.

"What exactly?"

"All of it? Any of it? I mean, it must seem weird to you," I say. Elija stays silent until we reach my kitchen. There, he steps around me to meet my eyes.

"It doesn't seem weird. It's a lot of new information and I hate that you have to deal with all that on a daily basis. Really, really hate it. But it's not weird. I do think that there must be a better way to deal with it than getting used to it, though, and it's your choice, but I'd like to help you in any way I can."

My chest grows all gooey and warm at his words. He manages to walk the tightrope between being overbearing and expressing his concern perfectly, letting me feel how much he cares. It's a feeling I've been missing dearly since my aunt passed, so getting it from him means so much.

I smile at him before rising on my tiptoes to press my lips to his. He leans down, pulling me closer and making me sigh against him. Here, in his arms and breathing the same air as him, nothing can hurt me.

Chapter 35

Elija

"My parents come home tomorrow," Florence whines as we walk out of school. We spent most of yesterday together, just reading as planned. Still, my girl doesn't seem to be sick of me yet seeing as she's dragging me to the parking lot where her bike is.

We both put on our helmets and off we go. Florence got me my own without my knowing, this one in black opposing to her beige one. It made me smile when she first showed me, but mostly because it means she'll wear hers from now on whenever I'm riding with her.

"What do you feel like doing?" I ask, sitting down on her bed.

"Watch a movie? We still have a few Harry Potter's to go," she says, joining me. By joining me I mean she pretty much lies on top of me, nestling close. I wrap an arm around her shoulder and press a kiss to the top of her head, anything to encourage her to keep using me as a pillow. I love it when she initiates a touch.

"Sounds good," I agree. She puts on the third one only to give me the first peck on my cheek about five minutes in. I smile at the show of affection and happily let her trail kisses down the side of my neck. It's definitely my sweet spot, my favorite place to be kissed so her lips there feel like heaven. I'm barely paying attention to the screen as Harry messes with his aunt.

When she starts sucking on my skin right below the jaw, my smile falls as I bite back a groan. She must notice my shift in mood because I feel her smile against my skin a second later.

"Your favorite movie is playing, Florence," I remind her before her teasing can lead my intentions astray.

"You can still watch it. Besides I want to take advantage of my last day being home alone. I don't know when my parents will leave again, and until then, you have to hide and be quiet when you visit," she whispers against my skin, leaving goosebumps in her wake. "Do you want me to stop?" she asks, her head coming up so she can look at me.

Do I ever? "The floor's yours," I tell her. You won't ever catch me denying this girl anything. Especially when it comes to this. Touching me. Kissing me. She has me wrapped around her finger and I'll beg her to keep going before I tell her to stop.

My girl shifts so she's straddling my hips before she goes back to kissing and nibbling my neck. I pretend to be watching the movie when really, it takes all my effort not to slam my lips to hers and forget all about it.

She reaches the base of my throat and tugs at my shirt. I help her take it off and ball my hands to firsts at my sides as her hungry eyes take me in. If I don't, I'll start touching her, and I'm trying to let her run the show. She continues her sweet torture, taking her time kissing every inch of my skin. Then, she reaches the waistband of my pants and her eyes find mine.

"Can you tell me what to do?" she asks softly. Damn but my dick twitches at that. I've been hard for the last fifteen minutes and her looking at me like this isn't helping.

"Are you sure? You don't have to do anything more than what you want. Just because you're in the mood to tease me and spoil me with kisses doesn't mean I expect anything more," I assure her, scared the people-pleasing side of her makes her think otherwise.

But she just smiles calmly. "I know that, Elija. I'd really like to do this. If you do."

"Florence, you could do about anything to me and I'd thank you for it, so don't worry about me." I chuckle. Apparently, that's the confirmation she needed before she starts tugging my pants off.

And so, there we are, me fully naked while she takes me in like I'm a statue in a museum. When she leans down, kissing me below the navel as I did to her days before, I grab the sheets tighter. It's been a while since I got any action and the anticipation is killing me, especially because this is *Florence* touching me. The girl I've been crazy about for months.

She gently wraps her hand around the base of my dick, stroking me twice before bringing it to her lips. She licks my tip, looking up at me shily and I decide to moan freely so she knows that I like what she's doing. There's no use in hiding it. I realize as soon as the heat of her mouth surrounds me that it's a battle I'd lose. I've never been particularly quiet about my pleasure.

She opens her mouth wider and starts sucking me in an inch at a time. When I hit the back of her throat, I groan.

"Fuck, Florence," I breathe out when she starts moving her head up and down, stroking the part she can't take with her hand. For all of her inexperience, she really doesn't need instructions. Knowing now what she reads though, I guess I shouldn't be surprised.

Before long, I can feel my release gathering at the base of my spine. I tap my girl's shoulder to give her a heads up before it's too late. I'd never just come down her throat without her permission and at least giving her a choice.

"If you don't stop, I'm going to come down that pretty little throat of yours," I warn with some effort. She doesn't stop, though. Instead, she speeds up, her cheeks hollowing out as she holds my gaze. I try to hold on to the edge, knowing it's embarrassingly early to lose it, but I can't prevent it for long. My eyes fall shut and I come with her name on my lips.

Florence swallows every last drop of my release, cleaning the edges of her mouth with her thumb as I slowly open my eyes. Then, she comes up to kiss me gently.

"Was that okay?" she asks softly. I cup her face, stroking her cheeks with my thumb as I often do.

"More than okay." Noticing she's still hovering above me, I take her by the hips and pull her down. She's sitting on my stomach, and as she makes contact with my skin, I can feel how wet the fabric of her panties is. My girl's wearing another skirt, and I wonder now if she planned this when she got dressed in the morning. I smirk at that. "Did that turn you on?" I ask her.

Her cheeks burn up and she tries to look away but I tilt her chin so she's forced to face at me.

"Maybe a little," she admits, making my blood simmer. Without a word, I flip us so she's below me. I let my hand travel down the side of her body before moving it up her thigh beneath her skirt. I wait at the edge of her underwear to see if she'll stop me but when she doesn't, I slip two fingers beneath the fabric.

"A little?" I tease her, feeling how drenched she is. She whimpers as I start rubbing her clit in tight circles. Before I can work her up too much, I move a finger up and down her slit to gather as much of her juices on my fingers as possible. Fuck, but feeling her so wet is a massive turn on. "I think sucking me off and making me come did more than turn you on a *little*."

Florence groans before tangling her fingers in my hair and pulling my lips down to meet hers. The kiss is desperate, tongues and teeth clashing. I store the knowledge that Florence apparently likes to be talked dirty to away for another time.

She starts grinding against my hand as soon as I slip a second finger inside of her. Then, she pulls away from the kiss and fumbles with her words. It's cute to see her this flustered, so I don't make a move to slow down my thrusts to make it any easier for her.

"Do you-" she breaks off in a moan as I press my thumb to her clit. "Can you go again?" she finally gasps out. I'm surprised by her words but when she starts moving against my hand, I make sure not to let my movements falter. Truth is, I got a semi as soon as I felt how needy she was. I don't doubt I could go again shortly.

Seeing the indecision on my features, she continues making her case. "We had our date. We're both sober. And I'm sure," she adds breathlessly. "Do you want to?" she asks. Is she asking me if I want to sleep with my smoking hot girlfriend? I nod slowly. "Do have a condom?" I nod again. Then, curling my fingers inside of her, I watch with a smirk as her eyes close and her back arches off the bed.

Before she can come, I pull my hand out of her panties. Her eyes snap open and she glares at me, making my grin widen. Now, there's the fire I've been waiting for.

"Really?" she asks, making me chuckle.

"Getting the condom, remember?" I tease her before taking my wallet from my pants to pull out a condom. I place it next to her and kiss her. I can tell she's confused but even if she's wet and ready, I won't rush this.

I only break the kiss to take off her shirt, then her skirt. Only in her underwear, she spreads her legs for me again and pulls me flush against her. Feeling her warm skin against mine has my heart pounding and I decide her bra needs to come off. She arches her back for me, apparently sharing the same thought.

I'd love to look at her the way she did me, but Florence pulls me tightly against her before I get the chance. Instead, I feel her stiff nipples against my chest and push her further into the mattress, high off the feeling of being so close to her. Skin to skin, our chests heaving in sync with our heavy breaths. She reaches for the condom and holds it out to me, breaking the kiss.

"Please," she whispers hoarsely, undoing me.

Chapter 36

Florence

Elija finally takes the condom from me, his expression as desperate as the undertone of my voice. At this point, I don't care that I'm begging him to have sex with me. I'm too needy to care. But it's his fault for edging me in the first place before deciding to go back to kissing for the next twenty minutes.

As he rolls the latex on, I take off my panties. Elija's the first one I've ever been naked in front of since I was a child and as I wait for him, I start feeling a bit nervous. Daylight streams in through the windows, so what if he doesn't like what he sees? Or what if I'm bad at sex? I couldn't even fit his dick all the way in my mouth, so what if I can't take him?

"You still with me?" Elija asks, snapping me from my chaotic thoughts. As I meet his eyes, my nerves calm. *It's him*, I remind myself. I don't have to worry when I'm with him.

"Yeah," I say honestly. He leans down to kiss me softly, covering my body with his entirely. One hand is braced next to my head and the other disappears between our bodies. I can feel him lining up with my entrance but instead of pushing in, he rubs himself through my folds and circles my clit once with the tip of his dick. I pull him closer and moan against his skin, the sensation of him, right there, giving me pleasure with his dick makes my blood hum.

His lips stall over mine as he leans closer, entering me the first inch only to pull back again when he meets resistance. I focus on staying relaxed even as he stretches me out each time he repeats the movement, kissing me softly as he goes deeper with every thrust. I barely kiss him back, too focused on what's happening between my legs. The books didn't lie, it does hurt as I try to adjust to his girth. Just not in an entirely bad way.

When Elija's finally all the way in, he stills for a beat, breathing heavily.

"You okay?" he asks softly, kissing the tip of my nose. I nod, trying to find my voice. When I don't react otherwise, my eyes still closed, he adds "Am I hurting you?" I force them open now, even as I nod. Elija searches my eyes and I can tell he's worried he's doing something wrong. I want to assure him, but he speaks first. "Do you want me to stop?" This time, I shake my head vehemently.

"Just move, please," I instruct him.

As he does as I asked him, I close my eyes again. I kiss him back this time, pulling him closer every time he's balls deep as the pain slowly eases up. Weirdly enough, the more he speeds up and the deeper he goes, the better it gets. I can feel myself getting wetter, and the pain finally vanishes entirely.

My hands roam his rippling back, his tense arms, fist his hair while his are on my hips, keeping me in place. I spread my legs wider, giving him more space to move. When he pulls me against him to meet his next thrust, I gasp out a startled moan.

"Faster," I demand huskily, too far gone to feel embarrassed. Elija follows my order and curses under his breath.

"You're doing so good," he tells me, moving faster and deeper. "You take me perfectly." The praise floods me with endorphins, drawing a breathless moan from my puffy lips.

One of his hands leaves my hips and his fingers start circling my clit as he keeps thrusting. My whole body starts tingling, my nerves buzzing with pleasure. I can feel the reminder of my earlier impending orgasm rush to the surface, gathering low in my womb. I stop kissing him and bury my face in his neck as I focus on the rising pleasure, eager to not let it slip through my fingers a second time. When I come, my back arches off the bed and bury my teeth in the cook of his neck before I know what

I'm doing. He stills, his groan sounding pained as he comes for the second time.

He stays where he is for a second as we both catch our breaths, peppering my face with little kisses. I revel in them and the afterglow of my orgasm, and all too soon, he pulls out of me. "I just have to take care of the condom. I'll be right back," he explains as he gets up. I bite back a needy whine, understanding it can't be comfortable to linger with the sticky condom on.

Before any rejection can settle in, he's back, no longer wearing the condom but still blissfully naked. He lies down next to me and pulls me into his arms, cradling me before covering us with my blanket. I sigh against his skin, content to be held.

"How was it?" Elija asks as if he hadn't been there. I laugh softly.

"You didn't see me twitch as I came?" I ask, making him join me with a laugh of his own.

"Just making sure."

"I know. Thank you. It was great. You were great," I assure him. Then, reluctantly since I hate to ruin a moment, I say, "I'm gonna go to the bathroom real quick."

"Of course," he says, letting me go. Getting up, I wince at the soreness between my legs. Then, seeing he's holding back a smile, I glare at him.

"Careful, boy. Otherwise, you're going to find out how I got away on Saturday faster than you can blink," I tell him, trying to be playful. When his face falls, I regret having mentioned it. I know he still blames himself for what happened after Jamie's party. I shouldn't have said anything.

Deciding to let it go, I quickly pick up Elija's shirt off the ground and put it on before going to the bathroom.

He's in the same position when I come back, watching Harry say goodbye to Sirius. Damn, we nearly missed the whole movie. And it's the last movie that doesn't make me sad in the series.

Right as I'm cuddling up to Elija, his phone goes off.

"My mom," he tells me before picking it up. He's close enough for me to hear what she's saying even though I don't try to. Not that Elija seems to mind.

Her exasperated voice fills the air between us as she exclaims, "Good to know he's alive," sounding an awful lot like Molly Weasley. "I've been asking myself if you were part of my imagination recently. Tell me, am I allowed to see my son again sometime?" she asks, making me stifle a laugh against his shoulder. He brushes a hand over my back and squeezes my shoulder, smiling too.

"Sorry, Ma. I've been staying-" his mom cuts him off.

"With Florence, I know. That's completely fine, but dad and I would like to go out for dinner tonight, and since Kai stayed home with the twins last time, I was hoping you could take over tonight. You can make it up to Florence by inviting her over for dinner tomorrow, okay?" she demands.

Elija shoots me an apologetic look and replies, "Yeah, sure. I'll ask her. See you later."

"Goodbye, Honey."

"Bye, Mom," Elija says before ending the call. Then, he turns to me, still caressing me. "I'm really sorry about that but I should really be there if the twins need to be looked after."

"Oh, don't worry about it. I totally get it," I assure him. While that is true, I don't blame him at all for having to take care of his siblings, the way his hands relentlessly stroke and caress me in one place or the other makes me want to stay curled up in his arms forever.

"I wish I'd known, though. I don't like leaving now. Maybe I can ask Kai if he's willing to take over again. I don't think he'd mind," he thinks aloud, already opening up his brother's contact to message him.

I stop him with a hand on his wrist. "There's no need, really. Besides, we do still have a bit of time, right?" I really hope we can cuddle just for a bit longer.

Elija looks stricken, clearly not loving the idea of not spending the night after what we just did. I really appreciate his concern, but I meant it when I said it's fine. I'd feel bad for inconveniencing the rest of his family by monopolizing all of Elija's time.

"Yeah, of course. If they're going out for dinner they won't leave before seven. I'll stay for as long as I can. Speaking of which, you heard what she said about dinner tomorrow, right? Would you like to come?" he asks, turning his body more fully towards mine so that his pecs are now right in front of my face and his arm acts as a pillow. I press a kiss to his pec just because I can't seem to stop.

"Well, my parents come home tomorrow so I probably won't be able to stay long, but I'd really like to come," I tell him. I'm not sure when my parents arrive but at this point, I'm sure they won't even notice I'm gone. We stay huddled together for another while, exchanging few words and loads of little touches. I soak it all up, basking in the comfort of being held.

Too soon, Elija gets dressed and leaves. He put it off for as long as possible, but he knew as well as I did that he needed to catch the right bus or he'd be an hour late. Since I really don't want his parents to dislike me for ruining their dinner plans when they're stranded without a babysitter, I all but forced Elija out eventually.

Now, alone at last, I'm unsure as to what to do. It's silly since I've spent most of my teen years entirely alone, but after being around Elija for so long, having him fill the room with his vibrancy, it feels dull without him. I should do some homework or study since I haven't been doing that in some time but I can't seem to find my motivation.

I wouldn't say my grades are bad, they're still better than 70% of the class, but they used to be even better. Since I started hanging out with the guys, I just don't have as much time on my hands as I used to when I had no social life.

My parents would say I should prioritize school, and they might be right. Still, I can't seem to do it. So here I am, reading my night away instead of studying for my test tomorrow, prioritizing my state of mind over the need to please them.

Because really, when have I ever pleased them no matter how hard I tried? Tonight, I decide it's not worth it to waste my energy.

"Flower girl!" May greets me, hugging my side.

"I'm coming!" Daniel screams as he runs around the corner, coming at me at full speed.

"Whoa! Hi you guys. It's good to see you too," I say. It is, but I really can't breathe with them squeezing me. They're five. How are they so strong?

"Florence, it's good to have you back. Come in, the food's about to be ready," Elija's father, Robert, tells me, his voice seeming much warmer than it did the first time I came to his house. It soothes my nerves. The thought that he didn't like me was gnawing at me, but just this short interaction banishes the irrational fears of him chasing me from his house. My mind can be so silly when given enough time to fret.

"Hi, Flo," Kai greets me, waving from his seat at the table. I wave back, smiling at the nickname, and then head toward the kitchen to greet Elija's mom.

"Hey, Amelia," I announce myself when I find her with her back to me, focused on what's in the pot ahead of her. She turns to me with the biggest of smiles, spreading her arms to hug me.

"Hi, honey. It's so nice to see you. How've you been?" she asks, pulling away enough to keep me at arm's length. My reaction to the motherly air that just naturally seems to flow from her hasn't lessened since the last time, and I find my heart swelling longingly as her affectionate expression fills my field of vision.

"I've been great, thank you. Although I am sorry for taking up so much of Elija's time," I say, hoping she doesn't notice the thick note in my voice. I'd been worried since hearing her on the phone yesterday that she would hold a grudge against me for keeping her son away from home, but it doesn't seem to be the case. She merely laughs and brushes me off.

"Don't be silly. It's been a long time since I've seen him this happy and I have you to thank for that. I know how it is to be young and in love. You have nothing to be sorry for." She squeezes my shoulder and my relief at her words is instant.

"Where is he, by the way?" I ask. He told me he'd meet me here, but I have yet to find my boyfriend amongst his family.

"I don't know but I'm sure he'll be here soon," she assures me, sounding pretty confident in her reply. I really hope she's right because by the looks of it, dinner is nearly ready. I already cut it a little close because of traffic, something that made me sweat the entire ride over, so for him to be even more late... It's strange.

Chapter 37

Elija

I'm hanging out with the guys, checking the time every five seconds. I shouldn't be here. Florence is probably already at my place, but the guys won't let me leave, insisting I'll ruin all of their night.

"Relax, Loverboy. Your girl won't die if you're a few minutes late," Jamie teases me. I flip him off.

It's not like I'm a vital part of this group right now anyway, contributing nothing to any of the ongoing conversations with my anxiety rising. Jamie's mooning over Orion, who's lying in his lap, looking like a content puppy. Liam has Sarah to talk to. They seem to be getting pretty serious pretty fast but it's actually – and I hate myself for thinking it but it's actually cute. And the added bonus that I don't have to worry about him going after my girl when he's happily occupied with his own is right there.

I can almost stand Liam's presence tonight with things like this. He hasn't baited me a single time or made any other pretentious remarks that usually give me the hives. It seems Sarah positively keeps him in check. Benji invited Miley over, the girl from the camping trip, which would have been cool if only she hadn't brought Joe with her. I've been firmly ignoring her as best as I could but it's still awkward. Even Marcus is busy cuddling with Jamie's flipping cat, leaving me to do absolutely nothing.

"So she's your girl now?" Joe asks, taking advantage of the beat of silence following Jamie's teasing. Her tone is so off, so laced with fake nicety that I can't believe I started liking her that one evening. Really, all the fresh air must've been getting to me at the time.

"Very much so," I reply. At the beginning of tonight, Joe was actually trying to get close to me, touching me and then using some lame excuse like *"Your hands are so big"* or *"I like that chain"*. Ugh. I was as rude as I could be without really wrecking the entire night and the other guys and even Sarah luckily helped me out, changing the topic or calling Joe away with some excuse.

Once it became clear that I was rejecting all her efforts, she resorted to being plain unpleasant.

"Heck yes, she is. Finally, I might add. Took them a while but you should see them together. Adorable," Jamie says to which Joe makes a face.

"I don't know. I'm not going to pretend to know her, but she gave off a weird vibe. Besides, I think she was looking a bit sickly, you know? Nothing like you, who fills out a t-shirt better than an Abercromby model," she remarks, making my blood boil to the point where it's all I can do not to snap at her. I refrain from hurting people, especially weak ones like Joe, so I grit my teeth and ball my hands into fists.

"Joe," Miley hisses. I'm glad I was right about that girl, at least. She seems genuinely nice and is clearly embarrassed by her friend's behavior.

"Oh, relax. I'm not trying to offend anyone. All I'm saying is that she could use a couple of pounds more, you know? Get some meat on those skinny little arms and legs. Provide Elija with something to grip. Don't look at me like that, Miley. We're all cool here. They understand I'm not being a bitch." The blond girl laughs. Alone, might I add.

"Actually, we don't," Sarah tells her, damn near growling. I'm glad I'm not the only one ready to snap. When I look at my friends, I notice all of them appear about as upset at this outright attack on Florence as I feel.

"And we're not cool," Marcus adds through gritted teeth.

"Yeah, I think it's time for you to leave," Orion offers about as calmly as a coiled snake, sitting up and looking as mean as ever. Joe swallows but doesn't make a move to leave.

"You heard him. Leave," Benji snaps. She gets to her feet, her face red.

"You're all weird anyways. Come on, Miley, let's go." Miley bites down on the inside of her cheeks looking at all our angry faces before staring at the ground, not meeting her friend's gaze.

"I think I'll stay for a bit," she finally whispers. I feel a pang of sympathy for the situation she's in. She reminds me a bit of Florence with the way she squirms under attention.

"What? No, you're not," Joe snaps but Miley doesn't move, still staring at her hands. "Didn't you hear me through that thick hair of yours? I said get your fat ass off that couch and follow me." *Nope, that's it.*

I get to my feet and walk up to Joe, glaring down at her. "I'd make you apologize if I thought your words were important enough. That *you* were important enough. But you're not, so I'm telling you to get the fuck out of this house and never show your face to any of us ever again," I seethe. Joe huffs, trying to meet my gaze defiantly but failing miserably. I can tell she's uncomfortable, but for once, I don't care that I'm the reason.

"Don't act like you don't know I'm right. You're so pathetic, bringing down the people around you in an attempt to feel better about yourself. Well, guess what, you're not better. You're just an insecure, body-shaming little imbecile with no personality and no real friends, and as if that wasn't bad enough, you just added racism to that list. Now, leave!"

The room is deadly silent and I keep all my attention on the shaking, red-faced girl in front of me. Finally, she screams, a broken, frustrated sound. She pushes me and I stumble back since I anything but expected to be physically attacked. The girl is not done with me though, coming at me again with her hand pulled back to slap me.

I barely feel the sting of her hit, the blood rushing in my head too distracting. *She's a woman*, I repeat to myself as my indignation rises. I don't hit people, no matter their gender, but I don't think I could live with myself if I physically harmed a woman. Even if it's self-defense. So I just back away from her with my vision swimming.

I'm faintly aware of my friends yelling things and movement around me, but I can't place anything. I simply keep backing away from the lunatic woman we mistakenly allowed into our circle.

"Elija, stop!" someone yells, and suddenly, the ground vanishes beneath my feet. *The stairs,* I realize when the first hard edge digs into my back. The wind is knocked out of me, and I lose track of what's above and beyond. My attempt to catch myself with my outstretched arms are fruitless and I keep falling until stars explode in my vision and a blinding pain shoots through my head.

I haven't stopped moving as everything goes dark.

Chapter 38

Florence

I've tried calling Elija five times, leaving three messages asking where he was. I texted him about a million times more as my anxiety steadily kept getting worse.

Me: *I'm at your place, where are you?*

Me: *Your mom said dinner was ready, what's the holdup?*

Me: *Come on, Elija. Please answer so I know everything is okay*

Me: *Your dad said we won't wait any longer but I'm too anxious to eat. Please just tell me where you are so I can relax.*

Me: *Come on, Elija. I feel sick already.*

Me: *I survived dinner but I feel horrible for your mom. She must've spent a lot of time preparing this meal and I could barely stomach anything.*

Me: *Okay forget about me and forget about your mom. Where are you?*

Me: *Kai went out to look for you.*

Me: *No one can reach you and it's hard not to freak out right now. Did I do something? Are you avoiding me? Because this is freaking out your entire family so you should just tell me to leave and come home to ease their minds.*

Me: *I hope you're ignoring me and not dead in a ditch somewhere.*

Me: *Shit, that was a horrible joke but I cope with humor. Only made things worse rn though.*

Me: *It's been an hour, I can't reach the guys so I'm coming to look for you myself*

Me: *Please be okay.*

I send the last message at the same time as the doorbell goes off. I jump to my feet, same as Elija's parents, and we all head to the door. The past one and a half hours have been tense as all of us were quietly worrying about Eli's whereabouts. I felt like I was intruding on a family situation and yet I haven't been able to make myself leave in case they got any news before me. Personally, I'm sick to my stomach, especially with my last meal so recent. I really tried to finish my plate and not make a scene. I regret that now.

Robert reaches the door first, blocking my view. "Who are you?" he demands roughly.

"I am here to pick up my daughter," a familiar voice replies. *Oh, shit.* Robert steps aside, looking at me questioningly while still blocking me from my mother's view with the door. I nod softly before stepping around him.

"Mom, hi. I didn't know you were back already," I try to appease her, smiling as if I was happy to see her.

"Yes, I figured that when I couldn't find you at home," she snaps. That's how I know I'm in big trouble. When this woman doesn't try to pretend we're a perfect family even in front of others.

"How did you find me?" I ask with a chuckle, trying to diffuse the tension. I step further outside to get this whole conversation away from the Mongrows. Their son is missing so the last thing they need is my family drama on top of things.

Luckily, my mom goes along, following me a few feet away from the door.

"That is beside the point. Your father and I give you all the freedom you want, only asking for you to do good in school, and this is how you repay us? By whoring around on a school night instead of studying?" my mom snaps, making me gasp. I've never heard her use such vulgar language and my cheeks heat up, knowing Elija's parents are witnessing all this.

"Whoring around?" I repeat incredulously, my voice as fragile and soft as a dying leaf in the wind. I must have heard her incorrectly. There's just no way.

"That's right. You know what I found in your trash, don't you?" my mom asks.

"You went through my trash?" I whisper, trying to keep up. My mom found our used condom, didn't she? I don't even have it in me to feel embarrassed about *that*. Not with the way she's acting right now.

"That's right. I knew something was wrong with you. I thought it was drugs, that you got in with the wrong crew but it's just a guy that's been distracting you. Guess what, that is over. If you don't keep up your end of the deal, then neither will we. Get in the car, now!"

"What are you talking about?" *Me doing drugs? What the hell?*

"Your report card came. Your GPA has dropped," my mother says as if it was the worst thing imaginable. *My grades*? That's what she's going on about. I don't know whether to laugh or cry at the absurdity of this entire night.

"It's still way above average," I try to reason. "I'm allowed to have a life beyond my studies. *She* would have understood that, and you know it!" It's a cheap shot to bring up the woman's dead sister – because we both know who I'm referring to – but I can't help it. I feel like she'd be so disappointed if she saw my mom and me right now, and it breaks my heart.

My mother's palm hits me right across the face, making my head snap to the side. My hand flies up to hold my stinging cheek as I gape at her, more surprised than hurt. My mother just hit me. She hit me *in front of strangers.* Where's the woman with the saccharine smile that showed up to all my school events if only to be seen by others doing so.

My mother straightens her clothes as if nothing out of the ordinary just happened. When she looks at me, she's calm, cool, and collected, like one little *slap* was all she needed to blow off some steam.

"Close your mouth, Florence, before you catch a fly. Nothing happened." My jaw snaps shut, but I don't answer. I don't go along and I don't make an excuse for her.

Turns out I don't have to since a soft hand settles on my shoulder from behind while a tall figure steps in front of me.

"It's time for you to get off our property," Robert tells my mother. She huffs, glances at me and the woman already comforting me, and whirls around as if deciding it's not worth the trouble. That I'm not worth the trouble. She might've acted like she came here to take me home but I know, clear as day, that she couldn't care less where I spend my time. She just came here to ruin my day.

I wonder if it's a compulsion by now. An addiction of sort, to put me down. She's been doing it awfully upfront recently, coming at me at random times and unprovoked. Tonight is just the tip of the iceberg, an escalation I'm not used to. *Yet.* I get the stifling sense that cutting words might not be enough for my mom from now on, and my heart races as I think it. Will it keep getting worse? Are we now entering screaming matches and slaps? What happens after that? Full-body beatings? I shudder. *What is happening?*

Maybe tonight is just cursed and all will be well by tomorrow. Elija will be home and fine, my mom will act the way she always did. No escalations. No rabbit hole.

"Are you okay, Sweetie?" Amelia asks right as something else captures my attention. I squint against the darkness at the dirty-blonde guy staring back at me from the sidewalk at the edge of the property.

He looks pale under the scarce moonlight and I can make out dark stains on his white shirt from where I am. Stains that look suspiciously like blood. My heart starts racing, the foreboding in the air thickening. Something is very wrong.

The guy starts walking toward me, looking distressed.

"Jamie?" I ask shakily. *Please, no more bad news*, I think. I can't handle anything else right now.

Without any sort of greeting, my friend starts rambling. "I – I'm so sorry. He didn't see the stairs and we couldn't warn him. I – He – he fell and then there was all that yelling and the blood." He breaks off with a shudder and Robert interrupts him.

"Jamie, slow down. Who fell? Where's Elija?" he asks, though I think we all know that answer.

"In the hospital. Elija's in the hospital. He had a fight with Joe and fell down the stairs. He hit his head really hard," his voice cracks as tears stream down his face. My heart aches for how devastated the happy boy I know looks right now, but I don't have it in me to comfort him. Not when it's starting to feel like a rug has been pulled from beneath my feet, hurtling me into a free fall.

"We went to the hospital with him, but we didn't have a phone and someone needed to tell you so I came back. He's not awake yet, I'm so sorry," he adds, sobbing now.

Amelia pulls him into her arms, trying to comfort him while Robert talks to someone on the phone. *Probably Kai*, I think, feeling strangely calm. Kai has the car, so it makes sense to call him. We need a car if we want to go to the hospital. The hospital, where Elija is. Elija got hurt.

This all feels like a dream. Like it's happening to someone else, and I'm just observing it through a screen. I can't hear the others talk anymore. I can't feel my heart pounding and don't even notice it when I'm being led toward the street. I obey quietly when someone helps me into the car but even though I see that my hands are shaking, I can't feel a single thing.

As soon as we walk through the hospital's double doors, everything comes rushing back. The massive headache and horrible nausea, the shaking, and the dizziness. I can feel my heart beating in my throat and my lungs being squeezed by an invisible iron fist when my brain catches up with where we are and why we're here.

I knew something was wrong. I felt it all evening and still, I did nothing.

I follow Jamie and Elija's parents on weak legs, barely able to see through my blurry eyes. I hate hospitals. And I hate that I'm reacting this strongly when this should be about Elija. He's hurt, and I want to be strong for him. Just this once, I'd like to be there when *he* needs *me*.

I force myself to breathe, ignoring the familiar scent of hand sanitizer and the memories it brings. Memories of my aunt connected to several machines. Memories of goodbyes.

I can't do this. As much as I hate myself for it, I'm not strong enough. I can't breathe. I can't see.

I find the closest wall, trying to be quiet as I gasp for air. Then, I walk until my hand hits the handle of a door. I open it and stumble into the room without having any idea where I am. It doesn't matter, though. I just need to be away from the others when this happens.

I fall to my knees, unable to support my own weight any longer. I can't feel the impact. All I can feel is the tightening of my lungs.

I'm still falling. I don't know what's up and down, so I curl up into a ball, trying to protect myself even though what's hurting me comes from within. I stay like that, hyperventilating until my head swims and darkness takes over. Until I'm no longer on the floor of that cold room.

Here, daylight is streaming through the window. It's a beautiful day. No cloud in the sky interrupting the sun's travel. It's warm outside but it doesn't reach this room.

No, this room is a cold nightmare. I'd recognize the interior anywhere.

"Florence," a soft voice says. I shake my head, tears gathering in my eyes as I fight my instinct to turn around.

"Florence, look at me," the voice repeats. Slowly, I obey.

In the clean, white bed centered in the room lies a beautiful woman. Dark brown hair, hazel eyes, and a loving smile on her lips. It's my aunt before she got sick.

"You're okay," she says, holding out a hand to me. I shake my head again, even as I take her hand greedily. My heart cracks in my chest. God, I miss her.

"Listen to me, you're okay. I know you're overwhelmed but right now, you need to suck it up. You can breathe, and you sure as hell can wake the fuck up. You're my little fighter, okay? My kind little fighter. You'll wake up now and be there for your boyfriend like you always used to be there for me," she insists, but I don't want to do that. I'm finally with her and I don't think I can handle this goodbye again.

"Florence, tell me you can do that," my aunt pushes, that old fire burning in her eyes. That determination and compassion all those hospital visits slowly snuffed out.

"I can do that," I croak over the tears clogging my throat.

"That's my girl. Now wake up."

My fight to regain consciousness feels akin to trudging through cold honey. My eyelids are heavy and my head swims as I sit up. I rub my eyes, breathing deeply before taking in my surroundings. It's an empty room apart from the vacant bed in the center. Thank god. It would have been horrible if I'd invaded a patient's room in my panicked state.

Slowly, I get to my feet, still shaking slightly, though it might just be from the cold. I wish I'd thought to bring my jacket.

With one last deep breath to fill my burning lungs, I get out of the room. *I can do this. I'm fine.*

With the help of a nurse, I find the guys and Elija's parents in less than five minutes. They blink when I arrive, asking me where the hell I've been.

"Sorry, needed a moment," I tell them with the faintest smile I can muster up. I must look like a mess, but no one here cares. For once, neither do I. "Is he going to be okay?" I ask, almost scared to hear the answer. I lower myself in the seat next to Benji. He puts an arm around me wordlessly, and I lean my head down on his shoulder, preparing for the worst.

"The doctor just left. He said they don't know when Elija will wake up but that he should be fine. He has a concussion but there's no internal bleeding. That's what's most important," Robert explains, sounding tired. "We'll go see him now. You guys should go home and get some sleep, we'll keep you posted if anything changes. No news are good news."

The guys all start getting to their feet, but I can't bring myself to do the same. Not even when Benji tugs at my hand, telling me, "Come on, we'll drop you off at home."

"That's okay. I'll just wait here," I tell him. Home is the last place I want to go right now. Anywhere but next to Elija is the last place I want to be.

My friend seems reluctant to leave without me, but Amelia comes to my aid. "Come on, Honey," she says, inviting me to go with them. I tell the guys goodnight and follow Elija's parents. Maybe I should feel bad for making them allow me to stay, but I don't have it in me. I need to see him for myself or I'll go crazy.

The three of us enter a room similar to the one I passed out in. The lights are on if not dimmed, and the bed isn't vacant. Instead, Elija lies there, his head bandaged but otherwise, looking peaceful. I hate it. It's only ever an illusion. Nothing about being hurt or sick is peaceful.

There's only one chair in the room so I simply stand next to him, holding his hand gently. It's already generous of Elija's parents to let me stay, so the chair, at least, is theirs.

"I'm getting myself a coffee. Can I get you something?" I hear Amelia ask.

"One for me as well, please," Robert replies.

"Florence?" the woman then asks. I jump slightly, having zoned out.

"Sorry, what was that?" I ask.

"Do you want something from the vending machine?" she repeats slowly. The sweet lady is staring at me all worried, so I try to smile softly as I shake my head. She has her own kid to worry about.

"I'm fine, thank you." The last thing I need is to give my stomach anything else to be upset about.

Amelia leaves, and the room falls silent. I keep watching her son, swiping my thumb across the back of his hand like he often does with me.

This is not how this evening should have gone. We should have eaten dinner together with his family. It would have been fun, and he would have been fine. He needs to be fine.

"You should try to get some sleep," Robert tells me from where he's sitting on the chair. He's right, I can feel how exhausted my body is, but I don't think my mind would allow me to sleep.

Still, I get down on my knees next to the bed, leaning my face against the side of it without letting go of my boy's hand.

I hear steps coming closer but don't turn around. Not even when I feel a heavy coat being draped over my shoulders.

"Thank you," I whisper uselessly, pressing my forehead harder against the thin mattress when I feel my eyes sting with unshed tears.

My kind little fighter. Be there for him like you always were for me. The reminder of my strange dream, my aunt's words in them has me blinking against the water gathering in my eyes. *Suck it up, Florence. You're better than this.* I've spent a lot of time putting up a facade for one sick loved one in the hospital, knowing the visits are never about me. I can do the same now.

Chapter 39

Elija

Holy hell, someone tell the psychopath in my head to stop carving out my brain. My head hurts so much, I can barely hear my own thoughts.

"Elija? I think he's waking up," I hear someone say. Even in my confused state do I recognize it, the voice that so quickly became my favorite one.

I try to force my eyes open, wanting to see Florence, but my body is protesting. Everything hurts so badly.

"Hey Champ, can you hear us?" a deeper voice asks. So my dad is here too. The question is just, where is *here*? I pry my eyelids open a crack and try not to wince at the bright light.

Before I can try to speak, someone's cupping my cheeks, directing my gaze to meet the most beautiful set of emerald eyes.

"Where am I?" I rasp huskily. Florence releases a wet chuckle.

"You're at the hospital. You fell down the stairs and hit your head," my mom tells me but I can't see her. I'm still looking at my girl, and a knot in my stomach tightens uncomfortably as I do so. Dark shadows circle her eyes, her skin is pale and her hair's a mess. Not that I care what she looks like but she's obviously exhausted and I hate to think it's because of me.

On its own command, one of my hands comes up to hold hers on my cheek, the need to touch her ingrained in my DNA by now.

Sommerstall Academy

"How long have I been here?" I ask softly. My throat is dry, but I don't want Florence to go away to get water for me.

"Since last night so about fifteen hours?" Florence replies, looking at my parents for aid.

"You've been here for that long?" She nods. "Have you slept at all?" I ask next. I hate that her cheeks glow pink at the indication, but she nods again, confirming my suspicion. "Have you eaten anything?" I ask, my voice lowered.

Florence tries to brush me off, but I have my answer right there.

"Very well. I already texted your friends you were awake so someone should be here soon. Would you mind if your mother and I went home to freshen up and maybe get some sleep? Kai came by a few hours ago to bring some of your essentials over. Your phone and headphones are here, just tell me if you need anything else. The doctor should check up on you soon," my dad says, finally making me look at him.

"That's good, thanks, and of course not, please go. Can you drop Florence off at her place on the way?" I ask. Then, realizing Florence is about to protest, I add, "You need some rest. I'll be fine here."

"You can come home with us if you don't want to go home, Honey. It's no problem," my mom says, making me furrow my eyebrows. Why wouldn't Florence want to go home? And what would my mother know about it?

"Thanks, but I'm okay here. Unless you want me to go? We don't have to talk. I'm sure your head is super sensitive right now." Her voice is even but there's a vulnerability in her eyes that she can't quite hide. I sigh, accepting defeat. To be honest, I want her to stay with me, but she needs sleep and food. Maybe if she stays here, I can at least keep an eye on and make sure she gets both.

My parents leave and the room falls quiet.

"You're an idiot," Florence finally tells me, looking completely serious.

"I am?"

"Yes! Do you have any idea how worried I was? God, Elija, your family and I spent over an hour not knowing where you were," she says, pacing the room and running a hand through her hair. Right as I was about to tell her to calm down, she takes a deep breath and drops her hands. She shakes her head to herself and in a much calmer tone adds, "I'm sorry. I know it wasn't your fault and I definitely shouldn't raise my voice at you right now. Tell me, how are you feeling? Can I get you anything?"

Okay, that mood change took place in less than a second, Florence going from stressed-out teen to a calm nurse.

"My head hurts a bit and my throat is dry, but I'm fine otherwise. Just aching a bit where I bruised other body parts on my way down," I promise, unsure what to do with her little outburst. She nods to herself before walking to a vacant chair and coming back with a water bottle. I accept it gratefully. When I'm done, I scoot to the edge of the small bed and tell Florence to lie down with me.

"Are you sure that's a good idea? What if I touch one of your bruises?" she asks.

"Then I'll survive, Florence. If you won't go home, then you'll at least rest here." Reluctantly, she snuggles up to me while muttering to herself, "I don't think I'll be able to rest in a hospital."

With a start, I realize I'm an idiot. She told me her aunt was sick for years before she died. It must really suck for her to be back here. Despite that, she stayed all night. For me. No wonder she looks wrecked.

"I'm sorry. You really don't have to stay," I tell her. She just scoots impossibly closer and holds me tight.

"I'm just glad you're okay."

I can feel Florence relax against me but just when I think she'll finally fall asleep, the door opens. My girl startles awake and tries to get off the bed when she recognizes the doctor, but I only pull her closer.

"Good to see you awake, Mister Mongrow. How are you feeling?" the old lady asks, not seeming to care at all that I'm sharing my bed. Quite the contrary, since she smiles fondly at the girl in my arms.

After a few routine questions, the doctor leaves again and I turn to look at Florence. Her eyelids are drooping, the whites of her eyes bloodshot, but she still smiles at me. I'm too worried to return it properly.

"I'm fine," she tells me as if reading my mind.

"You don't look fine, Florence. I don't mean to be mean, I hope you know that. I'm just worried about you. Please, just go home, eat, and sleep for a while. I'm not going anywhere," I tell her. She sits up so we can have a proper conversation, and I miss holding her instantly.

"I don't want to leave," she replies vaguely without meeting my eyes.

I frown. "Talk to me. Something's obviously going on."

"Nothing's going on," she insists half-heartedly. I get the feeling she's lying straight to my face and can't help but feel offended. Haven't I proven to her that she can trust me?

"Then why won't you go home?" I ask. "Your parents got home last night, didn't they? Are they giving you a hard time because you didn't go home all night? Or because you're skipping school? If so, I could try to talk to them," I offer, remembering the comment my mother made earlier.

"It's nothing, Elija. Don't worry about it. All that matters is making you feel better." But I am worrying about it. That combined with my massive headache does nothing for my patience. I try to sit up myself, ignoring Florence's protests. I can't talk to her if I'm lying down, and right now, I'm not dropping anything.

"Why are you lying to me?" I demand, unable to help myself.

"I'm not. Everything's fine," Florence insists stubbornly.

"You obviously are," I snap, raising my voice. The act makes the pounding in my head worse, only adding to my frustration.

"All I'm asking is for you to drop the act and be for real, just this once when I'm already in the hospital."

She frowns. "Please, Elija. You shouldn't get worked up. Let's just settle down and rest like you said," she tries to change the topic, her steady voice a stark contrast to mine.

"This conversation is making my head pound. You know how I feel about lies and now you just expect me to drop it and just rest? I can't do that with the possible explanations for your cagey behavior whirring in my head, Florence. It's so exhausting to try to figure out what you feel and think at all times because you won't communicate properly, and I honestly don't think I can do it right now. Just this once, please, don't be difficult!"

The girl across from me gets to her feet, shaking her head to herself and turning to face away from me. All the while muttering, "You don't mean that. It's fine." It only intensifies my headache. She's ignoring my every word.

"Of course I mean it. I told you I hated lies and acts and what you're doing right now is keeping things from me. Things that are obviously important." My head pounds so much that my visions blur. I lean back against my propped up pillow and massage my temple. This is the worst possible time to have this kind of conversation. Her pacing grates against the inside of my skull like a carving knife, evoking a sharp pain behind my eyes. It's what propels me to snap, "Stop walking! Just talk or fucking leave!"

I can barely keep my eyes open against the ache, but I hear that she keeps pacing. "You're just tired and injured. You don't mean that, you just need to get some sleep," she mutters.

"Stop making excuses for me. I'm not your parents, Florence! Just listen to me like I always listen to you," I insist before my anger gets the best of me, and I draw my next sentence out as if talking to a child. "I don't want to have to walk on eggshells around you and avoid talking about serious things, so if that is all you have to offer, you should. Just. Leave."

The last words taste bitter in my mouth, and when Florence turns to me, her eyes filled with tears and disbelief, I can feel my chest constricting.

Still, I know I mean what I said so I don't take it back. No matter how harsh that sounds.

"I'm sorry. I think we both should cool down," Florence says, her voice nothing above a hoarse whisper. I watch as she quickly gathers her things and mutters a silent goodbye. Then, she's gone.

The door closes behind Florence only to open again a few seconds later. I'm almost expecting my girl to reappear, but instead, Benji enters. I know I messed up when disappointment works its way through me.

"What happened? Why's Florence crying?" he asks.

"Wow, no 'how are you, Elija?'," I mutter. Another hot pulse shoots through my head, and I finally surrender to it and lie back down.

"I can see you're well enough. Now, what happened?" he repeats, his voice gruff with accusation. Well, this is just great. Really helping my headache.

"Shouldn't you be at school?" I drawl, ma tongue heavy and fuzzy in my mouth.

"I'm not missing more than I usually do. Stop avoiding my question. Why did your girlfriend, who stayed with your unconscious ass all night, just run past me like her ass was on fire?"

When he puts it like that, I feel even worse.

"We had an argument. I'll call her later. Hopefully, she'll be ready to talk then," I remark, unable to shake my lingering bitterness. I put so much effort into knowing her triggers and reading her body language, trying to accommodate her whenever I can and make sure she's as well as possible. Is it really too much to ask of her to be a bit forthcoming when I already admitted I'm in no shape to play the long game to get her reply? Honesty is so important to me and I've made it clear from the start. I hate feeling out of the loop.

Realizing how whiny I sound to my own ears, I decide it's time for me to stop complaining.

"Okay, I feel like there's a story there but I'm taking the hint now. Here, I snuck you in some food since I wasn't sure what they feed you here," Benji says, smiling sheepishly. When he hands me a whole Subway sandwich, I burst out laughing. The motion hurts so it's quickly cut short.

"Thanks, man. I really needed that," I tell him before taking the first bite. *Oh, hell yes.* It might be the concussion or the fact that I haven't eaten anything since lunch yesterday, but damn, this tastes good.

Benji keeps me company for a little longer, mostly with him telling me what happened after I fell last night. Joe ran, that rat. Not that anyone cared or really noticed since they were too busy freaking out over me.

I knew they loved me.

He also tells me that Miley won't be seeing her former friend again. Not after witnessing us stand up for Florence and her last night. That, at least, sounds like one good thing that came from last night.

No one should be treated the way Miley was last night. Especially by a friend. I like the idea of our group expanding a bit too, that way Florence will have some girls to talk to.

Of course, we need to make up first for that.

At about four pm, my parents come back so Benji can leave. I told them I don't need a babysitter at all times, but they don't care, saying they want to make sure I don't get lonely. Really, *lonely*? I'd be more than fine with some alone time and a break from all the talking.

After a quick scan of my room, my mom say, "Where's Florence? I brought her some of my clothes in case she wants to change. They won't fit, of course, but I thought I'd offer it either way."

I chew on my bottom lip, feeling guiltier by the second. I tried calling her twenty minutes ago but she didn't pick up.

She's probably still mad, so I'll give her some more time and try again later.

"She left," I tell my parents, which quickly gets their notice. They stop scanning the room and fix me with their undivided attention. It's kind of unnerving.

"Going where?" my dad asks slowly. I shrug.

"Don't know. Home, I guess." My mom and dad share a look, making my nerves act up all over again. What is it I don't know?

"Sweetie, are you sure?" my mom asks tentatively.

"Where else would she go?" Honestly, what is happening?

"Anywhere else? I'll ask Kai if she turned up at our place," my dad mutters.

"What? Why? She'd never just go to our place uninvited. Can someone please tell me what you're going on about?" I finally snap.

"Didn't you two talk about last night?" my mom asks, her eyes sad.

"She told me you were all worried about me, that's it. What happened last night?"

"Oh, well, if she didn't say anything, maybe we shouldn't."

"Mom, please," I say, but it's my dad who replies.

"I'm sure it's fine, Amelia. Elija, Florene's mother came to our place right before Jamie told us about you. She and Florence had an argument and things kind of... escalated," he explains.

I frown. Her mother came to our place? That's the last thing I would have guessed. How did she even know where to go?

"Escalated how?" I ask, a sick feeling gathering in my stomach. My parents share another look, making my blood boil. "Just tell me!"

"Well, I'm sure some things came out wrong, and then her mother kind of... slapped her," my dad says, his voice rough. Meanwhile, my jaw hangs slack. Florence's own mother raised a hand against her? My mind's going in a spiral.

Did that happen before?

What happened after?

Finally; where the hell is my girl now? I sure as fuck hope it's not somewhere within a mile of her parents, but at the same time, I don't know where else she'd go.

I grab my phone and send a message into the guys' group chat, asking if anyone knows where she is and if they can reach her. Then, I try to call her myself. She doesn't pick up.

"Elija, where did she say she was going?" my mom asks, probably noticing my sudden panic. God, I'm such an idiot for losing my calm with Florence like that. Last night must've been so horrible for her and I sent her away when she had nowhere to go.

"She didn't say anything. We had an argument and I just told her to leave but I didn't know," I tell her. I don't care that she sees the pathetic tears welling in my eyes. I feel like shit.

"Oh, Elija, I'm sure it's fine. She's a smart girl. She probably went to a friend's place. Or maybe she went home to work things out with her parents," my dad tries to reassure me. It really doesn't help, though. Especially when messages from my friends start rolling in, telling me they can't reach her either.

"You don't understand. She gets overwhelmed and has these really bad panic attacks. She's tired and hasn't even eaten anything." I try to get to my feet, but my mom's there, ready to hold me in place.

"Slow down, now, boy. You can't leave yet. How about this, we take care of finding Florence and keep you posted?" she offers. It's immensely generous to even consider spending their time going after her, but I still argue.

"And what, you want me to lie around here uselessly? She was crying when she left, and I did nothing!" I try to reason with her, knowing that I didn't just do nothing. I made her feel even worse with my outburst.

My mother's grip on me only tightens. "Elija, calm down. You're injured. You had a fight, it happens, that doesn't mean you get to jeopardize your health. You're staying here," she orders, leaving no room for argument.

There's something calming about it, the way she's staying collected. It's enough to make my frantic mind switch back a few gears to think logically. My mom's probably right. Florence is a smart girl. She probably just turned off her phone when I first called her, still upset and wanting more time to think. That has to be the reason why she's unreachable.

Chapter 40

Florence

I'm an idiot, that's what I am. Really, who runs off into the forest after a sleepless night and no meal? I just wanted to breathe and get away from all the people looking at me curiously. I know I look rough, okay? No need to remind me by staring as I walk down the street. I couldn't take it, so when I saw a walkway lead into the woods, I took the turn, eager to disappear from view.

But now, here I am, several crossroads later, with no clue which way I came from and no service. At least my detour has given me some time to think about my dumb behavior from earlier today. I should have just talked to Elija. I know that now. It's just that I was trying so hard all night not to think about my interaction with my mom that my immediate reaction was to distract and evade.

It's hard to believe that she raised her voice at me, not to mention slapped me. But I guess I'm overreacting. After all, she told me she was worried about me. Not her exact words but that's what her outburst really was, wasn't it? Besides, she didn't hit me hard. As she said, nothing really happened.

She hasn't tried contacting me since then. Neither has my dad. I'm not sure what to do with that but I guess they're busy. It's fine.

I'm lost in my thoughts when the sound of footsteps snap me out of it. My heartbeat spikes as I whip around, expecting some serial killer and ready to fight them. I release a shaky breath when it's only a dog. A big fluffy white one with the face of an angle.

"I'm so sorry. Don't worry, she doesn't bite!" a person yelps as they run up to me. "I really wasn't expecting to meet someone so deep into the woods, so I let her walk ahead."

"It's fine," I say. Reaching out slowly, I let the dog sniff my hand before softly petting her silky fur.

"I hope she didn't scare you. I'm Lex." They wave awkwardly. I smile even though it feels strange to do so right now. The action takes more effort than it should, reminding me that I really need to eat something soon.

"Florence," I introduce myself.

"Ehm, Florence, are you all right? You look a little lost, no offense. Your face is a little ashen. And-" I cut them off.

"I know. I know, I look as bad as I feel. I am lost, actually. If you could just point me in the direction of the hospital, that would be great. I can find my way home from there." At least, I think I can once I've eaten something.

"Ah, sure. It's that way." They point at a pathway leading away from where I was going but that makes sense. I've been wandering around for a while. "But, well... It takes at least an hour to get there by foot," Lex explains doubtfully.

I brush her off even as my stomach tightens. "I'm not in a hurry. Thanks for your help." With one last strained smile, I'm walking back to the hospital.

I mentally prepare for my conversation with Elija to distract myself from how sick I feel. I hate it when I get hungry to the point where I'm just as nauseous as when I eat, but there's nothing to do about it now. I'll just get myself something from the vending machine once I make it back.

I manage to keep my drained body going for about forty minutes before the world starts tilting and I know I really messed up. I dig my teeth into my bottom lip and bite down hard to get my adrenalin working. It won't help me for long, but I really need a few more seconds if I'm about to drop like a rock in the woods by myself.

I pull my phone from my pocket and see with relief that I have reception here. Blinking back my dizziness, I send Elija my location. I hope he's not still mad enough to ignore my message without context.

Worst case scenario, I'll just be knocked out in the forest alone for a while. What's the worst that could happen, right?

The familiar cold curses through my body so I try to lie down, knowing I can't fight off the darkness any longer. My blood sugar is too low, my body too drained.

I'm out cold before my body hits the ground.

I slowly come back to consciousness with a groan. I take a few deep breaths and look at my surroundings, remembering what happened and where I am. The first thing I notice is how incredibly uncomfortable I am. Good to know I wasn't competent enough to land on a nice patch of grass when I passed out. Nope, I had to fall face-first into the wet dirt.

I roll onto my back and try to wipe my face clean. The movement alone takes a lot of effort, my limps feeling incredibly heavy. That's the thing with passing out. It's not something you do to feel better afterward. Nope, I'm still as hungry, still as dizzy, and still as flipping cold as before. Just sweatier and paler

Why did I have to choose the coldest day of May to pass out in the forest?

With a pang of disappointment, I realize I'm as alone as I was when I fell. I sent Elija my location, didn't I? Yet here I am, no sign of him nearby. Sure, I have no idea how much time has passed, it could have just been a few minutes, but I can't fight of the wave of disappointment I feel.

I reach for my phone to check the time and maybe call someone only to find the cold gadget turned off. Dead. Great!

Okay, let's try not to panic. I should be, what, 20 minutes away from the hospital? Easy as pie. I can make it.

I try to get to my feet but as soon as my head is off the ground more dizziness washes over me in waves. I let my back fall down again, breathing heavily.

I won't walk, then. Whatever. *I can just crawl*, I think miserably.

That's when I hear the most beautiful sound. "Florence!" a familiar voice yells, and I nearly cry out in relief.

I hear his hurried steps until he drops to his knees beside me, touching my face and searching me with frantic eyes.

"You came," I state the obvious tiredly. His eyebrows furrow, a flash of hurt crossing his eyes.

"Of course, I did. I came as soon as you texted me, but I had to fight my mom off first. Fuck, Florence, did you think I wouldn't? Never mind, don't answer that. What are you doing here? Are you hurt?" he rambles. I shake my head a bit.

"I'm stupid, I shouldn't have texted you. You're injured. I'm sorry," I tell him, realizing how reckless it was of me. I could have texted any of the guys. I should have thought of that.

"Don't even go there. I'm glad you texted me. I was freaking out because no one knew where you were. If that's how you felt last night," he trails off, shaking his head. "Never mind. Are you hurt, Florence? What happened?"

"I just need to eat something, and maybe some sleep," I assure him.

"I didn't bring anything with me," Elija says, and I can tell he's still worried, so I smile softly. Before I can answer, I hear a car door being closed and realize we're not alone. How did I miss the hum of the engine for this long?

"Florence, are you okay?" Elija's mom asks as she hurries over. Oh, this is about to be embarrassing. I can feel my cheeks burning up already.

"Mom, do you have anything sugary in the car?" Elija asks.

"Just some old cola," she replies.

"Can you get that, please?" I wish I was in any position to tell Elija not to ask her that. I feel like such an inconvenience, lying on the forest floor, unable to move, and needing the help of others. His parents must hate me now for dragging Elija out of his hospital room before he was cleared. This is where they realize I'm not good for him. That I'm too messed up.

Elija gently raises my head so I'm leaning against his chest before he helps me drink the bubbly beverage. I usually hate soft drinks, but I won't deny that it really helps. In a few minutes, I'm able to get to my feet and walk to the car.

Robert's behind the wheel, looking at Elija and me worriedly through the rear-view mirror before driving off. No one speaks, and the radio's off. It's making me anxious. What must they be thinking? Finding me lying dirty and shivering in the middle of the forest. I'm such an idiot.

Elija, probably noticing how he always does, sets a hand on my leg and absently drums my rhythm with his finger. It does the trick and I relax into my seat, closing my eyes for a bit as I focus on only that.

Chapter 41

Elija

She's finally asleep. We're a few minutes away from the hospital but she's finally asleep so I tell my dad to drive to our place instead. He doesn't try to talk me out of it. They spent about five minutes trying to get me to stay in my hospital bed before finally agreeing to get to the location Florence had sent me. At this point, they know it's not worth arguing about, and I can tell that now that they saw her like this, they don't want to.

So on our way home, we are, all silent to allow her more rest.

"I'll carry her inside. Will you please go back to the hospital now? The doctor said she wanted to keep you overnight for observation," my dad says.

"But she needs to e-" I want to protest but my mom cuts me off.

"Enough, Elija. Please, let me drive you back. She's sleeping right now, and you can call her later," she says. She looks genuinely tired, and that's enough to make me shut up. She's right, I guess. I may not like it, but my parents are worried, so we'll do what the doctor said. I just hope we can handle the extra charges.

I hate this system.

I unbuckle my girl's seatbelt and my dad picks her up, gently so as not to wake her. Then, he walks toward our door and my mom and I drive off.

I text my dad to plug Florence's phone in only for him to tell me he already did. Then, I text Kai to check if we have green apples, wondering if I made a mistake by letting her sleep. Shouldn't she maybe have eaten something first?

But if she ate, she couldn't have lied down for some time, and therefore couldn't have slept. Fuck, this sucks.

"Hey, you feeling better?" I ask Florence the second she picks up. She just texted me she woke up, so I called her. I can hear her laugh over the line.

"I'm supposed to ask you that," she chides. "But, I'm better, thanks. Sorry for making such a scene, I didn't mean to freak you out. And your parents, oh god, I'm mortified."

"No one's judging you, Florence. Trust me, we're just glad you're feeling better. Now, did you eat something?"

"I texted you the second I woke up. When was I supposed to have eaten?" she points out, chuckling again.

"Okay, I get it. There should be green apples downstairs. My dad is out with the twins so you're probably home alone, so just take a look around in the pantry and decide what you want to eat, okay? No one will mind."

"I can't just eat your family's food. Besides, I should get home soon. My parents are probably worried," Florence tells me. I bite my tongue to hold back a comment about how she's still pretending nothing happened. Losing my temper won't help, so I take a deep breath and reply calmly.

"My parents told me about what happened," I tell her. The line goes quiet for so long, I check if she's still there. She is. "Did that happen before? With your mother?"

"No," she replies quietly. Man, I wish I could hold her during this conversation, but I promised my mom I'd spend another night in the hospital.

"Did she or your father contact you since?" I ask.

"Not really."

I clench my fist even as I force my voice to be even. My chest hurts hearing her subdued voice, knowing something that's out of my control is hurting her. "Why didn't you tell me?"

"I don't know. I guess I thought if I just didn't talk about it, it wouldn't be true. I'm sorry I lied," she says.

"Don't worry about it. I'm sorry I snapped at you. I shouldn't have pushed that hard. Now, are you eating yet?"

"Yeah, sure. I'll go downstairs now, but I think I'll really head home after." I hear the bed rustle and the sound of her quiet steps as she walks down the stairs.

"It'll be dark by the time you'll arrive, and you sure as hell won't take an uber again after what nearly happened. Just stay over at my place, please. You can have my bed and make yourself at home."

"I can't do that, Elija. I'd like to talk to my parents. I can't avoid them forever," she tells me. I groan inwardly. Not that I don't understand, I just don't like the idea of her being close to those assholes ever again.

"Let me at least text Kai. He'll give you a ride. Or one of the guys. Just promise me you'll wait for one of them, okay?"

"Fine," she mumbles but I can tell she's not happy about it. My poor girl, so bad at accepting help.

"Aww, don't pout, little one. That's not how good girls like you behave," I tease her to lighten the mood, only to hear her choking on something. "Florence, you okay there?" I ask.

"Yeah," she says after a while. A slow smile tugs at my lips.

"What was that all about?" I prod.

"Hm? Nothing," she denies, sounding very unconvincing.

"Yeah, you sure about that? You sure you didn't react to something I said?"

"I don't know what you're talking about," she repeats. Such a little liar.

"Mhm. Sure. You wouldn't mind if I kept calling you a good girl, then, would you?" I tease her.

"No," she squeaks. Guess I found a sweet spot there. I store that knowledge away for another time.

"Good to know. Now, what do you want to say to your parents?" I ask, getting back on track.

"I'm not sure. They'll probably pretend nothing happened, but I think I'll just be upfront and demand answers. They've been acting weird recently and I'm sick of being in the dark about it."

"You don't think they'll hurt you again, do you?" The words leave my lips with some resistance, and I hate to even think about it. Really, no one deserves to be abused at home. The thought of harm coming to Florence, especially in the place that should be her safe haven, sits very wrong with me.

"It's never happened before. I can't tell if it was a one-time thing, to be honest. My mother didn't really seem remorseful afterward, so we'll just have to see, I guess," she answers as if it was nothing. As if we weren't talking about her getting hurt.

The knot of unease in my stomach tightens enough for me to consider going against my word to my mother and leaving the hospital so Florence won't be alone with her parents.

"You can't mean that. There must be another way. You could report them or something," I try to reason.

"Because of what, one slap? They're my parents, Elija."

"So what? They are shitty people," I snap.

"You don't know them," she defends them.

"I know enough. I know they've been treating you like shit when you don't deserve it, and that's enough to make me hate them." Why can't she see that?

"They didn't use to be like that," she argues, her voice biting.

"You're just making excuses for them. People change, Florence."

"Which means they can change back!" she snaps back. I hate that we're fighting again, but it's just so damn hard to understand how she can't see my point. Does she care so little about her own well-being?

"That's not how it works. And even if it was, how long are they going to hurt you before changing again? Are you going to let them abuse you further? Not only verbally but physically now as well? When will you stop clinging to that small shimmer of hope and do what's good for you?"

"When I can't do it anymore! Don't you get it, Elija? They are my parents. They're all I have," she mutters defeatedly.

"Don't say that. There are so many people that care about you, me at the very top of them. But your parents? Florence, they're ruining you. You're already starving yourself. How much longer can you carry on? How many panic attacks and blackouts are you away from just not getting back up? I don't want to see you fade away," I tell her, my chest squeezing.

She sighs and sniffles. "I'm sorry. I have to try talking to them."

I swallow my next protest. Maybe she's right. Maybe I'm overreacting because I'm worried, and I guess if there's a chance Florence can salvage her relationship with her parents, it's worth a try. Doesn't mean I have to like it. "Well, Kai's on his way. Please text me when you're home or at least after you had the talk. I'll be on my phone, ready if you need anything. And hospital or not, Florence, don't worry about inconveniencing me. I'll always come when you need me."

"Thanks. For understanding. And everything else. I know I'm a mess right now, but I promise I'll pull myself together and things will be like they were," she promises, and if anything, her words are like a slap in the face.

She's promising me she'll hide behind those façades again, isn't she? That she'll do anything she thinks I want her to and behave so it's the most convenient for the people around her. Meanwhile, all I want is for her to be more selfish and put herself first.

"I know you think you need to be all right all the time, but that's not true. Please, don't shut me out because you think it's getting too messy for me or that I can't and don't want to handle it. I can and I want to help. Do you understand that? I don't mind repeating myself if you need to hear it again." I hear her chuckle softly.

"I understand. Thanks. Oh, your brother's here. Call you later, bye!" She hangs up before I get the chance to say anything else.

"Bye."

Chapter 42

Florence

"Hi, Kai. Thank you so much for giving me a ride. I know you probably have better things to do right now," I say as I walk up to the older Mongrow. I stop a few feet away from him, not sure how to greet him, but his smile is warm enough so I don't feel too awkward. He finishes the distance between us and hugs me.

"Hey. No problem, my girlfriend was in the mood for pizza anyways, so we were on the road," he tells me, pulling away. "You got everything?"

"Yes, thanks," I tell him. With that, we leave his home and walk toward his car, where two people are waiting. One East-Asian woman, who I assume is Kai's girlfriend, is in the passenger seat, and a short-looking man is in the back.

"Hi, I'm Miyu. It's nice to meet you," the girl says, turning her head to see me as I get in the back next to the guy. She's so ridiculously beautiful I need to force my jaw not to drop. That long, straight black hair paired with those striking, dark eyes and her otherwise pale complexion.

"Florence. The pleasure is all mine," I finally say.

"Easy, Florence. If you keep looking at my girl like that, I'm going to feel threatened. I'll totally tell on you to Elija," the other stranger exclaims humorously. Wait, *his* girl?

There must be a big question mark written all over my face since Kai laughs.

"We're poly, Flo. All three of us are in a relationship," Elija's brother tells me.

"Oh." I laugh. "Right, sorry. Okay, go on," I tell the other guy, who still hasn't introduced himself.

"I'm Alejandro and I'll be seriously offended if you don't gape at me like you did Miyu. Obviously, I'm the most beautiful in this relationship," he announces before laughing it off. "Just kidding."

I decide Kai's one lucky dude for scoring not one but two funny and attractive people. Not that I can complain, of course. I'm perfectly happy with my boy.

As the ride goes on, I learn enough things to make my head swim. For one, I'm told Alejandro is Mexican and has only been in the US for about ten years. Miyu is from Japan, though she was born and raised here.

I also get to know my boyfriend's brother a bit better. He works part-time as a swimming coach at a college nearby, which explains the shape he's in. On the days he's not there, he works as a barista. It's quite impressive.

Between Kai's sweetness, Miyu's sass, and Alejandro's sarcastic jokes, I completely forget to worry about what awaits me at home. Only when we stop in front of my driveway does the laughter die on my lips, reality crashing back.

The car goes silent the longer I stay frozen in my seat, and although I can feel three sets of curious eyes on me, I can't seem to muster up a smile and the courage to get out.

"Are you hungry? We're going for pizza, if you feel like it," Alejandro finally breaks the silence as well as the spell I was under. Apparently, I'm now visibly pathetic enough to be invited to forth wheel on a date. This is a new low, even for me.

"I should really get home but thanks for offering. Enjoy your dinner," I tell him before finally getting out. I'm not about to crash their date. Nope. Though, I don't doubt they could make it possible for me to stomach some pizza. They're really awesome.

Now, back to my task. I force my feet to keep going forward until I reach my front door. Aware of the car that hasn't gone away yet, I wave at them and enter my home, trying to put on a brave facade I all but feel.

The house feels cold and dead, more so than usual now that I've spent thirty minutes in a stuffy car with lively people.

"Hello? I'm home," I announce, trying to keep my voice even.

I hear a sound from the kitchen although there's no verbal reply and decide to follow it. Despite the fact that everything in me tells me not to. *They're your parents. Relax.*

As expected, both my parents are sitting at the kitchen table. My mom seems to be cooking dinner while my dad's on his phone. It's such a normal scene, I feel as if I'd stepped into the twilight zone. Both of them look up at me before returning their attention to their tasks as if I wasn't here at all. That's even weirder. All my life, there have been certain rules that everyone always abided to, and one of them was to at least act cordially at all times. It's obvious the rules are changing, but without the new manual, I feel entirely out of my depth.

"I think we should talk," I finally announce, gathering all my courage. My mom looks up, arching an eyebrow to prompt me to go on. "About what happened the last time I saw you. I get that you must've been worried after not finding me at home and that combined with the long travel back wasn't a good combination. Things were said and done that weren't supposed to. Still, I think we've reached a point where we should talk about it."

My mother sighs and her shoulders drop a tad. I can't believe it. The wary action almost makes her look human.

"You're right, Sweetie. I am so sorry about last night, there's really no excuse. It won't happen again, that, I can promise. Can you forgive me?" she asks. It's not at all how I thought this conversation would go, and it's such a pleasant surprise that I find myself nodding without questioning it.

We all make mistakes and if my mother says she's sorry, that's done. She has never once apologized for me, at least not that I can remember, so her owning up to making a mistake means something. What good would it do for me to hold one bad night against her? It's not like something horrible happened anyway. I think it just felt worse than it was at the time because I was overwhelmed with the situation and the evening with no trace of Elija. It was a bad combination and in turn blew things out of proportions in my mind.

"Just one more thing. Has everything been all right at work? You two have seemed a bit more tense recently," I add, hoping I'm not crossing a line. Whatever this treaty is, it feels fragile.

"We apologize for that. Work's been stressful and you haven't been around as much lately. I guess it's hard for us to see our little girl grow up, isn't it, Barb?" my dad asks.

"Absolutely. Now, tell us about that boy, why don't you? I hope it's all right for me to assume you have a boyfriend," my mother replies carefully. I beam at that, not only because thinking about Elija lifts my spirits but because my mother is showing interest in me. In my life. It's an unfamiliar feeling and one that wraps around me like a warm embrace. *Is this what it's like for Elija when he talks to his parents?* To think that so shortly after feeling envious of his parents, mine seem to finally start acting the same.

With my heart feeling twice its size, I start my rant. "I do. His name is Elija and he goes to school with me. You don't have to worry, he treats me really well, and he's always respectful, not to mention insanely talented. He makes me happy," I add shily, not quite sure how to go about this without precise questions they need answered. I've never talked to either of my parents about so much as a crush, so to say I'm unfamiliar with the process and the appropriate information to share would be an understatement.

"That sounds lovely. Why don't you invite him over for dinner soon? Seeing as you know his parents, it's only fair," my mom offers, her cheeks rosy as she smiles at me. A real smile. I don't think I've seen that look on her face, least of all directed at me, in a really long time. My chest swells further to the point

Sommerstall Academy

where I can hardly handle it. *Is this real? Or am I still passed out in the woods, my mind creating a reality based on my longings?*

"Really? I mean, of course. I'd love that. He just got injured recently, so it might take a few more days until he's up to it. Is that all right?" I ask, trying to keep my tentative excitement from my voice.

"Of course. How does Saturday sound? That way, he has three more days to recover," my dad proposes.

"I'll ask him. Thank you two so much, you're the best!" I tell them before hurrying off into my room. I quickly call Elija, eager to tell him the great news.

"Hi. Did you do it already? How'd it go?" he pounces the second the call connects, worry clear in his voice.

"I did it!" I squeal before pulling myself together. "It went so much better than expected. They apologized for their behavior and last night specifically. They even asked about you, and guess what. They'd like to meet you!" I announce.

When he's quiet for multiple beats, my excitement dies down a bit. "What's wrong? Why aren't you saying anything? Do you not want to meet them? I can tell them you're busy," I say slowly. Truth is, I'd hate that. For once, my parents want to be part of something I care about and canceling that would hurt. Still, if Elija doesn't feel up for it, I won't force him.

"No, it's not that. Just," he trails off and I hear him sigh. Foreboding sours my fragile good mood. "That's it? They apologized and everything is fine again?" he asks.

"What do you mean? They said it won't happen again, Elija. And my mother really sounded sincere, and they were nicer to me now than they've been in a long time. Maybe this talk was just what we needed, no matter the trigger. This could be the change into the right direction like I said. What do you want me to do, hold a grudge forever? Everyone makes mistakes."

"Not everyone hits their kids, though, Florence. I just think you should be a bit more cautious. You wear your heart on your sleeve, and it's one of your best traits, but this once, I think you should protect yourself. I'm not telling you to stay mad at them. If you believe their words were sincere, that's great. But be careful before getting your hopes up too soon," he tries to reason. Somehow, it makes me mad.

Why can't he be happy for me? Share my enthusiasm instead of warning me from my own parents when they clearly regret the way they've been acting. I force a calming breath down my throat before I dare reply.

"What you're saying might make sense to you, but I know my parents. They were different tonight, more sincere than I've seen them since my aunt passed away. Just tell me if you have time this Saturday evening. If you don't want to meet them, that's fine too. We don't have to rush anything," I assure him, glad when I find no trace of my irritation in my voice. The last thing I want to do is have a fight *again*.

He thankfully picks up on my dismissal of his change in topic. "Yeah, Saturday is fine, and of course, I'll be there. I told you I'll always be there where you need me to be. How long until you realize you have me wrapped around your finger, Florence?" He chuckles, lightening the mood.

"I do?" I ask, a slow smile spreading over my lips as the last whisps of my irritation slips through my fingers.

"Fuck, you have no idea."

"For the records, so do you. Me," I stumble over my words, caught on the deep timbers of his voice and his admission. *Agh, shoot me*. Seriously, I get a little flustered and immediately become a babbling idiot. Elija must find me very amusing since I can hear him laugh. One good thing to it, at least.

"I do you?" he teases me.

"That's not what I meant, and you know it. But I mean, I wouldn't say no to that either," I say, suddenly shy. Is it okay for me to say something like that?

"Fuck," Elija groans. "Don't say that when I'm so far away from you." Oh? I guess he doesn't mind my boldness, then.

"Why? Am I turning you on? Is your mind torturing you with memories of the last time? Memories of how good I felt stretched around you?" I ask him even as my cheeks burn up. I've read about characters saying similar things a million times, and yet, the words feel strange coming from my lips.

This is way out of my comfort zone and I'm not sure this is a good idea. Especially since I'm recalling those memories myself, intensifying my blush as my body heats.

"Florence, I swear to god I'll-" I cut him off, fueled by the low gruffness in his voice.

"You'll what? Come over here and fuck me until I can't walk straight for a week? Please do," I tell him, though I'm not sure I'm playing anymore.

My boyfriend groans again, making me smile. "Are you hard?" I wonder.

"Yes," he replies honestly. "But only because I know you're wet. The things you said turn you on just as much as they did me. You like teasing me."

Yeah, he's not wrong.

"I wonder," he muses, his voice teasing.

"What?" I prompt.

"Will you take care of it? Will you finish what you started and touch yourself imagining it's me? Fuck, even better yet, will you let me hear as you come around those sweet little fingers of yours?"

I answer with nothing more than a high-pitched squeak, my voice stunned away. Could I do that? I know I want to, but I'm hesitant. I mean, my parents are home.

But somehow, that last part only makes me feel dizzier. I just don't understand why. After all, them being around means I could get caught. Worst case scenario, they could hear me say something risky or even moan. That would be so awkward and horrible, so why is my blood running hotter at the thought that I shouldn't do it?

"Use your voice, Florence. Would you do that?"

Softly, I answer him. "Yes."

He mutters something under his breath before speaking to me again, his voice demanding.

"Take off your pants." I comply, feeling guilty but so flipping turned on at the same time. "Is your door locked?" he asks when I'm done.

"Yes," I breathe out, anticipation making it hard for me to speak.

"Good. Now, can you touch yourself for me?" Elija asks. I can almost imagine what he looks like right now, those dark eyes of his lidded with lust and his tattoos moving over his muscled arms as he clenches his fists. All because of me.

I bite back a groan as I let my fingers run along the inside of my thigh, stroking my pussy over my panties twice before moving back to my knee. "Are you doing it as well?" I ask Elija as I tease myself.

"Fuck yes."

"Tell me what you're doing," I beg, needing to hear his voice. To pretend he's right here with me.

"I have my eyes closed, thinking of you lying in your bed like you did that day. My fist is around my dick below the blanked like a pre-teen." I chuckle and he groans. "I'm imagining you're with me. That it's you touching me, getting wet by it like you did when you had my dick down your throat," he goes on.

I finally slip my panties aside and run my fingers up my slit to gather some of my wetness before circling my clit with it. I breathe out a quiet moan.

"You're drenched, aren't you? Fuck your fingers for me, Florence. Use two like I would." Again, I do as I'm ordered, the fact that it's really him getting me off rather than me a huge turn on. I keep circling my clit with one hand while I slip two fingers inside of my pussy. I clench down on them, pretending they're his thick ones instead of mine.

I hear Elija's breathing getting deeper, so I pick up my pace, making myself moan in the process.

"Shh, Florence, we can't have your parents hearing you. Be a good girl and keep quiet before you get us caught," Elija tells me. Damn him for knowing exactly what I need to hear. I bite down hard on my bottom lip to keep myself from making another sound. What I didn't expect was my pleasure to intensify at the sting of it.

I bite down harder until I taste the coppery tang of blood in my mouth. I release my lips and lick them, my toes curling.

What is wrong with me? I'm tasting blood and it turns me on? What am I, a flipping vampire? Shocked by the revelation, I quickly pull my tongue back behind my lips and stick it to the roof of my mouth.

"You're getting louder again. Don't make me hang up on you," Elija tsks.

"I'm close," I say, my voice nothing above a whisper.

"Shit, I wish I could see you right now. But I'll just have to remember all the dirty things I want to do to you until you're with me again," he mutters.

"Tell me," I beg, desperately grinding my hips against my hands. I can't remember a time when I lost my inhibitions like this while pleasuring myself. Usually, I'm so caught up with thoughts of what I should be doing that touching myself makes me uncomfortable. Right now, that's definitely not the case. All I'm thinking about is Elija.

"So bossy. Who would've thought my girl would turn out to be so dirty? Asking to hear all about the ways I'll make you see stars as I destroy that sweet little cunt of yours."

I moan, unable to help myself.

"Oh, she likes it when I say things like that. You're a moaning mess for me, aren't you? And all at the prospect of pain," he tsks. I ride my fingers more frantically, closing my eyes and losing myself in his voice and moans. "Oh, I can give you pain, if that's what you want. I can show you all sorts of things, Florence, all you have to do is ask. I bet you'll beg me nicely, won't you?"

I nod.

"Answer me," Elija demands, making me realize he can't see me.

"Ye- yes!"

"Good girl," he says. I clamp my mouth shut, my back arching and my toes curling as waves of pleasure rush through me. I keep moving my hands, my strokes desperate and jerky as I twitch and writhe.

Elija groans loudly just when my body finally slumps. For a while, both of us are breathing heavily as we come down from our highs.

"Holy shit," he finally mutters.

"Yeah," I agree tiredly. As I wait for my legs to stop feeling wobbly, I hug my pillow against my chest, imagining it was Eli. "I wish you were here," I tell him.

"Me too, Florence. Me too."

Before I can say anything else, someone's knocking on my door. "Dinner's ready!" my father yells against the wood before walking off. Meanwhile, my heart's pounding against my ribcage like a wild animal.

"Holy shit, that scared the hell out of me. Elija, I have to go. Love you, bye," I say before ending the call and hurriedly getting ready. I look in the mirror, taking in my flushed face and messy hair. I wash my hands and face, brush my hair quickly and throw on some proper clothes. Then, I leave my room only to stop dead in my tracks.

Oh god.

No, please no!

Tell me I didn't say what I think I did.

I told Elija that I loved him! Oh *god*.

Robotically, I force my legs to keep moving and shove the panicked thoughts aside. My parents are expecting me and I don't want to break our fragile good terms by being late. I step around the corner and face the living room, only to be faced with another surprise. We have guests I knew nothing about. The couple seems to be roughly my parents' age and after a quick glance at the strangers' hands, I figure they're married.

"Florence, here you are. Bob, Rose, this is our daughter, Florence. Florence, these are the Martins, our most esteemed business partners," my mother purrs with her perfectly polished smile. So much for enjoying an evening filled with more of their personal questions. I thought we could catch up since it's been forever since I really talked to my parents, but I guess it'll have to wait. It just would have been nice to get a heads-up, but my parents must have forgotten. Knowing this game, I smile politely at our guests and go to shake their hands.

"It's lovely to meet you," I tell them, my voice almost a tad too sweet. I haven't done this in a while, so it seems I'm a little rusty. Being paraded around in public used to be the status quo around here.

"The pleasure is all ours," Mr. Martin says, staring more at my chest than my face, even though my shirt doesn't show off any cleavage. With some embarrassment, I realize I'm not wearing a bra, and it takes every shred of control for me not to pull my hand out of his to cross my arms.

When I shake the man's wife's hand, I note she squeezes mine too tightly, despite her acting like she didn't notice her husband's wandering gaze. I let her play it that way without a remark, despite my disdain toward such snakes. I know my place here.

And so, the next two hours drag by slowly. I'm able to stay out of their conversations and mentally drift off other than the two times I come up. Once my parents mention how well I'm doing at school, and later, they say what big plans I have for the future. I pretend everything they say is true when really, they know nothing about me.

"Yeah, and she reads a lot of books," my mom throws in there at one point.

"Oh really? What kind?" Mrs. Martin asks, feigning interest as her husband takes in my body once more. It makes the bad kind of goosebumps prick my skin, and I suppress a shudder. It's been like this all night, with his strange leering making me feel dirty and powerless in my own home. Everyone else at the table *must* have noticed by now, but I wouldn't expect my parents to call who seems to be a very important business partner out on his behavior.

"The classics," I say, hopefully ending the conversation. I don't want to give the man sitting opposite me any excuse to look at me. I've hardly been able to get down any of the food my mother prepared. Not that I have a choice. It's simply not acceptable not to finish my plate, insult that would be. Nope, *just keep eating*, I tell myself. Even though I hate myself and my body more with every bite.

After dinner, the adults are quick to move their conversation to the couch, where one of my dad's most expensive bottles of bourbon is waiting. I help my mother in the kitchen as the other three people start discussing business.

"Can I go to my room after we're done? I'm tired and I wouldn't want to intrude," I say in a hushed voice so only she can hear.

"You'll stay for a bit. Then, you'll say you have work to finish for school tomorrow," she says curtly. I frown at the harsh contrast to her earlier niceties toward me but remind myself it's fine. Even the queen of acts needs a break from time to time, and maybe she's eager for the night to end as much as I am.

When the kitchen is all cleaned up, I follow my mom to the couch, only to sit on one of the chairs nearby. There's no way I'll get any closer to Mr. Martins. The four adults have already shared two bottles of wine and now they're drinking even more. I'll keep my distance until I can slip off.

I spend twenty uncomfortable minutes in the living room, wishing again I'd known sooner that we'd have guests tonight. I wouldn't have worn shorts and put on a bra. God, I hate men like Bob. My skin is itching with the stain his dirty eyes are leaving all over me.

"I have to excuse myself, but I need to finish a school project for tomorrow. It was nice to meet you, have a good night," I finally say. On my way down the corridor, the uncomfortable feeling of being watched makes my stomach churn. Only when I finally close the door behind me, do I relax.

I take out my current read and get lost in a world of pirates and hot female captains. Two hours pass in a blur, and I'm more than surprised when my dad calls out my name. It's after midnight on a Thursday morning, what could he possibly want?

I cautiously slip out of my room and walk up to the couch. Our guests are nowhere in sight, and neither is my mom. It's just my dad sitting on the couch in the living room by himself, slouching as he awaits my arrival.

"Come here," my dad instructs, his words slurred. I don't think I've ever witnessed my father drunk. It's unsettling to be met by those unfocused eyes, and the itch from earlier returns to my skin, a feeling of wrongness taking over every cell in my body.

Still, I step closer and finally distinguish what he's holding in his hands. It's a framed picture of me as a child, a toothless smile on my young face. I couldn't have been older than eight.

My father glances at it nearly, dare I say *melancholic*? He brushes his thumb over little me and sets down the frame on the desk, ready to face me.

"What is it?" I ask hesitantly, wishing I could return to my room already. There's a strange look in my father's eyes as he gets up and steps even closer to me. He doesn't make a sound, unnerving me. My attention is so fixed on his face, those firmly shut lips, I don't even notice the hand flying toward me until it's too late. The palm of his hand makes contact with my cheek like my mother's did not so long ago. Only this hit stings a lot more.

I choke on a cry as tears blur my view, then back away from the man. "Wha- Dad?" I croak, unable to form a coherent sentence. My father stumbles toward me, lifting both of his hands. I flinch and try to get away only for them to settle on my shoulders instead of landing another hit. I barely release a breath of relief, my adrenaline still spiking. *Run.* My instincts scream. *Danger.*

But I don't move. Can't bring myself to try and find a way to flee his strong fingers digging into my skin. When I meet his eyes, I'm stunned to see tears in them, mirroring my own. "You know what you did!" he accuses. I shake my head, having no idea what he's talking about. Shock keeps my mouth firmly shut, confusion warring inside of me.

"Don't lie!" he yells, spittle wetting my face. I cry harder.

"I'm not! I don't know what I did, I'm sorry," I say hurriedly. My father shakes my shoulders.

"You're playing dumb even though this is all your fault!" he says, his expression becoming one of deep despair. My heart aches at the thought I might have hurt him, but I haven't got the faintest clue of how I could be responsible for his pain.

"I'm sorry," I repeat hoarsely, eager to make it better. To make this weird moment pass and make things the way they were earlier. But it doesn't end, and my father pushes me back hard enough for me to land flat on my back. A hot pain shoots up my spine, but I ignore it as I scramble to a sitting position, trying to catch my breath. My wide eyes stay on him as he crouches closer.

"You deserve this for what you did!" he yells, still looking so damn anguished. My heart is beating in my throat as I try to move away from him, but he doesn't let me escape. Instead, he kicks me in the side once, making me curl up in a ball. That, in return, only gives him the opportunity to kick me across the back. My spine tries to bend, but I force my arms to tighten around my legs and curl up further.

"Please! Stop! I'm sorry!" I mutter against my knees between rasping breaths.

This is a nightmare. It must be a nightmare I'll wake up from any moment now. It has *to be a nightmare.*

"You deserve this," my father spits one more time before I hear his footsteps retreat.

Only when I hear his bedroom door lock, do my arms loosen their panicked grip on my knees. My adrenaline slowly subsides and the pain where I was kicked really flares up. I wince as I get up, trying to stay quiet so as not to get my father's attention again.

I lock my door and curl up in my bed, trying to breathe through the physical pain and the confusing onslaught of emotions. I don't get it. What was my dad so upset about? I must've done something really bad for him to punish me like this. He's never so much as raised his voice at me, not to mention threatened to harm me.

The sadness in his eyes haunts me as I close my eyes. *I did that?*

I stay up all night, crying until I can't breathe anymore. Then, it's overwhelming confusion that tortures me until my alarm goes off.

Chapter 43

Elija

"You look a bit tired, Flower girl. Rough night?" Jamie asks Florence when we've finally reached our 30-minute break mid-morning.

I've made the same observation about Florence but haven't figured out how to ask her about it without making her shy. Truth be told, I didn't get any sleep last night either, too busy thinking about what my girl told me on our call. About her parents' behavior, what we did besides talking, and of course, her last words before she hung up on me so suddenly.

I couldn't count the time I spent thinking about those three small words.

Florence chuckles. "Why thanks, Jamie. That's exactly what every girl wants to hear. But honestly, I couldn't set my book down all night." I take a closer look at her since I've barely been able to do that today so far. Her eyes are red and puffy and she really does look tired. If it weren't for the smile on her face, I'd be worried. As it is, my girl seems genuinely cheery, and I won't put it past her to have read all night.

I reach for Florence to pull her closer, the urge to hold her again taking over. It's been too long and I missed her all night stuck at that damn hospital.

What I don't expect is for Florence to stiffen in my arms before pulling away. She straightens her back awkwardly and smiles, leans over, and kisses me on the cheek before returning her attention to my friends.

Well, that was weird. My gut twists a little at the rejection, but I remind myself that she might simply not be in the mood for cuddles. We're at school, after all.

But as the break goes on, my suspicion that something is wrong rises. I can't help but notice that Florence is avoiding me. Not in the sense of moving further away from me physically, but she's not really looking at me and barely speaks to me. When the guys are busy talking about something else, I decide to ask her about it.

"Hey, are you all right?" I lower my voice and lean in a bit.

"Of course," she says but her eyes are bouncing around my face nervously, betraying her.

"Is it about what we did? If I took it too far or said something you didn't like, I'm really sorry. Please tell me if that's the case." She blinks at me, but after a second, realization dawns on her face. Red splotches creep up her neck and cheeks, and she smiles sheepishly.

"You certainly don't have to worry about that," she tells me with enough conviction to make me believe her.

"Then… is it about what you said?" I ask slowly. This time, my girl understands quicker and my stomach clenches in anticipation of her answer.

"Oh, that. Just forget about it," she says, not meeting my eyes and chuckling again. This time, I know she's nervous, though I can't blame her. My own heart is rising in my chest.

"Did you mean it?" I prod slowly.

"Yeah," she admits before quickly going on. "But I shouldn't have said it. I know it's too soon and it's really no problem if you don't feel the same way. I don't mean to pressure you or make things uncomfortable," she rambles. A swarm of butterflies comes to life in my stomach.

"Florence, look at me." I cup her face, relishing in the way she leans into the touch. I press my lips to hers, a quick and gentle gesture, but it does the trick since she seems to calm down.

Meanwhile, my heart is beating in my throat as I'm trying to gather my courage. I've never told anyone what I'm about to tell this girl, but I know it's the right thing. I know it's the truth so it's only fair to tell her.

"I love you," I tell her softly, watching my girl perk up further with every drawn out syllable falling from my lips. It's adorable. She looks about as excited as the twins do on Christmas, though I can tell she tries to be subtle about it.

"Really? Because if you don't, that's totally fine," she tries to assure me.

"I wouldn't lie to you. Not a fan of lies, remember" I try to assure her. Again, there's something unexpected in her reaction, a shimmer of what might be guilt passing over her features. It's gone so fast, though, that I think I might as well have imagined it. Then, she smiles at me again, and we get swept up in a different conversation.

After school, I quickly go home to change for a job interview. The doctor said I should take things easy for a while because of my concussion, but the date for this interview has been set for a while. Besides, I promised Florence I'd give her her aunt's guitar back eventually, so I better start saving up for my own.

"Come on, little brother. I'll give you a ride just like back in the day. Do you remember when I had to chauffeur your ass to your guitar lessons in middle school?" Kai teases me, ruffling my hair as he walks past me.

I push my hair away from my face and glare at him. "You know damn well I could drive myself if only our dear mother wasn't so worried all the time."

"Yeah, yeah. You just keep telling yourself that, big guy. Now, get in the car, I'm meeting my girlfriend later," he says, heading out of the house. I jog after him.

"Won't your boyfriend feel neglected?" I tease good-naturedly.

"Alejandro? Please, you know how he gets when he doesn't get his weekly dose of telenovelas. He told us if we so much as disturb his marathon with a text, he'll never forgive us." My brother laughs and I can't help but join. Yep, that sounds like Alejandro.

The interview at the local record store goes pretty well. It won't pay that much, but at least it's something I'd enjoy and that works with my school schedule. Besides, the old owner needs the help, and he thinks the teens coming here would enjoy seeing a young face.

If I need it, I can get a more serious job in the next break.

On my walk home, not too far from my house, something makes me stop in my tracks. Across the street, I see Marcus. It wouldn't be suspicious if it weren't for the other silhouette with him. Hood pulled down to cover the stranger's face, all I see are their hands as they pass Marcus something. Then, the stranger is gone, and my friend walks off in the opposite direction as if nothing happened.

I curse under my breath and pick up my pace to follow Marcus. When I'm close enough, I grab him by the shoulders and slam him into the closest wall so he's facing me.

"Hey! What the h- Eli?" he yells, his fist cocked and only a few inches away from my face.

"I could ask you the same thing!" I snap right back, not loosening my grip on him.

"What do you mean? And get off me!" he exclaims, shoving me hard enough to make me stumble back.

"Drugs, Marcus? Really?" His composure falters for a beat and I can see the hint of panic beneath the anger in his eyes.

"You don't know what you're talking about," he snaps.

"Yeah? Tell me, then. Tell me I didn't just see what I think I did." My friend's mouth clamps shut, making me heave a sigh. "Fuck, why didn't you tell us it was getting bad again?" I ask, my voice lower now.

Marcus got in a rough spot a bit over a year ago, not long after his mother's death. His father drowned himself in his work and his younger sister got sent away to a camp for troubled kids because of shoplifting. Feeling all alone and unable or unwilling to find another way to cope, he tried drinking excessively to ease his sorrows. When that reaction had an influence on his performance on the court, though, he stopped and switched to other things. Things that were much harder to quit.

His sister returned home after the summer, luckily. She means the world to Marcus, and it destroyed him to have failed to protect her. Having her back was what first made him realized he fucked up getting mixed up with drugs of all things. How was he supposed to take care of his sister when he couldn't even take care of himself? His father pulled himself together after realizing his kids needed him, and Marcus eventually quit the horrible habit of poisoning his body. Or so I'd thought.

"It's not the same. It's just because of soccer, I swear," he tries to reason with me, but I won't hear any of it. He's a fantastic soccer player, the captain of his team and top scorer. He doesn't need any enhancing shit if that's really what he just got. I won't let him fuck things up again.

"You don't need them, Marcus, and you know it. No matter the pressure you feel, down the toilet they go, okay? You can find another way," I urge. It's what the guys used to do whenever we found his stuff. Flush it away before it could tempt him.

Marcus lets his head drop forward with a sigh. When he looks back up at me, he nods, but I can tell he doesn't like it. He's under a lot of pressure, trying to get a scholarship and play professionally after our last year, so I get the underlying worry written across his features. But I see the shame too, and I know it's a good thing I caught him.

He can keep up with the competition as it is, without cheating and destroying his body in the meantime. No, he knows I'm right. And if he fails to remember that at times, I'm sure the guys and I will be there to make sure he doesn't slip.

We just need to keep a bit of a close eye on him for a while since he has trouble asking for help even when he knows he needs it. A tendency he shares with a certain girl I know…

Chapter 44

Florence

My parents don't come home until late this evening. That leaves me to pace my room, worried out of my mind about how we'll act toward each other.

This morning, they had both already left by the time I came out of my room, and they haven't tried reaching out over the phone, which is unsurprising. Therefore, I haven't heard anything from them since the beating I took last night.

Not knowing what else to do since I'm too anxious to read, I text Elija.

Me: Hello my super awesome boyfriend:)
Me: Oh god, let's ignore I said that.
Me: not that you aren't! You really are.

Great, now I'm rambling over the phone. I have no idea how Eli puts up with me.

Elija: Hello, super awesome girlfriend.

I snort.

Me: We totally are one of those disgustingly sweet couples, aren't we?
Elija: We are. And I don't care to change it. So, why'd you text me? Miss me so soon?
Me: Don't flatter yourself. I was just wondering how the job interview went.
Elija: You remembered that?
Me: Ofc! Why wouldn't I have?

Elija: *Idk. I mentioned it once like a week ago and a lot has happened since then. It went well, though. I think. Thanks for asking<3*

Me: *Love to hear it.*

Elija: *What r u doing?*

Me: *Nothing rn. Just waiting for my parents to come home so we can eat dinner.*

Elija: *How's that going recently btw? Good day, today?*

Me: *so far so good, thanks.*

There I go, doing the one thing my boyfriend told me specifically he hates. Lying. I consider telling him the truth, that today isn't a good day at all. That I was barely able to stomach freaking water without feeling my insides protest. I might've gone as far as telling him about what happened with my dad last night, but I never get to it, because just as my fingers hover over the letters, my parents come home.

"Florence? We brought food. Are you home?" my dad yells. My heart involuntarily starts racing, and my muscles tense. I need to answer. *Answer,* I think but my lips won't shape the words, and my legs won't carry me out of my room. It's like I'm stupefied, unable to control my body as a sudden wave of terror shivers down my spine

There's a knock on my door before my mother peaks her head through a crack. "Come on, Honey. Let's eat dinner," she says, a smile on her face.

Even though I'm confused, my body follows her command, and I follow her to the table wordlessly. No one speaks, and the silence quickly becomes awkward.

That is, until my father chuckles. Out of surprise, my eyes snap to his. I didn't mean to look at him, too scared I might see the anguished version of him that hurt me last night. Instead, I see the same put-together man that has been there all my life. The one I felt safe around.

"I got a bit carried away last night. Don't even remember Bob leaving. Honey, did I make sure he took a cab home? I can't have a partner like him dying in a drunken accident after having had him over for dinner," he tells my mom, his voice light.

"I wouldn't know. I went to bed early, remember?" she reminds him off-handedly, digging into her food. Meanwhile, my stomach is in knots at the thought of last night.

"Of course, of course." He turns his attention to me. "Well, you went to your room even earlier, right?" he asks, sounding the same as always. Everything seems the same as always now. So much so that I might have questioned if I dreamt the whole disaster of last night up if it weren't for the lingering ache the bruise on my back provides.

"You don't remember anything?" I ask, surprised by how even my voice sounds.

"God, I'm so embarrassed. Don't make me say it again," my dad groans, the gesture so human.

"I don't know either," I lie, a painfully fake smile on my lips. No one comments on it. No one cares.

"So, Saturday, we meet your boyfriend?" my mom changes the suspect. A quick, nervous glance at my dad is enough to notice the slight set of his jaw and his tighter-than-usual grip on the fork in his hand. The prospect of meeting my boyfriend apparently doesn't make him happy.

I guess I've heard before that fathers tend to be protective of their daughters, so it makes sense. Maybe it's a good thing that he cares. Only natural.

"Hey. Wow, you look so good," I tell Elija outside my front door on Saturday evening, running my hands up his button-down shirt. It's the fanciest I've ever seen him dressed, and it suits him exceptionally. I get to the tips of my toes to press a quick kiss on his lips.

"Why thank you. Figured I only get one chance at a first impression, so I better make it count. You look great as always," he replies. With a blush on my cheeks and my heart racing excitedly, I lead him into my home, where my parents are waiting.

"Hi, I'm Elija. It's nice to finally meet you," my boyfriend says, holding out his hand for my father to shake. It's my mother that takes it first, though, seeing as my father is merely staring at Eli.

"Pleasure is all ours," she says politely.

"Finally? How long have you and my daughter been together without our knowing?" my dad cuts in. I nearly recoil at that, never having seen him be so rude before.

"Dad," I mutter when I notice Elija pulling his hand back, looking a little lost for words. My dad's eyes meet mine in a flash, and I can see the unspoken fury behind them. I suppress a shiver but am saved from having to do something about it when my mom swoops in, telling us we should take our seats at the table.

My dad sits down at the head, as always. My mother heads to the kitchen and I get to my father's left, pulling Elija down next to me on the other side to act as a buffer. When my mother returns with the plates, a tense silence falls over us. Everyone digs into the food, but I can't, my anxiety too high.

Elija places a hand on my leg, just above the knee. It makes the cold in my bones recede slightly, and I shoot him a smile. Before I can get too comfortable, though, my eyes involuntarily meet my father's again, and it's all I can do not to inch away from him when he looks at me with such apparent anger. It seems my boyfriend's gesture didn't go unnoticed and my father does not appreciate the indecent touch.

"So, you still haven't answered my question. How long have you two been together?" my dad asks.

"A week, maybe? We've been friends and classmates before," I answer smoothly, knowing it's been longer. The lie slips past my lips almost before I could decide on it out of fear of angering my parents further by admitting how long I've kept my relationship a secret. My dad grunts, but doesn't say anything. Elija squeezes my leg encouragingly.

"That's wonderful. Florence tells us you're talented, what do you do?" my mother asks, and the cutest blush creeps up my boy's neck.

"I make music. Play the guitar and make beats and remixes, but I'm sure Florence exaggerated." He chuckles softly.

From there on, dinner goes more smoothly. My mother is acting really pleasantly, doing her best to get to know Elija and keep the conversation going. Even I'm able to relax until my dad has to ruin it again by bringing out a bottle of wine. My whole body tenses, memories of what happened the last time he drank flooding my brain until it's hard for me to breathe.

If Elija notices, he doesn't show it. I guess he's too busy being nervous to be attuned to my behavior for once.

When the four of us officially run out of things to talk about, Elija and I excuse ourselves and go to my room. He puts on some music and does another tour of my room, this time opening a few drawers. When he gets to the one containing all my nail polishes, he stops, slowly raising his eyes to look at me shily.

"Would you maybe- I mean, do you like painting nails?" he asks, fumbling with his words. I don't think I've ever seen him this flustered. It's adorable.

"Do you want me to paint yours?" I ask, getting off my bed to walk over.

"I don't know. Would you think it's weird?"

"No, of course not. Which color do you want?" I ask, wrapping an arm around his back to look down at the drawer alongside him.

"Black?" he asks, beaming hesitantly. "I keep seeing those pictures on Pinterest and it's got me thinking... I think I'd like to try it once."

I confirm and get to painting my boy's fingernails black. He studies me closely as I do it, and it's enough to evoke just the slightest tremble in my hands. Still, I force myself to do it well. Luckily, I work well under pressure.

When I'm done, he quickly swoops me up in a kiss, careful to keep his hands away from me like I told him to.

"Thank you," he whispers against my cheek, his warm breath tickling my skin. It's what really makes me wish I was home alone.

Since I'm not, Eli and I behave, doing nothing more than kissing and cuddling for a while.

"I should get going. But first, I got you something," he eventually says, pulling something from his pocket. It's a small box and as I open it, my eyes flick between my boyfriend and the object. I'm not really used to receiving gifts, and now my heart is accelerating.

When I see the necklace with its little guitar pendant within, it's all I can do to remember not to drop it to throw my arms around Elija.

"It's so pretty, Elija. You didn't need to do that," I tell him even as a smile spreads over my features.

"I wanted to. I hope you like it. I would've given you a flower one but you already have one so I thought a guitar might be a bit more personal, you know? Since you like to hear me play and the connection to your aunt as well."

My heart swells, happy tears pricking the back of my eyes. "I love it," I tell him truthfully. "Will you put it on me?" I turn around, already gathering my hair in one hand as I ask him over my shoulder. He silently takes the thin chain from me and does as I asked. His hands linger on my neck as he closes the clasp and then he turns me around and to seal the present with a kiss. I sigh into his mouth, relishing the affection he's showering me with. I'll never get sick of this.

"Okay, now I really gotta go. Do you think tonight went okay?" he asks, revealing a rare case of insecurity.

"You did perfectly, I'm sure my mom really likes you," I tell him.

"And your dad?"

I hesitate and make a sound. "Well, he's just a tough cookie to crack, but don't worry about it." I keep my confident and even, everything I don't feel as the memory of my father's furious eyes haunts me.

"I'll just keep trying," he says in earnest, warming my chest. He might not think the best about my parents but he's willing to try and make them like him for my sake. At the same time, I hate that my father's giving him such a hard time. Especially since Elija's family went above and beyond to make me feel welcome.

"I'll walk you out, come on." At the door, only my mother has the decency to tell our guest goodbye. Who knows where my father is right now, but at least my mother is being very polite.

"Don't let us wait for too long until we get to see you again," she even tells him as she closes the door behind him. To my great surprise, her smile doesn't fall as soon as we're alone.

"Good night, honey. I'm glad we did this tonight." she stifles a yawn. "Well, I'm tired enough to sleep through the end of the world right now. Sweet dreams" she wishes me before walking off with a pleased smile.

I focus on that smile and let it fuel my happiness about tonight's outcome. Most of all, I'm glad Elija said he was comfortable, but knowing my mom approves is the cherry on top. The night wasn't perfect with my father's open hostility, but I'm sure he'll warm up to the situation eventually.

Like always, I shut the door behind me, but before I can slump onto my bed, a silhouette in the far corner makes me stop dead in my tracks. My heart ceases to beat and my lungs seize as my eyes meet my father's bloodshot ones. He's drunk again. *In my room.*

"Dad?" I ask, slowly inching toward the door.

"You let him touch you," my father states, his voice empty.

"What? I- No." I shake my head, backing away. This feels wrong. So, so, so wrong. I'm not supposed to be scared of my own father. I never used to be. This isn't him.

"Don't lie!" the man snaps, coming closer and stepping between me and my way to out of this room. "Your mother told me what she found in your trash that night. I'm so disappointed in you."

He's back; the sad, broken man from last Wednesday. My blood cools to ice. The bruises he dealt me that night are only just fading, and I'm not ready for more. I don't know how to deal with this. I don't know what I can do.

"I'm sorry," I tell him desperately, panic lacing every syllable.

"You should be. You told me you've been together for only a week which means you either lied to me, or you were so desperate to give him your body before he was even your boyfriend. And still, you are desperate for more. I heard you on the phone the other night, and I could hear you tonight," he goes on, a visible shiver overtaking him. *He's* disgusted *at me.* But instead of getting away, he steps closer to the point where he's invading my personal space.

I want to protest. Tell him I lied earlier because I mixed the dates up or that nothing happened tonight, but my father slaps me before I can.

Pain engulfs the whole side of my face like the last time. The only difference is I'm not as caught off guard by the action tonight. The part of me not riddled with denial knew the moment I found him in here that this would happen. The realization only intensifies the ache.

With my jaw numb and buzzing from the slap, I weakly beg, "Please stop this, Dad." Tears prick my eyes as my backing away results with my back flush against the wall. He follows me, caging me in until I feel trapped and helpless. *Why is he doing this?* "Daddy –" he cuts me off before I can get another plea past my trembling lips.

"Do you enjoy it when he touches you? Taints you? Do you enjoy torturing me?" he roars, paralyzing me. Words evade me, my mind blanking at his menacing tone. All I can do is pray that my mother will hear. That the corridor separating our rooms isn't enough to block the sound of his scream. *Please, please* let her hear this time.

Suddenly, two big, rough hands are on my waist, squeezing me painfully. He yanks my petrified form forward, away from the wall so hard that I nearly stumble into him. My knees feel weak, my mind unable to keep up with what is happening. His *hands* are on me, and I'm too shocked to react, my thoughts too frantic to think of a way out.

When his hands start roaming my body, moving down the swing of my hips to squeeze my ass so hard I'm afraid he'll leave a fresh bruise, I start shrieking, my instincts finally kicking in.

I try to push my father's hands away, clawing at his skin with my short nails. When it doesn't work, I throw my weight against his torso, anything to get him off. It only gives him the opportunity to slide one strong arm around my waist as he squeezes my face painfully with his free hand.

His palm is wrapped under my jaw, his thumb and forefingers squeezing my cheeks so hard my mouth is pushed open. When his eyes drop to my neck, more precisely the necklace adorning it, fresh rage seems to fill them. His hand locks around the chain and rips it off with one hard tug. Freeing the pendant from the chain, he lets the latter part fall to the ground and walks off with the mini guitar, leaving me crying and shaking as my reeling mind replays the moment again and again.

Finally, my knees buckle beneath me, and I don't even feel my collision with the floor. The world simply goes black before I can even touch the ground, and I gladly let it.

Chapter 45

Elija

On Monday morning, the first thing I notice is that Florence isn't wearing my present. That does something mean to my heart and confidence, making a million doubts fly through my mind when I should be focusing on school.

Did she not like it?

Was it too soon? Too much?

Not enough?

Did it seem like I was trying to stake my claim?

It wasn't expensive, but it was all I could afford with the last of my savings. I thought Florence wouldn't mind the low quality but maybe she did. Not that it seems likely, knowing her the way I do.

I really don't like my brain sometimes.

Halfway done with our classes this morning, I can't stand it anymore. I interrupt my girl from reading, as much as I hate to do it. All morning, she hasn't spoken to anyone. Just a quick "Hi" before she fled into another world.

I tap her knee and notice her sigh before she looks up. Well, I wasn't expecting a much more enthusiastic reaction, but to say this feels nice would be a lie. Still, I'm determined not to show her any reaction and lean in to talk to her a bit more privately.

When she doesn't try to meet me in the middle but slightly stiffens as if uncomfortable with my proximity, the knot of unease tightens unbearably in my stomach. The fear of her not wanting me close is almost enough to make me pull right back, but I know I have to talk to her if I want to be able to focus on my other classes even a little.

"What happened to your necklace?" I ask, smiling slightly to diffuse some tension. She doesn't smile back. Instead, her eyes fill with tears and her bottom lip quivers as she moves her gaze away from mine. My chest constricts and my thoughts start racing some more. *What the hell happened? Why is she crying?*

"I'm sorry. It somehow got stuck in my helmet this morning, and when I took it off, the necklace ripped. I tried to find the pendant, but I think it fell down the street gully. I'm really sorry," she mumbles softly, not meeting my eyes. My stomach clenches but it has nothing to do with the gift. Hell no, I'm worried about my girlfriend, who can't seem to look at me.

I get up from my chair until I'm right in front of her hunched body, pulling her into a hug as I try to comfort her as well as possible. To hell with the curious glances our classmates shoot in our direction. I don't give a damn what they think.

Florence slowly melts into the embrace and pulls me tighter by the waist. She's shaking, but after taking a few measured breaths, it seems to get better.

The guys notice – of course, they do – but don't comment on it. They simply look at my girl worriedly before going back to minding their own business.

"There you go, no need to cry, pretty girl. It's okay. I'll get you a new one as soon as I can," I tell her, trying not to hate the way it sounds. When I *can*. I hate that I'll have to work for a few months until I can get my girlfriend a present. I'd like to spoil her until she knows exactly how precious she is to me. Being able to surprise her whenever I wanted to would be nice.

"I'm sorry. I haven't been sleeping well, and clearly, it's taking its toll. Please, don't worry about getting me a new one. You're saving up for more important things, and I don't want you to waste your money on me because I'm too clumsy," she tells me, attempting the smallest of smiles. It does a poor job of reaching her eyes.

"It wouldn't be a waste," I protest but she cuts me off.

"Really, it's fine." Somehow, the urgency in her voice shuts me up for good. Only makes my mind reel harder though.

Here are the facts as I see them; my girl hasn't been sleeping, she's been more distant, and she insists I don't spend any more money on her. The question I'm therefore facing is whether our relationship is stressing her out.

If not, what else is bothering her? Because something clearly is.

"When was the last time you ate?" I ask quietly enough for only her to hear. She looks so tired as she avoids my eyes, not uttering a sound to reply, and I have my answer right there. I feel sick. "Please, Florence, why won't you talk to me? I want to help you."

"I'm sorry. Everything is fine. I'm sorry," she says unconvincingly.

What happened to the bright and happy girl from just a few weeks ago? What could possibly have happened to dim that beautiful light in those green eyes of hers? More importantly, how the hell do I eliminate it?

"I feel like we haven't had any alone time in forever. How do you feel about coming over after school? I'm sure you've finished all your assignments already, and we don't have any exams for the next few days. My parents are taking the twins to my grandparents' place so they can go to the cinema, and my brother is out almost every night anyway. What do you say we enjoy the rare occasion of my being home alone for a change?" I ask.

My girl thinks about it for a long beat, oblivious that the wait is killing me. Finally, she bites her cheeks and smiles slightly.

"I'd really like that. I hope my parents won't mind too much, but they'll just have to deal with it," she mutters.

"That's right. What else are they going to do?" I ask jokingly, attempting to make her smile for real. I notice my mistake instantly when Florence's eyes fly back to the pages of her book, her leg bouncing wildly beneath the table.

Shit, is she thinking about the time her mom tried to get her from my place? The night she was *hit* by her mother. I'm such an idiot. And now, my own mood is dimming at the reminder.

It's just that after meeting her mother, it's a bit harder for me to imagine it. She seemed quite nice when I was over. Not that it's enough to make up for her earlier actions. She's making an effort, which is nice, but I won't forget that she raised a hand against the girl I love.

"It'll be fine. You can come over right after school, maybe tell them you'll be staying here late to study in the library or read in the park," I offer, hoping to be a little useful after all. She nods absently, which doesn't make me feel any better. "I won't let anything happen to you," I add, brushing my thumb over the back of her hand as I interlink our fingers.

It needed to be said. If Florence is worried her mom will try to hit her again, she shouldn't be. If she so much as tries, I'm done. Fuck trying to wait for people to change, I won't let my girlfriend go home to an abusive parent. She can stay with me. Any of the guys, come to think of it. I think we'd all rather sleep on our cold floors than have Florence in danger and hurt.

"I know," my girl whispers so softly I barely hear. God, I really need to talk to her tonight.

Chapter 46

Florence

I'm surrounded by laughter. My friends, telling each other stories and cracking up over them, being happy and relieved school is over for the day.

I try to smile along, to keep the façade up at least a little after the meltdown I had this morning. Like, really Flo? Crying at school? I really thought I was stronger than that.

With every nod, every "yeah, totally," and every fake laugh, I feel more like a fraud. I'm lying again. Always lying, and the fear of Elija, or anyone discovering that sets me on edge even further. It's the thing I know he hates most but can't seem to stop doing.

I'm caught in a vicious circle, and with every passing day of keeping secrets and making excuses, I feel myself sinking into it further. At this point, I don't know how I'll ever dig myself out of the hole I've made without making Elija lose his trust in me.

At least I'm not going home right now. I don't think I could handle it. Not after so many nights without sleep. The constant fear of my father sneaking into my room again, drunk out of his mind and with my pain on his mind makes it impossible for me to relax even with my door locked.

He hasn't hurt me again since the night Elija had dinner with us. Not physically, at least. Mentally, he's been destroying me and emotionally he's wearing me out. The uncertainty is the worst part. I don't know when or if he's going to come after me again, and constantly being on edge is tiring.

I'm so tired.

The people around me are getting suspicious, which I hate. I feel like I'm failing at something. Failing someone. I'm not sure who or why, but it feels wrong to bother anyone else with this. I hate bringing people down.

I zone back to the conversation when I see a hand flying my way. I flinch on instinct, my whole body stiffening and my eyes squeezing shut to brace for impact. My heart is racing, adrenalin making me dizzy, but the anticipated pain never comes. I slowly open my eyes again, and the whole scene ahead of me comes back to focus.

Elija is telling a story, moving his hands excitedly as he does, and my heart sinks. I just flinched for no reason. God, I'm so glad he didn't notice because he sure as hell would've been hurt and suspicious. It was bad enough when he asked me why I wasn't wearing his present earlier. I could see the confusion clear in his gaze, the vulnerability and doubt. He deserves answers. I'm simply too weak to provide them.

I'm just about to think that no one noticed my little accident when my eyes meet a pair of pale blue ones. Orion is staring at me, and I can tell from his expression that he knows. It makes my cheeks burn up with shame, and I'm forced to avert my eyes.

Suddenly painfully aware of Orion's attention, I notice him walking over to me. He touches my arm impossibly softly, making me stop as the others walk ahead. Only when they're a few feet away does he speak up.

"Your parents?" he asks, starting to walk again. I look at my feet as I follow at his side, matching his stride.

"What?" I play dumb.

"Is it your parents, Florence? It was with me and I know it's not Eli, so I just assumed," he adds, his demeanor as cool as always but his voice unusually strained. That's when my brain catches up with what he's saying. If we're talking about what I think we are, Orion just told me his parents hit him. My blood runs a little colder at the thought, and my anger spikes.

How do parents think they have the right to mistreat their kids like that? Please, let this be a case of miscommunication because right now, I'm mentally seeing little Orion getting beat up by his parents, and I hate it. I knew he had issues at home, but I never really questioned why he moved out at such a young age.

"Is what my parents?" I chuckle weakly, feigning ignorance because I'm panicking. I can't tell anyone. Maybe we're not talking about the same thing. What would he even do if he knew? Encourage me to move out as well? I don't have the means for that.

"The reason why you're flinching out of nowhere. I recognize that look on your Face, Florence, the sheer blind panic that shuts off your brain when you think the next hit is coming," he elaborates, unable to hide the murderous tone in his voice. It doesn't scare me, though. I know it's not directed at me. It's in my defense. It almost makes me want to confide in him, to talk to someone who might understand. "I can see the signs, Flo. I hope I'm wrong, but if I'm not, please, speak up. You don't have to endure it. We can figure something out," he tells me, finally looking at me. And it's so tempting. So dangerously tempting that I can feel the words on the tip of my tongue.

I swallow them.

I keep staring at my feet.

Then, I do what I've been doing best recently. I lie.

"Oh, god no. I don't know what gave you that impression and I'm really sorry, but there's nothing to worry about. Thank you, though, for looking out for me," I say thickly. He nods, looking unconvinced, and it feels like my heart is weighed down by a million pounds as I take my next step.

We catch up with the others, say our goodbyes, and our ways part. The long travel to Elija's place on my bike allows me to gather my bearings and relax a little. If only for a few hours, I'll be safe. I force myself to focus on that.

We hang out in his living room, lying on the couch and watching the next Harry Potter movie while my mood improves gradually. Enough so that, as the two of us lie with his front to my back and his arm around me to make sure I don't fall off, the sudden urge to do something completely different than watch TV surfaces.

Our bodies are connected all the way from my back down to my feet, one of Elija's arms supporting his head while the other is around my waist. Unable to help myself, I scoot impossibly closer.

Well, maybe not scoot closer as much as rubbing my ass against his dick. His dick, which I now notice is already hardening. Good to know I'm not the only one whose mind isn't with Harry's first challenge in the Triwizard's tournament.

"What are you doing?" my boy whispers against my ear, his hold on my waist tightening. Almost absently, his thumb starts caressing the small sliver of skin my shirt exposes, and I relish the touch.

"We're finally alone, and I can't believe I'm saying this, but there's something I want to do more than watch Harry Potter," I confess, trying not to let it show how desperate I am.

Truth is, I really want this – really want *him* and all the feelings that involves. I just want to stop thinking and worrying and being scared. Just want him to my mind taken off everything if only for a while.

Maybe my motives are wrong. Maybe it's not fair to Elija to use him that way, but when he tightens his grip on me and pushes his hips further against me, I know I won't stop him. All I feel is the heat of his body and the undeniable urge to touch him. All of him… With all of me.

"Bedroom?" I ask, my voice hoarse as all the things he promised me come rushing back to my mind.

Elija only grunts in reply, and the next thing I know, we're both standing. Then, I'm not standing at all but flying instead. Flying until my stomach presses down on Elija's shoulder, and he's carrying me toward his room.

I squeal and hit his back softly, but don't dare move otherwise. I'm not going to make carrying me any harder. I like my limbs intact and all.

In his room, Elija shuts the door and throws me onto his bed. The laughter dies on my lips when I see his expression. So scorching hot, so desperate and hungry that I have to bite back a sound of approval. I love it when he looks at me like that. It makes me feel like I'm the most beautiful girl out there.

The longer he stares at me, the more confident I get. That, and needy.

Feeling bold, I grab the hem of my shirt and pull it over my head, glad I'm wearing my pretty teal lace underwear set. There are small flowers along the edge of it, making it one of my favorites.

Elija takes me in for a good few beats before he curses under his breath. Finishing the distance between him and the bed as he pulls his own shirt over his head. He climbs on top of me.

"And I was wondering where they were," he mumbles against my cheek before kissing it. It takes a whole lot of concentration to pay his words any mind. Even more to speak.

"What?" I ask slowly.

"The flowers," he tells me as his finger moves along the lace around my ribs. "There are always flowers on you. Always, but I couldn't find them today. Now, I know you just hid them. Hid them only for me to see now." He groans, sounding almost pained as he pushes his body further against mine, pinning me to the mattress. "It's so ridiculously hot," he adds as an afterthought. My cheeks redden in delight. *He thinks I'm hot.*

"It would be even hotter if it was on your floor," I tell him. This is a torturous game, and I need more. Need him to touch me, and taste me, and finally make me feel the good kind of pain. For a change, I want it to be good.

"Impatient. So impatient," he tsks, clearly amused. "Tell me, Florence, what is it you want?"

"You. Please, Elija, always you," I reply, pulling his chest closer to mine.

"You want this?" he asks, kissing me gently. I try to deepen it, to bite or lick his lips, but he pulls back before I can. "Ah, I don't think you do. Is it the things we discussed that you're curious about?"

I nod, my voice gone. It makes my boyfriend chuckle, but then he pulls away a bit, and I whine pathetically. Instead of getting away from me as I thought, though, his hand slips between my back and the mattress to unclip my bra. Once he's thrown the clothing item away, he pulls me flush against him, groaning against my lips before kissing me hungrily.

He's holding most of his weight off me while his other hand slips between us, massaging my breasts. I moan when he pinches one of my nipples, arching against him.

When he pushes me down roughly and tells me not to move, a newfound dominance in his voice, I bite my lip to stifle another sound. This is what I need, I realize. To surrender my autonomy to him and let him take the lead.

My hands are roaming Elija's body like his are mine. I scratch his back, dig my nails into his arms, and pull on his hair.

Meanwhile, he's teasing me. Pinching me before stroking his fingers over the irritated skin to smooth out the pain, biting down on my skin only to lick it better, and placing his hand around my throat only to let it rest there without applying pressure.

Especially the last action is driving me mad, so I try to encourage him. I lean up into his hand and he finally tightens his grip on me just slightly, pushing me back down.

Then, he leans down and kisses the shell of my ear before whispering, "Do you trust me?"

I nod, trying to catch my breath. Trying to get my heartbeat under control before I die right here and now. There are worse ways to go, sure, but I'd prefer an orgasm or two first.

"Tell me everything you like, okay? And tell me when to stop," he instructs into my other ear. Again, I nod, and after another quick kiss, Elija pulls back.

His hands are on my waist in a beat, pulling my pants down with my help. Once that's done, he flips me around so I'm on my stomach before pulling me up so my ass is in the air. He arranges my limps as if I were a ragdoll, and I find myself more than happy to let it happen.

He gathers my wrists in his hand until they're resting on my lower back. When I eventually hear him taking off his belt, my heartbeat picks up in anticipation. With the utmost care, he ties my hands with it before giving it a tug.

"Is it too tight?" he asks, leaning over me so his breath is fanning against my shoulder. I exhale before shaking my head. "I have to hear you say something," he insists, placing a tender kiss on my shoulder blade. My knees nearly buckle.

"It's perfect," I tell him breathily.

He turns my head until it hurts and kisses me. Before I can complain about the discomfort, he pulls away and my forehead falls back onto the mattress. When his hands finally slide down the curve of my hips, all the way to my knees before moving up my inner thigh again, I'm ready to protest. What's with him and letting me wait until I'm ready to beg?

It turns out he's feeling generous enough to skip that part today, tugging my panties down to my knees before I can utter a word. I lift one leg for him so he can slide it off. I'm not about to ruin my favorite pair by stretching it out around my knees.

Once I'm completely naked, Elija seems to be done with the playing. Two of his fingers slide through my slit before he circles my clit like he's done the times before. But then he pinches my most sensitive part, and I moan in surprise, my back arching. He chuckles softly before soothing the pain by moving around it more slowly.

"Please, Elija," I beg. Once more. And I don't even care.

"What is it you want?" he asks, voice rough. I wish I could see him right now.

"You. Everything you can give, please," I whine.

"Oh, you'll get that. When I'm done playing. For now, I'm enjoying the way you squirm and moan for me, completely at my mercy. You'll wait patiently like the good girl you are, won't you?" he asks slowly, massaging my thighs and ass.

"Yes," I tell him even though my body is screaming at him to hurry the hell up.

He hums in approval. "That's right. And fuck if you don't look stunning while you're at it."

He spreads my knees wider and places a kiss on my backbone. Then, his mouth is on my pussy while his hands dig into my flesh to keep me from moving. But my legs are already starting to shake because I've been waiting for too long and now I'm finally getting what I asked for. Elija's not teasing me anymore. He's eating me out like a starved man. I should feel ashamed with how *everything* is on view in this position but all I feel is ecstasy as his lips move over my wet skin.

One of his arms comes around my waist and he squeezes one of my boobs. I'm embarrassed. Embarrassed that I'm so close to coming so soon when I really want this to last. I want this to last, but my body didn't get the message since I can feel that I won't be able to hold off the mounting pleasure for much longer.

"Don't hold back," Elija tells me before his mouth is back on me. I shake my head against the mattress, not even sure what I mean. "I want to feel you come all over my mouth. Don't hold back, Florence. No need to worry, we're not done," he whispers against my swollen lips. His other hand slides between my legs from the front and he rolls my clit between his fingers.

It does the trick. My body tenses, my back arches, and I'm not sure if I'm trying to get closer to Elija and all the sensations or away from them. I don't know anything at all other than the heat rolling over me in waves until my legs are weak and my breathing is comings in quick rasps.

Finally, Elija pulls his head from between my legs and leans over me again.

"You okay?" he asks, leaving soft kisses all over my back, neck, and shoulders. I chuckle breathily.

"Never better," I reply in a horrible British accent. Elija bursts out laughing.

"Really? Now?" he asks.

"We were watching Harry Potter before," I try to justify myself, laughing as well. God, it feels good to do that again.

"Are you still comfortable like this or do you want me to turn you around and untie you?" he then asks.

"This. I'd like to try this," I say, trying not to sound embarrassed.

"You're absolutely stunning like this," my boyfriend tells me, grinding against me to let me feel just how hard he is against his boxers. I decide to believe him and not let my insecurities ruin this. Even though the lights are on and Elija can see everything of me. Every last detail, but he still tells me I'm beautiful.

I can feel the mattress shift under his weight as he gets a condom. Then, I can hear his last piece of clothing hit the ground and I can hardly stand the wait anymore.

When his tip is at my entrance, I speak up. "Eli?" He freezes instantly.

"Yes?" he asks softly.

"Can you," I break off, my cheeks burning up. The boy behind me doesn't rush me. "Can you be rough with me? Please?"

I hear him mutter a curse and his grip on my hips tightens. "Yes, Florence. I can definitely do that. Just tell me when it's too much, okay?" he says. I nod again.

Then, without any further warning, Elija slams inside of me. I think I actually cry out a curse as my spine bends, and he stills for a second, spreading my legs even further. When I don't protest, he starts moving. He doesn't go slow this time but does what I asked him to, pounding into me with no remorse. And even though it hurts, I find myself meeting his thrusts halfway.

His nails dig into my skin and I moan. I try to move my hands, to grab something, to tug at his hair rough enough to make him hurt like he's hurting me. Not because he's doing anything wrong, but the idea of hearing him moan like he did the last time has me clenching around his dick.

"Fuck, look at you. My sweet, little whore," he tells me. And shit, the vulgar words shouldn't turn me on as much as they do. I moan louder, letting him know exactly how much I love the way he speaks to me. How I love the way he's thrusting into me like he hates my guts, leaving bruises for sure. Bruises I want to carry instead of having to.

"I- I'm," I stutter, unable to grasp enough letters to form a sentence. But Elija understands and his hands move once more. One comes up to my throat and he squeezes. Not enough to restrict my breathing but enough to show me exactly who is in control. His other hand finds my clit and he rubs it fast and hard.

Meanwhile, his pace picks up further to the point where I struggle not to fall forward. I don't, I push back instead, making him groan. He pinches my clit and tightens his grip on my throat, cursing as I come around him.

He keeps going for several thrusts. Then stills, finding his own release before collapsing along with me.

He rolls off to lie beside me and only takes a second to collect his breath before he unties my hands. He's so achingly gentle with me, my heart feels about ready to burst.

When he's done, he turns me so my head is on his chest and holds me tightly.

Chapter 47

Elija

Florence and I got dressed, and now I'm holding her again. She's adorably tired, and my heart can hardly take the way her soft breaths brush against my chest. Earlier, I had to help her into a pair of my boxers and my shirt. She didn't feel like putting her jeans back on and I love seeing her in my clothes too much to have protested.

I check the time on my phone, still stroking my girl's hand with the other. It's after eleven pm which means my parents will be back soon and Florence probably needs to leave. I don't know where she told her parents she'd be, but I'm sure they won't be thrilled if she's home after midnight. The last thing I want is for her to get into trouble.

So I kiss the top of her head and ask, "Do you want me to give you a ride home?"

Florence freezes completely, her whole body tense. Foreboding simmers in my gut as I say her name, again and again, asking what's wrong without receiving an answer.

I finally pull away to get a better look at her only for her to sit up as well, blinking like she just woke from a trance.

"No," she finally says softly. I'm too confused to speak, so I take a closer look at her. She's shaking, her face pale and eyes haunted. Haunted and so damn scared it triggers my own fear. My heart starts racing.

"No, you don't want me to take you home?" I ask slowly even though I know that's not it. Something else is happening right now, drawing this reaction from her. Something I don't think I'm equipped to understand.

Florence glances at the clock on my bedside table and despite all odds, the remaining color in her face drains away. She shakes her head, repeating, "no, no, no," over and over again. Her eyes fill with tears, making my head go into overdrive. I have no idea what's happening, but I can't just sit here like an idiot while Florence is crying.

I move forward to pull her back into my arms, to cup her face so she stops shaking her head, to do anything at all, but she is too fast. She grabs my wrists as I reach for her and puts them back at my sides, looking so damn miserable. "I'm sorry," she finally whispers.

"Florence, what-" I reach for her again, but she stops me.

"Don't, please," she mutters before turning away completely. She gets off my bed, hugging her shaking body, and I'm left staring at her back.

Meanwhile, a horrible feeling is settling deep in my bones. Like the suspicions I've been trying to ignore and the signs I chose not to analyze are back to bite me. Like this is some big crash I secretly knew would come but pretended it wouldn't.

And suddenly I'm having a déjà vu. A flashback from when Ricky confessed to me. Same tears, same "Don't touch me," same origin. It's always lies. Right now, I'd bet my balls that Florence is about to tell me she's been lying about something.

The betrayal settles in my chest prematurely even though Florence hasn't confessed anything.

I force myself to redirect my focus on the girl in front of me, and the anger recedes. I can't believe where my thoughts are headed. This is Florence. Not Ricky. She's crying and freaking out, and I'm sitting on my bed, wallowing in self-pity like a suspicious idiot.

"Florence, what happened?" I ask, trying to keep my voice calm. "What are you sorry for?" *Too familiar*, a voice in my head taunts me. *This is how it ends*, my anxious heart joins the chorus.

"You can't give me a ride home," she says quietly, her shoulders shaking with silent sobs. I fully forget my anger and suspicion. I forget it all and am left with a dull ache as I'm forced to watch her fall apart in front of me.

"Why not? How else would you go home?" I ask.

"Not at all. I'm sorry. I can't." She hiccups and her body jerks. Meanwhile, my hands feel like rocks at my sides. My fingers itch to reach out and hold her, but she doesn't want my touch.

Why is she pulling away?

"Why can't you go home?" I ask. I can feel the first lie is about to be revealed and brace myself.

"I didn't tell them where I was going. They know. I didn't say, but they must know," she cries.

"Your parents? Florence, what are you talking about? Why wouldn't you tell them anything?" I shake myself, realizing I'm focusing on the wrong things. "Never mind, it doesn't matter. Hey, it's fine. I'm sure they'll understand. I'll come home with you and help explain. Or we can make up an excuse, say your phone died and you forgot," I speak desperately, but my girl cries more.

"No, you don't understand. I'm sorry. I don't want to go home," she says, making absolutely no sense.

"Then spend the night. That's fine too," I try to reassure her. "Is this about what we just did? I didn't mean to kick you out, Florence. You can stay the night, of course. I thought you might want to leave, but you can always stay with me. I love having you in my space."

"Not tonight. It won't help if I don't go there tonight. He won't forget. You don't understand. I'm so sorry," she says, hugging herself even tighter and leaning heavily against my wall.

He won't forget? What the hell are we talking about?

"I don't understand. Please, calm down and start from the top. We can figure something out," I assure her.

"We can't. I lied to you. I'm so sorry, Eli. I lied so much. I don't know what to say," she finally confesses.

I knew it. I knew and expected this, but my heart still tears as I hear the words from Florence's lips. Sweet Florence whom I love and trusted so much. Whom I care about so stupidly deeply.

I stay silent, thinking about so much and so little at the same time. My girl is still not looking at me, and I am still so confused. I realize we're both too upset to have this conversation tonight.

I take a deep breath, making sure my voice is even when I speak.

"Can I please just give you a ride?" I ask. Florence sobs again and starts shaking her head. "Florence, we both need to cool down before we talk about whatever it is you lied about. You're not in the condition to explain anything, it seems, and I'm not sure I can comfort you right now," I add.

"Please, no. You don't understand," she says but I cut her off.

"Oh, I think I do. And I think I know what you'd say if you could. You'd tell me you didn't mean to do it. You'd say it just happened in the moment and that you're sorry, and Florence, I might even believe you. I just can't do this right now," I say tiredly. Florence finally whips around.

"No, that's not what happened. Elija, I didn't cheat on you," she tells me. Then her mouth clamps shut and she looks like she's about to be sick. She's shaking her head again. "I didn't want- It's not- Oh god." She presses the back of her hand to her mouth and turns away from me.

"Then what happened? Either tell me or let me take you home."

"I can't go home," she repeats quietly.

"Why not?" I demand, hardly able to keep my frustration from entering my voice.

"I'm scared of what he'll do to me if I'm home tonight," she finally whispers, running her hands through her hair and tugging at it.

Meanwhile, I'm stunned into silence, as her words slowly trickle through my frantic mind. I falter, too scared to think about the horrible implication of what she just said.

"What?" I breathe quietly. "Scared of – Florence, scared of what *who* will do to you?" I ask, feeling sick as the words leave my lips. Florence can't meet my eyes while the weight of her words really hit me.

My girlfriend is scared to go home because someone might do something to her there. The most disgusting story pieces itself together in my mind, and I feel tears stinging the back of my eyes.

"Your father? Florence, has your father been doing anything to you?" I ask. She cries harder, not looking at me.

Surges of rage and hatred flood my body, and my legs nearly give out beneath me. Something terrible has been going on at my girlfriend's home, and I didn't know. I didn't know because I was stupid and ignorant. I can barely stand to look at her right now. Not because I'm upset with her, but because she looks so broken, so defeated that it hurts to see.

"I can't do it tonight. I don't know what he'll do, but I can't," she breaks off, choking on her words. "I'm not strong enough. I'm sorry. So sorry, god, I didn't know what to do so I just kept lying," she reveals, leaning against the wall behind her for support. Meanwhile, I want to yell at her to use me, lean on me, and let me help her instead of the cold, dead surface.

"You should have *told me*," I tell her, my voice coming off rougher than intended.

"I know. I know, I'm sorry. Please, don't make me go back there," she then begs and it's the worst pain I've ever felt. She thinks I'd do that? Send her back to her father who's been doing who-knows-what to her? Who's the reason she's crying hysterically, and probably why she hasn't eaten anything in so long?

I feel sick. So, so sick I can hardly stay upright, but Florence mistakes my silence for rejection, and I can hear her sharp intake of breath.

"Please, Elija. I'm so sorry. Please, just for tonight. I promise I'll figure something out tomorrow," she pleads desperately over the sobs wrecking her body. She's panicking, only taking shallow breaths.

I look for my phone, wanting to put on her song but I can't see anything. I'm too dizzy, too worried, too confused, too angry, and too hurt.

When I realize Florence is gathering her clothes, preparing herself to go home, words finally burst from my lips. "No. You're not going anywhere. You can stay, Florence. You'll stay." My voice is too gruff, too loud, and too demanding.

"Are you angry?" Florence whispers. A cold, dead laugh rips from my lungs. Nothing is funny, and I don't mean to do it, but the pathetic sound leaves my lips no matter what. Does so as images of her piece-of-shit sperm doner laying his hands on the girl I love flood my mind, and it makes my blood run so much hotter in my veins.

"No, Florence, angry doesn't begin to cover what I'm feeling," I mutter, raising my hands to run them through my hair.

But Florence sees the movement and flinches before desperately trying to scramble backward. To get *away* from me.

"I'm sorry," she whispers as her eyes jump around the room, a wild expression on them. And my heart breaks. Literally crashes and shatters so hard I'm sure I could hear it if her breathing wasn't so loud. Her breathing! Shit, she needs to breathe evenly.

I forgot how horribly stressful her panic attacks could get and this seems to be turning right into one.

But I don't know how to comfort her because I have no control over my voice, and she is *scared* of me. Scared I'll *hurt* her.

"Hey, listen to me. Florence, you are safe. I'm sorry, I didn't mean to scare you. You know I won't hurt you. Please, you know that. You trust me, Florence. Please, breathe," I encourage desperately, taking a measured step closer.

She slides down the wall, trying to curl in on herself protectively as she whispers apologies and pleas. I realize she didn't hear a word I just said. I wouldn't be surprised if she mentally wasn't here at all anymore. If her mind has taken her elsewhere already. *Oh, Florence. What happened to you?*

I try to get closer again, panicking too. I need to tap her rhythm, to make her stop crying and start breathing, but when she sees me advancing, her eyes only widen.

"Please, Florence. You're safe. I'm not him. He'll never hurt you again. Breathe," I plead. It's to no avail.

That's when I hear the front door opening and closing. I look up from the curled-up girl in the corner of my room and back to my door.

"Elija? We're home," my dad yells. Florence flinches again, and with a muttered curse, I reluctantly leave my room.

"There you are. Is Flo here? I saw her Vespa. Oh, what's wrong?" my mom asks, noticing my distress, no doubt.

"Keep your voices down. Florence – she's in my room. I don't know what to do. She won't let me come closer, and she can't breathe," I explain hurriedly. The fact that Florence would hate me for involving my parents is nagging at my mind, but I'm too desperate to figure out what to do.

"Can't breathe? Where is she? What happened? Have you called 911?" my dad asks.

"No. It's a panic attack but she won't let me help. Dad, stop! You can't go in there!" I snap when the man tries to get past me.

"Why not? I can help," he says, but I shake my head.

"Not you. Mom, maybe it'd help if you tried. Tap this rhythm somewhere on her, okay?" I say, tapping the rhythm on the back of her hand. The woman nods solemnly and walks off.

When the door to my room shuts behind her, I exhale shakily and start pacing the living room. Only when my dad pulls me into a firm hug do I halt my fidgety movements. He tells me it'll be okay and not to be worried, but I am. I am sick to my stomach with worry and there are still so damn many unanswered questions.

Most of all, I really want to punch myself for reacting so horribly, and punch her father for being such a massive waste of space.

Chapter 48

Florence

I passed out after my panic attack. I hardly remember anything, but there was yelling at one point, and I think Elija left. He left when I was helpless and couldn't breathe, and I understand I must have hurt him by lying, but I never would've thought he'd do something like that. Not when I needed him most.

But I guess I overestimated how much he cared for me or the insignificance of my actions.

"You're up. Here, drink something," a familiar voice speaks. I realize just then that I'm no longer curled up on the floor but lying on a bed. Elija's bed. It's a punch to the gut. His mother must've found me at some point.

God, I'm so ashamed.

"I'm sorry," I say, not even attempting a façade. I'm tired and I feel weak. The last thing I want to do right now is act, and no matter how much I like this woman, I don't think I'll see her for much longer. Not if Elija and I are over.

So I let Amelia see my pathetic sadness. Sadness over losing her son and the closest thing I've had to a loving mother figure.

"Don't apologize, Honey. I'm just glad you're okay," she assures me, handing me the glass of water. I force myself to drink a bit, no matter how sick I feel. "Do you need anything else?" she asks me patiently, those loving eyes set intently on me. It's all I can do not to burst out crying. I just shake my head. "I'll get Elija, then, okay?" she's studying me closely. Too closely, and it takes my everything not to give her a reaction. I wonder what he told her my antics were about that she's studying me like this... I just nod, so she walks off.

In the time it takes Elija to get here, I sit up straighter on his bed, bracing myself.

When he steps into his room, he stares at me from the doorway for a good few beats. I force myself to meet his eyes. To gauge his reaction and figure out what's about to happen.

He looks away and walks further into the room, walking past the bed and taking down my aunt's guitar. He hands it to me slowly and wordlessly, searching my face as he does.

As soon as the old wood is in my hands, I feel like something snaps inside of me. I'm no longer clinging to some metaphorical edge, desperate to get back up. I've let go and I am falling. Flying. Floating. Everything and nothing.

I feel nothing.

Not my bleeding heart or terrified mind. I'm not angry or sad or hurt. I'm just here, accepting defeat.

I nod at Elija before getting up from the bed. I make a move to pick up my things once more to finally get out of here, but Elija stops me.

"What are you doing? I thought you'll stay here tonight?" he wonders slowly. That confuses me. He gave me back my aunt's guitar, that means we're breaking up, doesn't it? Over, done, no longer in a position to spend the night together.

"The guitar – I thought," I trail off. I watch as his eyebrows furrow and see the exact moment he realizes what I mean. A flash of hurt crosses his eyes as he jumps off the bed to walk toward me.

"That's not – Florence, I'm *not* breaking up with you," he insists urgently.

"You're not?"

"*No*. Oh, god no. Never that, Florence." He curses under his breath. "Can I please hug you?" he begs. His question confuses me; since when does he ask something like that? And what's with all that sadness in those pretty eyes of his?

I nod and he advances slowly, pulls me into his arms, and breathes me in.

"I'm sorry," he says.

"It's fine. Me too," I reply automatically.

"Don't be. You had every right to open up about this on your own agenda. God, I just – I have so many questions. Can we talk about it?" he asks slowly. I nod against him but stay quiet. I want to soak this moment up for a little longer and enjoy the comfort he's providing me with just some more.

"What do you want to know?" I finally mumble against his chest. He moves us over to the bed and pulls me just as close on there.

"When has it started? What happened?" He doesn't need to clarify. I remember enough to know I confessed about being scared of my father.

"It happened for the first time when I talked to them. Remember, I told you everything went well and then we had that call… My parents had business partners over and my father had a lot to drink. He," I break off with a sigh, my chest twisting with remnant fear at the memory of that night.

I remember the shock I felt. The denial. And how I believed he didn't remember a thing when he claimed so the next morning.

Elija shouldn't have to hear this, and I really don't want to talk about it. I know this talk will wear both of us down. But then, Elija squeezes my shoulder encouragingly and puts on the song he made for me, and my next breath comes a little easier.

"I was already in my room, and it was after midnight when he called my name. I knew something was wrong but went to the living room all the same. He was upset about something, I think. He slapped me and told me something was my fault but wouldn't tell me what," I catch myself and stop at that. My boyfriend's body is entirely tense and I decide I don't need to torture him further.

"The next day you wouldn't hug me or even look at me. Were you in pain?" Anguish clings to his words like a second skin.

"Yeah. I'm sorry, Elija. Really." He kisses my temple and shakes his head.

"Don't apologize. Just, why that long? Why didn't you say something?" Right on cue, there's a lump in my throat. *Yeah, why didn't I?*

"I don't know. I thought it was a one-time thing. Part of me even thought I did something to deserve it. And I felt so stupid because I got mad at you hours before for insinuating my parents weren't to be trusted. You were right."

"You didn't *deserve* that. You know that now, right?" he asks as if the mere idea was revolting to him. He faces me, scanning my face for any signs of deception as I nod.

"What about your mother? Did you tell her? Did she know?"

"I think she knew. I – I screamed for her when it happened but she never came. Then, the last time it happened, she kind of warned me that she was tired enough not to hear the end of the world. She seemed really content that night. I'm not sure if she knew or was in on it," I tell him. It's a suspicion I've had since the night Elija was over, one that goes against all my instincts to make excuses for my parents. I don't want to believe my mother was in on my father's attacks but I'm sick of being idiotically hopeful.

"How many times did he do something?" he asks.

"Two," I whisper.

"And he hit you? Did he do anything else?" he ponders, cringing as if the thought alone hurt him. His words before my panic attack return to me, his suspicion that I'd cheated on him. A cool sweat breaks out on the back of my neck, my anxiety rising.

"I – I'm sorry," I whisper, cursing myself when I feel his body lock up tightly beneath my touch. He's probably thinking the worst, so I quickly go on. "It wasn't much. He just… touched me over my clothes. It was nothing, I swear I didn't want it." My voice quivers as I speak. What if that's considered cheating? With his sore past with Ricky, I don't know where he draws the line.

"Fuck, Florence, of course you didn't. I'm so, so sorry I wasn't there to help. I knew something was wrong but I didn't want to push you, scared of what I'd find. I'm so sorry," he repeats miserably.

"Don't blame yourself." I don't want him to carry a burden that heavy. It wasn't his fault.

Ignoring my insistence, he asks, "Do you know what made him do it? If he never did anything of the sort before, what could have possibly triggered the change? Do you think it's part of a drinking problem he acquired recently?"

I bite my lip, really not wanting to tell him. It will only hurt him.

"You don't have to tell me but if you can, please do." I sigh and give my boyfriend a kiss on the cheek. A kiss for being so understanding and patient.

"The last time was on Saturday," I tell him.

"After or before I came over?"

"After. He snuck into my room. He told me he knew that we've had sex and that I was torturing him, too desperate for someone to touch me. But it wasn't your fault any more than it was mine. It's just his, okay? He only used you as an excuse to be a monster," I quickly add.

I hear the sadness in his voice when he replies. "Yeah. Yes, okay."

"Any more questions?" I ask him, turning my face so I can see him. He looks *wrecked,* so much so that I almost startle. I hate seeing him look so sad.

"Is there anything you want to say?"

"No, I think that's all. Thank you for letting me stay. I promise I'll figure out a long-term solution tomorrow," I assure him, but he brushes me off.

"We will figure something out, Florence. *We,* not you. You're not alone. I'll be with you every step of the way, okay?" He squeezes my arm with his hand then attempts a small smile that doesn't quite mask his somber mood. "Now, how about we eat something? We skipped dinner and after the workout we completed earlier, we need some energy. Are you up for it?" I try to get a sense of my body's state before I nod. It's been too long since I ate and it has become a lot easier to do with Eli around with him knowing all my triggers and the things that help.

He paid so much attention when I told him all about my issues that I never even had to repeat it. He just seemed to have the knowledge stowed away, ready to back it up whenever he knew he could ease my troubles.

Chapter 49

Elija

I fed my girl an apple and some crackers – all she wanted to accept despite my various offers to cook her something proper - and now we're back in my bed. My parents, although no doubt still awake and curious about the scene they walked into earlier tonight stayed in their room. I'm sure my father had a hand in keeping my mother away from us to give us some more space, and I'm really grateful for it. It's way past midnight, no time to force Florence to give up any more information after the toll of her panic attack, and I'll be damned before I leave her side right now. Hence, their curiosity has to wait.

We've been in my room for about twenty minutes, lying as if we were asleep even though I know we both aren't.

"What's on your mind?" Florence finally asks, raising her head from my chest so she can look at me.

Such a beautiful girl.

"Are you scared of me?" I ask silently, searching her eyes. She nearly recoils.

"What? No! Of course not!" she insists. "Why would you think that?"

"Earlier when I raised my arms, you flinched and tried to get away from me. I understand that what your parents did must've really taken its toll on you, but I hope you know I'd never hurt you. No matter how angry I was, I swear." Florence looks at me sadly and shakes her head before cuddling up to me again.

"I'm not scared of you, Eli. There's no one I've ever felt as safe or comfortable with. I know you wouldn't hurt me. I don't even remember what you're talking about, the whole evening is a blur," she tells me, and some of the weight on my chest eases.

"Your turn. Why are you not asleep?" I prompt, nuzzling the top of her head as I roll onto my side.

"Thinking about what I'll do."

"What have you got so far?" I ask her, stroking her hair softly.

"I don't think I want to go back to my parents," she says first.

"I agree one hundred percent."

"So, I'll try to get a job somewhere. In the meantime, I can live off the trust fund my aunt left me. It's been mine since I turned eighteen, and there's a lot of money in there. Enough for me not to worry about food and school any time soon. I'll start looking for a small place to live or whatever. Just don't know how to tell my parents yet," she mumbles.

"I mean, what you've got so far sounds pretty solid. Don't worry about finding an apartment just yet. I'm sure my parents won't mind if you stayed here for as long as you need to find something suiting, and with the end of our time at the academy coming closer, we could maybe bridge you over until you can move into student housing at college.

"But that's nothing we can or need to solve so late at night. Just know you're safe and you won't end up on the street even when you don't spend another night at your parents'. I got you, Florence. I swear they won't ever touch you again. Now, how about you turn off that pretty head of yours now, and we figure out the rest another time? We should try to get a little sleep before school starts tomorrow."

"Yeah, you're right," she relents, hugging my middle tightly and nestling closer. "Good night."

"Good night, my love."

"That is so messed up. I had no idea," Benji mutters through gritted teeth. The guys, Florence, and I are having lunch in the park – the other girls couldn't make it today – and Florence just told the guys about her parents. A really vague version, just that things haven't been good lately, and that she's moving out.

I'm proud of her for telling them. Squeezing her arm softly, I pull her tighter against me and kiss the top of her head.

The guys are very supportive as well. Like her own little squad of murderous puppies looking at her as if they are expecting any commands.

"What'd you say their address was? I think their car could use a little make over. I hear cut breaks are pretty," Marcus seethes. Looking this pissed doesn't suit him. He's usually more laid back and calm. Not when it comes to my girl, it seems.

I look to his right where Orion is sitting. He's strangely quiet but I know why. He grew up in an abusive household until he finally ran away at sixteen. He stayed with the rest of us for a while and eventually got his own place. To this point, he's working two jobs besides school trying to make ends meet, but he's making it work.

Now, he's looking at Florence with a mix of pride and obvious affection, though I can see the anger and sadness beneath that.

"Let me handle them. My lawyer will make them wish they had never even looked at you the wrong way," Liam chimes in. I'm still surprised by how I can look at him without feeling any resentment anymore. Quite the contrary; right now, I'm glad he's here. His financial situation and connections could come in handy should her parents look for any more trouble.

"Your lawyer my ass. Just call him dad," Jamie interjects. Then, he turns to Florence. "It's good you're leaving those bastards. Besides, you know what that means, right?" His signature grin is lighting up his whole face as he announces, "We'll all be roomies. My parents have been stressing me out lately, Orion already lives by himself, Benji's too high to know where he is half of the time, Marcus is only ever at his place to see his sis, Eli would follow you about anywhere, and we could use a sponsor like Liam. It makes sense on so many levels."

Sommerstall Academy

"Fuck you," Liam mutters at the same time as Benji says, "Fair."

"Of course, we'll need a giant place considering most of you will have your girls over all the time. Oh, please say yes! It'll be so much fun!" he squeals while Orion is looking at him like he just hung the moon. If Florence looks at me with half the affection, I'll die a happy man.

Speaking of my girl, she's currently looking at our friends in turns, trying to figure out if we're for real. We are, apparently. I can't believe I didn't think of that.

I'll have to tell my parents, and it might be hard to leave home, but even thinking about living with Florence and my best friends has my pulse racing in the best way possible. Besides, I'll still see my parents whenever I take care of the twins. Our place would have to be nearby because of school, so it's not that big of a deal.

"Really? I mean, you guys would do that?" she asks slowly.

"Don't say it like it's a chore. We've been dreaming of living together for years," Marcus chimes in.

"The amount of plans we've already made, house rules and financial plans included. We can swing it. And if we don't kill each other, it'll definitely be fun," Jamie explains dreamily.

Slowly, my girl nods. "Let's do it, then."

Chapter 50

Florence

"Are you ready?" Eli asks me when we pull up in the driveway of my parent's house. We went to school with his family's car this morning so I could get most of my stuff out of my old home already, considering I won't need it there anymore. I mean, I'm wearing Elija's shirt and underwear paired with my jeans from yesterday, but this look isn't sustainable. I need my things, so it's time to woman-up and do what I *really* don't want to.

Elija protested that there was no flower on me until I told him I was wearing my bra from yesterday. Then, he grinned boyishly and told me how good I looked in his shirt.

We get out of the car and stop again at the front door. *I'm really doing this*. Damn, am I really doing this? What if I didn't see this through? I haven't even started looking for jobs yet. How much of my trust fund will I have to use up for this?

Maybe I shouldn't be doing this.

A warm hand settles on the nape of my neck, massaging me slightly. "You're fine, Florence. I won't let anyone hurt you," Elija comforts me.

"Right. Yeah, you're right. They're probably not home anyway. It's just the nerves, you know." I chuckle, trying to shake the cold feet.

"Take your time," my boyfriend tells me calmly, as steady as a rock.

"I love you," I say, turning my neck to look at him. Studying his handsome profile, I can't believe how lucky I got.

Elija smiles. "I love you too."

With one deep breath, I unlock the door and push it open. Stepping inside, I'm greeted by someone calling my name.

"Florence? Oh, you finally made it home! Care to explain where you've been?" my mother demands, rounding the corner so she's standing in front of me. She's wearing the expression that used to scare the flip out of me as a child. The one where she looks at me like I did something wrong – like I'm something less than her. Now, it only makes me angry.

Manipulative woman.

"Oh, I should have guessed it was you she ran off with," she adds condescendingly, only now noticing Eli.

I can feel him tense beneath my touch, but he doesn't say anything and doesn't move a single muscle. He's here in case I need him, a silent reminder that I'm not alone and that I can do this. That I don't need my parents and all the pain having them in my life includes.

"I'm here to get my things and leave. Please, get out of my way," I tell her, my polite façade in place. I'm mocking her. I'm mocking the tyrant that has been making me feel bad about myself all my life, and it feels really damn nice.

That feeling quickly dies when my father joins us in the corridor. My façade slips, and it's all I can do not to back away.

Elija squeezes my shoulder encouragingly. I focus on that. On him and my goals. Mostly, I repeat to myself that I'm safe, and finally straighten my spine, meeting my father's gaze defiantly. I'm done cowering.

"Look who's back," my dad drawls, looking at Elija. "Leave, boy, I have some things to discuss with my daughter. Family things, you know. Very important."

I hate the chill that settles over me at the sheer sound of his voice. So much power. He and my mother still have so much power over me and I'm sick of it.

"He's not going anywhere, and there's nothing to discuss. Like I already told your wife, I'm only here to get my things," I tell them.

"Oh? And may I ask what you need your things for?" my mother asks.

I steel my spine. "You may. I'll need them seeing as I'm moving out. I'm done with you two taking your shit out on me like I'm your personal punching bag. I'm leaving, and you'll be rid of me for good. It's a win win, so *move.*"

"What? Don't be silly, girl. You can't just leave. Where would you even go? To live with him? Please, I've seen the hovel his family lives in. This is just the result of one of your moods. Typical teenager," my mother scoffs.

Oh, but she doesn't realize that the last thing she wants to do is disrespect my boy and his family around me. Not when there's a lifetime of resentment toward her bottled up inside of me.

I take a step toward her, staring her down.

"Where I go and what I'll do is none of your business. Anywhere is better than here. And just to be very clear, I'd sooner live under a bridge with Elija and his family than in a palace with you two. At least they know how to be decent human beings. More than decent, but that's why you're so jealous, isn't it?" I take my time looking her down and back up once, making sure to convey the disgust I feel. It's a look she's given me a million times, and I can only hope it makes her feel as small and worthless as it always did to me. "You're dead to me," I state, my voice venomous. Then, I look at my dad. "Both of you."

My parents are stunned silent, and I use the opportunity to push past them, ignoring the way my skin scorches where it touches my father. I go into my room and lock the door as soon as Elija is in. Only then do I release a breath and let my shoulders slump.

Elija's in front of me in a beat, wrapping his arms around me tightly. "You're okay. You can be so proud of yourself," he mumbles against my skin.

And so, we pack up my things and leave through the window. I don't care if it seems cowardly, I don't have anything more to say to my parents.

I pack up some of my clothes, my iPad, and some books I haven't read, along with my toiletries and other essentials. Leaving the rest behind feels like abandoning a part of myself, but it's just for now. I plan on getting everything else once the guys and I have our place. I just hope my parents won't do anything about it in the meantime.

On our way to Elija's home, I cry silently. He doesn't say anything and neither do I. He simply keeps one hand on my thigh and offers his silent support.

I guess this is really happening. Now, we'll just have to look for our new home, I have to find a job, and finish school. Easy, right?

Epilogue

Florence

"We did it!" Jamie whoops, raising his drink high in the air. The guys and girls around me cheer as we clink our glasses.

We're standing in the living room of our home. Our home where we've been living for a few months now. Orion, Jamie, Marcus, Benji, Liam, Sarah, Miley, Marcus' sister, Elija, and me. Strictly speaking, the girls don't live here, but let's be for real, they have their own drawers filled with clothes and toothbrushes. They live here.

We're toasting to the end of the school year. The end of an era now that we've finished the academy. I couldn't be happier.

"Stay with us, Florence," Elija whispers into my ears. I get up on my tiptoes to kiss him quickly. Damn, how I love this boy.

"I'm right here," I tell him. There's no place I'd rather be.

"Come on, Eli. Play something for us!" Sarah suggests.

"Yeah, Rockstar. Or are you too famous to entertain us simple folks now?" Jamie teases him.

Laughing, Elija grabs his guitar and stands up in front of us. "Any requests?" he asks, looking at me. Even now, my cheeks still have the audacity to heat up as I smile back.

"The one you showed me last night," I say, my blush intensifying as images of what else we did last night flood my brain.

Our friends chuckle, watching the interaction with apparent amusement.

"Let's not. We all know what you two did last night. Thin walls, remember? I'm pretty sure we're not ready for that kind of show," Benji says, nearly choking on his laughter.

"I sure as hell don't want to know what he did to make –" I cut Orion off before he can finish that sentence. It's likely to be the last thing I do before I die because of mortification.

"The song! Talking about a song!" I yell, covering my face with my hands. Oh, this is why you don't move in with friends.

"It's a draft. Unreleased, so let me know what you think," Elija says, amusement clear in his voice. He looks so proud of himself. *Traitor*.

And so Elija shows us a song he'll release soon. The song his followers have been demanding ever since he uploaded a short snipped of it. They've gone feral, demanding more of his songs even though he's already created and released half a dozen in the last few months.

He got lucky when the algorithm blew up the first ever TikTok I forced him to make. And all without ever showing his handsome face... To protect his privacy, we settled on filming his hands playing the guitar in the dim lighting of our overhead LEDs... it was an immediate hit, which is unsurprising considering his talent.

Once he saw the positive feedback of thousands of people on the internet, he finally started believing me that he was awesome. He released his songs on Spotify and the streams are still rising by the hour.

I couldn't be prouder.

I'm not doing too bad myself. Currently, I'm working at a local library, but I'm starting an internship at an architecture firm after this summer. I can't wait to start. But first, I'll enjoy some time off with my friends.

Luckily, it seems so far, no one will move out. Marcus is working out a contract with a soccer team in our region, the coach apparently eager to snatch up the promising your player, Liam will stay on track working for his father, Jamie's going to castings for any shows and movies nearby, saying he'll just figure out what to do when he feels like it, the safety of his family's money allowing him this freedom, Benji got into a local collage to become a doctor, and Orion will keep working at the retirement home as he's done for years. He doesn't plan on doing it forever, but right now, he's happy there, saying all the old ladies love his charm.

What I wouldn't give to see the alleged charm that seems to be exclusively reserved for those old ladies...

And that's it, I guess. That's my family.

My beautiful, messy, patchwork family standing in our living room and celebrating as if we just conquered the world.

Extended Epilogue

9 years later

Florence

Five minutes. The longest five minutes of my life. Even Mister Hank's classes couldn't compare. If those felt like forever, this is lasting an eternity.

I'm chewing on the skin around my nails, my leg bouncing as relentlessly as it used to back when I was a teenager. By the time my alarm goes off, my thoughts are a jumbled, unintelligible mess. With clammy hands, I turn off my chiming phone before getting up from the closed toilet seat to reach the sink.

I pick up the pregnancy test with the caution one might treat a foreign creature with. My heart sure is racing as if I was facing some unheard-of beast. I can't believe I'm doing this. Right now, of all time. When I really should be on my way to dinner with Elija, who is currently waiting for me in the living room.

After a second of holding the test without the world ending, I force my eyes to check the results, already knowing what I'll find. Still, my heart misses a beat as I take in the two lines. Two.

Positive.

I'm pregnant. My hand starts shaking more, and I hastily set the pregnancy test back down on the sink, taking a step back to collapse against the wall with a shuddering breath.

Okay. Deep breaths, Florence. You know this. After years of not experiencing even the faintest panic attack, I still recognize the signs. I will myself to relax. There's no need to panic. I don't even know what exactly I'm panicking about.

Even once I've collected myself, my heart doesn't stop racing. I don't know whether to laugh or cry.

Shit, I need to get out of this bathroom.

Grabbing the test, I hide it behind my back as I go to meet my boyfriend. Only to stop in my tracks when I see him lounging on the couch.

He hasn't noticed me yet, and I take the opportunity to take him in. Usually, he's so attuned to me that I can never catch him unaware. Now, my lungs are begging for air that doesn't seem to want to enter them.

He's so fucking beautiful.

His demeanor relaxed, his legs spread out as he leans back into the cushions. His eyes are focused on his phone, a small crease between his brows as he frowns. Still, I'm salivating as much as I would for his smile.

Strands of his dark hair are falling onto his forehead, but what finally catches my attention and keeps it are the rolled-up sleeves of his white button-down, showing off the tattoos adorning his golden skin.

I drink in the familiar designs, and my eyes catch on a particular patch of ink. A flower. A sunflower, to be more precise. One of his more recent additions.

Finally becoming aware of my presence, Elija's eyes meet mine, a spark lighting up in them as he smiles. "There you are. Took you long enough," he teases me. When I don't return his smile, the crease between his brows reappears. "Are you okay?"

Am I? I don't know. I'm nervous, that's for sure. "I have to tell you something. And I don't know how you'll take it," I admit slowly.

The man quickly gets to his feet, crossing the distance between us until he's close enough to cup my cheeks gently. He presses a lingering kiss to my lips, only pulling away when I melt against him with a sigh.

His hands drop from my face to settle on the sides of my arms. He smiles tentatively. "Okay, I'm ready. Hit me," he tells me.

If only I had the words to do so. Instead, any letters I might have known some time ago have fled my mind, and my throat is closed up, unwilling to let me make a single sound.

What if he won't react well? We haven't discussed children often, and whenever we did, it seemed like a far-away scenario.

I'm going to be sick.

Unable to handle it anymore, I hold out the hand clutching onto the pregnancy test, waiting for him to see for himself. With the same hesitance as me earlier, he takes the test from my hand and takes a closer look at the two lines.

Finally, when my heart feels like it's about to explode, his face breaks out into the biggest grin and he lets loose a startled laugh. The next thing I know, his arms are wrapped tightly around my waist and I'm lifted off the ground and spun in circles.

I clutch onto him, still unable to find my voice. Despite the relief that floods me at the sight of his apparent joy, I'm still freaking out.

He finally sets me down, grabs my face securely, and smashes his lips to mine. When he pulls away, he's still beaming.

I hate to see it dim as he studies me. His arm nudges mine. "What's wrong? How come you're not celebrating with me?"

"How come you are celebrating so readily?" I retort, unable to keep the hysteria from my voice.

"What do you mean? Why shouldn't I?"

"I don't know. We didn't plan this. I – We – I mean, we're not even married. We're getting the order all wrong. I don't know how this happened," I fumble for words, even more so when my man starts looking amused.

"Look at you freaking out. This feels just like old times," he teases me. I shove my hands against his chest.

"This isn't funny. We're talking about a child, Elija. A real human being. Oh, my god. There's something living inside of me." I break off, my eyes widening at the realization. A baby will grow inside of me. Dear. God.

"Florence. Hey, look at me. Baby, look at me. Just focus on me. It's all going to be okay. This is a good thing. Isn't it?" he asks, sounding more unsure with every word. "I mean, you want to keep it, right?"

I nod before my brain could register it, and I guess I have my answer right there. Elija loses a breath.

"Okay, good. Now, just wait here, okay? I'll be back in a second," he tells me, his eyes lighting up once more as he passes me with a quick kiss on my cheek.

I remain frozen in place, staring at the closed door of our bedroom, through which he just disappeared. *Okay*. I'll just wait here, then. It's a good time as any to *leave me*...

It's all I can do to hope that none of my friends are about to enter the living room to find me here. I wouldn't know what to tell them.

Of course, only Benji, Miley, Markus, Orion, and Jamie remain. Liam and Sarah built themselves a mansion right next door years ago, though they're happy to burst in here unannounced every other day.

With Jamie's ever-changing place of work as an actor, he and Orion travel often. Of course, they're not gone right now when I desperately need the chances of running into anyone to be as slim as possible.

"Can you come in here for a second, please? I could use a hand," Elija's voice rips me out of my thoughts. Use a hand? What is he doing in there?

I follow his voice, entering our room with a frown. Still in the doorway, I freeze on the spot, just staring down at my kneeling boyfriend.

"Hey, Florence," he says softly, watching my stupefied figure with a soft smile.

My gaze flicks between his eyes and the open box in his hand. I stare at the silver ring with the subtle gem for a moment, then focus on the kneeling man's face.

"Eli?" I breathe.

"I know, this isn't exactly how I planned tonight to go, either. I'm hoping you'll want me even without the grand gesture I'd planned. You are the one who spoiled it, after all," he says sheepishly.

"You? I?" I stammer. Tears are stinging my eyes, blurring the beautiful view, and I try to blink them away. "You planned this?" I finally ask.

"For months. Miley and Sarah were telling me to hurry the hell up ever since I asked them to help me chose a ring, but I wanted to do it today. You know. It being exactly nine years after you told me you loved me over the phone, and all. I know, it's cheesy, but we first kissed and got together on your birthday, and I didn't want to steal your day. And now you got me rambling. Please, say something," he pleads, half-teasing.

"I can't," I tell him.

"Why?" He chuckles, but I can tell I'm making it nervous. I smile a little.

"You haven't popped the question yet," I remind him, finally stepping into the room and closing the door behind me.

My man blushes. "Shoot. Right." He clears his throat. "Florence, are you ready to legally bind yourself to me until death do us part? To sign up for a lifetime of having me tag along when your inner Snow White craves another adventure, and to have me snoop through our bookshelf to find your most annotated books?" He sucks in a shaky breath. Meanwhile, my treacherous eyes are leaking tears like the damn party poopers they are. Is it too soon to blame it on the pregnancy hormones?

"Will you marry me, Florence?"

I don't even reply, and he knows me well enough to get to his feet before I throw myself into his arms, propelling the both of us onto the mattress behind him.

I try to kiss him, only for his face to swerve out of the way. I pull away to pout. That at least earns me a sweet laugh and a kiss on the tip of my nose.

"You haven't replied yet," he tells me. I let my forehead drop to his, closing my eyes.

"Yes, Elija, I really, really, really want to marry you," I say slowly, savoring every word.

Hey, you

You are beautiful

Printed in Dunstable, United Kingdom